"Fast-paced and wildly entertaining."
—*Chicago Tribune*

"An extraordinary Vatican tale—probably the best Vatican novel in recent memory."
—Tad Szulc, author of
Fidel and *Pope John Paul II*

liz R

Praise for WILLIAM D. MONTALBANO'S

BASILICA

Also by William D. Montalbano

POWDER BURN
(with Carl Hiaasen)
TRAP LINE
(with Carl Hiaasen)
A DEATH IN CHINA
(with Carl Hiaasen)
THE SINNERS OF SAN RAMON

BASILICA

William D. Montalbano

JOVE BOOKS, NEW YORK

This is a work of fiction. Names, characters, places, and incidents are either the product of the author's imagination or are used fictitiously, and any resemblance to actual persons, living or dead, business establishments, events or locales is entirely coincidental.

BASILICA

A Jove Book / published by arrangement with
the author

PRINTING HISTORY
G. P. Putnam's Sons edition / January 1999
Published simultaneously in Canada
Jove edition / January 2000

The Penguin Putnam Inc. World Wide Web site address is
http:/www.penguinputnam.com

ISBN: 0-515-12723-X

A JOVE BOOK®
Jove Books are published by The Berkley Publishing Group,
a division of Penguin Putnam Inc.,
375 Hudson Street, New York, New York 10014.
JOVE and the "J" design
are trademarks belonging to Penguin Putnam Inc.

PRINTED IN THE UNITED STATES OF AMERICA

10 9 8 7 6 5 4 3 2 1

In Memory

Vincent F. Montalbano
1906–1997

VATICAN CITY

1

THE GIANT COBBLESTONED square was deserted in the dark pool of Roman night, but he felt no unease. He knew the route well. Before him stood the Basilica, huge, immutable, encompassing, an embracing refuge for the saints and popes who lay in its crypts, and for sinners who begged on bended knee for peace and understanding. He was one of them, a man of internal contradictions, of flawed and sometimes wayward faith.

He climbed the broad esplanade of steps up to the giant bronze doors, then turned and walked to a darkened side entrance, the insider's secret passage to the world's largest church. Everyone who needed it knew where the key was. It is one of the many company secrets of the tiny religious state within the heart of Rome. The key clicked and the door yielded silently.

Inside, banks of vigil candles flickered yellowly and a swatch of gray from moonlight leaking through windows high up framed the main altar, but their effect was to magnify the darkness eerily. Shadows cast by a single blue flame played across Michelangelo's *Pietà*, the *Madonna* cradling her dead son. He stood quietly for a few minutes before one of history's landmarks, listening, feeling, thinking.

In the echoing stillness, he heard the shuffle of feet across the marble floor and a muffled cough from one of the side altars. Every night the men of God came to seek succor in the black bosom of their church. Each night that he had come, there had been others, the whisper of footsteps, the click of beads, sometimes a half-seen figure groping through the dark on its private mission of atonement.

"Bless me, Father, for I have sinned." Undulating through the gloom, the formal opening statement of a Catholic's confession eased his passage. He was not the only sinner there.

Although he could always sense their presence, he had never before spoken with another night visitor. Tonight would be different. Tonight he would meet a fellow supplicant.

There were hundreds of silent nooks in the church where a visitor could pray: pews, confessionals, quiet corners, stands of candles and flowers, at the base of statues, before or behind side altars. None of them suited him. Only one place could bathe his soul.

Walking softly down the right aisle, he came to an unmarked door, as never-known to casual visitors as the one that had granted coveted night entry into the Basilica.

This door, too, opened at a touch. Beyond it the darkness was complete. That was an integral part of his ritual. He reached his right arm out as far as it would go and then edged patiently to the right until his questing fingers touched the curved stone wall.

It was cold and compelling. With the wall as his guide, caressing it like a woman's cheek every black step, he began the long, breathtaking climb, a holy man on a private mission. At the top he would find fulfillment. He would refresh his soul, renew his commitment.

Seldom did anyone else challenge the spiraling passage. It was a secret within a secret, to be savored. And, that night, to be shared.

Patiently, but with growing confidence, he wound his way up the cold stone walkway. Near the top it grew lighter, as tentacles of false dawn fingered through the age-spotted windows. There, he was able to distinguish the dark bulk of the person who had asked to join his vigil, kneeling, head bent in prayer, further out along the Dome gallery than he himself usually ventured.

But he had a good head for heights, and soon the two figures were kneeling side by side as growing light crept into the crown of their church.

"God bless you, and ease your passage," the visitor whispered.

"And may light renew your faith," he replied. Such is the private litany of the keepers of the night.

Side by side they addressed the silence, a penitent and a murderer.

There was not long to wait, and when the light broke, it came with a flood. Standing tall, he thrust out his arms, and threw his head heavenward in appeal and abnegation, begging God for His love and forgiveness.

But he found death instead. A vicious shove; a panicked, futile clawing to deny that fatal plummet. An instant of pure lucidity, eternity beckoning, undeniable. Then nothing.

Amen.

That is the way it must have begun.

Later, I myself made that black climb. Something in the darkened church, on that never-seen and seemingly never-ending circular walk to domed majesty, pricked the hairs on the back of my neck.

When I, too, stood prayerfully as the first rays of a new day ignited the Dome of St. Peter's Basilica, I felt awed and fulfilled.

And frightened.

2

ONCE I WAS an on-the-edge cop, but now I'm a Roman Catholic brother, a kind of not-quite priest kicking around the back alleys of the world's largest church. Across the centuries, brothers have been the church's hewers of wood and drawers of water, more practical than spiritual; the callused blue-collar counterpoint to yeoman priests and high-dome theologians.

I had come to the church and to the Vatican late in life after some painful detours and a personality retread, so I especially welcomed the low-stress lifestyle. My job was to keep the peace at a residence of seminarians where I'm sort of a combination father figure and sergeant at arms. Beyond that, mostly I drift along, staying out of trouble, keeping my internal debris at bay.

But every now and then people around the Vatican with unchurchly problems ask me to help them. Which explains why I sat one soft Sunday morning in the garden at the seminarians' house called St. Damian's with an ice pack on my right shoulder reading the Vatican Police report of a mugging.

Across from me, one giant hand wrapped around a *cappuccino,* Luther chuckled. "My, but he does turn a phrase." Luther was a monk and a full-fledged priest. Like me, he had found his way to the church's bosom later rather than sooner. He didn't talk much about his en route stops either.

Luther was my second best friend in Rome, and he was one page ahead of me in the report that the Vatican cops had sent over. To tell you the truth, Luther was often a page or two ahead of me.

The report was as straightforward as bureaucracy ever approaches in Italian. It detailed an attack against an American professor named Frederick Worth after a day's research at the Vatican Library. The most rewarding part of the report was the victim's statement, written in tight, angry English. Worth was a medievalist of some note, and he expressed himself with the preachy pomposity you'd expect from a cultured man who'd spent his life rummaging among centuries-old manuscripts in ornate lettering and musty Latin. As liars go, he wasn't too shabby, though.

Professor Worth complained that he had left Vatican City through the Sant'Anna gate and had been crossing the street to a bus stop when he had been attacked from behind by two men on a motorbike, a *motorino* of the garden variety breed that is as much a trademark of Roman life as Catholicism. The two men had struck silently and were gone in an instant, the professor said, taking with them a briefcase that supposedly contained "research materials of inestimable academic importance but no commercial value."

The M.O. was classic Roman. The driver had maneuvered the *motorino* close to the victim and the rider on the back had snared the briefcase with a powerful yank. Professor Worth said he had managed to slug his assailant; to no avail, alas. Victims almost always say that, but it was usually not true.

"Both men were wearing helmets, making precise identification impossible," the professor wrote, "but the man who grabbed my briefcase was a stocky, almost apelike individual in a blue windbreaker. I had the impression that the driver, who was tall and well muscled and wore a sports shirt, might have been black, though I do not in any way wish this to be construed as a racist remark."

According to an accompanying list in Italian and English, the briefcase contained research notes on two yellow pads, a couple of magazines, a pair of reading glasses, an address book, a pocket knife, and a plastic bottle of antacid tablets.

Luther was watching with a grin as I finished reading.

"They'll never catch these guys, will they? Black Tarzan and his fat monkey?" he asked.

"Be a shock if they do." I shrugged the ice pack off my shoulder and gingerly swung a scuffed brown briefcase over to Luther. "Take a look."

Luther neatly spread the contents of the case we had stolen from Worth across the garden table. It was just as the not-so-good professor had said. Everything was there: pads, scholarly magazines, address book, notes, pocket knife, glasses, tablets. Luther, smart man, went right for the magazines. In each he found a manuscript page that had been lovingly illuminated by a monk dead now for nine centuries.

"Twelfth century, from the Gospel of Luke. Copied at an abbey in France. So says Father Albright at the Library."

Luther gently held the pages the way a father might cradle an injured child, concern crowded by anger.

"Albright says they're from the manuscript that Worth was studying. Looked as if the folios had been cut out with a razor, Albright said." Or the blade of a pen knife.

"Now what, Paul?" You could have cut a diamond with the edge in Luther's voice.

"I suggested to Albright we pay another short, sharp visit to the professor, maybe as he's walking back to his hotel one night after dinner."

"Good idea. You drive this time, take care of your shoulder."

"'No way,' Albright said."

Luther sighed noisily. "Me a priest, you a brother. We know he's right. Turn the other cheek; even if it stings. But what does Albright want? Ban the professor and forget about it? Pretend it never happened?"

What could I say? One of the earliest lessons anybody ever learns about the Vatican is that there are ways, and there are ways.

"Father Albright wants to give the good professor back the briefcase. Everything but the manuscript pages. The professor's a crook, but he's no dummy. He'll get the message—never to be seen again around the Vatican, Albright says."

"You buy that, Paul?"

"I think he's right as far as he goes, so we'll give the case back. But I'll confetti all the notes, though. In case they really are valuable."

Luther nodded, but he was not happy.

So I said what he was thinking. "Yes, it would be more satisfying to smash the asshole professor's nose and break his scissor fingers. To give him a couple of hospital days to reflect on his sins."

"You told Father Albright we wouldn't."

"That's what I told him."

"But we might anyway."

I shrugged. Some things are better left unsaid.

Luther is a strange name for a Catholic monk, but Luther was a strange monk. We'd met at a pickup basketball game one afternoon. He was from someplace in West Africa; hard to miss and harder to beat on the court. He looked like one of those giant veldt trees that grow into the sky with branches broad enough to obliterate the horizon. Take a rebound off Luther? It'd be easier to nail a list of grievances to the Vatican's bronze doors. Luther was as old as I was, and he'd once told me he had spent more than ten years at sea, but his beard was still black, his belly was still more or less flat, damn him, and with his great height, he made a patriarchal sight striding the streets of Rome in gray monk's robes and open-toed sandals. Not so much Moses on the mountain; more Moses *as* the mountain.

Luther was a preacher in a city full of priests, all of them preachers in one form or another, all of them coming to personal terms with the church that gripped them in the same and different ways. Some claimed they were born to religious life. Others struggled with doubts from the first day. Some never made it.

A few, like me, like Luther, trundled through life on another track, only to discover one day that a quiet itch suddenly demanded serious scratching. Luther told me once that he'd decided to become a priest because he had done everything else and so much of it seemed empty. My own imperfect vocation had arrived amid more anguish than conviction. I lived with that recognition, suffered with it, even: the present as penance for the past. Like the past itself, it is an essence that never strays far from me.

It was there that morning, pressing and depressing. Luther and I left the problem to marinate of suitable justice for Professor Worth, the manuscripts drowsing safely in a locked suitcase under my bed, and set off for our weekly stroll through what is probably the world's best walking city.

We walked a couple of hours most Sunday mornings after mass, wandering more or less aimlessly through ancient cobble-stoned streets, but usually pointing for the weekly papal blessing at St. Peter's. It was a pleasant, uplifting ritual for me, but marred quite accidentally that morning by a bunch of kids playing with stomp rockets in a piazza near the Tiber. They were jumping on squat plastic bellows that sent a column of compressed air into thin plastic cylinders, hurling them fifty or a hundred feet into the sky. A harmless amusement, I agree, and we stopped for a few minutes among a clutch of pedestrians attracted by it.

But the rockets whistled. As they lanced up, each gave off a thin shriek. It was part of the fun for everybody else. But I don't like whistles, and, no, it's nothing trivial, like hearing chalk scrape across a blackboard. For me, it's painful; a sudden, shocking reminder of the whistling sound that spells death.

If Luther noticed my discomfort he didn't comment, and within a few minutes we had reached the Vatican, where there were less hurtful things to talk about. Most Sundays, a few thousand people gather to glimpse the pope, but among the pilgrims that day protesters' banners made angry exclamation marks among the usual thickets of national and religious flags waved by tourists to attract papal attention. "History Cannot Be Rewritten" read one. "Save Our Saints" said another in rebuttal to a blood-red banner proclaiming "We Are All Saints."

"The debunkings," Luther grunted.

What else?

A few days before, the pope had stricken a long list of historic figures from the registry of saints. Artillery rounds would be landing for weeks among those who thought he had gone too far, and those who were sure he had been too timid. Around the Vatican, everything a pope does gores somebody's pulpit. This time the blow had been softened by saying that the debunked saints could still be regarded as figures of local esteem. But the pope had made plain he was spring cleaning his personal gallery of church heroes.

Gone the way of St. George the Dragon Slayer and St. Christopher the travelers' saint were the likes of Venerius and Homobonus, Crispin and Crispinian, Ludwyna and Arthur. Gravediggers, servants, tailors, tanners, locksmiths and swordsmiths, weavers and the falsely accused would henceforth all have to shop around for a new patron. In his wisdom, though, the pope had not also dismissed icons beloved of other groups of Catholics, including secretaries, paratroopers, undertakers, skaters, skiers, canonists, carpenters, ecologists, epileptics, dryers, or the dying.

"I can see the man's point," Luther murmured as we watched the piazza ballet, "but it's a shame to lose all that tradition, isn't it?"

Sometimes Luther wandered across minefields his namesake had visited all those centuries ago. Luther would say that while the teachings of the church were never wrong, Catholics would have to engage their own consciences in deciding how to obey them. That was anathema, of course, to the tight club of aging males that ran the Vatican. At least that was the way it had been since back into the reign of the Inflexible Pole. His replacement had cast no shadow, altered nothing, and impressed nobody. In another few years nobody would even remember his name, but after a pontificate as brief as it was undistinguished, Pope Nobody had done his church a mighty service by swiftly dying.

His successor was still new after only a couple of years in power, but—like the new century—he had the benefit of novelty. The new pope was the Americas' great pride and joy; the first pope, after two thousand years, to spring from the New World. His election had been a breathtaking surprise. Conclaves of cardinals at which new popes are elected are one of the Vatican's deepest secrets. Like everybody else, I knew the conclave had started as a head-to-head between a holy African from the Curia and a dynamic pastoral bishop from northern Italy.

It was a deadlock, apparently, because it had taken one hundred and eleven aging prelates ten days and who knows how many secret ballots to elect one of their number as the new pope. He had been a compromise candidate, a tall, polyglot, and photogenic cardinal who had been an activist leader of his church at home and had matured into an effective, if low-profile, head of one of the Vatican congregations in Rome.

The new pope had named himself Pius XIII, and "thirteenth" in Italian comes out as the hard-to-pronounce *"tredicesimo."* So "Tredi" he had instantly become to broadcasters, headline writers, and Catholics alike around the world. Always excepting, of course, the beads-tolling Holy Father–His Holiness crowd around the Vatican for whom no name was too hard to say and no change easy enough to accept.

The newest Bishop of Rome, latest pope in line of direct succession from the Apostle Peter, was the youngest and most vigorous pontiff in centuries. Just as well, too, for he had inherited a divided and fractious church, a difficult-to-govern community of believers more than one billion strong and active in virtually every country on earth.

Tredi, I knew, had played two sports at college, a fact neatly obscured by Vatican biographies for one simple reason: while the new pope undoubtedly hailed from Latin America, which has more Catholics than anywhere, he happened also to have gotten his college degree in the United States before going home to enter the seminary. The last greatest truism of the Catholic church is that there will never be an American pope. Tredi was as close as any pope had— or could—come.

Still, more than two years after becoming head of a mammoth but internally troubled church, Tredi's visage had made more impact than his policies. The sight of a vibrant pope striding purposefully hither and yon had dimmed memories of his doddering forebears. And even if Tredi hadn't done anything exactly revolutionary, there was a clear sense around the Vatican that fresh winds were blowing. Clean sheets had begun to appear on musty balconies. Some of the more obdurate and entrenched Curia cardinals had found themselves transferred to hinterland archdioceses. Pronouncements had lost the You Shall Never edge of John Paul II, and the Let's Pray Together fuzziness of a successor who had been intimidated by big shoes he couldn't fill. It was still early in his reign. Tredi had chosen his own name, and would go his own way. I'd bet on it.

I wouldn't have said there was exactly an atmosphere of menace in St. Peter's Square that morning, but certainly more tension than at any prayer meeting I've ever been to. I saw a hawk-nosed man in a black suit with a splash of purple at his collar and a heavy cross dangling from his neck standing a bit back from a chanting group of protesters. He might have been an observer, a prelate who just happened to be walking through the square, but I didn't think so, for saint-savers who were leading *"Salvai Santi"* chants twice drifted back to confer with him. Somebody had a bishop for an ally.

I didn't get it myself. "Luther, if you can pray to God, why waste time with saints?"

It was the sort of thing that only a simple brother could dare ask, of course. I'm not a priest and probably never will be. We brothers are helpers. Typically, a brother is somebody who wants to live a religious life but lacks the intellect and education to become a priest. That describes me to a Roman collar. Back in medieval times the brothers harvested the grapes, repaired the monasteries, and chased milkmaids while the smart monks sat close to the fire, illuminated manuscripts, kept learning alive, went blind, and generally pursued assorted spiritual delights.

Nowadays there are many fewer brothers than priests, but we run high schools in some places, and we administer a fair number of church institutions: a German brother manages the Vatican's biggest print shop, and brothers from a Spanish order man Rome's biggest soup kitchen.

We brothers take vows, the poverty, chastity and obedience thing, which makes us part of the Vatican team, all right. We wear the same uniform, but we're not technically clerics like priests. I can't say mass, or hear confessions.

Which is fine by me. Being a brother quenches my thirst without drowning me. I've got all the religion I want, but I haven't surrendered all my freedom. Sure I sin. Okay. But somehow I think it's less important than if I were a priest doing it. Maybe that's an illusion, but it's the way I feel.

At the end of a dark tunnel of years that I still find too painful to talk about, I did a two-year novitiate to become a member of the small American order called the Brothers of St. Matthias. In case it's slipped your mind, Matthias was the thirteenth apostle, elected by lot to replace the traitor Judas. And like Matthias, we came late to the supper: converts, widowers, guys like me who do other things they decide to chuck. Back in the States, we had lawyers and computer wizards and a doctor; businessmen, and a sprinkling of guys who never could get their lives together. We were men who didn't fit in the outside world, or no longer wanted to. Here in Rome we Matthians were just a handful of brothers with different jobs who hardly ever saw one another.

I was in charge of the St. Damian's residence, went to classes, mooched around, and sporadically made myself useful around the Vatican. Think of that as a carefully vague way of describing a discreet and faceless figure who straightens out problems that never officially occur. When indelicate things needed prodding, usually it was a quiet phone call that brought me with a stick. The heavy thinking I left to truly smart people like Luther—and the new pope.

"The church has always made saints important," Luther was saying as though to a slow student. "All Catholics are raised with pictures and stories of saints to ask for special intercessions."

"Sure. The big-favor figures—a key game, a make-or-break exam. But why would the pope mess with them now?"

"I'm only a poor monk, but I think maybe the pope has decided it's time to separate myth and the modern church. Get rid of the saints who were often only mythological figures anyway. Many of them were an early-days' Christian concession to polytheism: necessary then, but only a clutter today. The same thing is true in Africa today. In fact, I'm one of the pro-saints types who think they are more useful than harmful."

"That's pretty deep, Father Luther."

"I am a deep poor monk, Brother Paul."

There was a sudden swirl in the square where protesters behind a "Tradition Must Be Respected" banner were sassing some counter-demonstrators. The hawk-nosed bishop was gesticulating, waving his fist in the air. It looked like he was urging them on. The church is chary of political prelates, but Hawk-Nose was about as neutral as an Uzi.

We watched a file of cops lance into the melee, and for a minute I thought they would need reinforcements, but it was pretty harmless stuff, really, and in the midst of it a banner-draped fourth-floor window opened in the Apostolic Palace facing the square and a tall figure in a white robe appeared.

Tredi was only a foreshortened flash of white to most of the crowd below, but he was enough. Pilgrims cheered noisily, waving their banners.

The pope was a big, heavily built man in his fifties. His face was square-cut with a crisscross of small scars above his eyes. Depending on the angle, the scars could make him look quite fierce. And the pope was, in fact, a man accustomed to having his way. Tredi's eyes were black. They dominated his face, and nearly everyone he met. The eyes were his strongest feature—not counting the unflinching will.

All popes have commanding presence, but in Tredi's case there was a good-humored magnetism that seemed to scour the square of contention.

"God bless all the saints," the pope said into a pencil-thin microphone, "and all the people of God."

By the time Tredi had finished the brief *Angelus,* even the angry bishop seemed content to wander off with the rest of the crowd in search of Sunday lunch.

I went, too, for I could sense no threat that day except from my own memory.

Why did I care?

Because the most important reason I had come to the Vatican was to watch out for danger back along the bumpy trail Tredi had followed from the Americas to St. Peter's. We had traveled some of it together. I had been there when the scars on his face had been born in an angry explosion of glass. The new pope, too, understood about whistling death.

MIAMI

Fourteen Years Before

3

IN ITS WAY, Miami's light is as singular as Rome's, a clarity that lends dimension, excitement, insight, even, to those skilled enough to capture it on canvas. The morning light is best in Miami, as in most of the tropics. As the sun climbs, colors bleach, and it is the heat, not the light, that becomes dominant.

At Miami International that morning the best light was fading and the heat was building as a silver-painted executive jet taxied to a halt on the private aviation side of the giant airport. A small crowd pressed forward as a tall man in an open-necked, white-and-blue short-sleeved shirt came agilely down the steps. Four of the welcomers wore clerical garb. Three had come in business suits. Most of the rest carried cameras, for the Cocaine Cardinal was always news.

He also had an innate sense of timing, or maybe he was just lucky. The turbines were still winding down when the first panel truck came spinning round the corner of the nearest hangar, with two others right behind. Within a minute, a whole squad of men and women with automatic weapons in their hands and DEA on the back of their dark blue shirts had surrounded the plane, self-important pretend infantry.

Watching from the edge of the crowd, I could almost feel the cameras stiffen with excitement.

"Show biz," snarled Tom Slade, standing next to me.

"Pero coño, que cojones," said Pedro Benes from the other side. "This priest runs up and down the Caribbean like a vacuum cleaner, gobbling up enough shit to make whole cities high. Amazing he's still alive. But what balls as long as he is. *Coño."*

The Cocaine Cardinal and the DEA commander were chatting companionably, old allies, as agents boarded the plane and began to pass out black plastic garbage bags, carefully wrapped blocks and suitcases. Among them came a white plaster statue about four feet tall. Agents stacked the haul neatly on the tarmac so that it would most impress the cameras.

"Once again I am able to bring greetings and comfort to the people of the United States from their brothers in the islands of the Caribbean," the cardinal said from the top of a packing crate. "What you see there is cocaine. Not tons of it, which is what is out there, but at least hundreds of pounds. It has been seized by island peoples and their authorities who are infected by this cancer and determined to combat it.

"We speak Spanish, English, Creole, and French and we worship God under different names, but we are proud of our nations and our cultures. Smugglers who continue to use our islands as relay stations from their flights from South America should know that there is a risk. The risk is the outrage of decent people who will not tolerate criminals spreading poison in their midst."

A reporter piped up from the crowd, "This is your fourth

visit in six months with, uh, cargo. Is it getting easier to find, or is there more of it?"

"More and more people are calling their priests and their police to report knowledge and suspicions. Not a day passes without new seizures, by parishioners from caches left by smugglers, or by police from the arms of smugglers themselves."

"Is this vigilante justice?" asked a TV reporter, focusing more at her camera than at the cardinal.

"By no means. We are privileged witnesses to a popular revolt of the decent people in this hemisphere. The islanders of the Caribbean have a lesson to teach the criminals in South America who produce cocaine, and the Americans who consume it in ghettoes and country clubs. This is their gift to all of you."

A reporter asked, "But is all of this legal? Bringing this stuff in . . . who did it belong to? Is anybody in jail? Isn't this evidence . . ."

"Extraordinary times demand extraordinary measures," the cardinal said. "I remind you of the meeting of Caribbean heads of states last fall . . ."

On the fringe of the crowd, a clunky brown sedan wheezed to a stop. It might as well have had "U.S. Government" painted in pink on the driver's door. A tall black man got out and walked over.

"Mornin'."

"Andy," I replied neutrally.

"Becoming an institution, isn't he?" the black man said, gesturing toward the commanding figure before the microphones.

"A good man," I replied neutrally. Andy inclined his head at the tall, thin man at his side. "This is Sylvan Wilson, out of Washington." A bigfoot sent down to take over a case, Andy was saying. "Sylvan. Meet Captain Paul Lorenzo, Miami Homicide. Paul and the cardinal go back a long way."

"So we've heard. Nice to meet you, Paul." The Washington man's smile was tight as a snakeskin. He cut to the chase, very Washington. "Listen, buddy, we'd like to look after the big man this time. We've been hearing some threatening things and, well, we think it'd be better to keep him out of sight until he's ready to go back."

"Without even sweating him for his sources, right?" I tried to say it with a smile, but neither of us missed the edge. "Build up a whole network of informers with one Roman collar. What a coup. Two windows in that Washington office before you know it."

"C'mon, man. We're talking security. This guy is death walking. There's a threat."

"Sorry, no sale. There's always a threat. We've always handled it. We'll handle it this time. Amen."

What else was there to say? We watched in strained silence for a time while a young priest handed the plaster statue to the tall cardinal.

Benes broke the tension. "Time for a commercial," he sniggered.

The cardinal held up the statue.

"This is *Nuestra Señora de la Montaña,* an object of devotion to the Andean peoples of Peru, Ecuador, and Colombia. She is greatly loved. And now"—he paused for effect—"she has been basely defiled."

With a pen knife he cut a hole in the bottom of the statue. White powder spilled onto a sheet of newspaper held by the priest. The cameras rolled.

"I won't tell you on what island this statue was found, but I will tell you that another two dozen were there with her. They have all been destroyed," the cardinal said.

As the last of the cocaine trickled away, the bigfoot bluffed, "I'm afraid you'll be hearing from your chief about this one, Captain." My friend Andy tried to keep scorn off his face.

"The chief has my number, Washington Man. The cardinal's our package."

First the cameras left, then the reporters, and then, in tight convoy, the DEA vans. Two local patrol cars nosed up, and a pair of motorcycles.

The cardinal was talking animatedly with the priests when I walked over.

"Welcome back, Rico," I said. We embraced, the way Latinos do.

We had met more than a decade before when I had still been a young cop and found myself assigned escort duty for a photogenic and outspoken bishop who was already making waves in the Caribbean.

"How come?" I had asked then in an office overlooking an overworked Miami expressway. But I knew the answer. I was young and cocky, a still green sergeant. But I was smart, and I was a good cop, and marked for bigger things.

"You speak Spanish, don't you?" the patrol commander had replied.

"Doesn't everybody?"

"Catholic?"

"Not particularly."

"Then don't pray with him. Just see that he doesn't get into trouble."

"We have bigshots through here all the time. What makes this guy so special? He's only a bishop."

"You don't read the papers, right? Governments up and down the Caribbean say he's a trouble-maker; a rabble-rouser. I guess they'd call him a Commie if that meant anything anymore. I personally don't give a shit what he thinks about poverty or social justice, or human rights or the price of fish. But he's very political and a lot of people, including the wild-eyed right-wing Latino freakies around here, don't like him. No skin off my ass if he's Gandhi or the Second

Coming, I just don't want him offed on my turf. Do what it takes."

What it had taken was for me to persuade one muckraking bishop that it would be easier for both of us if the bishop rode as a passenger in an unmarked police car cum taxi. Across the years we had become friends. The bishop became a cardinal and the young detective clawed his way up the police ladder, but the original routine seldom varied.

"Lisa and the kids?" Rico was asking at the airport now.

"Great. Dinner tonight?"

"Absolutely. I should be free by eight. Maybe we can take in an inning or two of the Marlins before we eat." The cardinal tossed his head at the idling police cars. "Why all the cavalry?"

"You're not real popular just at this moment with the folks who produce the crop that America craves."

"Is that news?"

"A snitch told us that they might try something. Probably smoke, but . . ."

"A generic sort of 'Kill the bum,' or somebody special?"

"The Caballero crowd was what we heard," I said. The cocaine cartel's third largest family.

Rico was silent for a long moment. "I see," he said at length. "A fraternal welcome to the cavalry, then."

"They'll stay with you for at least the public part of the day. We'll tag along behind."

"Okay. Do me a favor and put those in the trunk of your car." Rico nodded toward two scuffed suitcases the pilot had unloaded from the nose compartment of the plane. "There's a bottle of rum and some stuff for the kids. I'll pick 'em up at your place tonight."

"No problem."

Rico spent most of his time before dinner with Sarah. She was Rico's honorary goddaughter, blonde and blue-eyed like her mother, seven years old, and autistic. Sarah needed full-time attention. She had short-circuited her mother's career as a magazine writer, and she had nearly cost us our marriage. Sarah's sister Nancy pouted; nine is a tough age to be left out.

But then Rico swept her up onto his shoulders, careened her across the backyard into a hammock, and told Nancy a well-tried Caribbean story about the sea monster who grew lonely in his cave on the shores of an azure sea. When they came in for dinner their eyes sparkled with laughter. Lisa grilled yellowtail and we ate it with green salad and a bottle of dry Chilean white wine and good talk, a relaxed meal, until Sarah started screaming from her room. Lisa bolted from the table without a word, her face pinched as if she had been scalded.

"She bangs her head against things sometimes," I said, not bothering to hide a father's pain.

"I'm sorry. It must be very hard."

"Harder and harder. At least I get away during the day. For Lisa there's no escape."

"I know."

"I suppose I should try harder to understand, but I'm too mad most of the time. Why? Why? I know you'll say it's God's way. What kind of God would do that to a little girl? If that's God's way, God sucks . . ."

Rico said nothing.

"Sorry, I didn't mean that . . . The wine talking."

Rico smiled: "The way we usually say it is that God sometimes works in ways that surpass our ability to understand."

"Then what? Prayer?"

"Lots of prayers."

"Sorry, man, I just can't bring myself to it."

"No problem, *chico*. I pray for both of us."

It was nearly eleven when I loaded Rico's suitcases into the trunk and pointed north toward the city.

The intimidating cavalcade of patrol cars and motorcycles had sloughed off before dinner as the Cocaine Cardinal ended a round of meetings and appearances. A single unmarked car had dropped Rico for dinner. Another, Slade and Benes, had kept watch outside. Nancy, one of her father's hats pulled low across her brow, pretending to be a spy, had brought them fish sandwiches and beer.

It should have taken twenty minutes for me to drive Rico back to the local archbishop's residence where he was staying.

We never made it.

"You see that guy, Tom?"

I spoke quietly into the radio, watching as I did the dark shape of the chase car behind us. Benes drove. Slade responded, "Black Buick, guy talking on a cell phone. I'll check the license number."

It didn't feel right. Cop instinct. "And watch close to see if we're followed," I said unnecessarily. To Rico, I said, "We'll skip the expressway. Sort of wander up through the Gables."

He was staring out through the night. "Trouble?"

"Always check out people who conspicuously ignore you. Probably nothing. But we'll take an unpredictable way home just in case."

We wound through lush suburban streets, past big pastel-painted houses where fear slept with money. All the back-yards were brightly lit; tight-locked front doors spotlighted and reinforced with burglar alarms.

"A gun in every night table," the cardinal said, reading my mind.

Neat, silent, armed-to-the-teeth suburban streets. The radio spluttered urgently to life: there was a shootout on Southwest Eighth, the main street of Little Havana.

My fingers tensed reflexively on the wheel. It was the kind of call I used to love; to dream about on slow nights when mist blew in off the bay, the air tasted of sea, and it was all you could do to stay awake. All it would take was a few words spilling from a tinny speaker; adrenaline coursing through the car, coffee cups tossed, butts snuffed, the flashing lights snapping on, like a stage; the siren howl becoming the cheer of the crowd. Alone, I would have gone, just for the memories. But Little Havana was off my route that night, too far north, and my cargo was too precious.

The radio dispatcher reported that two ambulances were en route. She called in more cars.

In a lull, Slade radioed from the chase car, "Hey, boss, that Buick was stolen in Dadeland coupla hours ago."

Shit.

"Any sign of anything behind you?"

"Not a thing. I think we're clear at least as far as the causeway."

I turned to Rico. "A lot of people know where you're staying?"

"It's no secret, but not many, I'd say. I didn't know myself until this afternoon. They said it'd be safer out there than in town where I usually stay with the bishop."

From Miami, a causeway piercing Biscayne Bay ran seven miles east and south to Key Biscayne, a boutique island suburb made famous initially by Richard Nixon, and latterly by tennis.

"Officer down, officer down," the dispatcher called. Tension tight in her throat. Every car in the city would go to Little Havana now, or try to.

We slid out of Coral Gables, into a bayside part of Miami called Coconut Grove, only a few minutes from the causeway entrance.

"Normally, I'd have somebody check out the causeway before we got on it, Rico." But not tonight.

"Of course, I understand."

"I think we're okay, but if I was going to run at you, I'd do it on the causeway."

"We're in God's hands, Paul."

"Just so you know."

Listening to the radio Babel, it never occurred to me that the shooting in Little Havana was a diversion to make it easier for a Colombian cocaine family to kill a priest. But it was.

After the blackened suburbs, the intersection at South Dixie Highway was awash with blessed light. Nothing behind them. I took a breath of relief; Rico short-circuited it.

"There's something you should know, *hermano*. The second suitcase back there in the trunk, the light one. It's full of money, more than a million, I'd guess."

I looked sharply across at the priest. It was hard to tell in the darkness, but there might have been just the hint of an abashed grin. "A million. How nice for you, Eminence. A special collection for the missions? Or just garden-variety currency smuggling?"

"How I got it, Paul, is less relevant right now than that until a few nights ago the money belonged to Sebastián Caballero and his family."

"Jesus . . ."

"So you love Him, too."

"Do you have a death wish?"

"Nobody *plans* to come across that kind of money belonging to a Colombian clan, Paul. Something crazy happened, and then something else, then something . . . you know the way it goes down there . . . and suddenly I had this suitcase. I didn't think anybody knew I ended up with it. I'm still not sure they do, in fact."

"I'd guess they might have a pretty good idea."

I flipped my badge at the lady tolltaker at the causeway, eased my pistol from its holster, and laid it on the seat between my legs.

"Close up," I radioed, and Benes jockeyed his car into the left lane tight on the unmarked car's left rear bumper. For seven miles, nothing would pass me, the archbishop, cardinal, or his money.

"What are you going to do with the money?" The thought flared unbidden: it would buy a lifetime of baby-sitters for Sarah, that kind of money.

"To be honest, I haven't even thought about it, since I never expected to have it, much less keep it," he replied. "But who would I give it to? I think the smartest thing to do would be to take it back home . . . it'd be most useful there. Put it under the mattress. When urgent things needed doing, bang, some money could turn up, whoosh! Hallelujah!"

"Black magic." We were driving past scrub pines and palms flanking a narrow beach. Catamarans and sailboards launched from there during the long hot days. At night, lovers parked. And assassins?

"Whatever works," Rico said, fighting the tension. "I remember one time in a little pueblo near where I was born, everybody was convinced that this one particular *campesina* was a witch. They might have killed her, too, except that the parish priest had a bright idea one day . . ."

I had been driving slowly, allowing the traffic in front to pull away. Now drivers were beginning to build up behind both unmarked cars. Good insulation; the road was divided here by concrete blocks and iron rails. I speeded up. If danger came, I sensed, it would come after the first bridge, when we would be easier to bottle up.

". . . so after the fireworks, this was in the days before television, remember, nobody ever bothered that lady again. In the years before she died, people had even begun sitting in the same pew with her at mass again. Mind you, they were neighbors she had known for nearly eighty years; they just took miraculous convincing, that's all."

We were on the long rise of the bridge now, moving well, safe from anything except a helicopter. To the left, two of America's great views: at eight o'clock, downtown Miami lit up the tropical night. At eleven o'clock, Miami Beach, shimmering backdrop for the dark sea.

"Why'd you become a priest anyway? I don't think you ever told me."

"I don't talk about it much; people see a cardinal, they think he was born that way. They say we're called, a vocation. That's true, I guess, but in my case I thought hard about it, no stars in my eyes before I decided. My family was well-off on an island where poverty was truly terrible. Governments came and left, there was violence, a procession of empty isms, but never any change. So I said to myself, 'This is wrong, there has to be a better way. I can help find one.' And so I followed the thought along those four paths that have always been most prominent in the Latin part of the world: politics, business, church, army. None of the other three appealed to me. So I became a priest, to make a long story short. Loved being a parish priest 'till, uh, bishop things got in the way; would love to be one again."

"And now the kids back home paint your name on the shanty walls: 'Rico for President.'"

"They're sweet, but whenever anybody asks I explain that I'm a cardinal; cardinals don't become president. They're not politicians."

"The hell they aren't."

Rico laughed. "Not in the traditional sense, at least."

As we came off the bridge, a garbage truck, left blinker winking, pulled out of the right verge up ahead and lumbered slowly on to the road in my lane. I had no choice but to slow, and as I did my right hand dropped reflexively from the wheel to the gun. From the tangle of traffic behind, an irate driver, probably a tourist, blasted his horn, flashing his lights at the escort car in the left lane. Through his outside mirror, I watched with a tight smile while Benes shot the tooter an elegant bird.

The garbage truck was punctilious and well driven. Once again its turn signal flashed, and it rumbled smoothly into the left lane. I decided it was jockeying for a U-turn by the Marine Stadium that would point it back toward the city.

But I was tragically wrong. What I should have been wondering was what a garbage truck was doing on the Rickenbacker Causeway near midnight, for the truck driver stood suddenly on his brakes. Rico and I were past in an instant, with just time enough to see the huge rear of the truck begin to rise and the truck itself slew back to the right until it straddled both lanes.

"What's going on?" Rico shouted in sudden alarm.

I never saw what spilled from the back of the garbage truck, canisters of some sort, tipping into the road like mines dropping off the stern of a destroyer.

Slade and Benes had no chance. They were almost under the truck when the canisters fell and a searing sheet of flame sprang up behind the truck. Years later I could still hear the crash of metal as cars began stacking up. Maybe I only imagined the screams.

Rico turned, half-kneeling on the front seat, to stare back at the carnage. "God forgive them and save them!" he intoned. From the corner of my eye, I saw him make the sign of the cross.

One desperate driver tried to squeeze past the garbage truck on the right. The truck, an elephant shaking a fly, sideswiped the car and crushed it against the right guard rail. It screeched there in agony until the truck released it. Then it slewed back on to the road, to be engulfed from behind by flaming tons of wreckage.

"*O Dios,* forgive them and protect us sinners." The cardinal was yelling in a mixture of English and Spanish.

"Mayday! Mayday!" I screamed into the radio, realizing even as I did that no help could come in time.

From behind, the bright lights of the garbage truck bored into the sedan. I watched as the back of the truck settled into place and I put my foot down as shots rang out from above the truck cabin. Whoever had been in the back had kicked out the canisters, and was now firing steadily at us. In the oncoming lane, traffic was stopping, people getting out to gape at the terrible fireball, running to help.

"Down, Rico, down."

The cardinal dropped below the level of the front seat as the first bullets plowed into the rear of the sedan. I began zigzagging, pulling away. If the truck was all there was, we might make it.

At least the road ahead was empty. The causeway broadened there to accommodate another parking area on the right and I steered briefly through it, running parallel to the road, to throw off the truckers' aim.

In another few seconds, though, I realized that the garbage truck was just the beater; there to drive out the game to where the hunter could kill it. The hunter lay before us.

Lights flashed on about a hundred yards ahead. I was able to make out the outline of a pickup truck, with what looked like a nozzle on its roof. Not a hose, but some sort of a light machine gun or recoilless rifle mounted there. A do-it-yourself tank destroyer to annihilate an underpowered city sedan with two pawns of the drug war trapped inside.

"Our Father who art in heaven . . ." Rico was praying.

". . . hallowed be Thy name," I continued silently.

My ears were pounding, blood boiling. I put the pedal on the floor and followed the stream of our own bright lights straight at the oncoming pickup.

Chicken. A teenagers' game.

". . . Thy kingdom come . . ."

Suicide run.

". . . Thy will be done . . ."

A last throw.

". . . on earth . . ."

I knew what I had to do. I had to stay exactly between the garbage truck and the pickup. That way, one of them had to break off; the risk of shooting one another was too great.

". . . as it is in heaven . . ."

Only a few seconds now. My right hand was welded to the wheel. I would not waver. I would never waver, not even for one heartbeat. I was going to drive as fast as I could go right into the heart of the pickup, one crazy *gringo*. The shooter above the cab and the driver both must understand that.

"Give us this day . . ."

The gunmen both must know in the depth of their souls that in another few seconds they would die as surely as Rico and I would. They must understand that there would never be any glory for them in killing the Cocaine Cardinal because they would be just as dead.

". . . our daily bread . . ."

The drivers' nerves must crack. The shooter's hand must shake. They must feel a spark of fear underlying the machismo that had brought them to this time and to this killing place, a spark nurtured over four centuries in Latin America that told them that in killing this cardinal they would go straight to hell. Forever.

". . . and forgive us our trespasses . . ."

Gunfire came from the pickup. But it was nervous, tentative. The best shooters never think. This one was scared. Fifty yards now.

Almost over. *Finis*. Turn, turn. No. Hand welded to the wheel. Can't turn.

". . . as we forgive those . . ."

The pickup fired again. A longer burst, but high. I felt the pressure of the lights from behind diminish and caught a fleeting glimpse of the garbage truck careening to the left off the road and across the grassy median past the stadium.

". . . who trespass against us . . ."

Now it was pure nerves. No more gun. *Macho.* The roof gun wouldn't deflect. They were too close. I had my gun out, firing left-handed against our own windstream. Less to hit than to frighten, to release the pent-up rage and the fear. I felt tired, weak, defeated. We were dead men, both of us.

". . . and lead us not into temptation . . ."

A dead man with his right hand welded to a steering wheel.

". . . but deliver us from evil . . ."

The pickup swerved an instant too late. It scraped the side of the sedan, pitching the shooter into the ground in a fatal tangle of arms and legs.

I felt a fierce burning. A fragment of metal, flying debris, had gouged deep into my face. Blood. I could hardly see.

The pickup flipped on its side and slid screeching back onto the road. The car spun like some demented top, round and round, out of control. The seatbelt jerked me sharply, but Rico snapped his. He ricocheted off the dashboard, against the passenger car door and finally slumped back with a groan, senseless.

"Don't roll, don't roll," I prayed silently.

The car didn't roll. Instead it pitched headlong into a stand of young mangrove along the shore, hurtling into the shallow black water with tremendous force.

I would never know how long I lay gasping amid the tick of angry metal and the roar of escaping steam, but it was the water that brought me back.

I was shivering. Even in winter, sea water in Miami is not cold, but the black water lapping at my ankles left me shivering. It took a minute to refocus, but my hands had remembered. I prised aching fingers from the wheel, freed the door with a shove of my shoulder, and struggled groggily out of the car. I still had the gun in my left hand, though it had done us no good. I jammed it in my waistband and leaned back against the car and clawed for a fulcrum.

In the bloody half-world of my vision, I could see the

pickup dark and silent on its side. The body of the gunman lay on the sand; the driver, presumably still inside, posed no threat. In the distance I could make out what I thought was the garbage truck. Was it heading back toward Miami? Maybe. And then, maybe, I could just hang on, not relax exactly, just enjoy the enormous luxury of doing nothing for a few minutes. Help was on the way, I could be sure of that. It would come not from Miami but from the Key Biscayne side, where the road was open; Dade County cars patrolled the causeway, and the island had its own small police force. Someone would come. They had better. I felt woozy and I needed a doctor. Rico would probably also benefit from a visit to the neighborhood emergency room. His head cracking against the door . . . He'd have a terrible . . .

Rico!

The passenger seat was empty, the door open. Rico lay still on his side in the shallow black water a few yards away. He was deathly still.

"Rico!"

Painfully, I inched to the back end of the car, and around to the right side. I scuttled to Rico, knelt down, and pushed him upright. He weighed a ton.

Breathing, no . . . yes, he was breathing, desperate, shallow little breaths like a baby's. Weak. Sporadic. Stopping. He needed help, resuscitation, an expert. There was only me.

"Please, God." I crawled around behind Rico. Had to do something, even if it was wrong.

With all my strength I squeezed under Rico's breastbone. Nothing happened. Again I squeezed. Cursing, squeezing, cursing. Painfully, I turned him around and began mouth-to-mouth. A bad position and a bad rhythm, but what else could I do?

It was an eternity later when water began seeping from Rico's mouth, life seemed to flow back to his muscles, and he started to cough.

"You're okay, *hermano*. Breathe deep. Breathe deep, man. We're okay." For me, it was a litany more satisfying than any rosary.

We stayed like that for a time, a frozen tableau under the moonlight, me on my knees in the water, supporting the priest; Rico alive at least, if not conscious.

I watched the forest of flashing lights and the ugly cloud of smoke still rising from the accident scene. Two police cars came shooting past from Key Biscayne, but they zoomed right by, heading for the carnage. I cradled Rico and thought about Slade and Benes. I thought about Lisa and Nancy and Sarah. And I thought about a million dollars lying twenty feet away.

When a car pulled up on the beach, its lights flooding him suddenly, I sagged with relief.

"Help." An agile figure jumped from the car and ran to the water's edge.

"I don't know how badly hurt he is; please help me get him out of the water and we'll get an ambulance."

The figure on the beach stopped and peered into the blackness, leaning forward from his waist as if he were near-sighted.

"That's the priest, the one they call the Cocaine Cardinal, is it not?" The man on the beach was a wiry Latin, around thirty, with long hair and heavily accented English. He made no move to approach. A wary peasant newly come to town. At least that's what I thought.

"Yes. Yes, that's right. There's been an accident. The cardinal's hurt. Please help. There's no danger."

"Hijo de la gran puta," the Latino exploded. "I have brought help for this *cabrón* priest, and some for you. One bullet for each."

"Listen . . ."

"My name is Pedro Caballero, priest. Do you know the name? It is my brother whose business you are ruining with all your sacred shit. It is our money that you have stolen, *cabrón.* It is we who will kill you. Perhaps you will send us a postcard from heaven."

I tried to shelter Rico, cupping him around the shoulders, shielding him from the filth that spewed from the beach in a profane mixture of bad English and peasant Spanish. I eased Rico's weight on to the right knee, shook a cramp from my left hand.

"Talk to me, priest! I demand that you talk to me!" Caballero screamed. "Do you not fear? Will you not beg for your whore life?"

"He's unconscious, he can't hear you. He's dying and in great pain. Your bullet would be a blessing."

"Talk to me!"

A bullet slammed into the water a few inches away, but I remember feeling strangely calm.

"He can't hear you. Let him die like a Christian. Your money's in the car. Take it and go."

Caballero spun to look at the battered sedan. "You're lying."

"See for yourself, a blue suitcase in the trunk."

"You lie!"

"As you wish. I'm not going anywhere until the cardinal dies. Then we can look together."

"You will die, too, priest-friend."

"I think the cardinal will wake before he dies. He will tell you, too. Perhaps he will even beg."

Greed and vengeance lapped at Caballero, in conflicting tides. Greed won. He raced over to the car, bent over just like in the movies, head turning one way and the other, trying to keep simultaneous track of Rico and the money. It took less than a minute. Rico moaned once. I sat very still, flexing.

Caballero cracked open the battered trunk with a mighty kick and scuttled back to the water's edge, gingerly tossing the blue bag on the sand before him.

"It's a trick."

"No trick."

"If it's a trick, you will die most painfully, but only after you have watched your whore priest friend dying."

There was nothing I could say.

Caballero squatted down and unzipped the money suit-case. His eyes were bright and wide as he studied the tight-packed bills under the moon. In that instant, I raised my left hand, aimed as carefully as I could from my awkward position, and shot Pedro Caballero four times.

Later, I dragged a groaning cardinal to the Colombian's black air-conditioned sedan with crushed velour seats. Shaking, bleeding, sobbing, I drove us back to the mainland.

It had taken only an extra few seconds to scoop up the millionaire suitcase and lock it in Caballero's trunk. Maybe I hadn't thought about it as stealing at that instant.

But who was I kidding?

In the few minutes that it took to drive Rico to a hospital back on the mainland, I was already worrying full-time about the money—my money.

"It's the cardinal, the Cocaine Cardinal. He's hurt bad, unconscious. Help him." I must have looked like a madman, bursting into the emergency room with Rico lolling in my arms.

I heard a Latina nurse twitter; she knew about Rico, all right, but a stiff-faced doctor dismissed me almost disdain-fully. "You shouldn't have moved him. Lay him on the table. Wait over there. Someone will look at the cut on your face."

But I didn't wait. Sprinting to the car, I drove home. I threw the suitcase in the eaves of the garage under a paint-stained tarpaulin. Then back to the hospital, less than half an hour, round-trip.

This time I left the car badly parked farther from the entrance. With the driver's door open and motor running, I walked in a pretend daze around the busy parking lot, until, a few minutes later, a cop recognized me and gently led me back inside.

My own injuries were minor, but Rico was critically injured; hanging on in the operating room with a concussion, broken ribs, lung problems, and possible internal injuries. In the coming days, while nuns and priests and crowds of everyday folk bearing flowers and candles and rosaries gathered spontaneously on the lawn outside the hospital to pray for a cardinal at razor's edge, I learned the meaning of irony.

In the garbled account the newspapers and my bosses jigsawed together, I became the hero of what passed into the lore of a vibrant and violent city as the Causeway Massacre. And nary a word about any suitcase, any money.

In those anxious first few days the cardinal nearly died more than once, and "miracle" crept into more than one news report. But Rico didn't die. Indeed, his doctors would eventually pronounce themselves proud of their cardinal patient. There was still some short-term memory loss about what they euphemistically called "the accident," but otherwise His Eminence would recover entirely, they announced with an air of self-congratulation.

"You saved my life out there, *hermano*. There's a lot I don't remember, but that's something I'll never forget. Count on me—anything, anytime, anywhere," Rico said softly once the crises had passed, looking at once wan and determined from a hospital bed that had by then made every evening news.

Within a few months, the Cocaine Cardinal was back crisscrossing the Caribbean in his lonely and losing crusade against drugs. Rico's warmth for me and my family never flickered. If anything, it deepened. I welcomed it but could never match it. After the causeway, it was a long time before I ever felt easy with Rico again, cringing mentally, waiting for a question I could not answer.

What about the money, Paul?

Rico never asked the question.

I would like to have believed that the concussion had driven recollection of the blue suitcase and its fortune from Rico's mind forever.

But the realest part of me, that spark which never really died even in the madness that was to come, understood that Rico did not ask about the money because he knew that his friend—his savior—had stolen it.

4

I STOLE THE money for my family; to take care of my daughter. She deserved it. We needed it. Sarah had worn us down. Poor, beautiful, lovable autistic Sarah, whom I loved with every fiber of my being. She had ended Lisa's hopes of being able to write from home; stretched my pay tighter and tighter until we lunged from credit-card payment to credit-card payment, never catching up. The money was for my family and its necessities. That is what I told myself.

At first it was true. With careful anonymity I used chunks to finance investments for friends felled on the causeway: the invalided Benes and slain Tom Slade's family. Then, for Sarah, I canvassed sources in the barrio until they produced the perfect find: a smart, patient, and caring Central American named Carmen. She came to live with us as a housekeeper-nurse and soon became part of the family. Carmen had come to the United States by walking across the Rio Grande. Like every one of the millions of illegal aliens in America, she lived in daily, quaking fear of *La Migra*—the Immigration Service. So I reached into the pile of dirty money and bought Carmen a green card, go-away-and-never-bother-me-again permanent residence. Maybe that was the best thing I did with the stolen money, but it came to ashes. Like everything else.

At first Lisa was delighted with the regained freedom that money bought. She was pleased with my new 4×4 and the playroom added to the back of the house. But then, as purchase followed purchase and our lifestyle grew beyond what a police salary could justify, Lisa began asking questions. My bosses at headquarters might have been asking questions, too, but if so, I never heard any. At home, I put Lisa off with wisecracks and inventions: a horse came home, poker winnings, a middling lottery win I had collected under a false name to avoid taxes.

I never convinced her, though. Somehow, before either one of us could stop it, a fifteen-year marriage began spinning out of control, faster, ever faster. Suspicion replaced trust in an almost classic unraveling of faith. I found myself spending as much time with the financial pages as with the once-fascinating, then-boring crime statistics that popped up in the office computer every morning. Lisa found more and more freelance assignments that kept her away from home. I did some drinking, popped pills when the mood struck; enjoyed an occasional snort. I began staying out, screwing around. For a few weeks, I had a passionate fling with a pair of black girls, twins studying for their pilot's license, whom I had picked up in a bar. With Lisa, the tension and fights climaxed finally, with the tawdry ritual of accusation and denial.

"You've been with other women."

"No, I swear." Lie, lie, lie.

"I don't believe you. You leave, or I will."

I left. I still saw the kids as much as possible, and Lisa and I learned painfully how to relate politely. Nancy would be a teenager soon, with Sarah close behind. Neither Lisa nor I, not even when the shouting became pushing and punching, had ever questioned the other's commitment to Sarah or Nancy. Only to one another.

One afternoon, after about six months, she called at work and said quietly, "Paul, I've decided it's time for me to begin dating. I wanted you to know."

"Sure, okay. Enjoy." What else could I say without revealing the vein of ice and anger that careened along my spine?

I was thinking of Lisa not long after that as I threaded through Friday-night traffic on my way to the house where I no longer lived. I had had a few drinks and I wanted to see my kids.

Lisa's car was there but the house was dark. I parked in a church lot a block away, walked back to the house, and let myself in through the back door. Funny, but I wasn't sure that Lisa knew I came sometimes to visit with our sleeping children, but she knew I had a key and she hadn't bothered to change the locks.

Nancy, my big girl, lay asleep on her stomach in a room that was cluttered testimony to preteen affluence. Clothes littered the floor and shadowed the portable computer on which she did her homework and exchanged gossip with electronic penpals. Books, homework, a half-eaten package of chips lay hither and yon. Her mother would have a fit in the morning.

I straightened my daughter's light blanket, and crossed a carpeted hallway lit by a tiny nightlight. As I let myself into Sarah's room, I could hear the light snores of housekeeper Carmen from a third bedroom. Sarah was a thrasher. She tossed and turned and often woke at night in fright. For a time she had pulled her hair out. She was restless that night as well, turning from side to side in search of a comfortable position, her thumb working in and out of her mouth as she wrestled with the demons in her mind. For a long time I sat patiently by the bed as I had so many nights before, crooning. I ran my fingers through her hair, along the curve of her cheeks and around beautiful ears lately graced by tiny silver starburst earrings. Never would have happened if it had been up to me, but Lisa and Nancy had insisted that ear-piercing was a fact of life.

It did not occur to me that Lisa was not also asleep in the master bedroom in the back wing of the L-shaped house, until a car pulled up in the driveway. Two doors closed. I heard Lisa's voice, and a man's. Too late to run. I should have strode from the bedroom and announced myself. But I didn't. *Voyeur.*

"I thought the ending was pretty lame, but it was a good movie," Lisa said, with a lightness of voice I had not heard for a long time.

"Yeah, but that part in the boat was sexy as hell." The voice was strong and rich, not educated, but confident.

Lisa laughed. "Yes, it was. But not tonight, George."

"Why not?"

"The kids are asleep. And so is Carmen. Rule number one, remember. We don't do it in this house."

"Rules are made to be broken. Right here. In the living room. On the floor. Clothes on."

"George, no." The excitement in her voice was unmistakable. "Stop," she said in surrender.

There was a shuffle and Paul could imagine two bodies easing on to the floor.

"Stop," she said one last time a few minutes later, and then, "Hard. Do it hard, George. Harder. There, there! Harder. No . . . Yes!"

Later, I crept away like a thief in the night.

The next morning, I ran the license plate of my wife's lover through the motor vehicles computer in Tallahassee. The car belonged to one Jorge Cuevas, who lived in a nowhere development out on the western reaches of the country that had been sawgrass, bass, and alligators when I was growing up in Miami. A police inquiry to the telephone company elicited an unlisted number. The voice I had heard the night before greeted me on the answering machine, first in English, then in Spanish. I said nothing after the beep. "Hard, harder," she had begged.

Cross-checking through the city directory produced a business address for Cuevas: a used-car lot along a strip of shady, buyer-beware con artists. A Latina who spoke peasant Spanish said that Señor Cuevas was in a meeting. I didn't leave a message. Between shuffling papers and beating off a request from a VIP security detail for the loan of some of my detectives, at midmorning I dropped Cuevas's name in the department computer.

Under "reason for inquiry," I typed "rape suspect." The computer didn't know Jorge Cuevas. A nobody used-car salesman? Oh, Lisa. For the hell of it, I asked the FBI computer about Cuevas, listing him this time as a suspected drug smuggler. The computer was down.

Near noon, I contrived to bump into an ambitious southern girl, a saucy blonde named Michele who had come to the police department with a master's degree and stars in her eyes. She had been coming on to me for months, truth to tell, working juvenile but thirsting for the day she could become a major-league detective. So I took Michele to lunch—stone crabs and white wine—and then fucked her blind in a borrowed hotel room on Miami Beach. Numb and sated, we returned in separate cars to headquarters, both understanding that an afternoon of lust had been a career down payment.

Late that afternoon, after one of these interminable department meetings that destroy hours, enthusiasm, and egos without resolving anything, I once again asked the FBI computer about Jorge Cuevas.

The machine worked this time.

Jorge Cuevas Infante, aka George, aka Bonito, aka Pretty Baby, had been born of Cuban parents in Union City, New Jersey. There had been a string of minor teenage arrests, a stint in the army with an early discharge, not quite dishonorable. The first time hard man George had gone to jail it had been eighteen months for bilking an old lady out of her inheritance. A gigolo. Not fresh meat, Lisa, is he? You can do better. Then ole Jorge had done two federal years after the Coast Guard had caught him off New Jersey in a fishing boat loaded with smack. Then nothing for the past five years. What happened, Georgie? A little hard time put the fear of God in you? More likely, he was into some new scam a bit slicker than the others and still hadn't been caught. I had read Cuevas's biography dozens, no, hundreds, of times before: South Florida teemed with petty hoods who drifted south from frostier climes like starlings seeking winter nests. There was a DEA cross-reference number at the foot of the FBI file. Probably the fishing boat arrest, I decided, but chased it anyway, wondering if my security clearance was high enough: the drug Feds were a jealous lot. When the computer sneered "Access Denied" for the third time, I surrendered and called Andy Ridgeway.

"Hey, *amigo,* did you hear the one about the rabbi and the parrot?"

"Weeks ago, and I'm just heading home for dinner. What is it?"

It took less than a minute.

"Peanuts," Andy announced. "Cuevas is small fry, man. There was this thing with the heroin on a boat. Then, the rest is all intelligence stuff: a suspicious series of trips to Puerto Rico; assistant manager of a video rental place in Brooklyn we think dispenses more than dirty movies; let's see, suspected associate the Matarazzi family in New York, and then . . . finally, why he moves in on us. Last entry about four months old, this one'll interest you: suspected associate/contract employee Caballero family, Miami. Whadaya know about him?"

It was a cheap headset and I was gripping it so hard the plastic cracked. Coffee cascaded across the papers on my desk as I shot to my feet, rigid with alarm.

"Nothing. Nothing hard, Andy," I managed. "His name came up is all. I'll let you know."

"Sure. See ya."

Fuck. I slammed my fist against the top of the computer terminal, wrestled with my jacket with one hand, and punched phone buttons with the other. Jorge and Lisa. No coincidence. The Caballeros had brought Cuevas to Miami. The score they were interested in was more than sex, a roll on the living room floor. I'd explain it to Lisa. She'd understand. She was not just an occasional lay for good-looking George.

She was his target. The Caballeros were tracking us.

I saw it clearly. I'd explain it to Lisa, step by step; make up something about driving past, seeing a strange car in the driveway, checking the plate. She'd be angry, but it would pass once she understood . . .

And then I'd pay a private call on George; send him to jail on a trumped-up charge or to hell in a coffin. Do it with my fists, a night stick, or my pistol, it didn't matter. As long as the Caballeros got the message.

It was nearly six. Carmen would be ready to feed the girls. Lisa probably would be home, too. No answer.

Why? Of course they were home. Where else . . . No answer. Go! Go!

I wrestled through the rush-hour traffic with siren wailing. Alongside me, the cellular telephone rang forlornly.

No answer. By the time I turned on to our street, a deadly certainty had settled over me. There was no hurry. I knew it. Too late. I knew what I would find. But I was wrong.

George and his vengeful Caballero friends had not butchered my family. They had murdered only loyal Carmen, slitting her throat in the kitchen where she had been preparing chicken and rice for dinner.

Of Lisa and the kids there was no sign. I turned off the stove and left without reporting the crime.

I went to my apartment to wait for the phone call. I was

sitting in the easy chair, still fully dressed, deadly still, staring at nothing, the phone on my lap, when it rang a few minutes before midnight.

"The money, scumbag. Your family for the money."

"Who is this?"

The voice was gruff, controlled. Accented to a trained ear, but not Jorge Cuevas. I had never heard it before.

"No games, *cabrón.* Check your mailbox."

The phone went dead.

It had taken the Caballeros more than two years to piece together what had happened on the causeway that night. I had always known that someone, someone less friendly than Rico, might one day come looking for the money. For months I had tensed each time the phone rang. But the call never came. Instead, Rico went off to Rome to become a Curia cardinal, the Vatican's way of getting him out of the line of fire, and time had built a cocoon of security around us in Miami. Gradually, it was no longer *the* money. It became *our* money. Mine and Lisa's and the kids'.

I figured I would find delivery instructions and a map in the mailbox. Instead, in a paper napkin atop a pile of bills and junk mail, there lay a small ear pierced with a starburst earring.

Sarah's ear.

I staggered out into the courtyard and retched into some bushes.

Then I went back inside and sat by the phone.

"Sorry I didn't get right back to you, *cabrón,* but it was my turn with Big Mama. That's one hungry lady. Fucks like a battery hen. How do you keep her satisfied? Too much for one man, I think. What do you think?"

"I want to talk to my wife."

"Not possible until Luis is finished. Then it's Jose's turn."

"I want to talk to my wife."

I hung up.

The Caballeros had lost track of the money when it had disappeared into the cargo hold of the Cocaine Cardinal's plane. Probably, they had been looking for it ever since, with ever-diminishing prospects of getting it back, but with a need to punish whoever had taken it: their family reputation demanded that. How had they found us? I had never told a soul about the money. Except, toward the end, Lisa. Pillow talk, Lisa? Sweet nothings to beloved George about my husband the cop who wraps himself in the financial pages instead of in me? God help us.

But really it didn't matter how they had found out about the money. What mattered is whether they knew if the thief had also killed Pedro Caballero that night. If it was just money they might take it and release my family rather than going to war. Every cop in Florida, every Fed, would go gunning for Caballeros if they fucked with the family of a senior Miami police officer. But if the Colombians also knew it was me who had killed their kin, bang, bang, shot him four times, bang, bang good riddance, then Lisa and the kids were dead already and I would be soon. All fall down.

Lisa called a few minutes later.

"Paul! Paul, oh, God, Paul." Her voice was octaves too high, on the edge of full-blown hysteria.

"Are you all right?"

"They . . . yes, oh, God."

"The girls, Lisa. Are you with the girls? How are the girls?"

"Asleep. They gave them a shot. Then they cut . . . Oh, God, help us Paul. I'm so ashamed . . ."

"Hold on. I'll come get you. Soon."

Liar.

"Paul, I love you. I . . ." She screamed and I covered my ear against sounds of the phone dropping.

"The money. All of it," the gruff voice demanded. "Tomorrow."

"Look, you know I don't have all of it anymore and that

it'll take me time to get what is left. It's offshore. I'll have to go get it early tomorrow. Unless you'll take a check."

"Don't fuck with me, *puto*. The next time I send you one of your wife's tits."

It was worth a try.

"I don't know why you're so angry with me. I'm just an intermediary in all this—a middle man, you must know that. It wasn't me who took the suitcase off the cardinal's plane."

No good.

"No way, *cabrón*. You have the money and you are the *hijo de puta* who killed Pedro. And I have your wife and two daughters."

Hopeless.

"I never killed anybody, I swear it. But you can have your money, no problem. Where do you want the money? When? I can get it in the morning."

"That I tell you tomorrow. Now it is my turn to spend a little time with Mama; she likes it rough, doesn't she? Then maybe the girls. *¿Quién sabe?* That little one, the one with the hearing problem, she's crazy, man. You need to learn how to discipline your women, *puto*."

All fall down.

"At the end of the block, turn left and drive down past the row of stores to the Stop sign."

Her voice was tightly controlled and she read like a slow third grader.

"Okay." Scanning the darkness, I tried to sound reassuring. "Can you see the girls? Are they with you?"

"Yes. At the Stop sign"—pause—"go straight until you come to some railroad tracks."

Kidnappers love mobile phones. For nearly two hours Lisa's captors had kept me driving through the piece of South Dade county where new residential development, shoddy one-story family factories, and workshops that made windows and refinished furniture huddled together one step from bankruptcy. Lisa was reading directions presumably handed her one snippet at a time.

"Let's see if Mama reads as good as she fucks," Gruff Voice had sneered as I had left my apartment with a phone in one hand and a heavy black leather attaché case in the other. "You play straight with us and Mama and the kids'll be fine—except, *cabrón,* you'll find her a bit sore. We just want the money."

No way, Jose. This was not about money. It was about death.

"Paul, when you cross the tracks, pull over on the right and stop."

Either they were waiting for a drop point to clear or they were shadowing me. Both, most likely. It was their play, and I would drive 'till kingdom come if that was what it took.

I had not slept the night before, instead I'd fled the claustrophobia of the apartment, ignored the call of a gaudy strip of bars nearby, and drove at last to the beach. I'd kicked away my shoes and walked alone among the stars. I had had choices to make, and by the time dawn crept in from a flat and oily sea, I had made them.

All the cavalry anybody could ever ask for—Feds, SWAT teams, helicopters, hot-and-cold running cops—was one phone call away. To get it, all I had to do was to make one simple declarative sentence on the way to jail from a dead career. "Please help me, I stole a million dollars and the cocaine gang I stole it from has kidnapped my family and wants it back."

No, I'd play this one alone. It was the only way. So I had spent the day making careful preparations, and so, presumably, had they. The Caballeros had insisted of course that I come alone. If they thought I had help they couldn't spot as they pushed me through the night like a rat in a maze, so much the better. Let them chew on it.

I had just finished urinating into the weeds by the disused tracks when the phone rang.

"Turn right one mile ahead and you'll see a gas station." Lisa seemed excited. "Parked alongside the outside pump is an empty blue Ford. The trunk is open. Put the money in there."

As I put the car in gear, I could feel a vein of tension pulsing in my forehead. I spoke slowly and clearly into the phone.

"The money goes in only after I'm sure they're safe."

The gruff-voiced kidnapper replied without bluster, all business. "No problem. A straight swap. I'm with your wife in a car from where we can see the Ford; a few hundred meters. When you approach, I get out; your wife and children stay inside. Once I see the money go into the trunk, I close the door and walk away. They can lock themselves and wait till you get there; flash the lights and sound the horn if they want to. Take you maybe two minutes to get to them. By then my friends and I are gone with the money, *adiós.*"

It wasn't perfect for either one of us. I couldn't be immediately sure Lisa and the kids were safe, but neither would the Caballeros see the color of their money before letting Lisa go. It would have to do.

"I see you coming, Paul. Hurry, hurry." It was almost a whisper.

At the gas station, I stopped well short of the parked sedan at the pump. From a parking lot about two hundred yards ahead, a car flashed its lights and I saw a bulky figure get out and stand near the front passenger door.

"That's me. Now you, *mierda mía,*" the gruff voice taunted me on the phone.

Getting out of the car and walking up to the Ford was suicide. A gunman waiting somewhere in the shadows, anywhere, could hardly miss.

I took a deep breath and got out of the car, the phone jammed between ear and shoulder. In one hand I held the bulky attaché case, in the other my gun. Braced for a bullet, I walked through stiff silence to the opened trunk of the Ford.

"Put the case inside," my phone commanded.

I waited, stock still, the attaché poised in the air above the trunk like some magician's prop.

"Lisa, tell me when he's out of the car and that you have locked the doors."

After a pause that seemed to last a century, her voice came, weak with relief and fear. "He's gone, Paul. We're safe. Hurry, hurry."

I laid the case gently on the floor of the trunk, turned, and sprinted back to the car. In a second I was driving toward the lot where flashing headlights marked Lisa and my girls.

A few yards away, a second car sprang to life and roared away, tires screeching. In the rearview mirror, I saw two men wheel the Ford to life.

"Lisa, Lisa." In another minute I would be there.

In the background behind her shouts, I could hear the girls. Another few hundred feet.

In the excitement, the exhilaration, I nearly deceived myself into believing that it might end happily. But I knew better.

It was never really a kidnap exchange. It was an ambush. It wasn't about money. It was about murder.

I saw the ignition flash from off to my right and the white tail of smoke. I stood on the brake and my heart broke.

The rocket-propelled grenade struck Lisa's car on the driver's door. The explosion was deafening, final.

"Better luck next time, *cabrón*," the telephone shouted.

Jerking the wheel, roaring like a bull in pain, I pointed the car toward a pickup truck where a solitary figure had dropped the missile launcher and was in the process of aiming a second one at me.

I put my foot on the floor. And I hit the pickup broadside just as the assassin fired.

The rocket roared off harmlessly into the sky as the truck toppled onto its side and skidded with a grinding squeal across the concrete.

When I prised myself from the wreck, I found the assassin near the pickup, a young man with thick tousled black hair lying on his stomach in a pool of blood.

"Help me, *madre mía, ayúdame*," the man moaned.

"What hurts?"

"My back, my legs, *aiyee Dios*."

"I'll help you."

Grinding my pistol deep into the assassin's ass, I fired once.

The man was still screaming when from the distance came a sudden crump, and a pillar of fire lanced briefly into the black sky.

Some curious soul had opened the attaché case.

It gets foggy after that. Even after all the therapy, all the years, more than a decade, mist still cloaks the hillsides. To put it bluntly, I flipped out. A basket case. But nobody ever learned that I was a thief. Even when it didn't matter anymore, I was always still a hero in the eyes of my department, of people who never had any inkling of the tragic justice that was meted out that night.

The solicitous city salted me away for a long time on public money in a fancy private place upstate where there were a lot of horses. People came to visit me, cops, old friends, even Rico once, but I never really connected with them. Too much going on inside my head. For a time I made friends with one of the other patients, a pilot who had walked away from an accident that had killed a lot of his passengers. We had much in common, though I never told him why, and he didn't seem terribly sick to me, but he must have been because one night he slit his wrists.

After that, I kept to myself. I never even rode any of the horses. But gradually, I suppose a certain healing began because I started to think not only about the past but also about the future. That was a good sign, the shrinks said, an end to a cloying stage of mourning and grief and the start of something better. But they wouldn't have said that, not at all, if they knew what future I was planning.

There must have been a trigger I never recognized, because one fine autumn night I knew that I was ready, and after more than two years among the shrinks and horses, I went AWOL forever. I simply walked out of my neat little room, climbed a wall more protective than intimidating, and within twenty minutes had hitched a ride south from a lady truck driver who certainly knew I was escaping from an asylum but didn't give a damn.

The next few years were ones I try not to think about now, a bleak time spent in a skin that seemed not my own, but some stranger's. I survived them, somehow. It was Rico who searched for me, Rico who found me at last, and Rico who helped to heal my soul until, five years ago, I came to the Vatican, dressed in my almost-priest suit and a reconstructed psyche.

Thinking about it, it doesn't seem so strange after all. A lot of damaged people find homes and useful citizenship as motes in Vatican shadows. I know that now. But who could ever have imagined it among the embers of three women I loved?

VATICAN CITY

5

LATE THAT SUNDAY afternoon, the day before the body of a murdered priest would rouse tethered demons, I was reading in my room when there came a tentative knock at the door, followed by a fresh-faced seminarian named Clarence, a Brit, and slick-as-sin.

"Brother Paul, I hope I am not disturbing you." He was a second-year seminarian, but not one who I thought would make it to ordination.

"Not at all, poised as I was between study and a snooze."

Clarence smiled. "About tonight, Brother Paul, the community meeting. I wondered if I might be excused. There's some pastoral work I've left hanging and I'd like to go out to the parish . . ."

Community meetings were once-a-week pray-alongs in which the seminarians, having gone to school all day, were afflicted with the usually dry and often banal spiritual musings of some invited professorlike priest. I hated them nearly as much as the seminarians but had to be careful about letting victims slide out or no one would ever go.

"Santa Rita, that's the parish where you are working, right?" I temporized.

"Yes, Brother, working class, out along the Via Tiburtina," he said, naming a featureless part of Rome that might as well have been Liverpool.

"You have classes tomorrow, right? Pastoral work isn't meant to interfere with studies."

"Absolutely, Brother. It's just that I've been doing some counseling and this afternoon I got a call from the person—"

"Clarence, it takes forty minutes by bus to get out there, doesn't it? And forty minutes back. Which means that you'll be late getting back—maybe late to class tomorrow."

"I won't be late. I promise."

Which probably meant somebody was picking him up on a *motorino*.

"Okay, Clarence, but this time only." I was feeling magnanimous, for I, too, had reason to skip that night's meeting.

"Thank you, Brother," he said, turning to leave.

"Oh . . . and Clarence . . ." He leaned back over his shoulder. "Give her my regards."

"Who?"

"That elderly parishioner lady you're counseling."

At least he had the grace to blush. Maybe he'd make a priest after all.

A little while later, I caught a bus from the Piazza Venezia and rode it across the Tiber to the end of the line outside the Vatican gates.

Dinner was the Spanish Caribbean at its best, *chico* black beans, rice, succulent fried plantains called *maduros*. There were morsels of fried pork and shredded beef, but I mostly ate grilled snapper that tasted as if it had come off a tropical reef that same morning. When you think about it, maybe it had. We had eaten together before at his place, but never this well.

"I know you don't eat like this every night," I said. "Nobody could. What's the occasion?"

"Soul food. I eat like this when I'm homesick and I think my cholesterol can stand the shock." Tredi laughed, rubbing a nascent belly. Hairy thighs strained against a faded pair of chino shorts. He wore no shoes.

"As a matter of fact," he said, worrying a fatty chunk of pork, "a lot of what we're eating blew in with a visiting nuncio from down that way."

"Anything special going on?"

"Little confusion in Cuba, but what's new about that?"

"You know that's not what I mean."

He sighed. "It was all a long time ago, Paul. Faces change, memories are short. Chances are, it's over."

How could he be sure?

"But no relaxing, Paul. Right? I get the official mumble-jumble, but you're Mr. Fixit. Poking around, listening. Old stuff, new stuff. I want to hear it all."

He had said as much before. I sometimes wondered if it was his way of assigning make-work to an ailing friend.

"Yeah, sure. But, that, uh . . ." I felt the old tightness. "Sometimes I still think lightning's going to fall out of the sky. It comes back. Not as often, but . . . And then when Jimmy Kearns died . . . it was bad for me."

It had happened a few months ago in the small apartment above the church where Father Jimmy Kearns had lived for more than thirty years, as much an institution in the heart of Miami as sunshine and violence. Like the church, the apartment had seen better days. Jimmy Kearns, though, had never changed. He was a legend, everything a priest should ever be. He spoke English with a brogue and Caribbean Spanish and Haitian Creole with atrocious accents. He spoke them infectiously all day and all night with street people who needed help.

If there was truly anybody who had no enemies, it must

have been Jimmy Kearns. But somebody had killed him anyway, carved the old man up slowly with a knife. Friends in Miami Homicide had sent me copies of the paperwork through an accommodation address in Panama—my only link with Florida for almost a decade. They thought the murderer had been a street psycho with a grudge against priests. But suppose Jimmy Kearns had been killed for information?

It is simple to explain why it was so important. I had made many painful stops on my zigzagging path between crazy Miami cop and usually sane Catholic brother. Jimmy Kearns and the friend with whom I had shared dinner were the only two who knew them all, knew that a journey of despair had ended with my back to Vatican walls.

My head told me the Miami cops were right. My fears told me that the memories and the hatreds out there were deeper than Tredi thought.

He threw me a quick change of pace. "Still seeing Father Ivanovic, Paul?"

I took a deep breath. "Regular as mass. Once a week. Twice when he has time." It was a friend's question; he already knew the answer.

"Good, that's important."

Mikhail Ivanovic had a long beard and a sharp-honed mind, and he kept my scars from festering. He bottled up the black side. He was the reason that I was a usually functioning and sometimes reliable servant of the church.

"Is he Russian, Ivanovic? Funny, but I've never asked him."

"Ukrainian, maybe. He sure ain't Irish." He punched my shoulder lightly, tickled at his own joke, wanting to lighten the mood, change the subject. "Keep the sunny side up, Paul, and a touch of private cynicism, and you'll go far in this town. Look at me!" He laughed again.

We drank Jamaican beer; like a soft moon rising over a summer sea. We talked about nothing, mostly, the way old friends do; politics, Vatican gossip, stories from around the

Caribbean. He was my silent partner in a fantasy baseball league, and we kicked around some ideas to improve the team, but we were both smart enough to realize that it wasn't our year.

"Is that *vivo* in the Secretariat of State going to win the pennant again? What's his name, Coogan?" he asked.

I nodded: "Hogan. From New York. An expert in offshore finance and the National League."

"Bears watching, does he?"

"Hogan's a comer," I agreed. Hogan was barely forty, a well-merited monsignor already. And a shoo-in for bishop, I reckoned.

We played a double-header that night. He was feeling good; so relaxed that I could feel myself unwinding, too. We could've played on the computer, as we sometimes did by modem when he claimed to be feeling trapped and manic: he had enough electronics on his desk in the next room to conjure takeout pizza from the moon. But we both liked the feel of the cards and that tingle that comes waiting for the careening dice to talk.

It was a table game that we'd first played nearly twenty years before, and while sometimes I'd remember to write away for updated player cards, mostly we played with old teams and old baseball memories. He was fast and reckless, a Latin American playing with intuition and brio and enjoying every minute of it. I plodded, mostly, played the percentages. We never kept track and he'd probably call me a liar, but I swear that I beat him six out of ten, year in, year out.

That night I cruised in the first game with the yesteryear Big Red Machine, raw bang-bang power, as ever. And I had hopes for a sweep with the original Magic Marlins, but my pitching was spotty and he rallied in the ninth.

One run down, he got a triple with one out. He sent up a pinch hitter. I changed the pitcher. I brought the infield in. He would call a squeeze bunt, the riskiest play in baseball.

He always called a squeeze in that kind of situation. I knew
that and he knew that I knew. Bad odds, but he didn't care.

"Squeeze," he called, warming the dice.

"Gee, how did you ever think of that?"

"Show some respect," he said, and tossed them. Routine
numbers. I knew what they meant without looking on the
results chart, and so did he, but he would have been disappointed if I hadn't, so I read: " 'Grounder to third, runner out
at home; batter safe at first.' "

"*Carajo!*" He scowled in mock exasperation.

"Two out, man on first. You're one run down and one out
from the locker room. Any more flashes of genius?"

"Don't gloat." He looked at the player card in his hand; a
wea :-hitting second baseman who had stayed so briefly in
the majors that even he hardly remembered it.

"Hit away," he said.

"He's awful. You must have somebody who can pinch-
hit," I offered.

"Hit away," he said again and threw the dice.

I had to look up the result this time, but before I read it I
peered across at him. Did he know? When did he know?

"'Inside-the-park home run,'" I read deadpan. And after
an appropriate pause: "Both runners score. You win, four
three. Nice game."

"Yeees!" He jumped to his feet, exploding into a one-man
victory dance across the oriental carpet, fists pummeling the
air above his head.

Then he looked at me with delight, the warrior visage dis-
solving into a grinning icon prized round the world.

"Who says there's no God?" demanded Pius XIII, Pontifex Maximus, Bishop of Rome, successor to St. Peter, ruler
of the world's one billion Roman Catholics.

We were in a big rectangular room on the fourth floor of the
long Renaissance *palazzo* flanking St. Peter's Square that is
known as the Apostolic Palace, because that is where the

pope lives. Mostly the palace is marble and tapestries and echoing corridors, but the sixteenth century had been banished from the room, except for the august dimensions and a Vatican-wide musty odor poised somewhere between sanctity and damp. There were inviting sofas, armchairs, lovely old rugs, bright *naïf* paintings, good reading lights everywhere, a big fireplace, a VCR and a television hooked to a grab-the-universe satellite dish on the roof.

Ricardo Sanchez de Arellano, whom everybody called Tredi, except to his face, filled the room, in bulk and presence. Well over six feet, he was perhaps twenty pounds heavier than when I had first met him, a trouble-making young bishop, but so was I, and he carried it well. A shock of gray hair punctuated the bottomless black eyes. He might have been a rich rancher like his father, a businessman, a politician, a movie actor, even, but he had become a priest, monsignor, bishop and cardinal in seemingly breathless procession. And then one day in an improbable puff of white smoke from the Sistine Chapel, he had become the first Latino pope. He was my friend, and a good deal more than that.

Tredi waved me onto a sofa facing the fireplace and handed me the twin to a glass he had filled with two ice cubes and about three fingers of crisp golden rum. I sipped.

"Babancourt," I ventured, in nasal appreciation that might have passed for Haitian French.

He smiled. *"Mais oui."*

"Call me 'Rico,' " he had said that long-ago afternoon in Miami. "Call me 'Rico' and don't get in the way of any trouble meant for me." So I had watched his back and called him Rico, even after we had gotten in the way of one another's troubles. I had called him Rico right through the red hat cardinal years, but now that he wore the Vatican's only white robe and was surrounded by obsequious souls murmuring "Your Holiness" and "Holy Father" all day, I mostly mumbled.

"How are you, Brother Paul?" He asked because he cared. The black eyes raked me deeper than any doctor's scanner.

"I'm good."

"You want to be ordained? A priest? Play in the Bigs?"

"No, thanks."

"Want to toss in the cassock and go back to live in the real world?"

"Not that, either."

We bantered. He asked about my classes and how I was coping with the seminarians in my charge. I asked him about his younger brother, the Arellano family black sheep, a harmless ne'er-do-well awash somewhere in the Caribbean.

"What do you hear from Bobby? Still into a chain of dive centers?"

"That was last month, *hermano,* or was it the month before?" Sadness tinged the pope's voice and the flashing eyes went momentarily dull. "Now it's fish farming, someplace on the coast. Tilapia, the fish of the future, Bobby says. A sure thing. If only he had a bit more investment capital . . . I've been praying for Bobby all my life, Paul, but somehow it hasn't 'taken' yet."

"Well, if there's anything I can do . . ." I felt I knew the pope's brother, though I had never actually met him, and occasionally I had served as a quiet link between them. Sometimes, Rico had found, as pope it is not always easy—or smart—to do things directly from the papal palace.

"Thanks, maybe I will drop him a line." I knew the pope well enough to know he worried about his kid brother more than he ever let on. I didn't think Tredi had anybody else at the Vatican he could talk to about Bobby. But I also knew that, in true Latin fashion, there would always be an unbridgeable chasm between Paul, the friend, and Bobby, the brother.

As the pope poured two more glasses of mellow rum, I passed along thirdhand Vatican kitchen gossip, most of which he'd heard, and a handful of Tredi jokes, which made him laugh.

"Apart from a few kind souls like you, I never catch any fresh breezes unless I get them off the news channels. Remarkable, when you think about it, how systematically and effectively the Curia has shielded popes from things like gossip, jokes, and unpleasant truths across the centuries."

I said, "You do realize, I know, that everybody around the Vatican analyzes everything you do and say and tries to figure out what it really means. How much pomp there was at your coronation, the length of your homilies, the politics of the people you appoint or don't appoint, what you say and what you don't say. How often you get your hair cut. Now everybody's bent out of shape one way or the other over the saints. Better you than me."

"Awful, ain't it?" He grinned, fanning his hand across the legend on the T-shirt I had brought him. "Preserve the Saints" it said.

"Or just normal. You're a new pope and everybody is waiting for the other shoe to drop. Will it fall softly or with a thud?"

He laughed and finished his rum. "What do you think, *hermano?*"

I didn't even have to pretend to think about it. "If I was one of those tightass people who hated all change, I think the first thing I'd do is learn how to defend against the suicide squeeze. Not your routine, tried-and-true missionary position play, is it?"

He liked that, but he had already gone mentally, drifted off. A mind that even his enemies regarded as one of the best of his time had skittered into some other dimension.

"You know, when I was a kid," he said, talking as much to himself as to me, "I used to love to go down to Paso Bernal and watch the big tankers go by. You been there? It's a narrow strait and the water is shallow enough and sometimes rough enough to make it tricky, but it saves a few hundred miles, the Bernal, and time is money to those big ships, computers checking everything a zillion times every second." He stared at one of the paintings: a barefoot black boy coming out of a grove of palms with a big smile and a string of fish on his shoulder. "What impressed me at first was how majestic they looked, sailing along like nothing could stop them, juggernauts, and anything that got in their way had better look out. There was a churchly certainty about them, wasn't there? I guess I was priest-bound even back then.

"But you know, Paul, what occurred to me later, what kept me going back, is what monsters those ships really are; half a mile long, some of them. Once they get going, how do you stop them? Reverse the engines Tuesday to stop for lunch Wednesday? Turn now to be able to take a left fifty miles down the road? A monster, tough to sail. Those captains get a lot of money and they're worth every penny. One bad mistake and wham, they're on every TV screen in the world with dead birds on the beaches. Still, they have to be steered, don't they, these goliaths? You can't just sit back and let them take you along for the ride. That's not what captains do—or popes. Right, Paul?"

"Uhm." I was awash in mixed metaphors.

"You chart your own course. But it's a bit like playing chess, isn't it? You have to figure out four or five moves in advance what the board is going to look like and what the enemy pieces are up to. It's not so much that I'm afraid of Vatican *apparatchiks,* but I'd like more of them on my side so that I don't have to zap so many. What I've been thinking about is . . ."

He talked for about ten minutes, airing his mind, and I sailed companionably along on the foredeck, enjoying his rum and his friendship. But the kitten broke his stream, emerging from behind the couch and crawling up Tredi's leg. It was, appropriately, mostly black with a white collar, but the thing that struck you was that it had one blue eye and one that was yellow. The kitten was not long weaned, but its pedigree was easy to spot, for it carried itself with that unmistakable arrogance that is bred centuries deep into the alley cats of Rome.

"What's that?" I asked stupidly, interrupting Rico's monologue. He encouraged the kitten on to his lap.

"You think maybe it's chopped liver? And please, Paul, not a word. I've heard them all already." He mimicked, " 'Your Holiness, if people know that you have a cat, then we will be overrun with cats. Well-wishers will send you cats from all over the world, Holy Father. What would we do with them? We couldn't keep them. Or kill them. To feed them. Imagine the cost! It will become a major embarrassment. A crisis!' "

The pope poured more rum and passed me the bottle. "This is the pope's cat, Paul. I found him one night while I was out for a walk. 'In the Vatican gardens,' people would say, but you know better. Actually there's nothing in the Apostolic Constitution that says I've got to wear the white robes day and night, and nothing that says I have to be a prisoner here, no matter what the security people say. So sometimes I go out, and shall we say, cat around. And one night I went for a walk up on the Aventine Hill and there on the sidewalk was this lonely kitten, so I picked him up and put him in my pocket and brought him home. His name is Santi, that's short for *Santissimo*. Hemingway said you should always have an 's' in the name for cats."

"Hey, that's cool. Santi, nice name. I've always liked cats. Of course at St. Damian's we can't—"

"Now that's one problem at least that I can fix with a phone call—"

"Thanks, but no thanks, I think a cat would be, well, not a crisis, really, but you know, a kind of complication—"

"I'm teasing. But it would be fun, when you think about it: issue a papal bull on cats."

Tredi plopped the kitten onto his shoulder and rose to his

feet, rolling his arms and the muscles in his back. It was near midnight. "I feel fine. Good games, good food, good rum, good talk, Paul. Sometimes I get lonely up here, a bit wired. Thanks for coming."

Tredi and Santi walked me to the door, and before I left the pope put both hands on my shoulders. "God bless you, *hermano*. And pray for me, will you please? I'm going to be sailing close to the wind. Pray for me, and watch my back."

I said that of course I would. But I could not have imagined how soon the moment would come.

6

THE DAY BEGAN in an ordinary enough fashion.

Every year I take two or three courses at pontifical universities that are scattered around Rome because my religious superior thinks it's a good idea. I suppose if you added up all my credits I could have some sort of degree, but, then again, if I was more committed I could also have been ordained a priest by now.

That semester my week began with a cock's-crow Monday morning class in numerology; not my idea, I promise you. The professor was a Dutch theologian of great dedication and no warmth. I had lost him that morning on the curve between six and seven, and the pretty Argentine nun sitting next to me hadn't even gotten that far, for she was deep into a doodle of a brooding, bearded figure who was either Che Guevara or somebody close enough to land her in big trouble back at her convent.

"The numbers in biblical times all had meanings that transcended their figurative values," the Dutchman bored in, saying the same thing for about the fifth time. There were maybe fifty students in the class, the usual mixture of seminarians, priests getting advanced degrees, nuns, and a few civilians: pontifical universities give good degrees and tuition's cheap.

"Seven is perfection. The House of Wisdom. Seven pillars of wisdom; seven capital sins." Hallelujah, hallelujah. By the time he got to ten, my skin was crawling: "Ten commandments. Perhaps there should have been twelve, or fifteen, or seventy-eight"—a dry smile—"but no, ten. The number will assert its spiritual value if you would, but consider the sum of the six Precepts and the four Canon Virtues."

Antonia, the Argentine nun, was wearing a crisp white blouse and a long floral skirt that had a lovely flow. She laid a hand on my forearm, leaned over with a conspiratorial gleam, and murmured in quick Spanish, "This is as boring as an elevator without a mirror."

"Coffee?"

I won a quick smile. Antonia and I were not the only students who abandoned the Dutchman at the break. We went into a brightly lit bar off the lobby, a bar being what both Italians and the Vatican call a coffee shop. I thought I was making a decent impression, when Antonia's eyes suddenly went big. Staring at something behind me, she nearly dropped her cup.

I felt a hand on my shoulder and turned to see a Vatican cop. He was a Swiss Guard. I knew him vaguely without remembering his name, but he had left his halberd home, along with the bright-colored doublet they say Michelangelo designed. Instead he wore a modern uniform of a high-peaked cap, gray trousers, and a navy jacket with a pistol on his belt. He looked like a highway patrolman, except Vatican State hasn't got roads enough, all twenty square blocks of it, to speed on.

"You got me," I said. "We were cutting class. But it's me you want. I made her do it."

Humor does not rank high among Swiss Guardly virtues. He never cracked a smile. Instead he saluted.

"There is a serious problem. Commendatore Galli would be grateful if you could come now," he said loudly, reading a script.

Loud and clear. Over and out.

I was running, every pore open, by the time we hit the piazza where the police car idled.

Please, God. Not Rico.

Normally it takes thirty-five minutes to get to the Vatican from the school by bus, which is how I usually go. The Guard—his name was Kurt—did it in thirteen flat in a tinny little Fiat he took down the hill like a Ferrari and squirted around crowded Piazza Venezia on two wheels.

"Where exactly are we going, Kurt?"

"There's been an accident in the Basilica."

"Who?"

He shrugged.

Relief washed over me. Not the pope. But someone, something, important enough for them to roust me with a five-alarm rush.

"Dead?"

"It's a long way down!" Kurt was enjoying himself. In the bucolic valley that has produced Swiss Guards for centuries, the profession is passed generation to generation, father to son. Loyalty to the pope is ingrained. Good posture is important. Good pasture is prized. Intelligence is optional. A *motorino* leapt from Kurt's path by a whisker.

"Nobody wins if we get killed," I snapped.

"Hah," he snorted, a feral Swiss growl whose sense escaped me, but not its meaning, for we came across Corso Vittorio flat out, safely breasted the cross traffic on Luongotevere because God is kind, and spilled across the river and onto the Via della Conciliazione with light flashing and siren howling.

At the head of the avenue is the largest and for me the most beautiful church in the world. There's been a basilica on the spot for seventeen hundred years, and I never tire of strolling through the current edition, a youngster less than four hundred years old. Before the church lies St. Peter's Square, so traffic has two choices when it reaches the giant piazza. Bear left toward the outer edge of Vatican City and the Porta Cavalleggerí gate which leads visitors to the new papal audience hall built under Paul VI. Turn right and you come eventually to the Sant'Anna Gate which leads into the papal apartment, the majestic Vatican Library, and government offices of the sort you find in any small city: the post office, the telephone company, the electric company, a big supermarket, a pharmacy which will sell you every remedy on God's green earth except condoms and the Pill.

Turning right is more interesting, but Kurt went left and after another few instants of terror, one of his Swiss friends was waving us through the tall black iron gate. We drove up parallel to the giant church for more than half its length, lurching eventually to a stop at an unmarked door guarded by two cops in plainclothes.

One of them beckoned and I followed him into the bowels of the Basilica. We passed the spot which archaeologists in 1950 had concluded was the tomb of St. Peter, the first pope. The cop ahead was almost running now through a gallery of grottoes, each the tomb of a different pope; ornate or starkly simple, depending on the tastes of the man and his time. We were under the altar of the Basilica, I knew, and soon we climbed a short flight of curving stairs to the main level of the church.

As many times as I have been there, it always takes my breath away. Man as ant. The church is built in the shape of a Latin cross, and the Dome, above where the arms meet the stem, sits over the main altar.

Its other virtues and shortcomings will be debated eternally, but when it comes to crowd control, the Vatican is as slick as Disney. The church was already open to visitors, but a large area under the Dome had been closed off with those metal crowd control fences that are a Roman staple. In the restricted zone was a smaller area cordoned off with more fences and white canvas curtains of the sort restorers use.

It was not hard to figure out why. I've never seen anybody deader than the man who lay on the marble floor before me. He'd fallen a long way, and he had not had a soft landing.

"Paolo, welcome, good to see you," called the voice of a man leaning over the body.

Marco Galli was a wiry man with a bristly black mustache that matched his eyes and, a lot of the time, his mood. He was the Vatican's best investigator.

"It is not a pleasant way to start the week, but perhaps you would like to take a look?"

"Sure."

What he meant was: I don't like what I'm finding here.

Even after all my Vatican years, given the choice between a corpse and biblical numerology, I'd almost prefer blood and gore all over the floor. Which, not to put too fine a cast on it, was exactly what Galli was asking me to contemplate there on the marble floor under the majestic Basilica Dome.

"Anybody see it happen?" I asked, squatting beside Galli.

"We have found no one who saw the departure, but a sisterhood of nuns was performing special early morning prayers in one of the side chapels. They heard the arrival; rather noisy."

Like an apple splitting.

"What time does the Basilica open anyway?"

"Not until much later for the public. For priests and other religious who want to pray, it is never really closed. There is a small side door with a big lock, but everybody at the Vatican knows that the key is kept behind a loose stone two hands-width to the right of the keyhole."

I hadn't known that; praying at home in bed was more my style.

"I don't suppose people who come to pray out of hours sign in, or something? A watchman who maybe logs them, keeps track . . ."

Galli stilled me with a look and a word.

"Paolo," he said with gentle reproach.

So I looked again at the body. I couldn't tell about prayers, but the rest was pretty apparent. "Jumped, pushed, fell," I said, although I could see enough amid the debris to rule out one of them.

I stared up at the sixteen-segment Dome. About a hundred and fifty feet above the Basilica's altar, there is a walkway where tourists can peer down. It isn't easy to fall from there, but it is final if you do.

The body was a mess. For his freefall the corpse had dressed in dark pants and a good quality Italian designer windbreaker over a blue cotton shirt open at the neck. One shoe was gone, but the other, a polished black loafer, was wedged on the right foot. I knew the style, also Italian, and not cheap. He had short black hair with the beginnings of gray above pale blue eyes, an early forties face that would have been easy enough to look at—an hour before. He had office worker's hands, with long fingers and well-kept nails. He might as well have been wearing a uniform.

It would take a pathologist to decide exactly what had killed him. I didn't know how many broken bones he had, either, but I didn't see many that weren't. It looked to me as if he had hit on his right side and then flopped over onto his back.

"Funny that the eyes are open."

"So what?" Galli asked.

"Lying like that"—I straddled the corpse, leaned back and peered up toward the peak of the great Dome, so far, so scary—"do you suppose he can see heaven?"

Galli muttered something foul in Roman dialect and began telling a nervous young man with a camera what angles to shoot. In the circle around the body, licking his lips as if to summon courage, flexing hands encased in clear plastic gloves, stood a squat individual with a ginger beard and a black bag at his feet.

"Go ahead and examine the corpse, Giuseppe. He won't bite you, but wait a second," Galli said, turning to the photographer. "Stand where he was standing," Galli gestured at me, "and shoot one down at the body and one up at the Dome."

"For art's sake, Marco?"

"Theological research," he rejoined. "Maybe heaven will appear on the negative." He was telling me not to be a wiseass.

Galli walked over to watch as the photographer positioned himself with the exaggerated distaste of a man wading through muck.

"Carabinieri get young and younger," I sympathized.

Galli griped, "These are not even Carabinieri. They are my own men; the Vatican's finest."

Vatican City is a sovereign state, of course, with diplomatic ties to more than one hundred and thirty countries. But it's also the smallest country in the world. Italian reinforcements arrive in a steady stream: computer wizards to crowd controllers, piazza cleaners to suicide recorders from the Carabinieri, the militarized national police.

"Any identification?"

"We should probably take a look up top," Galli replied.

"I know your men got names of everybody in the church; anybody who might have gone up to the Dome to pray. People do that, I suppose."

"The Dome is closed for cleaning."

I was beginning to understand.

"But no cleaners this early."

"Don't be silly."

The Vatican can be a confusing place, even to people who have lived there for years. But you didn't always need divine intervention to figure things out. Think about it.

Somebody nose-dives onto the floor of St. Peter's from a dome that is closed inside a church that is open only to insiders. The cop investigating his death doesn't call in pros to help. And avoids talking about identification. If the corpse is dressed pretty much the way I was dressed as I bent down to examine it, tell me, class: What did the dead man do for a living and who did he work for?

"Who is it?" I asked as we waited for the elevator that would take us up inside the Dome.

"Caruso, his name is. A monsignor in Justice and Peace," Galli replied, naming one of the most important departments in the Vatican Curia. We got in the steel cage and Galli pushed the button.

"Why would he jump?"

"Cancer, couldn't give up smoking, girl trouble, pope trouble. How can I know why he jumped?"

Marco Galli was a cop with a big headache.

"Okay, so he didn't jump."

"You saw the fingers and the nails as well as I did, didn't you, Paolo?"

"Maybe he changed his mind at the last minute." The fingers on those soft hands were bloody at the tips, the nicely rounded nails bent cruelly back.

"Don't joke about it, Paolo," Galli admonished. "Suicide is a grave sin, you know."

Murder's worse, he might have said.

If an up-and-coming young cleric forsakes his vow of celibacy in a moment of weakness, he'll find forgiveness, whether he sinned with a woman, a fellow priest, or—God help him—an altar boy. But if depression leads that same priest in another direction, to take his own life, say, well, that means that he has left this vale of tears in a state of mortal sin. That does not augur well for his immortal soul in the eyes of a church, which regards suicide almost with the same disdain as abortion and euthanasia. It's not too cool for the righteous reputation of the church, either. And if it should happen in St. Peter's . . .

Which is by way of explaining that if there was any honorable way my friend Marco Galli could conclude that the unfortunate Monsignor Caruso had tragically fallen to his death from the Dome, that's what he would do.

Galli might not ignore evidence, but he might be ordered to restructure it. For bureaucrats in the maw of an autocratic state, bearing the burden of bad news is the career equivalent of dome-diving.

"What was he like, Caruso?"

Galli thought about it. "Bright, well educated, a bit informal, extrovertish, even, but still a cinch for a bishopric. Probably they'd have sent him out to an archdiocese for seasoning in another year or two."

"How did he get up to the top, if it's closed?"

"Closed doesn't mean closed."

"Of course."

At the Vatican, nothing ever really means what it says. Everything's open to interpretation.

"It's closed because some of the safety fences are down as part of the cleaning and restoration. So it's closed even on the days when the restorers are not working," Galli said. "And," he added before I could ask him, "yes, there is a special sign at the entrance reminding visitors that it is particularly closed at night."

Okay, so the church was closed and the Dome was closed. But we both understood that any Vatican somebody could find his way in and find his way up; if not in the elevator then by trudging up the broad, curving walkway that had served steadfast pilgrims with strong lungs in the long centuries before electricity.

Visiting St. Peter's is free, but the Dome is an optional extra. The elevator is wood-lined, big enough for around twenty American-sized tourists. Normally an attendant rides it up and down, less because there's any need than because it discourages ecstatic pilgrims from committing graffiti.

When the elevator stopped, we obediently followed arrows round a corner and onto a narrow platform that circles the vault of the Dome. Giant mosaics glittered from the walls around us, patriarchal biblical figures bigger than life and stern as hell. They seemed disproportionate at close hand, but I knew enough to realize that was an artist's trick of perspective: distorted up here, the figure would seem normal enough when seen from below. Living in Rome, with so much art around you, there are some things you just learn, but that was something I knew because the Baroque and the Renaissance had become friends that helped me through my convalescence.

I had never been up to the St. Peter's Dome, though, in the same way that all those years I lived in Miami, I'd hardly ever gone to the Everglades. A mistake, I realized the second I followed Galli onto the walkway. It's a long way down, and breathtaking every inch of the way. What struck me was not so much the spirituality that the Dome was supposed to embody and reflect, I guess, but the vision and audacity of Michelangelo who'd conceived it, and Bernini who'd finished it for him, throwing it upward with cardinals and bean counters snapping at his heels every expensive brick of the way.

The tourist entrance leads visitors onto the walkway to the left of the main altar when seen from the front of the Basilica. Not quite halfway around the vault, another door leads people out; one-way tourism. There's a belt-high wrought-iron railing all the way around that is reinforced in the visitors' area by an eye-high safety fence of rigid mesh.

About fifty yards from the entrance, sections of the protective fence and the railing had been removed to be scraped for repainting. It didn't take great detective work to realize where Monsignor Caruso had departed for eternity, for a trail of angry scratches marked a newly laid marble floor, the sort of marks made perhaps on unpolished stone by fingers clawing desperately for purchase.

"O Dio mio," Galli muttered more to himself than to God, but an appeal for help nevertheless.

"You'd better . . ." I began, but Galli was already murmuring into his cell phone and I could imagine the scurry it would produce below.

"It will take them a few minutes to finish below and to bring the equipment," he said, closing the phone with an authoritative snap. They'd need pictures, fingerprint tests, scrapings from the floor gouges; the whole nine yards.

We edged around the marks on the floor to the exit door. Turning left, we could double back outside the curved wall of the Dome and re-enter the walkway. A right turn led up a narrow and curving flight of stairs: "Cupola, 330 steps" it read in a half-dozen languages. Straight ahead was most appealing. A door led to the huge flat roof of the Basilica, with amazing views of Rome.

"Che casino. What a mess." Galli dug out his cigarettes and ignited one with one of those disposable lighters the Bangladeshis sell at every traffic light in Rome. It made me wish I still smoked.

"Not pretty. Of course it could've been an accident, a slip, horseplay, a dare gone wrong . . ." I offered.

"Yes. But no." Galli took three nervous puffs and tossed his cigarette onto the roof.

"Paolo, I think it is best to assume that there is no one around. If you stay here, I will go up before the technicians come." Galli gestured toward the narrow doorway and its promise of three hundred thirty steps to the lantern of the Dome.

Was a murderer lurking there? Surely not. There had been ample time for a killer to have left the Dome down the broad walkway long before the first cops had arrived to gawk at the corpse.

Galli needed space and time to collect himself for the

ordeal that lay ahead. He had just fallen heir to a nasty cleri-cal murder in a very conspicuous place.

Better him than me.

"No problem, I'll play tourist."

That's what I thought.

7

THE MAIN ROOF of Christendom's biggest church is a wondrous esplanade dotted here and there by neatly fenced towers and architectural oddities. It is a lovely place to stroll in the sunshine and fresh air amid shapes and figures that undoubtedly have profound religious significance, but mostly are as nice to look at as they are plentiful.

Great place. As I walked and gawked, what struck me is that—amazingly—I was the only one up there in all the empty acres. Eerie almost, and a bit lonely once Galli's footsteps had faded in his long climb up to the lantern. When Christ cast the money-changers out of the Temple, do you suppose they moved to the roof? That's where an industrious order of nuns runs a religious souvenir store at St. Peter's Basilica. Blessed rosary beads, saints' statues, wall charts of the popes; tax included. But not that day. Without even the distraction of a cash register, I luxuriated in the view.

All Rome lay before me. By government edict, St. Peter's is the tallest structure in Rome. It was a clear day, and beyond the beautiful city center and its ugly suburbs I could see a glint of the Mediterranean from one side of the roof, and from the other the rounded Alban Hills south of Rome.

My mistake was to visit the front of the Basilica façade for a pope's-eye view of St. Peter's Square. It's not a bit square, as a matter of fact, but never mind. A lot of people smarter than I am consider it the world's single greatest public space. At the front of the church facing the square, the façade is capped by giant statues of Christ and the Apostles. Seen from below, the statues are righteous and powerful figures. From the back, though, they are just big hunks of stone, lumpen, uncarved—and still somehow impressive as hell.

Brother Paul the tourist was entranced.

Brother Paul the sometimes cop was a fool.

Talk about being out of shape. There was a time when I would have done the roof as it should have been done after a murder. Carefully. Maybe even with a gun drawn. Not like some overage, no-brain clerical schmuck lurching about wide-eyed when he should have been looking for a murderer. I was admiring the giant piazza in the refreshing shadow of St. Peter himself, my weight on hands braced atop the low ornamental stone wall, when I heard a faint shuffle behind me and then a strained silence.

Trouble. It couldn't have been Galli. Why would he try to be quiet? I came around quick and low, snapped into a strike position, and looked for a target.

Too late, tourist. I saw the blow descending—it looked like a short, thick club, but the man behind it was only a big black silhouette against the sun. I got one hand up. Too little. The club took me on the front of the head and a bit to one side. It drove me down and backward toward the edge of the roof. I was off-balance, windmilling desperately, on the verge of going over backward. In another second, Galli would have two homicides to investigate.

If Clubber struck again, I was gone. The most I could hope for would be to take him with me. Where was he? The sun in my eyes, the shadows, my splitting head. Nothing was making great sense. I flailed in front of me but came up with only air.

Then I was going over. Down. And there he was. I reached, but it was he who grabbed. No club this time, just a claw and something bright, golden . . . A ring? The claw ripped at my shirt and yanked me forward—away from the edge and certain death.

Out for the count. I was spread-eagled, my face against the warm roof tiles, as though a pilgrim in abject prayer, when Galli found me. How long? Five minutes? Too long. The headache was bad enough, but the humiliation was worse.

"Paolo, what? Did you . . . How . . ."

Galli wasn't thinking any better than I had been, for he had his arms under my right shoulder when his fingers should have been dancing on his fancy phone.

"Hit me . . . Tell them not to let anybody down."

And so he phoned, and an empty lot of good it did. When we eventually got back down to cathedral level, all we found was a red-faced cop standing at attention by the exit door. Galli understood.

"Who was it? Who came down?"

"It was nothing . . . I was told to stop people going up, I didn't know," the cop muttered miserably. He saw himself working six months of midnights.

"*Cretino!* Who was it?"

"Nobody . . . just a priest. He walked out, not running or anything. Normal. By the time you called, he had already gone." The Vatican cop waved vaguely into the vastness of the Basilica.

"What did he look like?"

"Nothing special. I didn't see the face. He was kind of average; a little smaller."

"What was he wearing, this priest? Robes, a gown of some kind? Was he a monk, a monsignor? Was there purple, red?" Galli demanded.

"Black. He was wearing a black priest suit, that's all."

Terrific. He had just described half the population of Vatican City.

The cop was as dumb as I had been.

A priest-murderer? Every cardinal's worst nightmare, and an inescapable conclusion. But a murderer with a conscience and a definite target. He had killed Caruso but yanked me back when I was as good as dead. A madman killer getting his kicks?

Poor Galli. He'd try to hush it up, but he might as well try to stay the tide. Beyond their God and a free nosh, there aren't many things that the distinguished corps of prelates at the Holy See prizes more than good gossip.

By nightfall, I was feeling better and a bit restless. I called a special friend of mine named Tilly but got only her recording. Tilly was the Rome correspondent for a big American newspaper, but the way she traveled she changed her answering machine message as often as some people changed their socks. What I got was the breathless "I've been called away suddenly" variety.

I skipped dinner with the seminarians. By ten o'clock, I was deep into a Cold War thriller, a blessed remedy for both headaches and abstruse textbooks. This time the caller was more solicitous.

"How's the head?"

"The pain is mostly psychological. I made a stupid mistake and got clobbered."

"Was it murder?" Pope Pius XIII asked.

"I'd say so."

"Not suicide?"

"Only if he changed his mind a few seconds too late."

"Terrible thing," the pope said. "I was over in the Basilica late this morning and they were still cleaning up."

A million different things go on inside St. Peter's every day, but I hadn't seen any of the usual sort of seating, deco-

ration, and panoply that signal a papal presence. Neither had
Galli mentioned it.

"A ceremony?"

"Nothing like that. Confessions," Tredi said. "Every couple of weeks I slide over to the church just before lunchtime,
when nobody's looking, and spend an hour or two hearing
confessions. Good for the waistline—and my humility.
When people say, 'Bless me, Father, for I have sinned,'
they're really asking for help, aren't they? That's the name
of the game, isn't it? People who work for me imagine that
Catholics really obey all the rules we set for them. All it
takes is hearing confessions to know different. God knows
what they *don't* confess."

"Did you see anything? You know . . ."

"'Fraid not."

"Reason I ask, the cops want me to, you know, help out in
the investigation."

"How do you feel about that?"

"A murder investigation. I'm not sure. It's been a long
time—"

"But maybe not long enough." Tredi finished the thought
for me.

"Exactly."

He was quiet for a minute, and then he said, "Paul, will
you find out who did it, please?" A pause. "If you think you
can do it."

I could sense him looking at me hard, the way Ivanovic
sometimes does. "I know it'll be hard, maybe even open
some wounds, but I need to know."

He was my pope and he was my friend.

"Sure, of course . . ." It was not easy to say.

"Knowing about Caruso would be a big help, Paul."

He knew that I'd risk new damage to scarred circuits, but
he obviously didn't want to talk about that, and neither did I.
So I asked, "Caruso. Did you know him? What was he
like?"

"Deep, very deep. And clever. Ask anybody. He reasoned brilliantly. And he wrote like a dream. He could argue his way out of anything."

Except a free fall from St. Peter's Dome.

"He was only a monsignor. How did you happen to know him?"

"An old friend. Sometimes he came to dinner; we talked. He was working with me on some things . . . church things . . ."

Maybe popes don't lie. But this one was being evasive.

"There's more, isn't there?"

He thought about it for a minute, nodded. "Yeah, but I don't think you need to hassle with it."

What was that supposed to mean? Then I thought exactly what it might mean. I said, "Forgive me for asking, but I suppose there's always the chance that it was a lovers' spat. Was Caruso gay?"

There was a long pause this time. "It hadn't occurred to me, to tell you the truth. But I doubt it. I would've said he was a ladies' man, if anything."

"You wouldn't have any idea who his lover might have been, if he had one, whatever the sex?"

"Priests tend not to share that sort of information with their pope, Paul. The most I can tell you about Luca Caruso is that I knew him as a valuable co-conspirator in the crew of the great ship of church."

Weren't we all? "Okay, I'll do my best."

"Thanks, if you need help, call me," the pope said. Then he hung up and I could imagine him padding with his kitten through the haunted old palace and back into the loneliest job in the world.

Rain clouds were dancing across the sky when I rang Ivanovic's bell a few hours later. He answered wearing an old-fashioned tank top undershirt and a baggy pair of trousers. His hair and his great black beard flared madly in all directions, but his eyes didn't look as if he had been asleep. They never do.

"Paul, what a nice surprise. I have you on my calendar for Friday at two in the afternoon but you come on Monday after midnight. Time flies, as they say. Come up, we'll have something to drink."

I couldn't sleep after talking with the pope. And I felt myself winding up, tighter and tighter. It doesn't happen so much anymore, but I still have bad nights.

"So, talk to me, Paul," Ivanovic said, sipping a tumbler of vodka from a bottle he'd taken right from the freezer. And so I told him about the murder and about the pope and about some of the other snaffles in my psychic pipes. Ivanovic carried a lot of my history around with him. He was one of the few people in Rome who knew about Tredi and me. He knew because Tredi had dumped me on him one day, piece by shattered piece.

"So you're worried about the pope's safety because of something that happened in Miami that you don't want to talk about. And at the same time you are, shall we say, roiled, by the prospect of becoming involved in the investigation of a violent death for the first time in many years."

Ivanovic had a way of reducing anything from mild confusion to utter despair into a few neat sentences. I could imagine a new entry sliding neatly into the file where he had archived Humpty Dumpty Paul. Not for the first time, I decided that one day I'd drop by Ivanovic's when he was out and take a magnet to his computer.

I said, "That's it, more or less. That, plus I don't give a shit about numerology."

"That at least is a sure sign of acute mental health. On the other hand, the fact that you won't talk about Miami is, uh, not helpful. As to the murder: Isn't it natural that you should be anxious about investigating a murder that may mentally take you back to previous experiences you have reason to regret?"

He watched me, gauging. "Don't you think that the best thing would be for me to call the pope and tell him that I— that both of us—think it would be unwise of you to do it?"

He was right, too. But also wrong. "I want to do it, don't you see? Tredi's my friend. He needs me, and I want to help him."

Ivan tugged reflexively at his beard. "I understand that, Paul, but at the end of the day every man is responsible for his own salvation. Pope and peasants like us. No difference."

I thought about that for a while. "The thing is, Mikhail, I really want to do it. Maybe not for Tredi, either. Maybe I want to do it, for me. But I'm scared of what will happen if I do— and if I don't. Would I still be here—a brother—if I succeeded? Could I be, if I failed?"

"Ah, well, that is a different game then, isn't it? The question you should ask yourself, then, Paul, is whether you think you can do it safely. Can you handle it? At the end, would we have to go back and start all over?"

"What do you think?"

He smiled. "Psychiatrists only ask questions, Paul. You must answer them."

Later, I walked slowly back across town, the Tiber bathed in moonlight, the city still pulsing in its ancient-young way; Rome, a city like none other and like all others, so distant, so alien from the white-robed figure it turned to only in time of need or fear. The clubs were humming, young people in tiny cars mocking half-hearted traffic cops as they darted past drowsing ruins of empire.

Amid the spirited swirl, St. Damian's was black and silent: the future of the church safe abed in pure dreams with both hands outside the blankets. I wondered if the British kid had made it back and whether his night out would make for a better priest or an early dropout.

And me?

How did I rank among the dropouts that floated in Roman eddies—the verbworn writers, stuttering actors, wine-heavy correspondents, artists without talent, out-of-work business wizards, dancers with fallen arches, and professors of classics with spotty Greek and fractured Latin? I was their kith in pathos; a failed thief who dressed as a priest while his mind danced with devils.

8

LUCA CARUSO WAS a neat man, as most priests are. As I am, for that matter. What we also had in common is that we both lived off the Vatican, but not in it. Vatican City is as full of priests as you'd expect, but not many of them actually live in its one hundred and eight acres; that's a privilege reserved for the pope, key cardinals, and other senior officials. Not even all of them make the cut, but that is no hardship. The church, which directly ruled Rome for centuries after all, still owns huge chunks of expensive real estate around the city.

The late Monsignor Caruso lived in a residence for priests about eight blocks from the Vatican, close enough for him to walk to work. There must be a couple hundred places like it in the headquarters city of the world's biggest religion, and they are all of a type: a common kitchen, usually staffed by high-cholesterol nuns or lay unemployables; a recreation room with a big color television and a lot of bickering about what channel it should be showing; communal bathrooms spaced along long, dark hallways that remind you of old monasteries or money-tight private schools.

The priests live in rooms that are a Space Age echo to medieval cells. Caruso's had a hard single bed, a desk, a phone, a combination closet-dresser, a bookcase, and a neat file marked "Correspondence," which seemed to contain mostly personal letters. Caruso also had a portable computer, neat stacks of high-gloss pamphlets that seemed at first glance poised between right-wing Catholic zealotry and anti-Semitism, and a handful of pornographic magazines under the mattress.

Caruso's room was depressingly familiar but not terribly forthcoming. There was no suicide note, phony or otherwise, no love letters, no lurid diary. But there were notes and phone numbers jotted on a yellow pad, one of those page-a-day loose-leaf desk calendars. I decided to take the pad with me, and the computer with its tray of diskettes. And why not the pornography? No sense sullying a dead priest's image. The religious pamphlets were in English and well thumbed. "Lock On" read the masthead. And under it: "Official Publication of the Society of the Sacred Keys." It belonged to one of those special pleading groups of commando Catholics. There are more of them around the Vatican than lobbyists in Washington. I stuck a sampling of the pamphlets into Caruso's computer case along with everything else, and left the dead man's room to catch a bus back home to St. Damian's.

What I had in mind was a siesta, which was a good idea, and to get to it I took a snorting orange number Sixty-four bus, which was a mistake. The Sixty-four is one of the most popular routes in Rome, running from the Vatican across the Tiber to the Piazza Venezia and from there up the hill to the giant Termini train station. It is probably also the most dangerous bus route in Rome, because it is invariably jammed with tourists and otherlifes—singleton vultures and coordinated teams—who prey on them. Normally, I mind my own business, but that day when I saw a young Latino maneuvering to strip the wallets from a pair of twittering nuns in old-fashioned black habits with blinder-like cowls, I pushed over next to him.

Placing Caruso's case between my legs in case I needed both hands, I said conversationally, "If you bother the sisters, I will break your arm." He looked at me for an instant, a flare of alarm in his brown eyes that vanished as quickly as it had come. Perhaps he decided he had not heard it at all, for in the next instant his hand disappeared into the purse of the nun with her back to him.

It was not as if I felt that my bluff had been called, nothing personal, but I trod hard on the Latino's instep. When he began to protest in broken Italian, I punched him once in the kidneys, a good hit; short but sharp. That left him gray and me feeling high one minute and like a fool the next, because when the man stumbled off at the next stop, so did his partner. And he was carrying Luca Caruso's black computer case.

Served me right, too. And if it had been something of little value, I might have let it go as a belated addition to my Roman education. But the case wasn't mine, and it was the closest thing to a clue I had in a murder investigation. I lumbered off the bus. The man I had hit was retching into the gutter.

His buddy was walking quickly down a quiet side street, the case in his right hand. He never looked back, but when he heard me pounding after him he glanced quickly over his shoulder and started to sprint. He had a couple of decades on me, but the case was heavy and awkward to run with and I was flying on adrenaline and self-disgust.

When he skidded into a byway that was more an alley than a street, I was right behind him. I grabbed for his collar, missed, and lost a step as he put on a frantic burst. When we came to a small piazza with a fountain framed by four bronze turtles, he threw the case hard against the marble base. I heard it slide down into the water with a tinny clunk.

Right then I should have stopped. Okay, I know that. But I was mad as hell, so I put on a burst of my own and over-hauled the little bastard before he could get out of the piazza. Then I went back and rescued the waterlogged case. It was leaking badly.

When I got back to St. Damian's, taxi this time, I found the computer in a dozen pieces; a write-off. But I quickly dried out the disks, the zealot magazines and—yes—the pornography. No harm done. What the thief did about his broken nose is his business.

The thief got off easy, for that night I curled up with a friendly bottle of something and swam through the stack of magazines I had taken from Caruso's place. At the end of it all I was feeling truly violent. Like a Commando Catholic. Half-recruiting poster, half-house organ, "Lock On" pro-claimed itself the "launchpad for committed-concerned Catholics in the computer age." Real Catholics, I learned, "Lock on to God the way a missile locks on to its target. God is our target, our only target."

Spooky stuff, right down to a picture of the Keys's Inter-net homepage, bristling with aggression and subscript. "Lock On" told CCCs how to get the home phone numbers and addresses of abortionists, and how to post them on the Internet. It offered model mail and e-mail messages to send to "baby killers," as it called them, and recommended just-short-of-obscene texts for phone calls.

The magazines told readers how to lobby bishops to "vote correctly in the common Catholic cause" at their national meetings. It urged parishioners to squeal on parish priests who were soft on birth control: "If you hear of a priest who gives absolution to those using artificial birth control, it is your duty to confront him."

One delightful article was headlined: "How to Denounce a Divorced Catholic Who Receives Sacraments to which

He/She Is Not Entitled." Mostly what you were supposed to do was to stand up in the middle of the communion, point a finger, and shout: "Stop that sinner!" But only after "giving the potential offender appropriate warning before mass, if possible."

The magazine counseled "direct action" in all matters affecting the one true faith. One article that I read with particular attention described how neighborhood watch committees should be created to check if clerics were respecting their celibacy vow. If it didn't actually preach violence, the Keys came with a whip of making violence seem not only righteous but also a downright homey way of defending our faith.

There's no shortage of hard-liners in the one true faith, but the magazines were certainly strange bedside reading for a Vatican comer who could reason brilliantly, according to his old friend the pope, and who was working together with Tredi on "some church things . . ."

The small man standing in a deep hole in the basement floor said testily, "As you can see, I am very busy."

I never bothered, but Vatican cops all went to charm school, and among them Galli was particularly smooth. "We are impressed by the importance of your work, Father," he said, "but as you will appreciate, the church is very concerned by this matter and your assistance would be most welcome."

With a long-suffering sigh, Gustavo Vidal clambered out of the hole, fished a filterless, black tobacco cigarette from the pocket of his sports shirt, lit it with a red plastic lighter, and dragged deep. He was in his late forties, short, barely five feet, with a flat face, furrowed brow, and thick black hair. His barrel chest and powerful shoulders sealed an unmistakable package.

Vidal was an Inca warrior who just happened to have been raised at an Andean mission of British priests, happened to have done archaeology at Cambridge, and happened to have been ordained a priest after studies of great distinction at the most intellectually demanding seminary in Great Britain. I was glad we were speaking Italian.

Vidal worked in the same Vatican congregation as Caruso, and they had also lived in the same residence with about two dozen other priests. That afternoon we had found him at neither place but in the bowels of a basilica called San Clemente, one of the most storied churches in Rome, a three-leveled marvel where pious Romans have prayed—to one God or another—for two millennia. Gladiators once sacrificed here before striding across the street to kill one another in the Coliseum.

At street level, San Clemente was a Renaissance church administered by Dominican priests from Ireland. Below were the remains of a fourth-century basilica on which it was built, and in its basement an altar to Mithras, a bull-god who had been worshipped mostly by Roman officers and their legionaries. Archaeologist Vidal, with his strainers, brooms and brushes, was working well below the level of the old altar floor, though, so maybe history was still being written.

Although it was murder, not archaeology, that had brought us to the church, Galli was an unctuous blend of sympathy and skill. "We can imagine how upset you are about Monsignor Caruso's death, just as we are anxious to find out exactly how he died. Can you tell us, please, Father, when you saw him last?"

"We had dinner at the residence the night before he fell, many of us together as usual."

"Did he seem upset in any way?"

"Not that I noticed. He didn't eat much, but Luca was perpetually worried about his weight." Vidal smiled sadly.

"I understand that you also worked in the same office at the Vatican." Galli was smooth as silk.

"Yes, normally we took a coffee after leaving the office

and went our different ways." Hardly surprising. The entire Vatican bureaucracy, in the best medieval tradition, begins work at eight each morning and shuts tight at two each afternoon.

"Were you close, you and Monsignor Caruso?"

"As colleagues, of course. But we were interested in different things professionally."

"Like what?" I interjected.

He looked at me, as if for the first time. "Luca did research and analysis on social policies of immediate interest to the church. My own work has a more historical context."

"But in concepts you were very close," I offered.

"I think we saw the church and her challenges in the same context, if that is what you mean," he replied.

"Can you imagine why he went to the Dome that night?" Galli asked patiently.

Vidal's eyes grew vacant. "To pray. I imagine that he went to pray and reflect."

"Have you ever gone to the Basilica in the middle of the night—part of what is called the Legion of Darkness?"

Vidal smiled. "That is a joke name, as you know. Yes, I have gone once or twice. It is very tranquil. But I have never been to the Dome, and, no, I didn't go to the Basilica that night at all. I was sound asleep."

He was getting on my nerves. "Did Caruso have some special friend he prayed with, by any chance, just the two of them up there alone in the Dome?"

Okay, I wasn't as smooth as Galli, and even before I felt his hand on my arm, I realized there might have been a smarter way to ask what was, in fact, a pretty good question.

Vidal didn't rise. He shrugged and squashed his butt against the ancient stone wall. He field-stripped it and put the paper in his pocket. "If you will excuse me, I must get back to work."

"Father, please . . ." Galli began.

I interrupted. In for a penny, in for a pound. "He went up

to the Dome with a woman, didn't he? And not for the first time. He often went up to the Dome with women at night, when they would not be bothered. They prayed, and sometimes they found God together in wondrous ways. Maybe the Dome turned for them."

Vidal's gaze burned like fire. "He went to pray. He went alone."

"Not on the night he was murdered," I pressed.

Vidal looked at me as if I had said a dirty word, but he did not reply.

"How long had he been going?" Galli asked.

"Quite often in the last few months, he was troubled. He would awaken long before dawn to go to the Dome. He said it was a wonderful place to pray and to reflect."

"Do you know why he was troubled? About what? Someone? Some thing?"

"Things . . . I don't know for sure."

I would have pushed him harder. I might even have squashed him against the wall and done a bit of clerical field-stripping. But when Vidal jumped back into his hole, Galli tugged me away.

The next day we went to see the hawk-nosed bishop. Walking across sun-dappled St. Peter's Square to his car, Galli asked, "Paolo, why were you so rude to Father Vidal? That business about a woman . . ."

"Call it an inspired guess. Besides, I wanted to shake Vidal. Supercilious dwarf—"

"Paolo! Father Vidal is a figure of some importance; the originator of a new kind of humanist freedom theology. He's a very influential thinker. Very well respected in the church."

"So? Maybe it's him. He and his buddy Caruso go up to the Dome for a prayerfest—to look at the mosaics, who knows what for. They have an argument; Caruso goes bonk. Charitably, we could even decide it was an accident. Case closed."

I had run all his red lights, but Galli was patient: "Paolo, one reason Father Vidal is so influential as a new thinker is that he is very close to the Holy Father."

Damn.

"Like Caruso," I thought aloud. Among Caruso's papers there had been a friendly note from the pope, thanking him for writing something or other. If he was another new thinker, then why was he so interested in the Keys, which represented old thinking of a very particular and closed-ended sort?

We were talking with people around Rome and the Vatican who had worked with Caruso or had known him socially. To little effect, I was thinking to myself as our path to Galli's office was cut off briefly by a long snake of Japanese, Rome's most relentless tourists. We waited as they catty-cornered the giant square two by two behind a bored-looking Italian guide listlessly waving a pink flag.

"One of my officers had a good idea," Galli said. "We're calling all of the people in Caruso's office phone book to say that the monsignor's family has requested no flowers, please, but would they like to have their name on a card of condolences, together with those of leading church figures, perhaps share some thoughts about Caruso that might be shaped into a general eulogy. Everybody seemed to like him—hard worker, good priest, team player. They tell us things about him and we learn some things about them."

"Nice touch, the calls." A lot of information for a small investment.

At Galli's office I had waded through the forensic report without much enthusiasm or luck. It would have been quicker to list the bones that Caruso hadn't broken. He had no sign of drugs or alcohol in his blood. In fact, reading between the pathologist's turgid lines, Caruso had been one of those poor souls who are splendidly healthy until they are instantly dead.

"When is Caruso's funeral?"

"The day after tomorrow in his home parish in the Abruzzo. He died the victim of a tragic fall. The local bishop will say the funeral mass; they were friends."

"Will there really be no flowers?"

"Of course there will be flowers. Great sprays of them; banks. Caruso's parents are country folk; they would be offended. We will send flowers—in the name of the Holy Father, and the entire church. A dreadful accident."

The hawk-nosed bishop was named Umberto Jésus de Beccar, and he lived in an old *palazzo* on a hill with a sniper's view of St. Peter's. Galli drove us from the Vatican in a lovely old silver Alfa, simultaneously breasting the madness of Roman traffic and establishing ground rules with more grace than I could have mustered.

"With Father Vidal, Paul, it—"

"I was a little rough, sure. Okay, I accept that. But there's something about that guy . . ."

"And while your Italian is quite faultless, I congratulate you, there may be times when the use of the subjunctive might not be entirely as apparent as if in fact it was your first or even your second language. So if I may suggest that when we talk to the archbishop—"

"I keep my mouth shut. I'll try, okay." We had talked to everybody we could find who knew Caruso, but it was my idea for us to see Beccar. He had been the cheerleader of pro-saint demonstrators in St. Peter's Square, and he led the Thou Shall Nots who seemed—improbably—to have so interested the late Luca Caruso.

"Is there something particular we want to know, Paolo?"

"How long Caruso had been working with the Keys and whether it was the sort of thing that might have made him some enemies."

Galli chewed at his mustache. "Do we know for a fact that Caruso was working with the Keys?"

"Let him think we do."

"Very well. But do listen closely, please." He tapped the horn and a wizened old man opened a tall iron gate onto a courtyard with cobblestones ground to submission by centuries of iron-wheeled carriages.

The long rectangular room on the *piano nobile* one flight up was paneled in dark wood. Once it might have been a refectory, or even a library, but now its intention was starker. At the far end of the room, one step up, stood a large wooden chair with a brocaded back and long arms. It was a throne, punctuated by a long and narrow ebony cross hanging from the wall behind it. This was the inner sanctum of the Society of the Sacred Keys. I felt as if I had floated centuries back into the past, when some priests saved souls by prayer but many others preferred torture.

"A great pleasure to meet you, Commendatore Galli, and your assistant, *Dottore . . .*" Bishop Beccar's voice was warm and perfectly modulated. I had a feeling it would be ever thus, even as he leaned over, whispering, "Repent my son, repent," while you writhed on the rack.

Galli was quick. "And a pleasure for us, Excellency. Your society and your work is known to all who labor on behalf of the church."

"How may I help you and our church?"

He was a central-casting bishop. His hair was wisdom-gray and every strand knew its place. He dripped purple, his skullcap, the thick cummerbund and the precise buttons on his tailored cassock all bespoke his rank and his pretension.

Beccar would never be pope, he was too controversial a figure for that. But behind the scenes he was a power to be reckoned with in the Catholic church, the shadowy leader of a semi-secret, quasi-militaristic organization sworn to safeguard orthodoxy from enemies outside and within. A protector of Ultimate Values in the eyes of his supporters, a scourge of decency and a threat to the future of the church, to hear outraged liberals like my friend Tilly tell the story.

Beccar was too smart to receive a senior Vatican cop from

his throne. We sat in a horseshoe of chairs in one corner of the dark and foreboding room, sipping coffee brought by an old nun. *"Gracias, hermana, está bien,"* Beccar dismissed her, and she vanished back into the dark womb of the palace as silently as she had come.

He had spoken in a sharp, high-tone Spanish, but the money behind his society, I knew, came not so much from Spain as from Latin America, where the Keys was the darling of the new right. The Keys never talked about its funding, or its membership, for that matter.

Was it dirty money trying to buy a conscience by funding religious fundamentalists without one?

You heard that around the Vatican. But softly.

According to a canny Jesuit named John with whom I sometimes sampled Rome's better restaurants, the Keys had been founded in the nineties by a Latin American bishop who was about as far to the right as you can get and not be drummed out of the church. Beccar, who had European charm and Curia savvy, had become the Keys's second leader when the founder had gone to his just reward.

"Secretive membership, shadowy Latin money, known to conspire against liberals," said John. "How actively? *Quién sabe?* But there are rumors—an activist Mexican cardinal murdered one night in his cathedral; a Peruvian bishop some people thought was too nice to coca-growing peasants. He was shot. Those sorts of things are often ascribed to the Keys. Wonderful gossip, though there's never been a shred of evidence," John had confided. "Like most of the soldier Catholics around these days, they probably bark worse than they bite. But the Keys have a big office here now, they have money, organization, a commitment. Around the Vatican, that all adds up to power . . ."

And to murder?

". . . and what a tragic death," Beccar was saying. "Yet his was not a fall from grace, for it is a beautiful place to die, St.

Peter's, to die contemplating the heart of the holy church. A terrible accident, that goes without saying."

"Did Monsignor Caruso perhaps collaborate with the society?" Galli was a dentist, probing ever so gently.

"Yes, I think I can safely say that he did," Beccar replied. "He was not strictly a member, but he offered us valuable counsel from time to time. We shall miss him."

"Of course, his collaboration with the Society would have been well known."

Of course it wasn't. Beccar digested the awkward question by doing what archbishops and other politicians sometimes do when they need a little time to calculate permutations. He rang a dainty silver bell, ordering more coffee.

The archbishop took three sugars, one more than for the first cup he had drunk with us. "I wouldn't say that Monsignor Caruso's work for the Society was well known, exactly," he said at length. "It was a quiet arrangement, if you understand what I mean. But not because that is how *we* wished it. We have nothing to hide. No, it was his choice. He, after all, had a sensitive post at the Vatican, did he not?"

Galli pressed. "So you would say, Excellency, that there was nothing about Monsignor Caruso's cooperation with the Society that might have excited enmity in certain circles."

"Are you suggesting that he might have been . . . that his . . . accident . . . might have had something to do with his work with us? Is that what you mean? *Ay de mí!*" The tone remained courteous, but anger flashed before the manicured eyebrows. "There is nothing about our work or our beliefs that might inspire violence among Christians, I assure you." He crossed himself, right there in front of us.

"Of course not, Excellency," Galli retreated.

Any chance one of *your* religious warriors literally knocked off Caruso? Killed him because for some pious reason you wanted him dead? I could think of many nasty questions. But I didn't ask any of them. I had promised Galli.

All I said was that I needed to go to the bathroom. I left
Galli and Beccar dueling with barbed courtesies; I wanted a
better sense of the Keys's lair. Another tinkle of the archbishop's bell and I followed the old crone up a two-level
flight of stairs, down a corridor, and into a high-tech bathroom. On the way, we passed a library full of dark and
doubtless moody volumes, and, next door, a brightly lit
room with a Plexiglas door that was obviously the Keys's
computer central. A clean-cut technician in a white shirt was
stacking CD-ROM disks in a tall, glass-fronted cabinet as I
passed.

From the front window on the second floor there was a
spectacular and suggestive view of the Basilica. Offices full
of busy people filled both sides of a long corridor. Through
the open door of one office near the head of the stairs, I saw
two burly figures in black priests' cassocks bent over computers, and between them the lovely profile of a young
woman.

Boys and girls together.

Marching lockstep for the greater glory of a new Inquisi-
tion deliciously akindle.

9

I WENT TO Caruso's funeral. The church was full of flowers, semi-important Vatican officials, and a lot of lumpy, red-eyed Italian women in black. I didn't see anybody who looked like a candidate to be Caruso's killer. There were no beautiful women with broken hearts cowering alone in the back of the church, no hard-eyed clerics who looked as if they were secretly glad he was dead. Vidal was there, looking sad in that intellectually superior way of his.

In the days that followed, I worked my ass off. I talked to Caruso's fellow workers, and to the priests who lived with him. I interviewed the doorman where he worked and the cleaning lady where he lived; the bar owner around the corner who made him coffee on his way to work every morning, and the large-busted lady who dry-cleaned his priest suits. I talked with his friends, and I would have talked with his enemies, but I couldn't find any.

An upstanding, well-liked citizen, Monsignor Caruso, until he became a free-falling one. Caruso's computer was kaput, but the disks booted up okay. I surfed them, but every file was about religion in some form or shape. To save time, I asked one of the seminarians, a South African computer wizard, to print them out for me. As a computer-friendly sort of guy, I could have done it myself, mind you, but it was tedious, and sometimes even lowly brother rank has its pleasures.

"So where are we, Paolo?" Galli asked over a Campari, after another fruitless foot-slogging day. "My bosses will be asking . . ."

"Say that we've reached a deeply religious moment in our inquiries."

"What does that mean?"

"We're praying for a miracle."

What I did have was a decent image of the man behind the corpse I had met on St. Peter's marbled floor. Caruso, it seems, was a provocative, even a radical, thinker. He was seen as a comer around the Vatican not so much for the volume of his work but because a lot of people seemed to think that he had the ear of the new pope. He was a creature of the Curia, all right, but closer to the great mass of Catholics on key bedroom and social issues than to Curia naysayers, many of them leftovers from the Never-Never Pole.

The litany of differences within the church was the same in the new century as it had been for the last decades of the old—just more divisive. Tens of millions of Catholics, quietly supported by thousands of priests, rebelled against the ban on artificial birth control, the exclusion of divorced and remarried Catholics from the sacraments, the unyielding insistence on priestly celibacy, the refusal to consider women priests, and the refusal to allow the participation of other Christians in Catholic communion. Tredi—wisely—hadn't tackled any of these issues so early in his reign.

What people told me about Caruso was backed up in the bulk of the computer files I'd scanned so far—daring, farsighted, change-with-the-times. But on the same disks were files that argued opposite propositions with equal vigor, expositions of hard-core, right-wing positions more acceptable to the Keys and their ilk than—I'd bet—to my friend the pope. Maybe the rest of the files would provide some clue when I got them back from the seminarian.

I was playing mental jigsaw, when Tilly turned my life upside down with a phone call. Not for the first time, heaven knows, or the last.

"Crusader Wright has returned safely from heathen lands and smiles anew on your sorrowful countenance, Brother Paul."

"Tilly! When did you get in? Welcome back."

"Come see my great new rug and have a drink. I command it."

"With pleasure."

Now I haven't said much about Tilly, and to tell you the truth I thought of leaving her out altogether, but in the end I decided that since this account is meant to be a kind of detoxification, I might as well try to be honest.

Tilly and I were close. But we had a fits-and-starts relationship. I won't say it was love, but it was nearer than a peripatetic correspondent and a housefrau cleric should get.

Sometimes Tilly was gone for months at a time. Sometimes she was in Rome for long stretches, but I seldom saw her, except maybe for an occasional coffee. She never announced them, but I knew when new men walked into her life, and I always knew when they walked out again. Over the years, Tilly and I had gotten to know one another very well. Too well, some would say.

Tilly lived in an old *palazzo* just off the Piazza di Spagna. The apartment itself was nothing special, but there was a glorious terrace with an angled view of the old Spanish Steps spilling into the piazza from the Trinità dei Monti, one of the best places to watch people, and to savor the daily ballet of tones and textures as the light changes over Rome.

She buzzed me up, and I breasted the four steep flights somewhere between aplomb and agony. The apartment door was open, so I walked through and onto the terrace. Tilly wore sandals and some sort of shapeless Middle East caftan. She greeted me with a kiss so sisterly that I immediately realized there was someone else there.

"Welcome home. Where you been?"

"Cairo, then Amman, then Ankara, wham, bam, thank you ma'am. My head's still spinning," Tilly said, as she led me to her guest. "Maria Lourdes Lopez del Rio, journalist extraordinary, this is piratical Brother Paul, Vatican-watcher and cleric about town."

She was a Latina, world-class. *"Buenas tardes,"* she said, with a smile.

"A drink, Paul," Tilly commanded.

"Bourbon, thanks."

The Latina was short and shapely, black hair cut above her ears, makeup cleverly highlighting violet eyes so that they seemed bottomless. We shook hands. Her grip bristled with life and energy; more than firm, athletic.

There was something . . . I had seen her before. Just as I was about to ask what sort of journalist she was, it came to me. Athletic. Of course.

"A great race." I meant it. "I was in a room full of guys and we were all on our feet cheering for you. Those final hundred meters were magic."

Great bolts of light lanced up out of the violet, warming, embracing. "Thank you. I never ran as well before, or since. I think maybe it was God running that day, not me."

The Australia games. One of the longer races. The favorites chewing themselves up, too fast, too early; a South American long shot bursting from the pack with a last desperate kick to win a heartstopping finish they'd show on Olympic highlights for decades to come.

Tilly came back with my drink and said to Maria, "Paul's an old friend." Her smile said "Keep off." To me she said, "Maria's with *Trompeta,* the big Catholic weekly in Santiago. She covers the Vatican."

"Are you newly arrived?"

"No, I've been here for some time, but the pastoral visit to New York will be my first trip with the Holy Father. I am very excited," Maria said.

"How nice. Next year, right?"

Tilly chided. "Stop teasing. It's sooner than that, Paul, and you know it. Here I've told Maria you understand everything about the Vatican and you pretend not even to know when the pope goes where."

"Mea culpa. Mea maxima culpa, Maria. I get so caught up in spiritual reflections that sometimes I lose track of the day-to-day. Will His Holiness also be going home to Poland?"

Wrong pope. They laughed.

"Are you going to New York, too?" I asked Tilly.

"Yes, sir, yes, sir, three bags full. On the papal plane with Maria. Come along, we'll carouse."

Matilda Wright was the best of the few remaining American staff correspondents in Rome. She covered the Vatican as well as a great swath of southern Europe and the Middle East; the Blood and Garlic Belt, she called it. Her apartment was also her office, though she was on the road so much she might as well have been based in Istanbul, Madrid, or Sarajevo.

One of the Pole's traditions that Tredi had kept alive and burnished in his own image was the high-profile foreign trip. Like John Paul II, he also traveled extensively within Italy, for that matter, and frequently visited Roman parishes. Tredi had invited me more than once, but I had never actually made a foreign pope trip. *Brutta figura,* as they say in Italian, bad form, at least for somebody who journalists saw as a Vatican insider. Which was a joke, of course.

Pay close attention to what happens around the hushed corridors of the oldest institution in the West, and after five years you might have a modest inkling of how things work in the world's last calculatingly opaque and unabashedly authoritarian state. I don't pretend to know the intricacies and don't particularly care. That might seem strange for someone who is a friend of the pope, but that's looking at things the wrong way around, as far as I'm concerned. Tredi was my friend, who also happened to be pope. And our friendship was our business.

Tilly raised her glass. "Actually, Maria and I have been sharing a drink in memory of a mutual acquaintance who died unexpectedly while I was away."

"I'm sorry."

"A monsignor who handled press queries for Justice and Peace. Luca Caruso. One of the very few over at the Vatican who not only seemed to enjoy talking with reporters but also played straight."

"He went to pray and fell from the Dome in the Basilica," Maria said to me. "A lovely, gentle man. Patient and very knowledgeable. I learned a lot from him. It is a great shame."

"We all liked and respected him." Tilly handed me a fresh drink.

Why hadn't anybody told me that Caruso talked regularly with Vatican journalists of divergent views and seemed to satisfy them both? Did it matter? It might. For the more I learned about Caruso, the less I understood which man he really was—new-thinking radical or hard-line zealot.

The women chatted about Caruso as an absent friend for a while and eventually I paid for my drinks by telling Tilly and Maria a few insider Vatican stories embroidered to suit the audience. With appropriate sympathetic irreverence, of course. On my third Bourbon I started to tell the one about Tredi playing golf with the successor to Mother Teresa. But I noticed that the violet fire had grown cold just as Tilly nudged me with her foot.

"And of course when Catholics laugh about their church it's with the same affection of lovers laughing at their own foibles," I concluded lamely.

"Gentle humor is always welcome, but the church and the Holy Father should not be objects of ridicule. Am I right, Brother Paul?" the Latina asked sweetly.

"Yes, of course."

A reverent journalist? An oxymoron. Like Catholic university. Holy brother. Working press.

"Maria works for a very traditionalist newspaper," Tilly interjected, signal flags flying.

"I try to be an observant Catholic," Maria said severely.

"I like to think that all of us are keepers of our faith."

Prudence is a brotherly virtue.

After another half-hour of banter, Maria left, pleading an interview. When she had gone, Tilly sat on my lap and put her arms around my neck. I gave her a chaste peck on the cheek.

"How's my favorite man of the cloth?"

"Tolerable."

"Did you miss me?"

"Always. Where'd you find Joan of Arc?"

"Maria? Journalists are a small tribe. I've known her for some time. She's nice, and she's really more political than as strict as she makes it sound. I would have said in fact, sire, that your poor eyes would be tired, having so thoroughly ravished her." She snuggled closer. I had to twist my head to save my ear. "So how's Tredi? You don't hear a lot about him out where Allah is God and Muhammad is His Prophet."

"He's fine, working hard, sends his love." The sun was nearly gone, but it was squirming hot there on the terrace. What the hell was his name?

"How's . . . uh." I knew he was Roman and had been around for a few months, but beyond that I couldn't have told you much about Tilly's latest flame.

"Back with his wife, the bastard."

"Sorry."

"No big deal. It was more overture than aria anyway." A

big enough deal to have broken the mood, though. "Let me see if I can find us something to chew on." Tilly levered to her feet and padded off. I went to stand by the terrace edge. Below, shadow was creeping across the piazza like an incoming tide.

"What about Caruso?" she called. "Are you working on it?"

"Officially, it was an accident. Unofficially—and off the record—yeah, I'm poking around."

"Does that mean he didn't just fall?"

Tilly came back with a bowl of cheese pieces, delicious-looking *peccorino*. She placed it on the edge of the chaise lounge and grabbed for her drink.

"He fell all right, but he probably had help."

The bowl tipped, spilling cheese across the terrazzo.

"Shit." Tilly began scooping. "Any suspects?" she asked.

"Yeah." She looked up sharply. "The chaise designer. If the plastic strips were closer together, the bowl would have had enough support."

"Stupid man. If Caruso didn't fall accidentally, and didn't commit suicide, then he was done, wasn't he? Do you know who did it?"

"Did you know him well?" Always answer a question with a question. No way I was going to tell her anything about the investigation—as if there was much to tell. What's more she knew it, too.

Tilly put the bowl under the chair, chewed some cheese, and pulled at her drink. "Fairly well. Talked with him once or twice a week; met him at receptions now and then. I liked his politics."

Another one. Tilly was out there on the wild-eyed end of the church that some people thought was progressive and others claimed was anarchical. Yet Caruso had admirers amid both fire and ice. Tilly and Maria. I knew journalists well enough to understand that love and commitment to their craft so unites them as kindred spirits that political opposites can be great friends—can marry, for that matter, and often do. But what spin could Caruso have been pitching that pleased both leftist Tilly and right wing Maria? To say nothing of the pope and the Keys bishop at the same time? How had the late Monsignor Caruso managed that?

It would have been smarter and ultimately more profitable to have dwelled more on that basic contradiction, but instead I followed Tilly when she walked to the terrace edge to watch day end. A mistake, for she pressed close, trapping my arms at my sides.

"How's my favorite man out of the cloth?"

"Tilly . . . I'm . . ." sworn to celibacy, I wanted to say, but . . . she was on fire, and so was I. The whisky or the sunset.

God forgive me.

When she kissed me, I kissed her back. When that was over, I wasn't at my most persuasive. But I did make one more try.

"Stop, Tilly. What about the new rug? I haven't seen it."

"You'll see it very soon," she murmured, hands working, "I laid it across the top of my bed to get the wrinkles out."

By the time I got back to St. Damian's, the weekly community meeting was under way. A German professor had come from one of the pontifical universities to lecture on "Sin in Everyday Life." I sat in the back and tried to look attentive.

Sorry if I shock you, but I'm not a perfect example of Brotherhood any more than I have been a perfect example of anything else I have ever been. I sin. Clerics are people, too. Some drink. Some gamble. Some have "housekeepers," wink, wink. Some smoke obsessively. Some succumb to homosexual urgings; a few are pedophiles. I am a raging heterosexual. I do my best to sublimate the urge, and regret it when I fail, but every now and then I wind up in bed with an attractive and willing partner for whom I feel affection. I go to bed against my vow of celibacy and cursing my own weakness, but that doesn't stop me from trying to screw her blind to our mutual satisfaction. Bless me, Father, for I have sinned. I sin and therefore I am.

I had a few quiet days to mull my transgressions. Life at St. Damian's had lapsed into a flat, grinding mid-semester ennui. Treadmilling between boring classes, bad meals, and long nights of study, the seminarians were mostly too whacked to cause me any trouble. Helping Galli had left my own half-hearted academic career in shambles, more's the pity, so I decided to pack it in for the time being. No one would miss me at classes, and I seldom took exams anyway.

Galli and I dutifully talked with more of Caruso's co-workers, his friends, even the cardinal who was his boss. We pawed again over the forensic evidence, reread reports of his other investigators, drank gallons of *espresso* by the thimble, talked to the trees. We reinterviewed the guards who had been on duty at the Basilica when Caruso had died in hopes of a better description of the priest one of them had seen leaving the Dome. We got nothing, *niente, nada, zilch.*

I kept my weekly appointment with Father Ivanovic. He had a big, sunny office on the Janiculum Hill on the Vatican side of the Tiber. It was such a lovely afternoon, though, we walked for about an hour in Villa Sciarra, one of the city parks. I told him a bit about the Caruso case and the old sorts of frustrations it had wakened. I think he found me restless and irritable, but no crazier than usual. At least he didn't push any of his magic blue integrating pills; I've swallowed enough of those for several lifetimes, thanks. I thought of talking to Ivan about Tilly but decided not to. Blackbeard's not my confessor, just my shrink.

Afterward, feeling a bit extreme myself and knowing Galli would not approve, I called Luther, and the next afternoon we bushwhacked Vidal as he left work. Emerging from the old *palazzo* in his black priest's suit and matching briefcase, Vidal looked every inch the Vatican bureaucrat, a far cry from the basement digger I had met a few days before. But no less aloof, or any more welcoming.

"Some things have surfaced in our investigation. If you have time for a couple of questions, we'd be grateful," I said, nodding toward Luther. "This is Father Clancy."

Vidal looked him up and down. "Clancy," he said.

"Black Irish," Luther said.

We sat at a sidewalk table on the Via della Conciliazione, the broad avenue that Mussolini had bulldozed at the cost of a whole neighborhood of medieval tenements to give himself a suitably imperial view of St. Peter's from the river. I nursed an orange juice, looking at the church. Luther and Vidal drank coffee.

"One of the things that puzzles us is that Caruso was obviously a great admirer of the Society of the Sacred Keys. He even worked for them, and that jars with everything else we have learned about him and his views."

Vidal shrugged. "Luca was a scholar, he had an eclectic mind; many things interested him."

"Would the Keys's views have reflected Monsignor Caruso's own thinking on church issues?"

"Of course not. He was at the other end of the rainbow, shall we say."

"And yet he wrote for them."

Vidal shrugged.

"The Keys's views would be also far from your own as well," I pressed.

"My views, my theories, the need for human awareness and dignity, are well known. They speak for themselves," Vidal said.

His eyes flickered, though, as he dragged on his cigarette, and I think he knew where I was going. It was Luther, inadvertently, who sand-bagged him.

The big monk had seemed half asleep but uncoiled with cheetah-speed and an exclamation. "Hey, I know who you are: 'Humanism and the Living God,' 'Spirituality with Dignity' . . ." He rattled off two or three more titles I hadn't read either. "My people like that stuff. It speaks to us in the head and in the heart," Luther announced—"his people" presumably a synonym for all of Africa.

"Thank you, Father, you are very kind." Vidal seemed almost human.

But I had done my Keys homework, waded through numbing hours of relentless zealotry. It was a perfect time for Direct Action.

I said, "Father Vidal, three years ago, before the new pope, the Keys was regularly denouncing you as a dangerous radical. Yet last year, it found some grudging praise for one of your ideas. Then, twice in successive issues the Keys magazine refers to the good Father Vidal as something less than the devil incarnate. And by the last issue, who is himself writing a big article? Why, it's Father Vidal. Has the apostle for change gone straight?"

I had his attention, all right. Luther had a funny look on his face. He must have thought I was getting wound up. Too bad.

"And who flipped first? Changed his stripes? You? Or Caruso? I think it was you, and I think Caruso chased after you—maybe because he was worried about his good friend suddenly turning his back on lifelong convictions. I think there was a lot of tension between the two of you. Bad blood, maybe. Arguments. A fight. Who knows?" I watched Vidal. "But I do know that nobody remembers seeing you at breakfast at your residence on the morning that Caruso died. So what do you think about that, Father?"

Vidal's answer was a long time coming, and it was calmer than I expected.

"I think it is wise to remember that in the life of the church, as in the affairs of her servants, there are many available avenues for analysis and information, Brother Paul. What may seem superficially conflictive may in fact contribute to the harmony and greater good."

He said it almost sadly, and got up to leave. I wish I had understood him. If I had been smarter, fewer people would have died.

I think about that often.

10

I HAD DINNER with the seminarians that night and was reading myself to sleep when the phone rang and a deep voice
demanded, "How's the church's most distinguished late
vocation?"

I came alert with a rush. "He's fine, probably. I'm good,
too."

"What are you up to? Studying?"

"Just hangin' out. Slow night."

"Me, too. Feel like taking a ride?"

"Sure."

"Largo Argentina, front of the news kiosk, fifteen minutes."

It had rained, more squall than storm, cooling the air and
leaving the city sweet-smelling. I walked through gleaming
streets, hopscotching puddles. At Largo Argentina, a large,
traffic-heavy square built about the ruins of Roman temples
hardly anybody ever bothers to look at, I sheltered in the lee
of the kiosk, not knowing exactly what I was waiting for. A
taxi slowed once, hopefully, and a police car purred pur-
posely past, but mostly it was just me looking at the ancient

ruins poking up from their home below ground level. After about ten minutes, a gray Fiat sedan flashed its lights from the corner and slid to a stop before me.

"Are you alone, big boy?" a voice called as the passenger door swung open.

I'd have shot back something witty and risqué, but he was the pope, after all, so I buttoned my lip and jumped in.

Tredi drove as well as he did everything else. No seat belt, of course, but that was not the only rule he was breaking that night.

"Nice car."

"Standard shift. Big engine, air-conditioned. It belongs to one of the curators at the Vatican Museum; he's away on a trip."

"Somebody behind us?" I looked through the mirror on the right door. No chase car.

"Naw, I slipped away. And yes, I know, my guys will be livid if they find out." He meant the Vatican cops.

Not my department, but I wouldn't let him out alone. Ever. It was dangerous. It was arrogant. It was stupid, particularly since the FBI had picked up some vague rumors about a possible threat against him, and passed them on to us. But he did that sort of thing all the time. I knew that from personal experience. And I also knew that no Vatican cop, no cop anywhere, will ever be any match for any pig-headed pope. But at least I could try.

"With all respect, I'm here to tell you that it's a dumb thing to do. And it's selfish. Those guys would give their lives for you, and you're mocking them."

He was my friend, but I knew that would make him mad. He looked at me sharply, opened his mouth to deliver a suitably papal reply, and I braced for a tongue-lashing. But then he just grunted, didn't want to hear it.

I had to insist. "How about that threat the Americans warned you about?"

We darted into the narrow mouth of Via del Corso, a lone

traffic policeman studiously ignoring us as we followed a few other cars into an area supposedly restricted to taxis and bigshots with special permissions.

"Nothing really new. Hard to pin down." He smiled. "The Americans."

"They didn't happen to say by any chance from what direction they heard it. Miami? Further south maybe?"

The pope grinned. "Nice to get out. Air the mind, stretch the mental legs. Relax."

Isn't there something in the Bible about preaching to a stone? I shut up, but I wasn't happy.

Every now and then a rumor surfaced in one of the Roman newspapers that Pope Pius XIII would sometimes steal away from the Vatican to wander anonymously by night through a city he had gotten to know well in nearly a decade at the Curia. In those simpler times, he had driven a *motorino* of his own.

"I've been reading about tilapia," the pope said. "An amazing fish, really. Great implications for poor countries as a cheap and reliable source of protein. They're hardy little things, too. Probably could grow them at the Vatican if we wanted to."

He was talking about his errant brother Bobby, one of the world's lost souls. Lumbering like some giant turtle through Caribbean waters in search of a fortune that he'd never find.

"They breed pretty quick, don't they? Has there been a first tilapia harvest?" I asked gently.

"Oh, no. It's still far too early for that. But Bobby says the infrastructure is nearly ready to put in. Won't be long, he says."

We all have our blind spots. His brother Bobby was the pope's. I had learned that over the years. Before the fish farm, there had been coconut and nutmeg plantations decimated by bugs, time-sharing schemes with leaky roofs, and schooner charters that somehow never sailed. I had a feeling that deep down my friend the pope understood that none of Bobby's grandiose projects would ever work.

On the nights that I rode with the pope, it was because he wanted space and time away from the punishing pressure cooker of larger-than-life responsibilities. Deserved it, too. The Vatican press office never commented on rumors of papal excursions, of course, so officially they never occurred, since as far as the Vatican is concerned no pope ever does anything except officially.

"Amazing, this," Tredi said, bending low over the wheel to look up at the passing *palazzi* as if seeing them for the first time, talking mostly to himself. "Here in one square mile, give or take, is the heart of a whole country. The key ministries, the big banks, newspapers, political parties."

We passed a bank, a church, and an insurance company, one, two, three. I don't know how often he snuck out, or who else went with him, but I understood the impulse. Whatever else he is, a pope is a prisoner of the Vatican, locked up, in the name of God, in a prison as confining—and perhaps as soulless—as any other. I accompanied him on what he called his "breakouts" every month or so, and it was almost always him doing the talking. Letting his hair down, or in his case, stripping away the constrictive white cassock that marked him—scarred him?—as surely as any brand.

Tredi had his window open, and cool air snapped refreshingly past. On the left, an ancient Roman column drifted past, a newspaper office behind it, then Palazzo Chigi, the prime minister's office, and beyond it Montecitorio, the parliament, stately old-ochre *palazzi* softly lit and lightly watched by carabinieri in parked vans and on foot patrol with automatic weapons and bulletproof vests. He drove slowly, checking it out, the way a stranger might. Or a mayor. Why not? The pope is the Bishop of Rome and the Bishop of Rome is always the pope, after all.

"Is the Vatican really very different from all this, Paul?" Tredi was thinking out loud. "We've got a lot of the same institutions, except maybe for a parliament, because the Vatican's a dictatorship. All power in the hands of one man in a white robe who never needs to run for re-election. Apart from that, we've got ministers, even if they're called cardinals. Got a bank, a newspaper; a big radio station, all the trappings.

"We've got branch offices in practically every country on earth, and trouble at nearly all of them. The in-fighting that goes on: horrendous, I'm here to tell you. Not always just words, either. A friend of mine, a tough old cardinal, was murdered in his cathedral in Latin America a couple of years ago. Cops arrested a homeless man; they say he confessed and maybe he did, but it wouldn't have surprised me if it had been politics, maybe even church politics, that killed him." That was a shrewd guess, as it turned out, but the full truth was even more sordid than that.

Tredi followed the road around to the right and we drove past one of those Roman anomalies, the only department store in a city that lures tens of millions of shoppers from around the world every year.

"Good thing the apostles didn't all leave diaries: you can be sure that late at night over a skin of wine they squabbled between themselves over exactly what He said and what He meant. Only natural. There have been factions, cabals, alliances, knifing differences of opinion ever since. We've fought a lot of wars in God's name, haven't we? Stupid, every one of them. If you have to compel somebody to believe what you believe, it's pretty senseless, isn't it, Paul?"

I wondered if he was rehearsing a homily—and where he would dare deliver it. We were running along Via Tritone now, a narrow shopping street that spills into Piazza Barberini, with its Bernini statue of the sea god Triton tooting his horn. The right door mirror showed a clean and empty street behind us.

"The trick is to convince people you are right, not to frighten them. People shouldn't sin because it's wrong, an insult to God and to their own dignity; not because they'll burn in hell. I could never say that, but it's true. There are certain fundamental truths if you want to be Catholic, but beyond that—it's mostly Parcheesi. A lot of rules imposed to suit political currents that flowed and ebbed centuries ago. Good riddance, but I can't really say that, Paul." He looked over at me in the darkened car for a long instant and I wondered what he was seeing. "Or can I? Suppose I was to tell people the truth: that God is God. Reach out to Him the best way you can; He'll be there for you. Anger a lot of people, if I did that."

He turned left at the head of the piazza and we climbed a gentle sweeping curve to the left. We passed one of the city's great old hotels, and a former queen's palace that is now the American Embassy. The light was green and he eased through and on to Via Veneto. A few people were sitting around sidewalk tables shielded by lean-to awnings.

"La Dolce Vita," the pope said. "What a movie. And the name. It became shorthand for a street, an era, a country, a way of life that never really existed but people are still nostalgic for. People of a certain age, I mean. You say you live in Rome and they say, *'La Dolce Vita,'* with a not-so-secret smile meaning how nice that you can manage to sit around all day admiring Anita Ekberg's profile. The idea you might actually work hard in a city that's noisy, dirty, polluted; dangerous, even. There's no room in their reality for that. I knew Fellini. Did I ever tell you that?"

"No."

"We met a few times, receptions and things when I was a cardinal, and one day out of the blue he called me up. Did I know a priest he could talk to? So I sent over a worldly one; a Jesuit, maybe. Fellini looked awful. Never said what he wanted, just started talking, a kind of living biography: all the women he had screwed, all the producers he had hated, a lot of bad things he had done, wished, plotted, stolen. A stream of consciousness, almost, interrupted now and then for another glass of something. At the end of it, he said, 'Well, that's my confession, Father, I feel better.' And the priest, who wasn't stupid and could see what was coming, said, 'Federico, confessing means saying you're sorry. Are you sorry?' Fellini thought for a while and he said, 'I'm sorry for a lot of it, because I see now how petty most of it was. Except for cheating thieving producers—and the women. I'm not sorry about any of them, because I never thought there was anything wrong with it—and neither did they. Does that mean I'll go to hell?' A few weeks later he was dead."

Ahead of us, a Lancia that had been parked in a crosswalk roared off into the night. In the best Roman tradition, Tredi nosed in slickly to replace it. We were more than halfway up the Veneto, not far from the Porta Pinciana gate.

"So let's say you're the priest, Paul. And here's the final examination question for your ethics course. Do you give him absolution, the almost-sorry *Signore* Fellini, who hadn't set foot in a church for sixty years but was scared to die without a priest?"

He killed the engine and looked across at me.

"Absolution, sure. But I'm only a brother." I don't know if I would have passed the exam, because I don't think Tredi heard me. He was already sailing on another tack.

"Fellini and his women, like all Italian men, I suppose. And you know, all those ring-kissing, pope-loving Italian Catholics produce proportionately fewer babies than any other place on earth. Should I yell at them, Paul? That's what Wojtyla did—for all he accomplished. Maybe I should just say it's your bedroom, whatever position you take in it is your business. Can you imagine what that would do to all the traditionalists? Outrage! Condemnation! Maybe even schism. Still, you ever heard of anybody impeaching a pope? They're stuck with me. Till death do us part."

He went quiet, fingers playing a light tattoo on the steering wheel. I am a simple brother, but I am not stupid. So I said, finally, "You're into something big—and you think you might be whacked. What? Who?"

He glanced over sharply again, and this time he spoke. "It's vaguer than that. I don't even know for sure what I want to do, or what it would trigger. I'm still thinking. When the Americans feel something in the wind, it's worth thinking about. And you're right, I'm being selfish. I'll apologize to my security guys in the morning."

"It is never wrong to do the right thing," I said, teasing. It was one of his favorite lines.

"Right on," the pope smiled, "but now let's have a drink, *hermano.*"

"Here? Now? The Via Veneto! C'mon!"

"Trust me. Tonight, I've actually got money, borrowed from Don Vincenzo," he said, naming an aged and tight-fisted priest who oversaw household accounts at the Apostolic Palace. About six months before, we had shared a midnight bottle of wine in a working-class bar on the slum outskirts of the city, and a moment of panic when Tredi'd realized he had no money. Fortunately, I had had enough to pay.

"Do I look like a movie star?" He had donned a pair of dark glasses and a shapeless felt hat above the tan windbreaker he wore.

It was madness. And exactly what was I supposed to do about it? Stuff the pope in the trunk and hustle him back to the Vatican?

"No, sorry. Anita's virtue is safe," I said, meekly following him from the car. "But you don't look like the pope, either, I'll say that much."

"So much for small favors."

Tredi had an uncanny sense of knowing what he could get away with. He knew that people see what they are accustomed to seeing. He took advantage of that. That night, we sat at an awning-covered sidewalk table in a half-lit corner.

If you had asked the waiter, the way reporters and cops did later, he would have said that two middle-aged men had stopped for a nightcap. Spoke good Italian but not quite Romans; Spaniards or Latin Americans maybe, businessmen, international bankers, priests even. Men of a certain carriage and substance, clearly, but nothing special about either of them.

I had a nervous Campari. The pope sipped a clear, cold *grappa* made from Alpine pears. I gobbled peanuts while he demolished a plate of jumbo green olives with his brandy.

Down at the corner, TV lights and camera flashes bathed the entrance to a big hotel, recording Beautiful People parading in and out in evening dress. At the tables around us, groups of American tourists, some of them the worse for all that Chianti at dinner, were comparing their non-existent Italian with great hilarity. The Americans were of the triple-chinned jumbo variety, big-boned men with bellies spreading over white belts, large women within loose clothes with a lot of paint under never-never land blonde hair. Nice folks, if you got to know them, I suppose. Of an age not only to remember *La Dolce Vita* but to have seen it at college.

"Do you know what I'd really like right now, Paul?" the pope asked, adding another olive pit to the pile in the big glass ashtray. There was no instant when I thought he might say "Anita Ekberg," but he surprised me anyway. "A batting cage. I'd like to step into the cage with a light bat and hit a hundred pitches. I could get my rhythm back with a hundred pitches. Probably raise a blister, but I could use gloves, they'd help. I hit nearly three hundred one year, did you know that?" I knew that. He had told me that first day we had met in Miami—and about half a dozen times since.

We gabbed and I could sense the tension flowing out of him. When it came, he sipped his second *grappa* with appreciation. "Olives and cold pears. What a combination. One sure thing about God—She loves olives and pears. Trust me on that one, Paul." He laughed at his own weak joke. "You know, Paul, when I was a kid, back on the Island"—he always called his country the Island, although it wasn't—"I played ball every chance I got. I knew that I was born to play in the Bigs, but by the time I was sixteen, reality intruded.

Like nasty curveballs in on the hands that left me paralyzed
and feeling like a fool. So I became a priest—what else
could I do? Still . . . of all the pleasures in life one of the
greatest has got to be getting Good Wood. You know what I
mean, don't you? The pitcher throws smoke and you turn on
just so and there's a crack! That's more electrifying and honest than most other things in this world. Good Wood. *Sí,
señor.* What's better than Good Wood, Paul?"

"Sex."

"Why did I know you were going to say that?"

"I could never hit a curveball, either."

"Did you ever see my batting stance? Look," the pope
commanded. He sprang to his feet, locked his right hand
around his left thumb, half-crouched and folded his arms up
close to his cheek. "I used to stand fairly wide and cock the
bat about here. Now that I'm old, I'd have trouble getting
around on a fast ball, so I'd compensate this way, a more
precise stroke. Forget the long ball. Go for the line drives."
He swung, a nice precise stroke.

"Strike three!" called a good-natured American voice
from among three couples of tourists at a nearby table.

"He's out—to lunch," I said.

It should have ended there, except that the tourist, a bulky
white-haired man, face flushed with wine, levered out of his
chair with elephantine grace. Popping a pair of olives and
blocking the sidewalk, he announced, "A good batting
stance depends on the wrists, and also on transferring weight
from the back leg to the front at just the right moment.
Watch."

Talking all the while, the man took his stance, strode forward, and brought his arms through the arc and snapped his
wrists.

"Going, going, gone, Archie," one of his friends called,
and the others clapped.

"Nice swing," I said and turned away. It was time to put
Tredi on the road. The next thing, they'd invite us over to

their table so Archie and the Bishop of Rome could swap baseball lies.

But the pope was still watching the American, and when a woman screamed "Archie!" I spun around and understood why.

The man was collapsing, face red as a beet, hands to his throat. A dreadful rattle leaked from his throat; a dying sound.

Shit. I leapt up, but the pope was already around me. In three giant strides he was behind the American. He knotted his fists under the man's breastbone, and as I rushed forward to support the man, I could see the muscles in the pope's arms flexing. He jerked. The sound from the American's throat changed to a high C, but nothing else happened.

"Damn olives!" I heard the pope mutter. He squeezed again and this time two slimy olives fired from the man's mouth. One grazed my eye and the other bounced off my cheek. It might even have been funny, except that the American's eyes rolled up into his head and he went from choleric red to flaccid gray in a few scary seconds. The pope and I were both on our knees, the man between us, with a knot of yelling Americans, waiters, and passersby clustered around.

"It's his heart!" I heard a woman scream. "Pills! In his trouser pocket."

I fished out a plastic vial and Tredi forced a pill under the man's lolling tongue. We laid him gently onto the sidewalk and cradled his head with a white cloth one of the waiters had ripped off a table.

Bells were ringing in my head. I didn't know this man and, sorry, I didn't care what happened to him. I had to get the pope away.

That was all that mattered.

I reached across to tug him up, but once again Tredi was too quick for me. Cradling the man in his arms, the pope began mouth-to-mouth resuscitation. Blessedly, the light was poor and the old hat shadowed his face.

What a mess. The Americans were screaming, excited Italians trying loudly to calm them. The manager came out of the bar to announce that an ambulance was on its way.

I hunkered down to shield Tredi. He had a good rhythm going, counting softly to himself in Spanish, breathing, pinching the nostrils, letting the air escape, the pope giving the kiss of life to a stranger on a Roman sidewalk.

It seemed forever before cops showed up and pushed people away to make room for the ambulance and two competent-looking paramedics. Maybe we'd get out of this after all.

When I stood up to give the medics room, I realized that even if I got Tredi away quietly, he'd still be on every TV set in the world because a two-woman camera crew drawn by the sirens was hurrying toward us from the hotel. Somebody was bound to recognize him. People stood aside as I walked a few unsteady paces away from Tredi and the cops, wincing and stretching my tired back.

I leaned heavily against an abandoned chair and watched as the medics firmly replaced the pope just as the TV crew came rushing up.

Could I have known that the chair would skid away from me or that I would fall heavily onto the sidewalk directly in front of the running women? Or that they would go tumbling over me in a tangle, camera flying, as I caught just a glimpse of Tredi rising, understanding all in an instant, vanishing into the crowd?

It took me a few minutes of confusion and apology to get clear, but I had no trouble finding Tredi double-parked on the road that parallels the top edge of Villa Borghese Park.

"The American was breathing on his own when they put him in the ambulance."

"Oh, that's good. I was saying a little prayer for him when you came up." He put the car in gear and pointed down the hill.

I was a mess. My breathing was ragged; my nerves jan-

gled. "That was too close. And you know it as well as I do,"
I gasped. "If somebody had been gunning for you tonight,
you'd be dead. And if the papers once catch you out of the
Vatican, you'll never be able to sneak out again. They'll
haunt every gate every night. No more, damn it. Please, no
more."

The pope gave me a big smile. "There are tunnels only
popes know about. Besides, as someone famous, maybe
even me, once said, 'I am who I am. I do what I must.' " He
had enjoyed himself. "Why, *hermano,*" he teased, "if you
think that was a near thing, you should have been with me
the night I was walking a beach out near Ostia when suddenly there was this couple, and she—"

"Oh, get a life!" I snapped, which must have been exactly
what he expected, because he laughed a to-the-soul belly
laugh I had only heard a couple of times in all the years I had
known him.

"Okay, okay," I surrendered, "it was fun and I'm sure it
beats sitting around the Vatican surfing the Internet. But,
please, please, don't take any more chances, until whatever
threat that's bothering the Americans gets sorted out. And let
me find you somebody to stay close. I have a friend, Luther,
an African monk. He's got moves you wouldn't believe."

"The security mavens have already thought of that one,"
Tredi said. "I've got a new personal assistant, a priest no
less, who apparently knows forty-six ways to kill with a
communion wafer. Nice kid, too. Latino. Diego Altamirano
is his name. Come by and meet him, see what you think.
We'll work your Father Luther into the rotation, too, if it
makes you feel better. But wait and see: the threat will turn
out to be hot air and smoke. They always are."

"There must be something I can do."

"I need you to find whoever killed Caruso," he said quietly.

"Is there a connection?"

"I can answer that only once I know who killed him,
Paul."

"Did you know that Caruso was mixed up with the Keys? Not the sort of people I'd expect a friend of yours to be running around with."

I think I had hoped to surprise the pope, but he disappointed me.

"I know all about it."

I started to tell him what I was thinking, but he suddenly switched tracks. "I know you've got Father Vidal in your craw, but don't dwell on him. Keep looking."

Small world, the Vatican.

"What else?"

"Be close for the next couple of months. There's no end of fast-reflex folks itching to strike a blow for their pope, but a scarred old dog with good instincts would be an even greater comfort."

"Sure." Right from the start, Tredi had known how to make me feel good.

"It's still a ways off, but I put you on the list to come with us on the plane to New York; gave you a phony title. Keep your eyes open."

"I will."

We were near the bottom of the hill and I'd get out before he cut back across the bridge to the Vatican. I was beginning to unwind.

"It was you, wasn't it? The worldly priest?"

Tredi smiled. "Which one was that?"

"Fellini. Did you give him absolution? You did, didn't you?"

"Had it been me, I couldn't say. Secret of the confessional, Paul." Another big grin. "Do me a favor and take care of this for me, will you, *hermano?*" He handed me an air mail envelope addressed to his brother Bobby, the kind you might use to send a check for seed capital to raise fish.

Then the pope gave me a friend's tap on the arm and drove off into the night.

There was a paragraph in *Il Messagero* the next morning

about how a good Samaritan had saved the life of a visiting
American dentist, and a fifteen-second snippet on the noon
TV news in which the man's wife said, "We are so grateful
to that man and we want to say *'Grazie'* from the bottom of
our heart. He looked so familiar; I'm sure I've seen him
someplace before. He might even have been a movie star,
but all I know for sure is that he was big and he was handsome and"—giggle—"my husband Archie remembers he
had real bad breath. We'd really like to help him with that if
we could. It's a little problem, really, and Archie is such a
good dentist."

Maybe She never mixes frozen mountain pears with her
olives.

11

WE HAD A dawn crisis at St. Damian's the next morning. I
followed the rector, a small and precise Spaniard named
Diaz who reminded me of a sparrow, along sterile and
gloomy corridors past the identical brown wooden doors of
the cubicles where the seminarians lived. About three-
quarters of the way down, we encountered a tubby seminarian from India named Gilbert, who would have sold his
mother for a rector's smile.

"He's been screaming," Gilbert reported with self-
importance. "Terrible things."

No one gets to be a rector of a big seminary in the Vatican's shadow by being slow-witted. Diaz stood authorita-
tively aside and I went in first.

On the bed, knees to his chest, sat a blond German kid
named Schmidt. Beside him lolled a can of red spray
paint.

"Fuck God" said shaky red letters reeling across the
bile-green wall. I wondered why he had written in English.

"Ay, mi Dios," muttered Diaz. He crossed himself, warding off evil.

Except it wasn't evil, only mid-semester burnout.

"Fuck Matthew, Mark, Luke, and John!" Schmidt screamed.

He was coiled tight as a spring, one fist knotted in his hair. I took the spray can away and he stared at me with fevered eyes that saw some other dimension.

"Fuck Mary!" he screamed. Diaz and Gilbert drew back with matching gulps of horror.

"And the horse you rode in on, pal," I said.

Schmidt was rigid, but a little pressure around the elbow softened him up smartly. He hardly dragged his feet as I frog-marched him down the corridor. We must have made quite a racket, but nary a door opened nary a crack. Curiosity is not encouraged in seminaries.

At the communal bathroom, I stood Schmidt under the shower. He began crying as the cold water cascaded down. Later I got him dressed and took him by cab to a special clinic the Vatican never talks about. He'd be okay, I thought, but they'd never let him back.

Not after Fuck Mary.

At Vatican Police headquarters later that morning, I found the happiest man in Rome.

"Paolo, it is fantastic," Marco Galli bubbled. "The Caruso case is solved. Have you been praying? I have been praying. Truly, prayers are sometimes answered. We have a confession, a confession!"

"Who has confessed?"

"You will see. Hurry. I am anxious to begin my interrogation."

I hurried. A cop solving his first homicide is a bit like a kid on his first date: a lot can go wrong.

There are exactly two cells in the Vatican police station, and one of them held stacked cartons of prayerbooks that morning. Galli had installed two strapping Swiss Guards in the narrow corridor beside the other cell to watch the poor wretch within. He was spectral, a short, gaunt, and travel-stained man whose face spoke of hardship as eloquently as his rough hands told of manual labor. He wore a threadbare black priest's suit shining with age. Sharp black eyes surveyed me for an encompassing instant and then fell dully to resume their study of the terracotta floor. No way you can tell a murderer by looking. But this guy had been in jail before. I knew it.

"Who is he?"

"He says he is a priest, but not much of one, I'd say. From someplace in what used to be Czechoslovakia. It's all here." He tossed me a manila folder.

Written in a round school boy's hand and rotund prose by a Swiss Guard, the single sheet proclaimed that Father Jan Pevec had appeared at the Sant'Anna gate the night before to say that he wished as a matter of conscience to confess that he had bludgeoned a man with a souvenir carved wooden statue on the roof of St. Peter's Basilica.

"That's me! He's the guy who hit me."

Galli smiled a winner's smile. "Exactly."

I returned to the folder, turning to the next page. It was blank.

"Where does it say he killed Caruso?"

"He hasn't said it. Not yet. But he will. We will interrogate him; peel him like an artichoke, one leaf at a time."

"Marco, does this guy speak any known language?"

"His own, of course, but not Italian, alas. He has spoken with the Swiss in German." Galli looked at me hopefully. I shook my head. "His prayerbook is in Latin. My own is a bit, shall we say, disused. Perhaps you . . ."

"Get serious."

"I suppose there remains the remote possibility that he may know some English."

In fact, Jan Pevec spoke clear, concise English. He sat on a stiff-backed chair, rigid as a pole, feet primly together, hands locked on his lap. The only remarkable thing about him was a big gold ring he wore on his right hand. It was out of place, out of character. Otherwise he was the perfect prisoner. And he confessed.

He had been a priest for many years, Pevec said, but this was his first time in Rome. He didn't say why, but I think we all understood it was because that of all the satellite states of the Soviet Union during the Cold War, Czechoslovakia was by far the nastiest in suppressing the church.

In the aftermath of the Wall, it seemed, among the relative handful of long-suffering Czech priests who had survived communism, a private tradition of pilgrimage had grown up. They came to Rome to celebrate the birth of a new day—and their church's new dawn—with prayers from the Dome of St. Peter's. For years, Pevec said, he had dreamed of making that journey. It had become almost an obsession.

Even in the dark, Pevec said he had easily found his way into the Basilica, thanks to the not-so-secret key to "the Priest's Door." It was easy, only a venial sin, to slip past the warning signs on to the Dome walkway. He had enjoyed the Dome, a majesty that surpassed even his imagination, and at dawn had headily taken the additional liberty of touring the starlit roof. He had stayed there, intending to leave by blending in with tourists in the morning. When he'd heard the footsteps of a lone man, though, he knew it could not be a tourist. He had hidden himself, but when the man had come too close, Pevec confessed that he had hit him, then fled back down the ramp. It had been evil and it had weighed on his conscience ever since. He had committed grievous harm without cause, and he was sorry. He had come to confess and to accept his punishment.

Why had he hit a stranger without warning or reason? I asked. Pevec stared at me impassively without answering. He had met more skilled interrogators than I. But then I understood why.

"Ask him why he killed Caruso," Galli urged.

I asked him something else.

"When were you ordained, Father?"

"In 1948."

"In Czechoslovakia, under the Communists?"

The barest of nods.

"How long were you in Communist jails, Father?"

There was a long pause, and when he spoke, it was so softly I almost missed it.

"Twenty-seven years, four months, and nine days."

I had expected something like that. But not a lifetime. O Lord! Twenty-seven . . . for the crime of being a priest.

"For the faith, it was nothing," he said, with a dignity as awesome as it was unassuming.

"Where did you get the lovely ring, Father?"

He twisted it nervously with his left hand and said quietly, "It was a gift that came after I was freed. From the Holy Father . . . not this one, but before."

We might check, send faxes back and forth to Prague or Bratislava or whatever corner of a no-more country he came from, but I knew that it would be senseless; a bureaucratic imperative. It was the truth, improbable but unassailable. Galli recognized it, too. This saintly man had never killed anyone.

The silence grew in the small room until it became intolerable. I stared at the manila folder until my eyes danced. Pevec looked at nothing.

"Father Pevec," I said, when I couldn't stand it anymore, "your presence in the Dome does not interest us. Or your actions on the roof. I was the one you hit, by the way, but I have a very hard head . . ."

For the first time, the man behind the twenty-seven-year

prisoner emerged. "You! I don't mean to strike so hard. And then you were falling . . . I am so terribly sorry—"

"But let me tell you what I think happened. You saw something happen on the walkway around the Dome. When someone came—me—you attacked him because you were afraid that somehow the Authorities"—a pause to suggest that Authorities would all be like the ones he knew under Communism—"that the Authorities would seek to involve you, even blame you for it. You hit me, and you fled down the ramp, the way you had come up . . . "

The silence was Pevec's this time.

At length he said, "It was just a few moments after first light. They were talking, arguing. Then . . . he fell. What could I do? I ran onto the roof. The rest . . . you are right. I am terribly sorry."

"Who were they?" I pressed.

"Two people, men, I think. I was far away on the opposite side of the Dome walkway . . . my eyes . . . but I thought, assumed, they must be priests, but perhaps I am wrong."

"Faces?"

"Too far."

"What happened?"

"They were standing close together, almost as if in an embrace. Then there was some shoving. I heard loud words—Italian, I think. One man fell and the other person ran away."

"The one who ran away. How was he dressed?"

"Black pants, white shirt. A priest without his jacket or collar, I thought. He left quickly; a graceful walk."

"Was he tall? Short? What color was his hair?"

Pevec shrugged: "I'm sorry. It happened quickly, and I'm afraid I was watching more the one who fell. Then I went to the roof to hide."

I took him over it twice more without a lot to show for it.

"It was strange," Pevec said, almost to himself. "The one who fell. He never screamed."

"Would you have screamed?"

"It would seem so natural." He thought about it. "But perhaps not in the Basilica."

In the end, Galli and I took Father Pevec to lunch. When the cops gave the old priest back his stuff he rummaged through a plastic shopping bag and produced a round object around eight inches tall wrapped in tattered newspapers. A wooden statue of Francis of Assisi.

"I think you should have this, Brother Paul." I took it. A nice souvenir, even if Francis's right arm, always shown raised in greeting, had snapped off, the worse for violent collision with my head. We drank a lot of wine at lunch.

In the shank of the afternoon, I strolled over to the Piazza di Spagna to find a tense and irritable Tilly. Her editors, it seems, were demanding a profile of the pope, and she was in a foul mood, elbows deep in press cuttings and Vatican documents.

"Look at this stuff. Tredi smiles and bobs and weaves and looks good and sounds intelligent. He's young, energetic, and personable—but that makes him even more disappointing. Because if you take the trouble to look coldly at his papacy, it's clear that apart from debunking a few old dead-for-centuries saints he's done nothing. He's a dweeb. Boring, boring, boring," Tilly snapped.

"Nice guy, though," I tried.

"Nonsense. I hate him. If there really was a God, He would give us an interesting pope. Wojtyla was hateful, but at least he was interesting."

"Haven't you heard that Tredi might soon break new ground? Drive-by confessions? Internet masses? The ordination of women and precocious children?"

Tilly snorted. "Those are rumors started by bored people like me. Tredi wouldn't cross the street without a signed consent order from the College of Cardinals. He's a eunuch."

After a suitable period of groans, curses, and theatrical sighs, which I endured with a private smile from the terrace, Tilly filed her piece. It was boring all right, but she cheered up afterward. We had a few drinks and later, as the sun set over the piazza, we rode together to pleasant places. Skipping the prickly new rug, hallelujah.

The next day was a Saturday, and while the seminarians were at their morning classes, I packed up poor Schmidt's stuff and rummaged through the debris in my mental attic.

Two priests had climbed in darkness to the heights of the Basilica. For prayer time gone bad? Maybe. Or did the other priest lure Caruso to the Dome to kill him? The murder was premeditated then. What could it have been about? Sex? But by all accounts Caruso was drawn more to girls than to boys. Could the other "priest" then have been a woman? I had suggested that to Father Vidal as a red herring, with no luck. Suppose the argument was between two men and it wasn't about sex. What was it about? Not money, surely. Religion? As in religious politics?

I decided to play hooky from the Vatican police, though I did call Galli. Not a happy camper. "Ay, Paolo, as we suspected, Father Pevec is a saintly man, a heroic figure in his country. *Mio Dio!* I do not need a hero; I need a villain. Cardinal Dupré called again this morning . . ."

"What did you tell him?" The cardinal was a waspish Frenchman with administrative responsibility for the Vatican Police.

"That the investigation was proceeding, that clues were being examined, information analyzed, hypotheses pursued."

"Did he believe you?"

"Of course not. But all cardinals understand about lies."

On my way to the St. Damian's staff lounge for a mid-morning *espresso,* I bumped into the seminarian I had asked to print Caruso's computer disks. He was a stocky kid from

Natal, a quick study; St. Damian's best hope for a future theologian, to hear his teachers tell it.

"There is a great deal of material and much of it is duplicated on different disks. I will need another couple of days to give you the rest of it, Brother Paul."

"Is it interesting stuff?" He colored. "You are reading it, aren't you?" Of course he was reading it. "I want you to read it. Tell me what it says."

His face cleared. "It's a strange mixture, as if two different men were using the same machine, except it is clearly written by the same person. The phrasings—"

"What about the contents?"

"Oh, mostly essays and speech drafts about church issues. And that's the problem. On a couple of disks the ideas are very puritanical, hard-line, old-fashioned. On most of them, though, the ideas are new and audacious. They call for change and turn some important current teachings upside down. Quite revolutionary."

Just as before: Caruso writing out of both sides of his mouth. Why? If I could figure that out, then I might be able to figure out who had a motive to kill him. I chewed it over, got no answers, took it to the playground with me.

He always moved to his right with a basketball, and so I shaded him that way. Had him well in hand, too, until the new guy blocked me out and he slithered past toward the basket.

"Pick up," I hollered. Luther slid across and matched the drive, step for step, slapping the ball away at the last second as it arced toward the basket.

Luther stayed with my man as a lucky rebound gave him another try. He came across the middle this time, jumping high inside the key, one of his favorite moves. Again Luther rose in front of him, leaping effortlessly; a panther, stuffing the ball back to earth. It bounced out of bounds. As a teammate retrieved the ball, the shooter, red-faced, his T-shirt wringing wet, turned to Luther in exasperation.

"Damn it, Father Luther, I am the pope!"

Luther grinned. "Hold the ball out in front of you and the devil will take it every time, Holiness."

Tredi laughed. To me, he said, "Bring more friends like this one, Paul, and I'll have to try another sport."

We were playing geriatric three-on-three in afternoon shadows on a very private outdoor court whose very existence is one of the Vatican's lesser secrets.

I don't know how often Tredi played, but I got a Saturday afternoon invitation every couple of weeks. Players came and went, but typically I guarded the pope and we played on teams with off-duty Swiss Guards, as punctilious and boring on the court as off.

This time was different because the invitation had come, not as usual from Tredi's desiccated and stuffy Japanese private secretary, but from a new, young voice who introduced himself as Father Diego.

"The Holy Father invites you to, ah, shoot some hoops," he said in good English underlain by Spanish.

"I'd be delighted. Do we know one another, Father?"

"I think not. I am Diego Altamirano, the Holy Father's new assistant."

Aha. The penny dropped. The martial arts wizard who could derail regiments with the flick of his rosary. I asked, "Will you be playing as well, Father?"

"The Holy Father suggested that I might . . . but basketball is not really my best . . . And, well, do you think I should? I hope you don't mind that I ask, but I am new."

"If he invited you to play, then it is because he wants you to play. Please say that I accept his invitation and that since he has you as his new recruit, I will be bringing reinforcements of my own."

As Tredi sized up Luther in a lazy man's pregame

warmup, I took stock of Diego. I liked what I saw. A Latino, black hair, stocky build, a couple inches short of six feet; an athlete, unconsciously bursting with muscles and good health. A centerfold, if it hadn't been for the scar on his cheek and the fact he was a priest. Basketball wasn't his game, he had said; probably meant he had turned down a pro offer to go to the seminary. He had a good eye, soft hands, and legs that pumped like springs. Normally, Tredi and I set the pace among the Guards. That day we were the supporting cast. Luther was top draw, and taller than Diego, but older—and slower. He had his hands full.

"I have an audience to give. Next basket wins," said Tredi.

Luther stayed on the pope. Their Guard brought the ball inbound to Altamirano. A lovely pass behind his back to Tredi. He crouched, facing Luther, faked, drove left. Left! Since when left? Wrong-footed, Luther never caught up. Tredi went high and slipped in a lovely layup.

"Holy smoke," Luther grunted.

"And the devil take the hindmost," said the pope.

That night, Luther and I took Diego Altamirano to dinner. Diego, it turned out, was a Latin American orphan raised by priests after his parents had died in a car crash. "I could not wait to become one of them," he said.

A familiar story; recruits were lagging, but around the world the church still harvested a steady stream of young people, nuns and priests alike, from live-ins raised at her bosom. Clearly his bishop back home had marked Diego for greater things. He'd been in Rome for about two years, studying for a licentiate in theology. Then, one day, Vatican central casting had cranked up its computer, identified him as the most likely priest-as-bodyguard, and Diego found himself a shadow for the Pontifex Maximus.

"It is a bit perplexing. I know that I am supposed to help protect the Holy Father," Diego said, "but no one has told me from what or from who. It is not easy."

"Trust no one," Luther said, with avuncular certainty, from the depths of an engaging Barolo.

Diego looked startled.

"What Luther means is: keep your eyes open. Question anything and anyone that strikes you as not quite right and don't worry who you offend," I said, and I meant it.

A fine one to talk. I should have taken my own advice, for two nights later I was walking back alone from dinner at Luther's place when the violence and duplicity of my past rose up and engulfed me.

Okay, I should have been paying more attention. All I can say is that it was one of those soft, moonlit Roman nights when the world seems at peace, and that I am not as young or as quick as I once was. It happened as I was crossing the Campidoglio, the square before the city hall that Michelangelo designed for Rome. It was late, and the big square, flanked by an archaeological museum and the old palazzo where civil marriages are performed, was deserted except for a pair of lovers strolling out the back end toward the ancient Roman Forum.

I skirted the modern bronze replica of the statue of Marcus Aurelius that dominates the piazza and pointed toward the long and broad stone stairway that abruptly descends to the street below.

I never saw him.

Later, I worked out that he must have followed me from Luther's and then, guessing my route, maneuvered past me. There are some bushes alongside the head of the stairs, and that is where he must have waited, for I caught only the slightest glimpse of a hurtling form out of the corner of my eye just as I reached the top step.

He slammed against me with tremendous force from behind, striking between the waist and the top of the knees. In football, it would have been clipping, but at the head of a stone staircase it was an assassin's blow, driving me forward and down.

I might have saved my balance, except that as I staggered forward, I tripped against an unseen barrier that upended me and sent me, a rag doll, sprawling down the stairs and into darkness. The next day Luther would find the remains of heavy monofilament fishing line tied to one of the stone balustrades.

12

CLOTHES REALLY CAN make the man. Lounging around the papal apartments in cutoffs and a T-shirt, Tredi could pass for a middle-aged suburbanite with a weekend off. In his white robe on a bright Sunday morning, he fulfilled everybody's image of the Supreme Pontiff. Or the pope-as-linebacker, for he was a tall, rangy man who carried himself with telegenic grace and assurance. Greeting people in what looked like a movie-set piazza in the Trastevere neighborhood of Rome, Tredi towered over his retinue and the faithful who had come to cheer him.

"Viva il papa!" a woman screamed, as he worked his way toward her along metal fencing, shaking hands, kissing babies, exchanging smiles and wisecracks. The pope as politician in a cobblestoned square with a backdrop of ochre-colored, four-story *palazzi,* as Italians call not only their palaces but also their apartment houses. Picture-perfect. A handful of TV cameras had come for the show, despite the hour, despite the Sunday.

One of the most important of the honorifics that comes

with being pope is his title of Bishop of Rome. Smart popes never forget that. For holy reasons, sure, but also because the *Romani,* as they proudly know themselves, are the strongest popular ally any pope can have. The Holy Pole, an actor early in life and a consummate stage walker for all of his extraordinary reign, carefully polished his Roman credentials. Most Sundays, in the sleep-it-off, lazy breakfast hours of the morning between eight and noon, he'd visit a Roman parish. There was inevitably a lot of ceremony, ringing of bells, pillars of incense, but the *Io sono romano* message couldn't have been plainer. It worked, too.

Tredi had kept the tradition alive. That morning in Trastevere, he had said mass to an SRO crowd in a baroque parish church that probably seldom drew a hundred people all weekend. Tredi had come in his Class-A uniform, saintly white from the round *zucchetto,* fastened with a discreet hairpin to his salt and pepper hair, to the fine silk socks. The shoes were shiny black loafers that had drawn a lot of press comment in Italy. The Pole had worn clunky brown things that surely had Polish forebears. Tredi's shoes shouted: *Italiane!*

The pope moved with ease along the metal fence, pausing every few yards to chat with people, to answer questions, and to ask them. The crowd was only three or four deep in most places, so nearly everyone got a chance at least to squeeze a papal finger. One young woman held up a baby; an older woman next to her pushed forward with an ugly lap dog. Tredi blessed them both. A little further, he convinced a little boy to throw him a soccer ball and deftly tapped it back with his head. It was like watching a carnival: an I Love the Pope commercial.

It suited Brother Paul just fine, thanks, for I was happy just to be there. And fortunate, too, that there was still some watchdog saints Tredi hadn't debunked, because I can't imagine what else had saved me. I'd bounced down that long flight of stone stairs like a bowling ball, careening from step to step, one harder than the other.

Blackness.

Cops had found me unconscious three-quarters of the way down. Probably they would have taken me to jail as a drunk, but I had a Vatican security pass in my wallet and that had made the difference: they'd called an ambulance. Nothing was broken, amazingly, but I'd lain for days in a black-and-blue cocoon of pain. While Luther fluttered and doctors probed for concussions and internal injuries—shh, lie still!—I'd drifted between anxious sleep and hard-time thinking.

Physical damage. Psychic injury. One. Two. My past, the thin-scarred anguish of fury, madness and death born in Miami, had come home to the Vatican.

My body was battered, but my mind was as clear as it ever gets. The scum had murdered Jimmy Kearns, this is how it must have been. And now it was my turn. I was frightened. For me, and because Tredi might also be in the line of fire. Hadn't the Americans warned him? Could the menace be from the same drug lords? They had reason to hate him as much as me. Did we face two halves of the same threat? Tredi was a prized target for anybody craving vengeance or a headline, but he lived at the heart of an elaborate security net. They'd go first for the minnow, not the whale.

I lived alone. Easy prey. So I was scared. Once I had been quick and young. Now I was a jury-rigged psychotic in new clothes. A loser who had exchanged mayhem for a church, his badge for a dog collar, violence for never-enough prayer. The man who hunted me would be tough, fast, and confident, a *macho* juiced on revenge, burning with passion.

We would be playing on my turf, but the odds would be in his favor. He'd probably get me. So be it. But if he made even the slightest mistake, I'd kill the motherfucker.

That Sunday morning in Trastevere there were still twinges, but all the pieces were moving more or less in rhythm. The day before, I had even jogged twice around the Vatican to prove it. I stood in a large uncrowded area reserved for the press; Vatican-beat photographers mostly, mixed with a sprinkling of thoroughbred staff correspondents. Tilly had come, and also Maria, and one or two European reporters with whom I had a nodding acquaintance.

I made small talk with the two women, but the professional part of me was measuring the security around Tredi. Two Vatican security cops in business suits preceded the pope, then Diego Altamirano, slightly ahead of him. He had a smile on his face, but his eyes patrolled the crowd with patience and wariness. Tredi had said his young new aide was an expert in unarmed combat and I could believe it. I wondered if he also carried a gun hidden by the jacket of his black priest suit. Two more plainclothes Vatican cops completed the envelope around Tredi. There would also be a couple of young cops in jeans sprinkled around the piazza, I knew. At the back edge of the crowd loped a tall black man in the gray robes of a monk. Luther had found Sunday employment that seemed to suit him as well as preaching.

"Every time I see the Holy Father he seems more handsome. But is he the man who will save our church?" Maria asked, a trifle breathless.

"Ignore her, Paul. This is her first pope; Maria's in love," Tilly teased.

Maria blushed prettily.

I said, "Must be tough to be a grizzled old veteran, Till."

She smiled. "Well, I confess that he does make me a bit . . . well, you know. Even if I *am* disappointed in his lack of new policies. He's got presence, but we'll just have to wait to see for some substance before I'd surrender *my* maidenly virtue." Hot air, for "boring" or not, radical Tilly was as pope-bit as traditionalist Maria. Her face was flushed, and she hadn't taken her eyes off Tredi since he'd begun his walk through the piazza.

While Tredi dawdled over coffee with local notables, Maria and Tilly had teased me mercilessly about my dog collar and black bib, the black pants, the whole nine yards. Mostly the clothes moldered in my closet until there came a churchly event to which I would give offense to someone more religious than I by going in jeans. I thought I cut a rather dashing figure, as a matter of fact. Still, the women dropped me like last week's fish at the first sight of Tredi.

"I could marry a man like that, if he was truly strong," Maria said softly.

"I did, once," Tilly said, mostly to herself, and so low I wasn't sure I had heard it.

The by-play of friends and political opposites watching the same man from diametrically opposed perspectives ricocheted pleasantly around me for another few seconds.

Then I was over the metal fence and lumbering toward the pope.

An angry knot in the crowd had burst like a boil a few yards in front of Tredi just as he approached. People scattered. People shouted. I saw a hand raised high and something dark rise against the bright sky. In the instant it took me to clear the fence, I saw Luther slash into the heart of the melee. In front of the pope, Diego Altamirano had snapped into an attack position. Either he had no gun, or he had confidence enough not to go for it. I recognized the position: it is called Serpent Coiled in an old Chinese system that is little known and hardly ever seen, because it was designed for killing, pure and simple. Diego was very good.

The Vatican cops folded in around the pope and began to shoulder him away from the disturbance. From the fringes, carabinieri began running in their red-striped trousers, hands grappling with their holsters. The dark shape was arcing through the air, dropping toward me. If it was a grenade, we were all dead. But it wasn't falling in a clean arc like a baseball. It twisted, more like a Frisbee. It floated. I caught it, slightly hampered by a shoulder bag I was carrying, and tucked it against my chest, spinning away from the pope in the same motion. In that second, I realized it was not dangerous; no grenade.

It was a wig.

"Porca miseria!" Old ways die hard. In a heartbeat I went from being frightened to a rage that launched me into the crowd, waving the wig like a trophy scalp.

"Is this a joke? Does somebody think this is funny?" I spotted a small man of about fifty cowering like an altar boy who'd been caught stealing from the collection plate. He wore a shiny black suit and a starched white shirt with one of those designer silk neckties that cost the earth and looked like it. He had a big gold watch, a thin-line, count-the-hairs mustache, and a gleaming pate.

"Is this yours? *Cretino! Brutto!* How did you lose it? Did you sneeze? Did it fly off in the wind?"

I was screaming in a babble of languages by then, the release of tension, you see, and I probably would have stuffed the greasy thing down the little man's throat, except that I came across Luther. It was like bumping into a wall.

"Easy, Paul, easy. No sweat, no problem at all, cool it," Luther soothed. He had one hand fastened around the bracelet-festooned arm of an ugly woman with red hair and a bad mouth. A wig-ripper if there ever was one. A screaming shrew in full cry.

"For the pope you dress up, Giuseppe, you comb your plastic hair and you stick out your scrawny chest. Whore's son." The little man cringed, cheeks flaming in humiliation. "Come home at four in the morning, steal into my bed like a thief. Don't you think I know about her? The one you bought the wig to please. Your slut! Young enough to be your granddaughter! Now the pope knows, too! Everybody knows!"

"Bit of family trouble; a spot of discord," said Luther calmly. I felt the adrenaline ebbing, the heart settling back in my chest. I handed the poor wretch his wig. I expected him to put it back on, but he didn't, diffidently sticking it into his coat pocket instead, for his gaze slid over me entirely, and when a friendly hand settled firmly on my shoulder, I knew why.

"You okay, Paul?" I nodded. "Nice catch, *hermano*. Take a couple of deep breaths. It always helps," Tredi counseled.

Did they think, Luther and Tredi, that I had lost it, flipped out over a wig, for Christ's sake?

"Thank you for asking, Holy Father, I'm fine," I said, a bit louder than I should have.

But by then Tredi was wading fearlessly into the shoals of marital strife. I left him talking with the harridan and her victim and sidled back to the press area. I should have known better, for Tilly and Maria fell on me like two halves of the same cyclone.

"Paul, what happened? Why did you go running off? Who . . . did someone attack the pope? How did you get out there?" Maria windmilled.

"What was that thing that you caught? Was it a bomb? Did you talk with the pope? What did he say? Tell me, Paul, damn it," Tilly demanded.

God knows how many lies I might have told, but I didn't have to, for Tredi himself sauntered over with a smile and stood in front of the cameras. He didn't lie, exactly. Speaking lovely Italian, he simply charmed the reporters, ignoring the individual questions with generic pontifical gloss.

"I think that these parish visits are one of the most important things that the Bishop of Rome can do. I know they are certainly among the most enjoyable parts of my own week. It is an emotional thing for me to be able to meet my fellow Romans in the churches where they pray each week. And emotional for them, as well, I am pleased to say. Here at San Rocco's, a man and his wife who came to share my visit on this beautiful day became suffused with excitement and emotion. I was happy to be able to spend a few minutes with them," Tredi said.

Bravo! I could see the reporters switching gears. An

overexcited couple at a papal walkabout might make news. Unlikely, though, if they were married to one another. Reporters began hollering questions from their own agenda.

"Holy Father, do you have any message for Catholics who are distressed to see age-old traditions of the church challenged and even discarded by some Catholics themselves?" I heard Maria ask in pointed reference to Tredi's assault on saints.

"What other changes are you contemplating to haul the church closer to the concerns of its people?" Tilly harped in dogged counterpoint.

Popes leave the protective walls of the Vatican far less frequently than American presidents leave the White House, and usually when they do travel, it is with security arrangements that would make your neighborhood Secret Service agent weep with frustration. Still, papal trips are not the catch-can, ramshackle affairs they were when John Paul II first hit the road. Reporters traveling with the pope get bottom-of-the-rung plastic badges with their pictures on them. Members of the official retinue get a discreet colored lapel pin. The papal security team gets a second pin, and the handful of men closest around His Holiness wear a third color. Members of the two innermost rings are wired, and if Vatican technology is never quite state-of-the-art, at least radio receivers no longer look like hearing aids, and minders don't shout into their neckties as they did in the Holy Pole's day.

The insider's pin for the parish visit was a white dove of peace on a gray background. Since I was wearing one, I had no problem mooching around Tredi's limousine when the time came for him to go home. By tradition and predilection, the pope appears in his study window above St. Peter's Square at noon on Sunday to say a midday prayer and to greet pilgrims. Tredi, whose virtues were not quite limitless because punctuality was not among them, usually hurtled back into the Vatican by the skin of his teeth.

That morning, the motorcycle escorts were already mounted and anxious by the time the pope wrenched free of his last admirers and strode to the gleaming black Mercedes with its SCV 1 license plate. Altamirano trailed behind like a terrier, leading a clerical pack that included the parish priest, the Vatican master of ceremonies, and Curia functionaries of middling rank.

Tredi was quick on the uptake.

"Need a ride, Brother Paul?" he asked, casting an appraising glance at the thick envelope I had drawn out of my bag.

"Please, if there's room, Holy Father."

The envelope contained some of the other files the seminarian had printed out for me of Caruso's. I had had a chance to read them while mending. Suspicions confirmed.

What bothered me most about the late Monsignor Luca Caruso was that in investigating his death—his murder—I had uncovered two different men. One was an agenda-setting thinker who called for a more open church under new leadership in a more modern structure. The other was a revanchist pillbox theologian ready to torch any Catholic who challenged Vatican authority.

Monsignor Janus. No way to reconcile such opposites as the work of the same man; not if he was sane. Except that it had belatedly occurred to me that Caruso was really some sort of a script writer—like those guys in Hollywood who write comedy one day and horror the next. Caruso, a variation on the theme, was alternately revolutionary and reactionary. Was he writing the revolutionary stuff for the pope, and the fire and brimstone for the Keys?

If Caruso was the inspiration for liberal reform, then a fanatic might want him dead: the Keys, or a madman among the Vatican autocrats who fear that all morality will collapse if a pope sneezes without an approved script. On the other hand, if Caruso was the Keys's secret philosopher king, a freak on the woolly left of the church might well have given him the shove. But I was at the bottom of the Vatican totem pole. The pope, up on top, could work out the permutations faster and smarter than I'd ever manage.

As we pulled smoothly away from the piazza and its waving crowds, Tredi rolled his shoulders, leaned back into the plush leather with a contented sigh, and surrendered to a guffaw he had obviously been husbanding.

"I know there's infinite room in heaven, but I hope the good Lord in His wisdom doesn't put that woman on my floor."

"I could do without Giuseppe, too," Diego cracked.

"How will I ever explain it if she strangles him with the wig over lunch? Suppose she says 'the pope made me do it'?"

Their laughter sounded a companionable counterpoint to the growling sirens as the papal caravan turned onto a main road parallel to the Tiber for the run-up to the Vatican.

It was time for a reality check in the spiritual locker room. I said, "Sure, it was funny, but it could have been serious, and if it had been serious, you'd be dead, Holiness. The security can never be tight enough if you wander into crowds. No more parish strolls until we get a real fix on what's going on. Please."

Diego Altamirano sat up very straight. I guess he was not used to hearing the ecclesiastical equivalent of a corporal lecturing the pope. Too bad. By then I had decided that I didn't like Diego much. Okay, he was young. But he was too self-impressed and too cocky to suit me.

Tredi waved away my concerns with an expressive brush of his hand. "I do what I do, Paul. Always have, always will. You, if anybody, should know that."

"Yes, I do," I said, "but please remember that a priest who was close to you is dead. Tell me what game Caruso was playing. It would help find out who killed him." I handed Tredi the envelope. "It's stuff we took off Caruso's computer. Could you look through it, please?"

"Yes, Paul, of course." The pope was suddenly very serious. He fingered the envelope thoughtfully. "No good suspects?"

I thought about the elegant, arrogant Father Vidal, but the pope had warned me off. I said, "This stuff will either put you to sleep or give you sweats, because it seems Caruso was a right-thinking friend of the pope who also, unfortunately, happened to be masterminding secret anti-pope attacks for the wild-eyed right. Big-time schizophrenia, maybe, but it's more than that. On top of it all, you've had a threat. And. . . ."

The pope looked at me shrewdly "And you have felt somebody's breath on your spine, too, haven't you?"

Tredi and I hadn't talked all week. I had decided not to call him about my spill, preferring to do it in person. But he'd always been able to read me, and I was sure a few bruises still showed.

"Somebody helped me down a nasty flight of stairs. I was lucky."

Clearly uncomfortable at hearing things not meant for junior guard dog priests, Diego said, "Holiness, perhaps I should get out. I can walk . . ."

"No, Diego, stay. Paul and I go back together to the dawn of time, when there was some trouble that we hope will never come back to haunt us. Probably won't either. We're just being extra careful."

"Yes, Holiness," Diego said primly.

"Tell me about it, Paul," the pope commanded.

And so I did. Short and to the point.

As I talked, his mouth drew into a tight, angry line. The lines under his eyes deepened. Color rose in his face. He was angry, but he was also alarmed, and I could guess the sort of thing he was going to say before he said it.

"I think we ought to build you some space, Paul. There's something important I need done—a papal mission. Tokyo, I'd say, or Cape Town, if you prefer. Will you go do it, please? Take a coupla weeks."

"No sir, I will not."

"I am your pope, Paul."

"I am your friend, Holiness." He understood that the stalkers would never be content with just the minnow.

Diego stared straight ahead, wide-eyed.

It was the pope who surrendered.

"We'll play it your way, *hermano*. I'll be more careful if you will."

"A deal. And do me a favor, okay? Let Luther hang close until we work this out. With Luther and Diego together reinforcing the formal protection, I'd feel better. Will you do that?"

The pope raised an eyebrow at Diego. "How does that sound?"

"I would be pleased to work with Father Luther, Holy Father," the young priest said, straining to please.

Tredi made up his mind. "Paul, ask Luther to come by tomorrow morning and ask for Yomuri," he said, naming his chief secretary. "He'll invent something to tell Luther's superior that will keep him around until things cool off."

It was two minutes before noon when the limo knifed through the Vatican gates. At the Apostolic Palace, Tredi slapped my shoulder, said, "And thanks, Paul, for bringing this stuff. I'll read it and we'll talk." Then he was gone with a wave that could have been a blessing. His young aide made to follow, but I took Diego's arm and pulled him aside.

I think he expected me to remind him that my conversation with the pope had never happened, but I said something else. "Tell me about the gun, Diego," I demanded.

He went pale and his head dropped to examine the ancient cobblestones.

"A thirty-eight?"

He nodded. I had seen the holster when his jacket had ridden up on the ride back.

"Can you use it?"

He looked at me, all Latin pride. "Very well."

"But the pope doesn't know you've got it."

"No, Brother Paul."

"The pope doesn't like guns."

"No, sir."

"And he'll raise holy hell if he finds out."

"Yes, sir."

"He'll take it away from you; send you away to some-place unpleasant."

"Yes, Brother Paul." He looked at me like a puppy caught with his paws in the birthday cake.

"I won't tell him you've got it. But I don't want to see it again."

"Thank you, Brother Paul."

I walked back across the river and bought myself a chunk of pizza and a beer over near the Pantheon. It was hot as I sat in the sun in the bowl of the lovely piazza with its nearly two-thousand-year-old temple, but I didn't take off my black priest jacket.

Discomfit is a price you sometimes pay when there's a Beretta quietly riding your belt. It had been many years, but I would get used to it again. I was being careful, just as I had promised my pope.

13

THAT NIGHT, WHILE St. Damian's priests-to-be were snug
abed, their pope had called with more to talk about than
baseball. I won't say he was drunk, but Tredi's voice was
thicker than usual, and he spoke with less precision. I would
have bet on rum, but I am only a simple brother.

"Diego and I have been sitting here reading the Caruso
stuff. It is all over the lot, isn't it?" I could hear ice tinkle.

I want to be right up front about this. I felt jealousy then,
more than a twinge. Not rational, Ivanovic would say. Yes, I
accept that. But there it was. Tredi in his magic palace with
an amber glass of Caribbean gold, his bare feet propped on
some priceless piece of Vatican hassockry, sharing confi-
dences with Diego Altamirano, a yes-man-come-lately who
couldn't decide if he was a praying mantis or a killing
machine.

"Yes, Holy Father, Caruso's stuff is minestrone: carrot,
potatoes, onion," I said neutrally.

"Right, Paul. Some of it is cutting edge stuff; some

Torquemada rides again. A bit schizophrenic, I have to agree."

"One's real, the other's smoke—"

"And."

"And I think—" But he knew what I was going to say, so he said it for me. Probably so his pal Diego could catch on.

"And you think that some of it, one half or the other, made somebody mad enough to kill Luca Caruso, to pitch him off the Dome."

"That's what I think."

"Think it was the Keys, Paul?" I caught a note of urgency in his voice.

"Maybe." He wanted me to say yes.

"Paul, there's something you should know. Hang on . . . " and Tredi said, "Goodnight, Diego, thanks for the company."

A few seconds later, I heard a swallow, and the pope said, "Okay, let's start from the top, Paul. Luca Caruso and I went back almost right to the beginning, back in the good old cocaine-smashing days. His first assignment as a priest was as a missionary down that way. Did you know that?"

"No, I didn't." And I should have checked, damn it.

"Caruso was one of the local priests who helped me, Paul. Took incredible risks and never blinked. Ice in his veins."

"Made the druggies mad at him, too?"

"I'd say so."

A chill was beginning to play up and down my back. I heard the flames and smelled my family's burning flesh.

The pope was hoping that Luca Caruso had been the victim of religious madmen. It was much worse if he had fallen victim to the violent, drug-stained past we all shared.

" . . . promoted Luca and brought him here to the Vatican; a safer place, really. He was good enough at what he did, Paul, but in the end Luca got bored. I could see it. And so to give him something extra to do, I asked him to do me a favor with a little problem. Sound familiar?"

"You asked him to infiltrate the Keys—"

"Yes, and God forgive me. So he started writing all sorts of right-wing junk, and they loved it; took him on board lickety-split, particularly since I let the word out that he was a friend of mine. Some of this stuff you've brought me from Caruso's computer is what he really thought, but all the Commando Catholicism stuff is gibberish. He wrote it for me—all of it. The Keys thought he was writing what I believed but couldn't say. They printed it, including a lot of nonsense they wouldn't have dared touch from any other source."

"Caruso was your agent and he was able to feed you a lot of insider information about the Keys."

I may be a slow learner, but I am not stupid.

The pope drank some more. "Including the fact that a lot of the money—too much—is flowing into the Keys and that most of it seems to be coming from drug families in South America."

Oh, shit. I thought of the fancy computer room at the Keys headquarters.

"And Vidal?" But I already knew the answer.

"Another old friend. I sent him in after Caruso. He built a 'respectable,' suitably conservative religious front to get close, but mostly what he's doing is tracing the money back. He's a Latino; has great contacts all over South America. That makes it easier."

"As long as you're absolutely sure about Vidal."

A long pause then, and when the pope spoke again, it was with a voice and a tone I had heard only a couple of times before.

"Paul, listen to me. I am your friend, and I'm your pope. Vidal is a soul brother, like you."

Look Jane. See Spot. Watch Brother Paul shot down in flames.

"Father Vidal is in South America for me right now," the pope was saying. "He should be back in another few days and I want you to work with him, okay? Please don't go near the Keys until he gets back."

I didn't. In fact, there were lost days in which I don't remember that poor Galli and I and all the Vatican cops managed to accomplish anything memorable. It happens that way sometimes in a homicide investigation. But it always rankles. The only useful thing was that Luther slid quietly into the pope's retinue and clearly liked being there, for when we met one night for dinner he was flying.

"How's life at pope central?"

Luther waved his hands the way Italians do when they want to describe something complex and hard to explain.

He said, "Man earns his money, that pope. Never stops, day and night. Loves his job, lives his job. A holy man, too, I think."

"Really?" I never thought of Tredi holy, somehow.

"Not because he tries to be, but somehow he is."

"He's really impressed you, hasn't he? An old cynic like you."

"You talk to the man and you feel good, what can I tell you, Paul? The other day he finishes his last appointment and he says, 'Luther, walk with me back to my apartment,' and he kicks off his shoes, gets two glasses, and there I am, drinking beer with the Bishop of Rome. We start talking and I find that I'm telling him things about Africa, about life, about me, that I hardly ever told anybody. You, a few others. Scarifying, Paul, the pope's a scarifying man."

Like me, Luther had come to the cloth the long way around. My own excuse was trauma, but from the fragments Luther had told me over the years and the pieces I had mentally assembled of his life, his might as well have been exhaustion. I knew that at one point or another he had been a farmer, a soldier, a government official, a teacher, and a fisherman-smuggler, but the sequence escaped me. Maybe

Luther, too. It was a tribute to Tredi that he could make a man like Luther open up, but that was not what he had gone to the Apostolic Palace to accomplish.

"What about security? Is Tredi safe?"

Luther replied promptly enough, but I could see his mind working some other field. "Of course he's not safe, Paul. You know, I know, he knows, Kennedy knew. He's dead, somebody wants him bad enough. Diego Altamirano follows him around like he was on a leash, and he means well, but . . . I guess if somebody came wearing a big sign that said 'Assassin,' the Vatican cops might hold a meeting, take a vote, send up smoke signals. But against somebody serious—"

"But you'll be there. Tredi wants you there. He needs you."

"I'll be there, Paul. But I've got to talk with the pope again."

"You talk to him every day, for heaven's sake."

"I mean really talk to him. He's got to know . . ."

I asked him, "What? What does he have to know?" But Luther was off rummaging somewhere in his mind.

We walked in companionable silence through crowded streets, enjoying the cool evening. At least I did. I don't know where Luther was. He didn't come back until we had walked nearly home. We were skirting the old Circus Maximus. When Luther suddenly pointed into the giant oval, I followed in silence. When I caught up, he was hunkered down at the base of the old statue in the center of the ancient race track. He was sweating, eyes bright. I thought he might be sick, but it was more than that.

"Paul, listen. Hear me. I want to tell you something about Africa . . . It's not easy. Just listen, will you do that?"

Luther closed his eyes and told me a story.

"Nobody knows this story, Paul. It's the sort of secret you never talk about; there's too much shame. I never told anybody, but now I have got to tell the story. Like a confession, Paul. Do you understand?"

"Yes." But I didn't.

"Will you listen to my story, Paul?"

"Of course I will."

Luther smiled. "You're my brother, Paul."

Then he wandered off again without moving. A breeze sprang up and it grew chill under the statue, but I sat patiently until Luther returned and began to talk about a cruel place he called Eden.

"When I walked into the clearing that afternoon, it was so beautiful that my first thought was that it was perfect. It was so lovely. Paul, you wouldn't believe the beauty. Flowers, fruits, neat rows of crops, a brook with a mountain in the background, a village of neat houses, and a whitewashed church. On the hill behind it, an old stone abbey must have been there since the earliest colonial days. It was the sort of place a man could go and think about life, or God, in perfect peace. It was a four-day walk from the nearest gravel road, but somehow I sensed that the people who lived there never worried about that, because they recognized that they were not far from anywhere.

"But it was no Eden when I got there, Paul. God forgive them. You probably read about it, or others like it. The brook was full of bodies, and the church. Macheted, most of them, though a few had been killed with shovels and hoes. The church was full of women and children and a few European nuns who had tried to protect them. Wrong tribe, Paul. Terrible thing in modern Africa to come from the wrong tribe. A killing offense."

Luther was a continent and more than a decade away. He wrapped his giant hand around my arm and grasped it hard. "I was supposed to be a peacekeeper, wore a blue helmet and all. What a joke. I killed a lot of African people in the name of peace, and I would have shot a lot more that day, but I didn't shoot anybody because the ones who did it had already run away.

"The stench was terrible, worse than ever, flies, maggots,

big fat dogs angry at the intrusion on their feast. What we needed was a bulldozer, but of course there are no bulldozers in Eden, are there? My soldiers shot the dogs and built a big fire for the bodies; so many kids, Paul.

"I walked up into the abbey. There were seven priests there, white men, all of them wearing this robe I'm wearing today. Old men. How had they ever hurt anyone? Throats slit, bodies mutilated, every one. I thought I had seen it all, but I hadn't. I stayed in the abbey for a while with the dead priests, and then I walked back down the hill and I sent the soldiers away, told them I'd follow, but I never did. They were happy to get moving before dark, God knows; the devil had come to Eden and we all knew it. That night I stayed alone in the abbey with the dead priests. I didn't sleep because if the devil came back I wanted to be ready. But he didn't come, and the next morning I buried the priests. Then I put my gun away and I took off my uniform and I decided to stay in Eden. Couple of times in the first few weeks, they sent soldiers back to look for me, but I hid. They didn't look too hard. One more dead officer, so what? Plenty of wars to make more officers for.

"I stayed there a long time, a very long time; just me and the missionaries' books and their spoor. Nobody ever came back to live in Eden, Paul. Bad ju-ju. But not for me. I was happy there. Days came and went, seasons changed, even in Africa you can tell about the seasons. I watched them slip away and I never thought much about it, because all the time I was learning from those dead priests. I read all the priests' books, one by one: history, religion, literature. All of it, whatever came to hand; language has never been a problem for me, you know that, Paul. I learned a lot about the world, about God, about me. I began to think I was there for a reason. I guess that I began to feel that I was the heir to those priests. They had come hoping to do good and instead they had died in mindless violence. For me to carry on could somehow right the terrible injustice. Sounds crazy, doesn't it? Maybe it was. So what? I learned everything about those priests and their faith. In the end, is it mad to imagine I became them? Does that make sense? I thought it did; think it does. One day, I don't know why I knew, but I knew, it was time for me to go. I went into the abbot's room and I took out the big ledger that he kept. I took it with me and brought it to the missionaries' headquarters here in Rome. That's how I got here."

He released my arm and leaned his head back against the cool marble statue base.

After a time, I said, "That's a wonderful story, Luther."

"I've got to tell the pope."

"He'll be moved."

"No, Paul, I don't think so."

"But—"

"Because what I've got to tell the pope is that I signed up to march with a dead battalion; wrote my name in the abbot's ledger with the others. Said I was one of them, a member of their order. When I got to Rome, the ones here were happy to see me, figured the trauma had knocked a lot out of my head; the theology, the ceremonials. So they retaught me things that in truth I never had learned. I just drifted along, it was easy, after living with all those dead holy friends. But now suddenly it's different, Paul. I've got to tell the pope. The pope has to know that I'm not really a priest."

"I've been expecting someone like you for some time now," she said, no compliment intended. Teresa Longhi was a striking woman, challenging: sharp cheekbones, green eyes, long black hair swept back and cascading down the back of her white lab coat. Around forty, maybe. Very much a surgeon, very much the professor of nuclear medicine. Very much a woman.

There had to have been a woman in Luca Caruso's life. It just had taken me too long to get to her. Galli's detectives had gone through Caruso's personal effects, but not thoroughly enough, it turned out, when, in frustration at an investigation going nowhere, I'd pawed through them myself. From his personal address book I'd extracted the names of about twenty-five women. Little by little, I'd winnowed them down. Then I went calling on the ones who seemed most promising. Two days of false alarms, but I learned a lot about Luca Caruso along the way. I was beginning to like him, in fact.

Veronica Urlo, a dumpy brunette of around twenty-five without much between her ears, worked at the Vatican telephone exchange. She was not expecting me, and she was nervous, but after I talked to her earnestly in my best avuncular fashion over a *cappuccino,* it all came spilling out. Veronica was what we used to call an easy lay. Not being terribly bright or awfully pretty in a city that bursts with women who are both, Veronica cultivated companionship the best way she could. There was no shortage of companions around the Vatican, she made clear.

"It's, like, you know, fun, going out to movies and all with important people. Big people. Even if some of them were priests, they never dressed like it when we were together, and I kind of felt it was our secret. I always like the things we did anyway, most of them, I mean, you know."

"You go to bed with them."

"Well, you know, not always exactly to bed. We did things. But we always prayed."

"And Monsignor Caruso? Did you and he make love, and uh, other things in strange places?"

"Luca? Strange places?" She giggled, seemed to come alive for the first time. "Oh, no, you don't understand. Not him. We just talked. We talked a lot. He thought that what I was doing was wrong. He said people were taking advantage of me. In my heart, I know he was right, but, well, you know . . ."

Among the other women who had found their names into

Caruso's book, two were typical. One was a grandmother who had enlisted Caruso's help to get a job for her husband. The other was heavily pregnant. Caruso had presided at her wedding, it seems, and she seemed genuinely distraught that he wouldn't be there to baptize her child.

Hard, slogging, frustrating, disappointing police work. But then I met Teresa Longhi. For the first few minutes after I walked into her office in the medieval city of Siena about three hours north of Rome, she was silent, pretending to study the X ray of a skull on a lighted box fastened to the wall behind her.

"This dark part is a brain tumor." She tapped it with a pencil. "I have spent hours examining it, thinking about it. I can see it even without the X ray. I turn it in my mind, this way and that, looking at its facets, front, back, side, seeking some way to attack it. There is no way. None at all. That is a death sentence. Six months, perhaps only four."

"I'm sorry," I said. But I wasn't the patient and I was looking for a murderer; somebody who had pitched Luca Caruso from the Dome of St. Peter's. Teresa Longhi looked strong enough.

I said, "If you know why I've come, I won't disturb you for long."

She looked at me for the first time. Intelligent, hostile. There was passion enough for a murderer.

"You are here to ask about me and Luca Caruso."

How did she know? Guilty conscience?

"I will make it easy for you, Captain . . . It is captain?"

"Brother. I'm just a brother."

"A brother detective. How quaint." She smiled without warmth. Beautiful, but there was an undercurrent. Danger? No. Anger.

"Very well, Brother. I confess. Luca was my lover. We lived in the same town and knew one another as children. We became lovers when we were fourteen. He became a priest, I became a doctor. He went off to Latin America to be a missionary. When he returned and went to work in the Vatican, we became lovers again."

She glared at me. Taunting. Defiant.

"We remained lovers until he died. I loved him. I don't care who knows it. Publish it in *Osservatore Romano* if you like, Brother Detective."

"Did you see Caruso before his death? Did you ever go with him to the Dome of St. Peter's?"

"No, alas. It would have been wonderful to make love there. But we saw one another no more than four or five times a year, when we could contrive a few days together. In the mountains, on a beach, someplace out of the country if we could arrange it. No priest, no surgeon. Just a man and a woman. We would make love night and day. In Rome, almost never."

"I see."

I thought that she was one of the most attractive women I had ever met.

"I doubt if you see at all. It was bliss. Paradise. I was married for a time, but Luca was the only man I have ever truly loved."

"I'm sorry."

She rounded on me. "Do you think it is wrong for a priest to love, Brother? To lie with a woman? Are you one of those? Do you not think about it, alone late at night, imagining what it must be like? I will tell you: it is magnificent, wonderful; a blessing. Go away and let me grieve."

"If you can satisfy me that you were not in Rome when your friend died, I will go away and never come back, Professor."

She had been expecting that question from someone like me she knew would come.

"I was in Milan for a conference that weekend." She leafed through an agenda on the desk before her and wrote down a phone number. "Talk to Professor Di Rienzo or any of the others."

"Can you think of anyone who might have wanted to do Monsignor Caruso harm? Anyone who knew about the two of you, for example? Who might have been offended?"

"Italy is a modern country, Brother. No one except a few old men at the Vatican care if a woman sleeps with a priest or a priest with a woman."

She was right, too. Just as I was sure she had been where she said she was in Milan the day that Caruso died.

"No one then. Who might have—"

"It must have been the Flower Man. The Flower Man murdered Luca."

She took my breath away. The Flower Man? And she quickly realized it.

"Surely you know about him, Brother Detective. Has no one told you? None of Luca's friends? Perhaps he never told them, either. How every month a single red flower would be delivered to the residence for Luca?"

"No one told me."

"A shame. The flowers came with a card—every month the same card."

"What did it say?"

"There was no writing. Only a hand-drawn picture. The picture of a smoking gun."

"Did Luc . . . Monsignor Caruso say what it meant?"

"He said it was a reminder of an old debt."

"How long had he been getting these cards?"

"About a year, I think. Perhaps longer. You should look into it." I nodded dumbly, and she continued, "Would you excuse me please, Brother Detective? I have a patient."

I was at the door, a terrible weight pressing, when she called softly, almost an apology, "Do you pray, Brother?"

"Every day, Professor."

"Pray for us, please." She looked at me, fierce and proud,

but her voice was dust. "For me and for Antonia." She pointed at the X ray. "She is our daughter, Luca's and mine. Antonia is seventeen. Soon she will be as dead as her father. I don't believe in your God, Brother, but I will pray that He lets me join them."

14

STANDING ON A hill not far from the Vatican is a walled complex that testifies to the historic wealth of the church and its current weakness. For decades, the compound was the bustling training center for New World seminarians studying for the priesthood. Mostly Americans, but also Canadians and a handful of Latinos from Mexico and the Islands. In nearly every diocese the bishop would trawl the pool of student priests and select one of the brightest to be trained in Rome. They became marked men: as future leaders of their church at home, and as bridges between North American Catholics and the Vatican, after five centuries as suspicious and uncomprehending as ever of all things from the New World.

Once, there had been fierce competition for admission. By the time the twentieth century limped to a close, though, like most other ecclesiastical centers in Rome it had empty classrooms, closed wings, and a severely shrunken enrollment. The church, more adept during change-nothing papacies at bandaging than rebuilding, had responded by changing the name of the college to the Leadership Center, and filling it with conferences by learned and often boring churchmen explaining to one another why the number of priests was diminishing even as the number of world Catholics grew daily.

I walked to the Center, puffing up the steep hill through lovely late-afternoon shadows punctuated by sunlight glinting off the Tiber below. All my way up the hill, big air-conditioned sedans slid past me in steady procession, black-crammed with church heavies. A flash of photographers and church groupies clustered around the tall iron-barred gate. I counted four network TV trucks with bright silver dishes on their roof and a gaggle of reporters being filtered through metal detectors. Tredi was attending a seminar of the leaders of missionary societies at the Center, but I hadn't fought the hill to a breathless draw because of the pope. I didn't have enough rank even to sit in the back of the conference hall, for one thing. And for another, it wasn't Tredi who had invited me, but Gustavo Vidal.

When we had spoken on the phone that morning, it was almost as if we were friends. His arrogance and his hostility had vanished. We were both the pope's men working on the same side of the fence, Vidal's new attitude made plain. Things might have turned out differently if Tredi had gotten around to telling either of us earlier.

"I'm just off a plane, but etiquette demands that I join the welcoming committee for the Holy Father at tonight's seminar," Vidal had explained. "Still, I'm anxious to talk about Caruso—and the Keys. I have big news, decisive news, from South America. We need to act quickly. Once the Holy Father is installed, perhaps we can have a quiet few minutes."

At the conference center, the small priest seemed com-

pletely at ease, commanding even, at the vortex of a swirling
crowd of church luminaries, prowling reporters, and remnant seminarians.

Vidal greeted me with an *abrazo*. "Sorry, if it's a bit
chaotic now," he said. "The pope is meeting privately with
some of the bishops, but things will calm down once he's
seated in the conference hall."

We made small talk for a few minutes, and when young
Diego Altamirano drifted past, looking out of place and over
his head, I introduced them, reflexively speaking Spanish.

"I have read many of your books, Father. I am honored to
meet one of the great minds of the church," Diego said
smoothly.

"Thank you. I heard that the Holy Father had a new
Latino assistant, and I can taste the Andes in your voice. I
myself have returned only this morning."

Diego and Vidal were exchanging do-you-knows when I
caught sight of Luther standing off in a corner with a good
view of the front door. When the crowd kaleidoscoped for an
instant, I realized he was talking with Tilly. She wore a simple white cotton dress with a scooped neck and a hemline
that stopped about four inches short of her knees. A hammered silver necklace and matching earrings shown off by a
swept-back hair-do completed the package. Tilly wore no
makeup. She didn't need any.

Vidal interrupted my feast. "Diego and I have many
friends in common and I was just explaining to him that the
Holy Father and I have been friends since he was still a
bishop. I'm sort of his private emissary in Latin America for
quiet things that the church doesn't like to talk about pub-
licly. In fact, I'll be calling on him tomorrow to report on my
trip."

Diego smiled. "Until then. If you will excuse me now . . ."

Turning to me, Vidal said, "I must get people moving,
too. Perhaps we could meet in the library in, say, twenty

minutes. Down the stairs to the left, past the big recreation room."

We all three shook hands and wandered away in different directions. Before she could also vanish in the crush, I nailed Tilly with some overdue questions about Caruso: her name was among the women in the dead monsignor's address book.

"Luca? Didn't I tell you? He was one of us, once—sweet, caring, gentle with a puckish sense of the ridiculous. Then, zoom zoom, he motored over to the extreme right," she said. "Pissed me off, too, though I never got around to telling him. He kind of dropped out of journalistic sight at around the same time, come to think of it."

I should never have asked the next question, I know that. It just came out. "Did you ever, I mean, Till, did you and he . . ."

She looked at me narrowly, poised between being flattered because I might be jealous, and angry because I was sounding like a cop.

"Listen, Bro, who I take to my bed is my business, even when it's you." She tucked me under the chin. "Tomorrow night. Dinner first. Around eight?"

Well. Why not?

It was time for her to join the big domes, but Tilly had more on her mind.

"Tell me about the pope's dog," she challenged.

"What dog?"

"He's got a black-and-white puppy. That's what I hear. I need one more confirmation before I can print it. Tell me."

"No dog. To the best of my knowledge, the pope has no dog. Honest Injun. I don't even think he likes dogs."

She regarded me narrowly. Would I have lied if she had asked about a cat? Probably.

With Luther and Diego watching the pope's back and the future of the church safe in finer minds around a rhetoric-laden table, I prowled the library and the big recreation room, with its pool table, piano, and giant TV set, even poked into the pantry.

Vidal never showed up. I finally got bored and went looking, but there was no sign of him anywhere. Finally, I went home. The hill was easier going down, but no less lonely. As I would later tell Galli, the last time I saw Gustavo Vidal alive, the pope's secret emissary was shepherding stragglers into the conference room.

"I want to play the piano. I have the right to play the piano; I play every morning. But this morning I cannot play the piano." He was crying, nearly hysterical, talking to the air. Ivanovic could have given a whole seminar on this guy. "And do you know why I can't play the piano? Because Father Vidal is in the piano. Why is Father Vidal in the piano? It is my turn to play."

"Who is this screaming mimi?"

"Priest named Little. Lives here. He found the body," said Marco Galli, once again heading a dispirited bunch of Vatican cops who had not yet managed to solve their first homicide.

I knew exactly how they felt, and it was hard enough to concentrate without the caterwauling. I walked over to him. "Father Little. Sit down and kindly wait quietly until we are ready to talk with you."

Offend their dignity. That is a sure way of getting the attention of most people. It certainly worked with Father Little, jarred him out of his shock.

"Do you know who I am?" He pulled himself to his full height, a bald man around sixty-five with black-rimmed glasses and a big belly.

"You are a distinguished academic"—a fair guess—"who has many friends in the Curia." He nodded. "I congratulate you on both accounts. Sit down and shut up." Galli laid a restraining hand on my forearm. "Easy, Paolo," but Little reeled peaceably away.

The medical examiner ran a thermostrip across the corpse's neck. She read the results, juggled numbers in a palm-sized computer, and announced, "Dead twelve hours, maybe a bit less."

I could have told her that. Twelve hours before, Gustavo Vidal, a tiny priest with a big brain, had been alive and well in the midst of a large crowd, anxious to talk with me. I thought he knew who might have killed his buddy Caruso—and who was financing the Keys from Latin America. I suspected that it was all tied together, and he might have given me the pieces I needed.

Too late now. An eternity too late.

His killer had jammed Vidal into the guts of the big upright piano and closed the lid. It must have happened while the pope was at the conference upstairs. Probably Vidal had already been in his tomb when I'd passed the basement recreation room en route to the next-door library where we'd agreed to meet.

The coroner had the annoying habit of giving a running commentary, as if it was a soccer game. "No wound visible, no bleeding. But the bowels seem to have . . . could it have been poison?"

Of course it wasn't poison.

"No, not poison, I think . . . ahh. This man's neck has been broken," the examiner proclaimed.

That made more sense.

"But a shorter fall."

Galli winced. I shouldn't have said it.

"Paolo, you were here last night. Tell me who else."

"Oh, just the pope and all his security. Maybe a dozen cardinals, bishops by the bushels, reporters, factotums, seminarians, waiters, jugglers, jesters, pickpockets, pimps, anybody else you can think of. I didn't see any warlocks, but I couldn't swear . . . What a mess."

Galli sighed loudly. I asked him, "Did anybody see anything, hear anything, suspect anything before Liberace here
wandered into the show?" I gestured at Little sitting rigid in
the chair as if chained to it, shooting me daggers, fingers
beating an angry concerto on his chubby thigh tops.

Galli shrugged in defeat. "Nothing. Nothing at all." He
shrugged his shoulders. "There are no witnesses. And
what do we know? Was the killer a man or a woman? Was
it the same person as in the Dome? Talk to me, Paolo,
please."

Poor guy. He sounded as desperate as I felt.

"A woman might have killed Vidal, but I don't think so.
There were not many of them around last night, and Vidal,
like his friend Caruso, was killed by somebody he knew;
somebody strong who thinks well. He saw a chance, broke
Vidal's neck, and then very coolly hid the body. A particularly strong and athletic woman? I doubt it. I'm sure it was a
man, and the odds are that it was a priest. There weren't
many people around last night who weren't."

"And the motive?"

"Your guess is as good as mine, *amigo mio*."

In fact, I had a better answer, but I needed to talk with the
pope first.

That was never really hard for me to arrange, and that day
it proved easier than ever, because just then Diego Altamirano came plunging into the recreation room, trailed by a
Swiss Guard who had obviously whisked him over from the
papal apartments.

"Brother Paul." He came rushing over. "What's
happened . . . The Holy Father . . ."

Diego caught sight of the piano and its burden and I
thought for a moment he'd lose his apostolic breakfast right
there.

"Father Vidal. Oh, my God. What? How?" He crossed
himself.

There are times to be avuncular and supportive, but this

was not one of them. I took the young priest under the arm, marched him right through the smell, right up to the body. I pointed.

"Look, Diego. Look hard. Vidal's neck has been snapped like a chicken bone. You're the Vatican's gift to unarmed combat. Is that hard to do?"

His face whitened. He glared at me, eyes wild.

Galli was hovering, edgy, worrying. Was he scared I'd bruise the pope's sidekick? The hell with him. He should have protected Vidal. The hell with both of them. I squeezed the young priest's arm a little tighter.

"Diego, answer the question, damn it."

I guess he realized I was serious, for he really looked at the body for the first time, bending down to examine an angry, angular bruise on the neck. Then he looked at me, chewing his lip.

"It was done by a right-handed person. It was a demanding but not a technically difficult stroke. Father Vidal is, was, a small man. It would have required more precision than strength."

That was something, at least. I was about to thank him, when Diego challenged me with frosty disdain. "If that is all you require, Brother Paul, I think that I should return to the Vatican to inform our Holy Father that another of his friends has been murdered. Shall I say that you have a suspect?"

"I'll tell him myself, if it's all the same to you."

A few minutes later, I rode back to the Vatican with the pope's shadow. Diego sulked all the way. I didn't mind.

The pope kept me waiting. It can happen when you drop in unannounced on one of the most powerful men in the world in the middle of his working day. They stuck me in one of those for-middling-dignitaries waiting rooms with lots of baroque marble, hard chairs, and the inevitable crucifix. It could have been worse. After about an hour, one of the nuns who looks after the pope, a tall and stately woman from Peru named *Hermana* Lucía, poked her head in and gestured me to follow her. We wound up in a small, spotless, and hyper-modern kitchen she ruled more completely than Tredi would ever rule the church.

"The Holy Father said you like fish," she confided.

Hermana Lucía fed me an amazing *ceviche* followed by a black tuna steak. By the time a gentle bell sounded in the kitchen and Lucía led me into Tredi's apartment, I had also drunk two cold beers to soothe my jangled nerves.

Tredi spoiled it, right off the bat. "Caruso and now Vidal. This has got to stop, *coño.*"

He scowled at me for a long, tense instant, standing only a few inches away. Then he slapped a meaty hand on my shoulder. "I'm sorry, Paul, this whole business has me down."

In the living room, he scaled his skullcap onto a table and rested his shoes atop an antique coffee table, sliding them off quickly when *Hermana* Lucía appeared with the coffee. She was that sort of nun.

Tredi spooned sugar into a cup of ink. "Let's talk, *hermano.*"

I thought all along he had known more than I had, and I was right. "It's Miami all over again, isn't it?" I asked more softly than I felt.

The pope nodded. "I think so. The same bad guys again. But the game is much more complex." He waved a stern forefinger at me. "And there's another difference this time around. We have to handle it differently. We play it cool." He said "we," but of course he meant me—loose cannon Paul. "Keep a grip, Paul. I really need you. This can't be like Colombia."

I nodded emptily at him, but I was drifting away. Colombia. My hands had begun to sweat. I had a tiny china coffee cup in my hands and I raised it to my lips. But it was not coffee that I tasted.

I tasted the dust on the mountainside. I felt the rough fabric of the knotted rope. I saw the sun, dappling a gentle trail through the trees.

I heard the hoofbeats.

COLOMBIA

Ten Years Before

15

ONE AFTERNOON WHEN a tropical storm too small to have a name thrashed across the Caribbean, a Canadian businessman with long sideburns named Dave Scanlon flew from Montreal to Panama and checked in electronically at one of those big hotels on the Pacific coast of the isthmus. That night he transacted some quiet business in a ramshackle house in the old part of the city with a man who had dealt discreetly for three decades in private matters and had a filigree of silent friends throughout Latin America. The Canadian was expected. He asked few questions, answered none, paid cash, and left little lasting impression. Dave Scanlon checked out of the hotel the next morning as anonymously as he had come.

He was never seen again.

There was nothing to connect him to a stooped Spanish businessman named Ignacio Cruz who got off a dusty bus in San José, Costa Rica, two days later. Cruz left no trace in San José and bore scant resemblance to the bespectacled Uruguayan called Gerardo Fuentes who flew into Ecuador on a sleepy Sunday afternoon, connecting to Medellín from Guayaquil.

It was another traveler, blond and broad-shouldered, a German, perhaps, who collected a sturdy and carefully loaded four-wheel-drive van from a suburban parking lot there, fishing the keys from the exhaust pipe as he pretended to tie his shoe. The blond disappeared, too, along with the van and its cargo; unremarkable really, for in their northern reaches, the Andes are mysterious and concealing mountains. People come and go with few questions. Much of what happens there exists outside the bounds of laws and governments. If you know where to look, sophisticated weapons are plentiful and as easy to harvest in the majestic Andes as coca leaves.

Three months later, spring bathed the lush Colombian mountains, and with it an inviting sun that coaxed new growth from the red earth and smiled on remote villages that had squatted for centuries in arrogance and isolation, ignorance and violence. It was an uplifting Saturday morning, a lovely day for a horseback ride, and for murder.

Squatted along the dirt roadside, the peasant peered intently at the contents of a small leather bag. It looked as if he was counting something important, lips moving dumbly in painful concentration. He started with guilt when the horsemen came trotting around the turn of a dusty track on the shank of a green hill that was not quite a mountain.

Wrapping his cloak around him and shoving the bag into the pocket of stained and baggy trousers, the peasant dove furtively into the brush, but there were three horsemen and they caught him quickly and chivvied him back to the road.

The riders were rich men, dressed in imported tweeds and soft leather, come on an inviting morning from the town of red-tile roofs in the valley below to ride their lands as landowners have done in Latin America for four centuries. Their horses were high-strung and expensive beasts; symbols as carefully selected, as proudly and casually used, and, ultimately, as off-handedly discarded as their clothes, or their women.

Two of the riders were young men, and they bullied the peasant, who was dirty and smelled of the earth and cowered before them. They pushed him this way and that with their horses, lashed him with their quirts.

The older man watched a few paces away as the breathless peasant, arms raised to protect himself, lost his balance and fell awkwardly. The young men laughed as he painfully recovered his feet, his face streaked with dirt. The peasant whipped off his hat and stood mutely, staring at the earth while the riders circled him.

"You are trespassing."

"Forgive me, Señor."

"Do you know whose land this is?"

"It is not my land."

"Do you know who he is?" A gesture toward the older man, who was igniting a slim cigar with a sculptured gold lighter, glittering in the sun.

"He is *Don* Patricio, the *patrón*. It is his land."

"And who am I?"

The peasant looked up fearfully at the fair-haired young man on the snorting black horse.

"His son, Señor Ernesto, who is at school in America."

"What are you doing here?" the second young man demanded.

"I was lost. I'm sorry."

"Liar! You know where you are. You know that strangers are not permitted here," the one called Ernesto shouted. He lanced forward with the quirt, landing a blow that brought blood from the peasant's forehead.

"Forgive me, I did no harm," the peasant said, his eyes never lifting.

"Your accent is funny, not from around here," the other rider said accusingly, one hand effortlessly controlling a plunging roan. "Where are you from?"

The peasant pointed east across a corrugated tangle of steep ridges and narrow valleys that stretched hundreds of miles to the sea.

"What's in your pocket? What have you stolen?"

"Nothing."

From an oiled holster that had cost more than a thousand dollars at a specialty shop in Beverly Hills, the roan's rider jerked a pistol with an ugly long nose as black and as oily as the hair tied behind his head in a ponytail.

"What's in your pocket? Last chance."

The older man said softly, "There is no need for that, Carlos. This is not a security matter."

"He's an animal, a thief." Carlos was angry. The Colt had snagged when he drew. The clerk had promised him that the holster had once been worn by Doc Holliday, and yet the Colt had snagged.

The older man said, "He does us no harm. Looks as if he hasn't slept in a week; longer since he's washed." Then, to the peasant, "Show me, *amigo*. Show me what you have."

"*Sí, Patrón.*" There was no hesitation.

With dirty fingers blunt as spades, the peasant prised the bag from his pocket and passed it through wreathes of smoke to the *patrón* called Patricio.

Painted bits of clay, a worked bit of bone, and a deeply scored black stone spilled onto Patricio's soft palm.

The *patrón* regarded the peasant's hoard silently.

"Junk," said his son Ernesto.

Carlos jammed his gun back into the traitor holster and cuffed the peasant on the head, almost as an after-thought.

"I thought he might have found something valuable," he said.

The two young men lit cigarettes.

"Where did you find these things?" the *patrón* asked after a time.

The peasant shaded his eyes and pointed higher up the hill. "There is a cave."

"Why did you go to the cave?"

"I was looking for snakes." The peasant was frightened. He mumbled. "Snakes. I kill snakes, sell the skins."

"And eat the meat, too. Am I right?" the *patrón* asked. The peasant nodded. "What else did you find in the cave, Señor Snakecatcher?"

"It was very dark. I found these and I saw some other things too big to carry. I had only a small light. I was frightened. It is your land, I am sorry. Take it—a—gift."

Ernesto scuffed out his cigarette and said, *"Vamos.* I need some jacuzzi time." Carlos obediently pointed his horse two steps back toward the trail.

"Wait," commanded the *patrón.* "Will you take us to the cave, Snakecatcher?"

"If you wish it, *patrón.* It is not far."

"Shit, *Papi,"* Ernesto complained. "Why waste time in a smelly cave? We can buy whole museums full of that kind of junk if that's what you want."

"Shut up," the *patrón* commanded. "These are Indian artifacts. The stone has been worked, it may be prehistoric. This is our land, this is our heritage—yours, too, College Boy. For how many generations has our family lived better than our friend the snakecatcher? Not many at all."

He dismissed the gunman. "Carlos, go back and tell the cook to hold lunch, perhaps for an hour." To the peasant, he said, "Snakecatcher, my son and I will follow you." Carlos spun the lovely roan and was gone.

They tied the horses to a bush and walked about twenty minutes uphill, the peasant without effort, the frayed woolen *ruana* that was his coat and his sleeping blanket flapping lightly against him.

Once it had been coffee land, but now it was mostly scrub, the rich red volcanic earth untilled and untended. The father and son struggled to keep pace. When they at last crested a rise and lurched into a nearly flat clearing shaded by a large mahogany tree, the peasant was waiting.

"This is as far as we go."

"Thank God for small favors," the son said. He mopped his brow with a silk handkerchief.

"I don't see a cave . . ." the father began but stopped when he saw what hung from the mahogany tree.

The snakecatcher had shed his hat, his stoop, his peasant servility, and his country accent. He had become a stranger with a rasping voice and a commanding manner. Only the dead eyes had not changed.

"Who are you?" Patricio Caballero asked quietly.

"I told you. I catch snakes."

My Spanish was rougher. I abandoned melodic tones and softer vowels. What I spoke was no longer poor man's Andean Spanish but a harsher tongue that was unmistakably Caribbean. I was home.

"Sometimes I imagine I'm Justice, big J. I've been waiting for you; weeks. If you hadn't come today, you would have come tomorrow. It might have been somewhere else, but we would have met. I have been waiting for a long time. What is another day, another week?"

"*Papi,* what is this?"

"Shut up, Ernesto." Caballero had recovered his breath. He reached into his shirt pocket for a fresh cigar. "You have names, a Christian name, a surname, perhaps, *Señor* Snakecatcher?"

"Names don't matter. But I want you to know who I am. That *is* important. I used to be a lawman in Miami."

"Now you are DEA? Or freelance? A bounty hunter, perhaps? A cowboy come to kidnap us, hustle us on to a plane? Do you really imagine that is possible?"

The peasant's smile never reached his empty eyes. "Oh, no, nothing so elegant."

"*Papi,* I know him! I know who he is." The boy was babbling in fear and excitement. "He's the thief cop who killed Pedro, stole our money. You remember! About two years ago Santiago killed his family, but we never saw the money. You must remember him!"

The *patrón* had gone very still. He asked softly, "Did you kill my brother Pedro?"

"Yes."

"And we killed your wife and children. I remember." The smoke hung heavy in the still mountain air.

"He's the crazy one. *Loco!*" the son screamed, an accusation. "When the other cops got there, they found him rolling around naked on the ground. *Loco!* You're crazy, man," Ernesto Caballero blurted again, spittle flying.

The peasant never moved.

"Are you crazy, Snakecatcher?" Patricio Caballero asked.

"Crazy." I thought about it, tracing an arc with my sandal in the dirt. "It's not so bad. Crazy creates its own clarity. Yes, let us say that I am. *Loco.*"

The father gestured at the mahogany tree. "Is that madman's art? Or intimidation? A prop, perhaps? A reminder of what could happen if we don't go quietly? We'll go quietly. But you'll never get out of this country alive, I think you know that. You're on a suicide run."

I shrugged. "I'm not crazy enough to worry about that. It's the tree. The tree is where it ends."

"You can't kill us! I mean . . ." The boy was grappling for a fulcrum, on the edge of panic. He screamed, "Help! Help! Carlos, Manuel. Help us! For God's sake! Help us!"

Patricio Caballero seemed embarrassed by his son's outburst. He controlled his fear. He was the *patrón.* "So. No extradition, no fair trial, no American Way. You're going to kill us—just like that? Our death is the price for your family. Am I right?"

The father was edging in front of the blabbering youth. Soon he would push him aside and rush the peasant. Not a bad plan, if the boy was smart enough to run.

"You're just the beginning," I said softly. I wanted them to know. "I'm going to kill all the Caballeros."

"Impossible!" Caballero was angry now. "We will hunt you down to the ends of the earth. Nothing can save you. You're a dead man, too, and not just you. All of your tribe. Parents, brothers, uncles, cousins, friends, people who never heard the name Caballero. Whoever they are, wherever they are. All of them will die. If not tomorrow, then next week, next year. That is our way, the Caballero Way." Caballero tossed the cigar into the brush. It was a signal, a challenge.

I had thought of that.

"There's just me; nobody else. Too bad, Caballero." I watched the first tendrils of smoke feather out of the weeds where the cigar had fallen.

I ended a long silence with a short gesture of my head.

"Time to go."

The patriarch said, "I don't suppose it would help if I apologized about your family. Or if some settlement—"

"Money, you mean. Unmarked bills, or a nice quiet account in the Caymans or Switzerland."

"If you wish. We can talk this through. We are both civilized men. Lamentable things happen." A breeze had sprung up, and it caressed young smoke beside the Caballeros. "Things that we regret later. That is life," the *patrón* continued, "but there is always the possibility of making amends. I am sure you understand that. Even pain has its price . . ."

He didn't understand, did he? "The settlement's on the tree. Time to go."

"He's *loco, Papi,* a madman. He can't do this. Let's get him."

"Careful!"

"He hasn't even got a gun."

"He has a gun."

"He can't stop both of us," the boy shouted. But he was wrong.

The youth leapt, collapsing six feet short in a howl of pain as a bullet smashed his shoulder.

"Turn around." I clubbed the father with the pistol butt and bound him before he could recover. The boy writhed on the ground, forgetting to be brave. He cried when I jerked the wounded shoulder back to tie his hands behind him. My girls had not even had time enough to cry.

"I understand your emotions. Any father would," Caballero pleaded. "Take me, let my son go. He's just a boy."

"Over to the tree. Help your son."

"I prefer to be shot," Patricio Caballero said, with some dignity. He ran a few lumbering steps before I tripped him.

"That offer has expired."

The fire was burning in earnest. White smoke washed me and I fitted the nooses.

"Adiós."

"Fuck you," the father cursed.

The son, who had wet his pants, sagged as if in exhaustion until the rope's pressure brought him up short.

"Papi, Papi," he screamed. "This isn't happening. This can't happen. Tell him to stop. Save us."

"Forgive me, my son. Try to be brave," the father said.

I walked over to where the rope ends were tied to the pommel of a tall brown horse. I mounted and urged the horse forward, away from the tree. The horse set off with a stumble but adjusted easily to the strain. After a few paces, I reined in. The horse skittered, but I calmed it and sat quietly as it became accustomed to its burden.

My back to the tree, my vacant eyes scouring the distant green hills, I ignored the terrible noises behind me and the growing roar of the fire as it took hold through the dry brush.

After a time silence returned and wind carried the fire down the hill, away from the crest and its gallows tree.

Soon, a pair of songbirds flitted past the swinging figures. High above the neighboring valley, a hawk patrolled.

I cut the ropes with a sharp knife and rode away without looking back.

16

THE CABALLERO FAMILY filed from the church in a thin and impeccably dressed black line; raw silks with Italian labels. My binoculars were the best money could buy, but I scarcely needed them. I knew them all; every face, every bio, and most of the crimes. I had killed the patriarch and the third son. Two older sons remained, Horacio and Eduardo, lining up now as chief mourners before the two gleaming caskets being carried from the church by squads of retainers.

The fourth and youngest son, Luis, still a gawky teenager, stood one step back with two sisters and their husbands. There was a long train of mourners, staff, and country folk, but the burial itself would be just immediate family. The portable radio that was my only link to the world had promised me that. Like the binoculars and the camping gear and the knives and the ordinance, it was the best that stolen cocaine money could buy.

It had been almost a year, and I had learned much since slipping over the tall brick wall at the mental hospital. One thing I had learned is that it is truly amazing what a determined man can accomplish, given time, money, and a cause. A few hundred thousand dollars and a point of view. That is a powerful combination. And the potency is tripled, quadrupled, if the man is also willing, even anxious, to gamble, to surrender, his own chance of survival.

With plenty of money and unlimited time, I had started slow and low. First, had come Jorge Fuentes aka Cuevas; the last hard man my wife Lisa had ever known. I found him living in Alabama, selling mobile homes at an air base to kids who couldn't afford them. Before he died, sniveling Jorge had told me where to find the gruff-voiced kidnapper. He was a distant Caballero cousin, it turned out. Stop number two. As his life trickled away in a Connecticut basement, the gruff voice turned shriek; he had sketched an insider's view of the Caballero clan family tree.

Drug cop Andy Ridgeway had filled in the details, responding to a telephoned appeal with a floppy disk packed with prime Fed intelligence documents. A favor, one cop to another. And never a question asked, never a take-it-easy Paul, where-are-you, come-in-let's-talk. God bless Andy.

By the day of the funeral, I had been in the Colombian mountains almost three months, a camper with a mission and a one-way ticket. The blond German who might have been a journalist or a coffee buyer had vanished; become a scruffy and perhaps dissolute traveler who could, when the time came, segue into one more anonymous *campesino*. The traveler was seldom seen, hardly ever visiting country towns, and then only long enough to buy supplies, and once, a horse. If some inquiring soul asked where he was from, the traveler would flick his hand and gesture toward a remote and imprecise direction. He slept rough and moved with the solemn speed and deliberation of a tortoise, sampling the air and the lay of the land, absorbing the local accent and the local color, picking his spots.

Watching. Waiting. Watching some more.

I made a plan. I worked out the times, and the places. It

had not taken long to learn that on Saturdays the *patrón*
liked to ride his showy stallion along country trails with
pride and passion. It was just a question of waiting along the
right trail at the right time. It had taken three weeks. The
squealing son was a bonus.

At first the hard life had honed me, but then I had fallen
sick, bad water, lying for one painful day after another under
cover. I grew rail-thin and wild-eyed. Then came a fever. I
dosed myself with expensive drugs, and maybe it went
away. But maybe not, because for days I shivered when the
sun was at its zenith.

The Caballero family cemetery lay between me and the
chapel at the peak of a gentle rise with a lovely panoramic
view of the countryside. It was as new as the family's
wealth. Caballero had chosen the spot when his third wife,
not the mother of the children, had driven her canary Ferrari
off the side of a cliff in a fit of overcoked exuberance. She'd
been a beautiful woman, a former Miss Colombia, who, it
was rumored, owed her title to an assembly line half-hour
backstage in which she had displayed more than bathing suit
talents to five election-night judges.

Patrón Caballero had given his young wife everything in
life, and spared her nothing in death. Six workmen from
Italy had spent months building her baroque mausoleum.
Later, Caballero had had his parents reburied there as well.
Now he and his son would lie among them.

I counted eight in the security detail around the church
and another dozen spread out between there and the cemetery. Just after dawn, two men with rifles had come within
yards of where I lay with my raw memories and hunter's
illusion under a blanket of forest debris. They'd searched
carefully, just as they had searched time and again in the
tense two days since father and son had been murdered on a
burning hillside. But they had never found even a trace of *El
Patrón*'s killer; not then, not on this sad burial day.

The early morning searchers were outriders of the funeral

security net. Instincts told me that they would not be back, but I was wrong.

The Caballeros walked to the cemetery. That surprised me, honestly. I had expected ostentation, an ornate, high-wheeled glass hearse pulled by caparisoned black horses. Maybe walking was a family tradition; the Caballeros were not far from peasant roots. Latin American peasants walk to country cemeteries because they are often too many and too poor to get there any other way. I watched the family string out behind the fat young man in full ecclesiastical regalia whom the newspapers called the "designer priest." The dirt road led slightly uphill and it was good to see him sweat. The designer priest gave earnest newspaper interviews, describing his "mission to the troubled newly rich." It was all part of a New Era Christianity, he said, seldom bothering to mention that he had never been a real priest at all, or that in ministering to the likes of the Caballeros he had acquired a large drug habit and a remarkable fondness for young boys.

Knots of people left standing at the church began to break up and drive away from the Caballero compound as the chief mourners and coffin bearers walked in single file, black ants behind the puffing priest. The funeral was falling behind the mental schedule I had set for it, but it didn't matter. Let them walk. It really made no difference.

The attack came without warning.

He was a heavy but lithe man, a *campesino* who smelled of dung and wielded the heavy butt of an old rifle. If he had not been a peasant he probably would have shot me, but Colombian peasants do not lightly kill strangers; not a stranger who has fancy binoculars and who might, God forbid, be a friend of the Caballero family or even be a fellow security guard nobody had bothered to mention.

I flung myself to one side, the butt missing my skull but landing with a numbing thud against the top of my left

shoulder. I kicked the *campesino,* once, twice, then levered
to my feet and drove forward before he could swing again.

We rolled like animals in the dirt. The *campesino* hammered at my head and back with the rifle, but I scarcely felt
it. When my hands closed on his throat, he let the weapon
fall and switched to a bear hug. The man was strong and he
was willing, but he was unschooled. I focused and struck for
the carotid artery. After a minute I pushed myself clear of
the still form and paused, wheezing, to catch my breath.

I saw the tail of the funeral procession entering the grave-
yard gates and was reaching for the binoculars when a
rustling in the brush from behind made clear that I had made
another mistake: Caballero retainers patrolled not in ones
but in twos.

I sprang forward to counter another attack, but the second
man was smarter. I caught a glimpse of him scuttling away,
an ochre shirt retreating through the trees. Chase him down?
There was no time. Besides, the man was running away, he
posed no threat. It would take him half an hour to get back
and raise the alarm. By then it would be finished.

Except . . . I heard a high-pitched voice shouting in alarm.
Then came answering squeals that could only have been
from a walkie-talkie.

"Shit."

Below, white-shirted pallbearers, villa and rancher workers, I saw, were withdrawing respectfully from the cemetery,
leaving only the fat priest and the immediate Caballero family. I counted the three sons, a cluster of their women and
other men in a black knot, and a handful of others—first
cousins, probably. The priest made the sign of the cross over
the two coffins lying side by side and began reading from his
prayerbook. I could see his lips move; watched the others'
heads bow. It was nearly time.

In the end, I have to admit that I was lucky. The security
chief Eduardo was about a hundred yards from the cemetery
when the electronic hysteria from the hillside reached him. I

watched him hunch over suddenly as if in pain, with the walkie-talkie pressed to his ear. Then he jerked upright and sprinted wildly for the cemetery gates.

I took a final measured look at the tight group around the two caskets. The priest, the mourners, the dead.

A great target cluster.

The security honcho reached the cemetery entrance. He was shouting. The mourners' heads jerked up in alarm, their bodies stiffened. One of the sons reached into his jacket and brought out a machine pistol. A lot of good that would do him.

I took a deep breath, aimed at a spot in front of the priest and between the two caskets. Rock-steady, I fired the missile.

I ran for four days, hungry, weak, sweating, shivering. It never occurred to me not to run, but it was not survival I sought. It was release that I craved, and that would come in its time. So I ran until it did. I had to abandon the horse early one day, and twice Caballero's men nearly caught me. Once I had to shoot two of them, and the second time lucky long-distance fire from a rifle caught me a glancing blow in the side.

On the third day, soldiers crashed the party, tough mountain troops who knew their craft. I couldn't figure out who had sent for them, or why, or what their role was supposed to be, but when the helicopters came I knew that I'd never escape the net. It is possible to hide from helicopters in jungled mountains, but it is hard to run far enough from them if they are supported by good troops on the ground.

The soldiers were choppered in before nightfall on the third day and almost immediately got into a sharp firefight with my pursuers. At first I wrote if off to battlefield confusion: they were hunters who could only be seeking the same prey. Still, the shooting bought me a few hours.

By the afternoon of the fourth day, though, everyone must have understood as well as I did that it would end soon. By then, I was reeling in exhaustion, muttering to myself, talk-

ing to my wife and daughters, arguing with people I had
killed and some I'd never met, humming bars of tuneless
music with no beginning or end.

The helicopter spotted me just after the sun passed its
zenith, and after that it became a pest, dogging my tracks
like an impertinent mosquito as I climbed slowly. There
were a dozen times when a marksman in the open door
could have taken me, but no shots came.

When at last I reached the crest of a high, knobby mountain spur, I slumped in exhaustion against a rock slanted just
enough to offer some shade and cover. I would have sold my
soul for a cup of cool water.

It was a lovely eyrie, the sort of place that painters and
poets celebrate. What better spot for a thief's last stand. The
air smelled sweet. Across a narrow valley, framed by the
first of a series of misty peaks, a condor floated lazily, enjoying the day. Gingerly, I inched down a narrow slope to where
the ground ended and eased myself into a sitting position.

Letting my feet dangle, I leaned forward.

The drop was sheer; eight hundred, a thousand feet; far
enough. Glistening in the dappled sunlight below I could
make out the pool of water where a river spilled into an
amphitheater of boulders. A twinkling bull's-eye. I felt
dizzy, with fear. I felt giddy, with relief and exhaltation. My
subconscious must have taken me there: this was the
jumping-off place.

The helicopter startled the condor. It hovered level with
me a few hundred feet away, bouncing a bit. Either the air
rising from the distant valley floor was turbulent or the pilot
was spooked.

I had tossed away the rifle the day before when the
ammunition had run out. I still had a pistol; a long shot,
mind you, but I still might have hit the chopper. But why
bother? I couldn't concentrate anyway. For some crazy reason the interplay of helicopter and condor made me remember an afternoon I had taken my boat into Biscayne Bay to

fish for mackerel. As I was loafing along to Marker Twenty-three, a pair of frolicking dolphins had turned up. They'd played tag with the boat for more than a mile, a ballet of grace and beauty a few miles from some of the meanest and deadliest streets in America. What made me think of that? I wondered then, and I wonder still.

Off to the right came fresh shooting. At me? At the helicopter, more likely, for it spun decisively off its hover to settle over a tiny clearing below and to my left. A rope ladder snaked out and two soldiers dropped agilely down, followed by a bulkier figure in a white shirt and less certain feet.

Who was he, the sheriff?

Curtain coming down. *Sí, Señor.* Not hours now, just minutes. I understood it. And I welcomed it. Dopers and soldiers on one side. Soldiers and the sheriff on the other. No place left to climb. No way out. Trapped! Oh, horrors! Why, it's all downhill from here! I laughed, a cackle that rebounded off the hill, startling a flock of parrots.

More shooting from the right; a round pinged off a rock some distance away. They lack not the will, just the range and the angle, I decided. The angle of the dangle equals the square of the mass of the ass; that's what they used to say around the school yard when I was in high school. But was it true?

It was tempting, floating there, free as a condor, to revisit the women I had known to see if it was true, but it was not a good idea. A bad idea, because while the shooters on the right still had a long way to climb, the ones on the left would be on me quite soon. I regarded them narrowly, watching with rapt attention while the two soldiers and the sheriff conferred in an urgent knot.

Then . . .

What was this about? The two soldiers hunkered down by the base of a tree, their rifles cast negligently aside. The sheriff climbed on alone, making heavy weather of the slender path and steep incline.

Grandstanding, Sheriff?

Want to go before the cameras as the hero who brought in the *loco gringo* single-handed? Sorry, but it would never happen. The varmint was about to vamoose, Sheriff.

Another burst of nonsense shooting from the right, answered this time by the crunch of a grenade and disciplined fire from what sounded like serious heavy weapons.

Now what? Soldiers fighting dopers, that was pretty clear, and I was beginning to understand why.

For, off to the left, what a strange sheriff.

I could see the figure quite clearly as the man scrambled painfully up, on his hands and knees most of the time. He had a canteen slung across his chest, and something metal glinted at his throat.

But the sheriff carried no weapon.

Some sheriff.

Finally it sank in.

I scrambled to my feet, screaming, "Leave me alone! This is not your place. Go away and let me be!"

The sheriff stopped in his tracks. I studied the face, wreathed in sweat, streaked with scratches from rocks and brambles. It broke into a well-known grin.

"Nobody plays solitaire when I'm in town, especially not you, *hermano,*" hollered a prince of the Catholic church and a friend I had always called Rico.

"And if you're planning some operatic exit, at least wait till we've had a drink. Cardinals are built for comfort, not speed. I've had a hard enough time just getting this far."

My anger ebbed as I watched my friend scrabble nearer, each step more trying than the last. Once he nearly fell. Another time, he slipped and embedded himself in some thorny-looking bushes.

It had been a long time since we had seen one another.

Rico had aged.

"Damn Vatican," he complained when he at last lurched

on to the ledge, breathless with effort. "Soft living—you get drawn in little by little. 'Your Excellency this, Your Excellency that,' and the next thing you know, whoosh, there's twenty pounds you never had before and you're looking for elevators every place you go."

The eyes hadn't changed.

They glinted like flint, tough, calculating, a hawk assaying its prey.

Gradually, the cardinal caught his breath and made a ceremony of unslinging the canteen. He drank deep before offering it over.

"Been a long time, hasn't it? Wish I could say you look good, but the fact is you look like hell, *amigo.*"

"You shouldn't have come."

"Drink it all, if you like. You need it more than I do." He walked a pace toward me, but I stopped him with a warning flick of the pistol.

"Close enough. Just slide it over."

I swigged but immediately spat it out.

"This isn't water; it's rum."

Rico laughed, "You don't imagine I could have climbed down a rope ladder from a helicopter and hiked up this brute of a mountain on water, do you? You're the only one here who's crazy, *hermano.*"

"Don't fuck with me, Rico. I'm here because I want to be here, and this is as far as I want to go."

"Whatever you say, Paul. Take it easy."

"How'd you get here? Why?"

"Well the world does turn, you must understand that. Even at the Vatican we get a little glimmer now and then. Now, if *El Jefe* Caballero and his college son had died in a car crash, maybe I'd have said a prayer for their souls and one of thanksgiving for deliverance. But when Señor Caballero and his boy are lynched, well, for some reason that made me think of an old friend of mine who dropped out of sight with fire in his eye. I wonder why?"

"They squirmed. It felt good."

"So as soon as I heard about it, I jumped on a plane because I was afraid my old friend, who's a mean *hijo de puta* when he wants to be, might not stop with two corpses, and I thought if I could get there in time I could help him before something worse . . . " He shrugged. "But I was too late—for that part of it, anyway. That was a terrible thing to do, Paul, to Caballero and his son, and at the cemetery."

"Eye for an eye, that's what the Bible says."

"Wrong testament, *amigo.* It was a terrible thing—and I think you know it."

I drank, cautiously this time. The rum coursed like fire. I felt as if I could fly.

"Why don't you give me the gun, Paul?" Rico asked softly.

"Sure. I don't need it. Not now. Here." Rico caught it. One by one he extracted the bullets, tossed them over the precipice. He stuck the gun under his belt.

"I thought I might use it one last time, but then I decided it'd be more fun to feel the breeze."

"You're not jumping, Paul."

"Oh, yeah. Free-fall with a double twist, maybe three." Witty. "A terrible thing, huh? Some may say it was wrong, but it wasn't their wife, not their daughters. I feel good."

"I don't think so, I don't think you do at all, Paul."

"Well, maybe I'm *loco,* but that's the way it was, this is where it ends."

We sat in incendiary silence for a few minutes, but there was one more thing I had to say. "Something short and sweet, Rico, then I'll finish the rum and you can turn your back and walk down to the helicopter and catch a ride home."

It was hard to say, even after all the pain, the terrible years. "The money, that night in the car. I stole it." I was crying.

"I know, Paul," the cardinal said quietly. "I forgive you. I forgave you a long time ago."

I felt breathless, watched my deepest most shameful secret spilling out into the mountain sunshine. "Why didn't you say something? You should have said so. It wouldn't have made any difference, maybe, but . . . I thought the money would help; Lisa and the kids. But it didn't . . . It was the reason that they, that I . . . for all of this . . . "

Rico said softly, "One thing you don't know about that money, *amigo,* is that I stole it first. Someday I'll tell you all about it."

What? What? The rum. And the tears. The universe spun. Let go. Just a nudge. *Adiós.*

"Sit still," Rico commanded. "Stop feeling sorry for yourself and listen to me: this has never been about money, Paul. You're what matters to me. You're my friend. I haven't got that many. I won't let you slip away. One day you will be sorry for this, too. And you will be forgiven. Just as I was forgiven."

"Stay away! Any closer and you'll go with me!"

"Neither one of us is going anywhere, not today."

"You're a fucking cardinal, worth something. I'm a thief, a killer."

"Everybody's soul is the same as everybody else's. Jesus was crucified next to a good thief, wasn't he?"

I hurled the canteen into space, leapt to my feet, screaming through the tears.

"Don't lecture me. I don't need any catechism lessons. I fucked it up, Rico, all of it. And this is how it ends. Don't kill yourself, too."

The cardinal was on his feet now, yelling, arms pounding the air like pistons.

"You saved me, Paul, pulled me from that car when I was drowning. I won't let you go without a fight."

"Bless me, Father," I pleaded, "for I have sinned."

And stepped into space.

At that instant the cardinal launched himself diagonally across the jagged edge. He caught an arm, spun with it like a demented discus thrower, redirecting my momentum, clawing desperately with his feet for a fulcrum, willing the two bodies back against the mountain, away from the void.

We teetered for what seemed an eternity, both of us screaming then like the madmen we were, locked in an almost primeval struggle between a force for life and a wish for death.

Rico won.

It was all a question of physics, really. Of force and counterforce, thrust and gravity. Maybe there was even an angle of the dangle, but when all was said and done, it was basic physical laws that kept two men from falling to their deaths. That must have been what happened.

Neither of us would ever talk about it to anyone. But neither of us would ever believe that it was that simple.

One instant I was falling.

The next I was sprawled with my back against a prodding splinter of rock.

Puffing, his face red with exertion, Rico crouched on one knee above me. The last thing I remember was watching Rico yank the pistol from his belt and how prettily the sun's rays glinted off it as it came hurtling toward my head.

VATICAN CITY

17

SHAKILY, I PLACED the coffee cup back into its saucer. The pope was standing over me, his hand on my shoulder.

"You okay, *hermano?*" he asked with concern. I think maybe he understood where I had been.

"Fine, I'm fine," I lied, battling for a fulcrum. After an awkward few moments, I managed to say what I felt. "You know that I'm with you all the way on this one. And if I feel my grip is starting to slip, I'll get Ivanovic to stuff me like a turkey with those wonderful blue pills."

Tredi smiled. He knew all about broken minds and blue pills. He had whisked me from the mountaintop in the helicopter that had brought him, and he must have worked great magic. Before long—no questions asked, no murders to confess to—I'd found myself in a church-run asylum in woodlands near the border between the United States and Canada. I was Paul there, just Paul, and I've been Paul ever since. I don't think anybody knew much more about me than that I was very screwed up. I spent countless hours with a doctor named Jennifer, with horn-rimmed glasses and a prim black bun, a soul mate of Ivanovic's.

She'd helped, but I'd never told her everything. I read a lot, though, walked in the woods, thought about things I had never given much time. God, for one. Jimmy Kearns, bless him, had been my link with the past. He'd call me at least once a week, and sometimes—marvel of electronics—Rico would be on the line at the same time, though one of them was in Miami and the other at the Vatican. It was a brutal winter, but I never stopped walking, and midway through a short and glorious spring, old Jimmy had bounced up from Miami with a spring in his step and a glint in his eye.

Kearns had handed me an envelope with one of those big smiles. "Your ticket to freedom, Paul my lad." More a halfway house, really, this time an ancient *palazzo*-refuge run by Catholic brothers in the mountains of northern Italy. I'd chopped wood, worked in the forest, read a lot in the Gothic-vaulted library. It was there I'd met Ivanovic for the first time and there, on one of his flying visits, that I told Rico that I felt that I might have a vocation. More years of study and thinking time here and there, until I'd found myself at the Vatican in a black almost-priest suit having tea with my friend the cardinal who would, to his own astonishment and—I think—secret delight, one day be pope.

"Let's see if we can put this thing together," the pope was saying. "Tell me everything you know about Caruso."

I took him through the Caruso investigation, step by frustrating step, routine, witnesses, the whole business. Once he reached into a diagonal pocket in his white cassock, pulled out a silver pen, made me spell a name, and made a quick note.

I said, "Vidal wanted to see me. Do you know what he found out in South America?"

"He wanted to talk about the Caballero family. I told him you had a particular focus on it," the pope said quietly.

The target swimming into range, finger tightening.

The pope explained, "From what he had been able to pick up here by phone and computer, Vidal thought it might be the Caballeros back in the game. I sent him to South America to find out for sure. That's exactly what he found."

Gentle pressure. Squeeze.

"They're history, the Caballeros."

Wonderful release.

"History."

The pope said, "It seems not. Maybe it's the women. *Quién sabe?* I didn't get a chance to see Gustavo when he got back yesterday, but he came right here from the airport, dumped a stack of documents and computer disks. My backroom guys are looking at them now. The note he left came right to the point: 'Caballeros and the Keys,' it said, 'two faces, one devil.' "

"The Keys. I don't see the connection. Why would drug lords care about a bunch of religious fanatics? They wouldn't know what hand to use to cross themselves."

The pope poured us more coffee. "It's been about the Keys from the very beginning, Paul," he said, with a sigh. "It started out innocently enough, but it has become a movement that is repugnant to me and dangerous to the future and the unity of the whole church. I believe its long-range goal is to split the church and to eventually gain control of the hardline, authoritarian branch they want to drive away from Rome—away from me. I'm afraid the true believers, including the Keys leaders here, are being manipulated intellectually and financially."

Tredi was pacing the room, eyes cold, voice strained. "Imagine the windfall, not just drugs, if a criminal gang controlled a worldwide network of militant Christian fundamentalists from behind the scenes. They know I'll fight them with every ounce of my strength. Maybe another pope wouldn't feel so threatened—or threatening to them."

He finished the coffee, big hands cradling the delicate blue and white cup. "So I sent two friends, good priests, to find out more for me. A sin of arrogance—and of ignorance. My sin. They were smart, they were brave, and I sent them to their deaths, God forgive me."

"Rico, I . . ." The pope was in pain.

He brushed past me. "I thought it all out, Paul. Caruso is the quiet one; they know he's a friend of mine and he encourages them to imagine that I'm sympathetic to their views. He writes extremist garbage that they rush into print, thinking the ideas might be mine. Caruso becomes their secret weapon—and mine. He tells me what he learns about the Keys and when I'm ready I can hang them as schismatics for what he wrote.

"Gustavo Vidal, God give him rest, was Mr. Inside. He's famous; they love having him around. Forget all those social justice beliefs he's had. Our buddy Vidal's really been a Keys conservative all along. He smiles, he listens, he snoops. But he was my man. He never forgot anything and he was wonderful with numbers. So from two sides my friends burrow into the Keys and they bleed it."

The pope had it all worked out. But he hadn't planned murder.

"They're dead and I'm responsible. It's as if I killed them, Paul."

"No, Rico, no," I said uselessly.

There were tears in the pope's eyes. With a crack, the tiny cup exploded in his fist. Dregs of coffee splattered his white robe and the Persian carpet, but he seemed not to notice.

I turned quietly to the door. Alone, I knew that he would mourn. But I also knew that Tredi would move earth—and, yes, heaven if he could—to see that his friends, his priests, had not died in vain.

"You're batting third, Paul. We've got to finish it. But no paybacks, not this time," he called softly. "I'm prepared to forgive whoever killed Caruso and Vidal, as they would have forgiven their murderers. But find out who is behind all of this, Paul. Find out, and I'll destroy them my way. Destroy them and all the evil they have created."

He walked over and gave me a fierce *abrazo*. Then, he strode back on stage to his role as the world's high priest.

I would find them. But forgive them? No way. I'm no pope. Just a simple brother. Vengeance is more my style.

On my way out of the palace, a fussy papal chamberlain intercepted me, as he sometimes did. Without speaking, he handed me a letter-sized air mail envelope. I took it to the post office and mailed it to Bobby. In the midst of a crisis he feared could sunder his church, the pope was sending his can't-get-it-right brother Bobby another payment for a fish farm.

18

WHEN I GOT back to St. Damian's, I thought the doorkeeper looked at me funny. Then I caught a couple of seminarians smirking in my general direction. In my room I discovered why. On the door was a note in the rector's spindly handwriting, never a good sign.

On my bed, carefully wrapped in florist's paper, lay a single red carnation. The card had no writing. Just a careful ink sketch of a smoking pistol. It looked like a .38.

The note from the rector said, "Brother Paul, I am sure that you are as aware as I am that flowers are not suitable gifts to send—or to receive—at a residence for seminarians."

Be okay, though, if the Flower Man sent a nice bouquet to my funeral, wouldn't it, Rector? Caruso had been warned by the Flower Man, I had the testimony of the alluring Teresa Longhi for that. Vidal, too, I could only assume. My turn.

Two days later, Vidal was buried. The pope went to the funeral. So did the head of the Keys: how deeply, with what reverence, he had bowed to kiss the pope's ring.

At my urging, Galli was quietly running full checks on

everybody who had anything to do with the Keys. So far there was nothing firm, but he had turned up two or three young blades, one of them a priest with funny-looking identity documents who worked full-time at the Keys headquarters. They'd be worth talking to. And maybe Luther and I would make a quiet night visit to the old *palazzo* that was the Keys headquarters. We'd done that sort of thing before.

I thought about Tredi, a holy, commanding, lonely figure, and I thought about the others who had shared his vocation, turning their back on the world for the rewarding but often thankless loner's role as priest. It is hard to become a Catholic priest; harder still to live up to its strictures. Caruso had a weakness for women. In Vidal's room we had found some hashish. Galli, who was a gentler and more human man than most cops I've known, had seen it and immediately developed an urgent need to talk on his cell phone.

He'd walked away, I'd flushed it. But I told the pope. We were speaking by phone most days, both of us sensing that the pace was accelerating, that we were hurtling toward some climax in a script only a deadly, unseen enemy had read.

I must have said something that wasn't funny about the hash because Tredi grew suddenly stern: "We are men, Paul, only men. Don't you think I sometimes have a glass or two too many? Don't you think I sometimes have what we priests like to call 'impure thoughts'?" he had demanded.

"Don't you think I wake up with a tumescent penis sometimes? Caruso battled all his priestly life against a liking for women. Vidal had a brain big enough for a whole village locked up in a tiny body. Maybe sometimes he succumbed to a yearning to step out of it for a little while. Don't be too tough on Caruso and Vidal. Or on yourself. We're all of us frail but wondrous creatures in His image."

Nothing as refreshing for the ego as being lectured on morality and common sense by the world's high priest. Particularly when you deserve it.

• • •

I was still licking my psychic wounds when I met Luther later that terrible week, but he was high enough for both of us. He surveyed the thick menu with gusto that surpassed hunger. "I'll have one of each, right from the top."

"And I'll have whatever you've been smoking, drinking, or inhaling."

He flashed me a giant smile. "Paul, I feel good, real good. I'm the lion that just killed an antelope."

We sat at a sidewalk table in what was once the fish market of ancient Rome. It was on the shores of the Tiber then, but now it is a few blocks back, centuries of engineering having tamed a river that over the centuries has claimed more lives than any other outside China. Our table was next to a weathered Roman column, but whether it was a classical remnant or the inspiration of the trattoria owner I couldn't say. What I did know was that the food was authentic.

Luther ordered *carciofi alla giudia,* small artichokes deep-fried whole. I had *fiori di zucchini,* squash flowers, wrapped around a fillet of anchovy and mozzarella and lightly fried. We shared a chilled bottle of Pinot Grigio, a bit sweet for my taste, but it was Luther's treat.

"A night off, how come?"

"Pope's home tonight, all buttoned up. Said he'd manage to stay alive by himself. Chased us away, Diego and me. We needed some time off, he said."

Luther vaporized the artichokes and gnawed at a thick slice of crusty bread. Looking around approvingly, he said with his mouth full, "Great place. I like it. Magic."

"Luther, we've eaten here a dozen times, more."

"Lots of history, though. I like that, history. Cultures mixing."

Jews have lived in Rome since before the birth of Christ. If you've ever heard about St. Paul's letter to the Romans, it was to the Roman Jews that he wrote. A persistent, valued, but not often easy presence. For more than three hundred years from the sixteenth to the nineteenth centuries, popes locked the Jews away in a Ghetto near the Tiber, the gates closed and guarded every night. Today, the old Ghetto is proof of the two-thousand-year-old truism: to go "home," a Roman goes out into the streets to socialize.

The neighborhood where we sat is one of the liveliest of old Rome. Streets around the big nineteenth-century synagogue, Catholic churches on three sides and its back to the Tiber, brim with people theater *al fresco,* old women in straight-backed chairs gabbling with one eye on grandchildren flirting from the saddles of their *motorini.* As darkness fell, we sat there at the sidewalk table as spectators in a popular circus as buoyant and as eternal as Rome itself.

Luther had *spaghetti alle vongole,* small juicy clams in a sauce of oil, garlic, and *peperoncino.* I ate *fettuccini con i funghi porcini,* ribbon-flat pasta with fat mushrooms.

"I talked with the Holy Father," Luther announced as the pile of shells on his bread plate mounted precariously. "Got it all off my chest."

I nodded. Big chest.

"I told him the story—everything. I talked for two hours, Paul; he sat for two hours, the Bishop of Rome, and he listened, never took his eyes off my face. He knows more about my life than anybody, even me, maybe, because by the time I was finished talking I understood myself better. But I had the sense he was one chapter ahead of me the whole time. I told him about the women, the violence, about that night on the freighter off Nigeria that I'll live with for the rest of my life.

"I told him how when I was on the university faculty we'd teach kids how to hijack food and equipment from the army, how we'd sell it on the black market, use the money to pay salaries and electricity to keep the school open. I told him things I never told you, Paul. Shit, I told him stuff I didn't even know I remembered."

Luther must have seen a twinge of jealousy flash past my

eyes, for he laid a big hand on my arm. "The thing is, Paul, he's the pope. He's got things to do, promises to keep. You're my brother; I talk to you anytime I want to, tell you anything. Like now. But he's the pope!"

"And one hell of a priest."

"A great man, Paul. A holy man."

We drank to the pope. I ordered another bottle of wine. As a main course Luther had *saltimbocca alla romana,* veal with ham and a bit of cheese, a dish invented not far from where we ate. I was as traditional, ordering *abbacchio arrostito,* roast lamb with a side order of *broccoletti in padella,* broccoli fried lightly with garlic and just a suggestion of red pepper.

We swapped Tredi stories, watched a gray-haired man on a motorbike grimly duel for street space with an angry young woman in a flashy Fiat, and drank deep of the gentle white wine. Finally Luther pushed his empty plate away, said, "I ain't mad at nobody," and cut to the chase.

"When I got to the part about Eden and the monastery, living there"—Luther stared at the white tablecloth, as if embarrassed—"it was the hardest thing I think I've ever done; told the pope that I was not really a priest.

"I was a fraud, a liar. I waited for him to react, to say something, chase me away. But his face never changed, or his eyes. I couldn't tell what he was thinking. But I'll tell you something, Paul. I was scared like I've never been scared. I wanted this man to respect me, but I had to tell him I was a cheat, a liar, a pretender."

Now it was my turn to comfort Luther. I knew how he hurt—knew it exactly. "He understood," I murmured. "I'm sure Tredi understood."

"Oh, yeah, man, he did." Luther's voice was a whisper. "When I finished, just sort of ran down, there was a long time when nobody said anything. I thought 'Maybe I should just get up and leave. Slink away somewhere. Complete my disgrace. It's what I deserve.'

"But then he asked me a question, just one question. 'Luther,' he said, 'since you began pretending to be a priest, have you lived like a priest?' And I said, 'Yes, Holy Father, I have,' and it's true, Paul, I swear to you that it's true."

"I know it is, Luther."

" 'Are you sorry for the bad things you have done, Luther? The sins, all of them.' I said that I was, and he said, 'I have heard and accept your confession. Now make a good Act of Contrition.' I did. He forgave me. I'm whole now."

"Way to go. He's not great. You're great. I'm proud of you," I said. And I was. Luther had confronted his demons better than I had ever managed. I teased him to defray the tension.

"So what happens now? Are you defrocked?"

"No, he said I could still do what I do, wear what I wear, the robes and all, just not dispense the sacraments. That's maybe the worst thing I've done, though he didn't say so."

Luther drained his glass. "So what happens now is that we get all this business over with, the threat to the Holy Father, you figure out who killed Caruso and Vidal, we do New York. Then the pope says I go away to a place he knows, think a lot, really learn all the priestly things I just pretend to know. Then he says he'll ordain me. Make me a real priest."

Tredi had made the same offer to me. But I had not taken him up on it and never would.

"That would be great, Luther. I'm sure you'll want to do it."

"More than anything I've ever done in my life, Paul."

We skipped dessert, drank coffee, and set out to stroll through cobblestoned streets whose crowds had begun to thin out. It was a beautiful evening, a memorable night. It had been a meal of great joy, for both of us.

We were about two blocks from the restaurant and Luther was talking about going home to Africa as a missionary one day, when suddenly he stiffened in alarm.

He was quicker than I was, always quicker.

I was flatfooted, had barely caught sight of the gun barrel

resting on the roof of a car across the street, no image of the dark face, sighting.

"Paul!" he shouted, and he shoved me so hard that I fell headlong into the street.

In that instant, the shot rang out and Luther fell like a toppled tree.

When I got to him a few seconds later, his eyes were rolling up into his head.

I knew he had taken a bullet meant for me, and I knew he was gone.

I guess I was crying, because when the pope burst into the hospital a few hours later he looked all blurry to me.

Luther didn't die right away. There's a hospital not far from the Ghetto, and when an ambulance finally came, they took him into the operating room and kept him there for a long time.

Then the surgeon came out and talked with me, her face gray with fatigue, eyes knotted in pain.

"We have done all we can," she said. "Your friend . . . I am afraid there is nothing more . . . I am sorry." She said it like she meant it. "I am going home now to my children. But my colleagues will be here . . . " Her hands fluttered an amen. "I am so sorry."

They wheeled Luther into a small private room to die and the hospital chaplain, a wizened Italian priest with a sweet face, came in and administered Extreme Unction, the last rites, with weary authority.

I sat there holding Luther's hand for what seemed a long time. I'm not sure there was anything in my mind. I was crushed, empty. Maybe I was praying.

Tredi smashed into the room like a blitzing linebacker. Quite a crowd forced its way in behind him: Vatican and Italian cops, doctors, nurses, the chaplain.

"Out!" the pope commanded. "Everybody out."

They left. I got up to go, too.

"Not you, Paul," he said in a softer tone. "You're with us."

The pope carried a black leather bag. From it he took a battered prayer book, his stole, oils, and a communion host. He lit a candle and handed it to me.

"Luther's dying, Rico."

"We'll see."

"The doctor said—"

"I heard what the doctor said."

"The chaplain already gave him Last Rites."

"This is not Last Rites." His hands were flying through the wafer-thin prayer book pages.

"He pushed me out of the way. That's why he's lying here."

"I heard what happened."

"*They* did it. Back again—here. It's started all over again." He knew what I meant. History come back to life. First me. Then him.

"It's not important right now," the pope grunted. From a slash pocket in his white robe he fished out a half-frame pair of spectacles and put them on. I had never seen him in reading glasses before; I don't think anybody had.

"Hold the candle still, Paul," he said impatiently. "You are my witness."

He started reading in Latin. I could tell right away that it wasn't Last Rites, but I didn't know what it could be.

Special prayers?

What?

It took me a while to work it out while tears cascaded and the candle wobbled in my nerveless hands. It was a ritual as old as the church; passed in traceable, witnessed, direct, and unbroken line from Christ through two thousand years of bishops. Luther was being ordained.

I don't know how long it took, but by the end Tredi must have grown tired of squinting at the small Latin letters, for he closed the book, laid his hands on Luther's head, and said, simply, a few words invoking the Holy Spirit.

The pope smiled tightly.

"Welcome to the club, Luther," he said. He bent over and kissed Luther on the forehead.

I was too broken up to say anything, to react at all. I never felt the hot candle wax falling on my hands.

Tredi stood before Luther's bed for a long minute, his head bowed in silent prayer. He crossed himself.

"This is just insurance," he said quietly to the still body on the bed. "Some day we'll do it right. A big church, a lovely organ, the whole works."

Then he turned to me. Strength, determination flowed from him in compelling waves.

Maybe he was a holy man.

"Rico, he's dying," I began. "What difference—"

"Please shut up, Paul. And blow out the candle, or you'll burn the place down."

I tried but couldn't.

He blew it out, came over, and wrapped me in an *abrazo*.

Then the pope kissed me on the cheek and said in a conspirator's whisper, "Luther will make it, Paul."

It was 12:31 a.m. on the machine that monitored Luther's vital signs when Tredi left in the same controlled tumult with which he had arrived.

I heard the cars start up outside, imagined the flashing blue lights on the escorts, the radio traffic that would empty Roman streets for Tredi's return to the Vatican.

Within a few minutes, the whole hospital, it seemed, had found a compelling need to visit the room where the pope had prayed. After the first few, I closed the door with a scowl fierce enough to discourage the rest.

Then it was just the two of us, Luther and I.

And whatever aura Tredi had left.

At 2:23 a.m., Luther's heart stopped.

An alarm sounded, and at his bedside I jolted to my feet with a guilty start, wondering in panic what to do. But a nurse and a doctor with a long needle were there almost immediately. They must have seen it coming on a monitor at the nurses' station.

They did something and beeps returned, the green lines dancing again on the screen.

That is when I got down on my knees, laid my head against the bed, and started to pray.

At 4:41 a.m., the alarm sounded again.

This time the nurse and the needled doctor took longer to come and seemed to work with less urgency. Again the lines of life resumed their quiet ballet, but the doctor and the nurse left without saying anything, an eloquent silence.

I knew it was almost over.

Rico, where are you?

I must have opened my eyes every few minutes for the rest of that longest night, but the lines were always still there, slowly dancing.

Once, when I pressed Luther's hand, I convinced myself there was some responding pressure.

At 7:03 a.m., I came fully awake.

The surgeon who had worked on him the night before had returned. She was standing stock-still at the head of the bed, watching the monitors, studying the silent, blanket-shrouded form. I never knew how long she had been there.

When at last she looked over at me, I saw that something akin to awe had replaced the pain that had etched her eyes the night before.

"What happened to this man?" she asked quietly.

An icy blade lanced deep into my soul.

"He was shot. You know that." I focused despairingly at the monitors. "He's not . . . he can't be dead. Look, the lines are dancing. The lines are still dancing, don't you see?"

She looked back at Luther.

"No, he is not dead," she said. "He should be dead. But he is alive, and it may be that he will live."

I sat for a long time in the darkened church. Rome is a city that never denies sanctuary. Every neighborhood in a city of churches has quiet corners where it is possible to shelter from the storm of daily urban life. I needed refuge that morning. I was bone-tired, my nerves were running on empty, and I was madder than I had been in a long time.

However psyche-jarring, the search for killers of priests had been a professional exercise; even the protection of Tredi. But now someone had stepped out of my past into the streets of Rome to kill me, and Luther had been hit instead. That was personal, doubly personal. I didn't know who he was or, exactly, who had sent him, but I knew who some of his friends would be. I would see to them. Not rationally, I knew that. But I would collect payment for Luther's pain and my fear. Biblically.

Two old women in black walked down the middle aisle and lit candles on a stand by the baroque altar. A priest in an old-fashioned cassock walked the inside perimeter of the church, a cop on the beat, his gaze raking the side altars as he passed, checking, probing. He glanced over at me. I must have looked as rough as I felt, for I could sense him dropping me into the mental box he carried for "bums, unprayerful, hiding from the noise." I was prayed out. That much was true.

Either you have faith or you don't, and if you have it, there's no way to explain it to someone who doesn't.

Luther lived. I believed.

A suture of surgeons had followed the first one through Luther's room. They had asked her a lot of questions, looked at the monitor, stared hard at Luther, as though the fact of his living somehow undermined the fundament of their science. Eventually, the doctors had shrugged, thrown up their hands, and walked off. They were Italians, after all, weaned in the conviction that most things are understandable, but that others, a few, just happen. Medicine has limits. Luther's survival was a game played on some other field.

After the doctors left, the cops came. Three bored young Roman detectives appeared. They all wore fancier clothes than they should have, and knew less. I told them Luther had been the victim of a random shooting. Urban rage. A mugger. Mistaken identity. No, I didn't see the shooter, even a glimpse, and did it look to them like Luther himself was in a position to answer any questions? They didn't believe me, but none of us cared.

Later, I would call Tilly and tell her the same story. As news, it wouldn't make more than a few paragraphs in the local papers. If somebody heard a rumor of a late-night hospital visit by the pope, the Vatican Press Office could be counted on to deny it.

The cops had barely left when papal messenger Diego Altamirano hurtled in. "How is he, Paul? The Holy Father—"

"He is very gravely wounded, but the doctors now believe he will survive."

"Thank God." He seemed genuinely moved. "I must go quickly then. His Holiness is . . . well, he's been praying since before dawn in his private chapel. Please tell Father Luther that, that . . . well, you'll know what to say."

There were a lot of things of my own I wanted to say to Luther, but they'd have to wait. He was sleeping, licking his wounds someplace that Tredi had reached but I could never go.

By midmorning I was tossing in the spine-testing chair alongside the bed when a friendly hand nudged me awake.

"Go home, Paul, and get some sleep. You look worse than Luther."

His name was Mitch and he came from Norway. He wore the same open-faced sandals and gray woolen robes as Luther, had the same work-hardened hands and that air of assurance that only some people ever get.

"We'll take care of our brother now," said the second man. He was a monk named Louis, and he was an East African. I could never remember if he was a Hutu or a Tutsi, but Luther liked to brag that Louis was the best poet in Rome.

When I got back to St. Damian's, it was nearly noon, and Mikhail Ivanovic was sitting on the steps, fingers idly combing his great black beard. What a coincidence.

"How are you, Paul?"

"Fine, great. It's a lovely day."

"Tough night, though."

"No big deal. Luther got shot, Tredi made a miracle. I bounced around in the turbulence. Routine."

"But Luther's going to be all right. You, too."

"Of course I am. I was thinking of calling you, in fact. Just to talk things through."

"Smart man. But the reason I stopped by, in fact, is that I'm driving up to the mountains for a few days. Thought you might like to come along. Luther's in good hands. You know he's strong as an ox, and his people will be with him round the clock. We could walk, talk, drink a few gallons of that amazing Valpolicella."

We both understood, of course, that he had "stopped by" because the pope had dragged him out of bed and told him to haul his hairy Jungian ass over to soothe star shrinkee Brother Paul.

"I'd really like to, Mikhail, but there's Luther, and other stuff. Two murders—"

"Paul, a few days of fresh air; that can all wait. You deserve a few days off." Need, he meant. "A long weekend and you'll be back, a new man."

I knew he was right and I did not want to go, but it was a no-win situation for crazy old Brother Paul. I could dig in my heels and Ivanovic would go away, but that would anger the pope. Tredi might not send guys after me in white coats and a net. But he had before. Besides, when I thought about it, being out of Rome for a few days would suit me fine. Neither Tredi nor Ivanovic had to know that. So I let myself be persuaded.

"Okay, let's do it," I said at length, after Ivanovic had waxed lyrical about everything from the purity of the mountain air to the assumed impurity of the broad-hipped serving wench in the priests' house where we stayed. "But I've been up all night. I need a shower and some sleep, and there's an important staff meeting here tonight at St. Damian's and a lot of administrative junk to do afterward. Remember that time we left really late? Let's do it again. One, two in the morning. Easy driving then, and we'll get there in time to see the sun rise over that cleft in the mountains."

That warmed my Ukrainian shrink's romantic soul. "Great, I'll be ready anytime after midnight. Give me a shout. And let me leave you these. Just in case you have trouble falling asleep."

He handed me a paper bag with a flat box inside. I didn't have to look.

"The blue things? Again?"

"Maybe just for a day or two."

"They kick like a mule, you know. Make me forget where I forgot the other half of me."

"That'll be the day. See you tonight."

Back inside St. Damian's, I did take a shower. And I did take one of the blue tablets out of its foil pouch. But only to flush it down the toilet. Ivanovic wanted me to smooth out the wrinkles of my corrugated mind. I wanted to feed my anger.

I slept until the shops reopened around four in the afternoon. Then, on a borrowed *motorino,* I visited a half-dozen different hardware stores and garden supply shops in different parts of the city. For an hour I sat alone in the basement at St. Damian's. I was all thumbs at first, fingers balky, but the skills had returned by the time I was finished. Some things are never forgotten.

That night I made a point of being visible and voluble at the staff meeting. Then I went to the hospital. Luther was resting comfortably, the doctors said. In his room, two monks sat companionable watch. One of them had a thick wooden club on the floor next to his chair.

Around eleven, I left a sleeping St. Damian's and stole through the night. I cut my hand on some glass a little while later, but the windows were easy, there was only one balky door and two stubborn locks.

And an embarrassment of riches at rainbow's end. An easy run, considering.

I did some serious scurrying after that, including a quick and anonymous stop at the Vatican, but I was waiting on the steps of St. Damian's, feeling about as loose and as calm as unstable Brother Paul ever gets, when Ivanovic pulled up around one in the morning.

Normally, by that hour, even Rome begins to get a break from its traffic monster. Not that night.

On the Luongotevere heading north from the center, it was bumper to bumper. Three times, screaming police cars fought their way past with impotent fire trucks in their wake. By the time we crossed the Tiber at a bridge statued by Mussolini and pointed toward the *autostrada,* we could see the reason: smoke spiraling from a hilltop *palazzo.*

"A nasty fire," Ivanovic said.

I nodded without speaking, for I was lolling in the embracing cocoon of an integrating blue pill. My cut hand hurt like hell and a shoulder muscle was aching. It had been a high and nasty wall. But my mind was at ease and my conscience drowsed companionably alongside.

19

ON THE WAY to Naples the following week, I fell asleep on the Vatican bus, head pressed against the glass as the *autostrada* unfolded south from Rome. I had shrunk nicely, thanks, cosseted by Mikhail Ivanovic from early morning until the moment the blackberry *grappa* claimed its price late in the mountain darkness. When Mikhail's chin folded into his beard, I'd drag us both off to bed. The first few days, I slept twelve hours straight. Little by little, I felt my head coming back together. By the fifth day, I had run out of the blue pills, and when I asked Ivanovic he said never mind.

What I never told him was that the whole time there in the mountains I kept replaying the death curse that Patricio Caballero had laid against me as I led him to the hanging tree. Ever since the cemetery slaughter—Focus, Aim, Steady, Squeeze—I'd have sworn there weren't any Caballeros left to come looking for me. But I must have missed one. So be it.

Back in Rome, I had gone straight to the hospital. Luther looked gray, old, and tired. But he was very much alive, sitting up in bed when I walked in, reading his breviary. He brightened immediately. "Paul! Welcome back."

When his guardian monks wandered off in search of a *cappuccino,* Luther regarded me appraisingly.

"How are you? I've been worried about you."

Me! "I'm fine. You're the one—"

"I'm a walking miracle, that's what people tell me. The hospital priest's gaga, all the nuns. Doctors don't know what to say. It's great, except it's nonsense. Nothing miraculous about an ornery sonofabitch surviving one more bullet . . ."

"Luther, I don't know exactly how to say this, but I owe you—"

"That's what I told the Holy Father when he sneaked in here the other night. I said, 'I hope you haven't come to check your miracle, Holy Father, because it isn't,' and he burst out laughing. 'Luther,' he said, 'people die when the good Lord decides. He must have something more in mind for you.' I said, 'Well, I certainly wouldn't want to die before I was ordained, now that I've come this far.'"

I nodded encouragingly. Ecclesiastical niceties are for popes to sort out. "How was the pope?"

"Fine. We talked for a few minutes and he left, zoom zoom. Came on a *motorino,* Paul, can you believe that? Wearing a big helmet. Nobody looked at him twice. Maybe he left Diego downstairs. Hope so. I sure don't like him out like that . . ."

He ran down and I could see that his wound was aching. There was just one thing.

"Luther, that shot was meant for me. I . . . There are some things about me—"

"Paul, listen. I caught a glimpse of the shooter: young, in a red baseball cap with a long brim, standing in a doorway. He shot me because I was the first target, the easiest target. Either one of us would have suited him fine. Or both. Watch your ass."

Tredi's office had invented a meaningless and suitably

vague title for me as an excuse to tag along on his quick-hit visit to Naples, so I rode the two hours down from Rome in the bus carrying the Vatican retinue and security agents.

On the way, resplendent in my not-quite priest black-and-white suit, I had absorbed the *Il Messaggero* account of the pope's sortie to beatify a thirteenth-century nun who had apparently died rather than surrender her virtue under duress. Another front-page story quoted Rome's fire chief to say that arson was responsible for the fire that had damaged the headquarters of the Sacred Keys. Imagine.

In the fullness of time, the Vatican retinue bus and two trailing buses full of reporters spilled under a heavy Mediterranean sun onto an Italian air base north of the city. No long bus rides for His Holiness. He'd join us by helicopter and lead the caravan from his popemobile as it entered boisterous Naples itself. Papal prerogative. And safer, too.

There was a VIP lounge at the base, but most of my fellow prelates ignored the sandwiches and inviting glasses of white wine. Instead, almost as one, they headed for the toilet. Papal visits can be an agonizing test of endurance for aging males in long skirts. Bathrooms on the road are often few and far between. I was washing my hands, when in the mirror above the sink I saw a familiar face and turned to find Bishop Beccar, prefect of the Sacred Keys, waiting his turn.

"Good morning, Your Excellency. How are you today?"

"Well, thank you." I had worn street clothes to meet him with Franco Galli, but he placed me immediately nonetheless. He didn't like me—and he didn't know the half of it. "I trust you are also well."

Not often you pack so much hypocrisy into two sentences.

"I was sorry to hear of your loss," I said.

"The Lord tests us all. We shall endure," he said, with a thin smile that he wished would turn me into a pillar of salt.

After a while, pope visits are a bit like dancing. You can sometimes add a wrinkle here or there, but it is basically a one-two-three. Amid tight security in Naples, Tredi would ride to the cathedral for a meeting with local priests and nuns. Then lunch with local notables and leaders of other religions, followed by the main event, the outdoor beatification mass in the Palazzo Reale in the heart of old Naples. In late afternoon, he'd spend some time at a youth rally and—chopper, chopper—home again in time for dinner at the Vatican. The rest of us buslings would be lucky to get back before midnight—or encounter much dinner along the way.

I wandered out of the lounge and onto the tarmac where the reporters waited for the pope's arrival in a not-too-military-looking helicopter mooched for the day from the Italian Air Force. It was a beautiful day with only a few puffy clouds. Off in the distance I could see the sun glinting off Naples Bay and, beyond, the majestic cone of Vesuvius.

In the crowd of reporters, Maria was impossible to miss. She had let her hair down, black tresses cascading along her back. She was vivacious and relaxed. As a middle-aged cynic needing no evidence, I put it down, wistfully and wishfully, to her discovery of regular sex. Probably I was wrong, because underneath the new exterior beat the same molten converter's heart.

"Brother Paul, how are you? I've been hoping to bump into you today. Do you have a second?" To make sure that I did, she tugged me by the arm over to a quiet corner.

"Travel obviously agrees with you, *linda,* you look wonderful," I offered, when she had alighted in a strategic spot that allowed her simultaneously to see me and the approaching dot that was Tredi's chopper.

"You're very kind. It's nice to get away from Rome, but I'm exhausted. I've been working with volunteers at the Keys house, cleaning up the mess."

"I'm sorry about the fire."

"The fire itself was the least of it. It was small and only destroyed the computer center and some nearby offices. But the sprinklers went crazy and there is a lot of water damage, plus the smell of smoke everywhere. I scrubbed myself for hours afterward, but I can still smell it. I hate that smell."

"Terrible thing, fire." Ouch. And more damage than I had intended. There hadn't been time to copy the Keys's computer disks, and sometimes a small electrical fire can cover a multitude of sins. I had called in the alarm a few minutes after it had started. In retrospect, if I had known about the overexuberant sprinklers, I might have thought of something else.

"But the fire won't stop us, Paul. Bishop Beccar says we must rise like the legendary phoenix, to fly higher than ever."

Then, in a rush she must have rehearsed, Maria floored me: "It is the Sacred Keys that I wanted to talk to you about, Paul. I know that you love the church and that you have an open mind. I'd like you to come and meet some of my Keys friends one night when we get back. Just to listen and to chat. Come with me. I'd like that."

A recruiting pitch. Brother Paul, religious storm trooper. *Achtung!*

"Well, I . . . but Maria . . . yes, I'm committed to the faith but—"

"You're a man of God, Paul, a man who has a special relationship with the Holy Father."

Aha. The Holy Father.

"We want you for yourself, of course. And if you came to know the truth about us, about our society and our dreams, who knows, one day you might be able to show the Holy Father . . ."

She wanted a spy! Was espionage a contagious Vatican disease? I thought of Tredi, his cockamamie scheme of sending two priests against the Keys. And look what had happened to them.

"Maria, I'm flattered. I know you don't make this offer lightly. But what is it that I could ever show, or tell, the Holy Father about your society that he doesn't already know?"

"That's the point. You've hit it!" She was excited now, reaching across to take my hand. "We, I, think he may be suspicious of us, that he does not understand that we want only the best for the church. Don't you see?"

"Yes, I think I do," I said slowly.

Careful, Paul, careful.

"I'm not much on politics, Maria, but I have the feeling that the Keys—you—are not convinced of the Holy Father's plans for the church and the direction in which he may lead her?"

"Lamentably, that is true. We believe that the church must be able to count on the Holy Father, to trust him for proper leadership and direction. If not—" She stopped.

"If not, what?"

Find a new pope?

"Then we do whatever is necessary to persuade him. We are the one true faith. Without the unified leadership that only the Supreme Pontiff can give, we are as the savages, no different from any other religion."

"And you think I might be able to be a bridge, to bring things together."

"Yes, Paul, yes."

"I'm honored that you've asked me, *linda.*" I took her hand. It was sweaty with tension. "I'll think seriously about it."

When hell freezes over.

When next I saw the pope, Tredi was on show and in great splendor. He stood tall, a smiling, universally recognized figure waving to the faithful as his popemobile cut through the huge throng along the Naples waterfront.

Any pope is most exposed at large outdoor ceremonies. The most dangerous time is usually in those few minutes in a *piazza* or stadium or race track when the pope rides the outlandish, see-through machine the world knows as a popemobile. As you might have guessed, the Vatican decided that popemobiles should have sides right after Wojtyla was shot riding open-sided through St. Peter's Square in 1981. And if the sides in contemporary popemobiles look like glass, they are indeed bulletproof. But there are bullets, and there are bullets. Security agents and snipers monitor every instant of his passage. Every cop holds his breath until the foolish thing is empty again.

Anything-goes Naples is a city whose middle name is Chaos, but that day the pope's mass there went smooth as silk. Striding from the popemobile, Tredi mounted a forty-foot-high altar backed by an artist's conception of what soon-to-be-beatified Sister Concetta might have looked like seven centuries ago. Moon-faced, pining, and suitably virginal.

With dozens of his fellow bishops concelebrating at the altar around him, Tredi honored the old nun with obvious commitment. His homily was about the power of brother-hood and the virtues of justice, the sort of pronouncement calculated to make a point in a city gripped by a violent, cunning homegrown Mafia called Camorra.

As Tredi reached the climax of the mass, the consecration of bread and wine into the body and blood of Christ, I went backstage to find an alb to put over my priest suit. Brothers cannot consecrate; that is reserved for priests. But brothers, like lay Catholics well schooled in Catholic dogma, are wel-come to dispense communion once the hosts have been con-secrated. So many thousands take communion at a papal mass that it is all priests and look-alikes on deck when it is time to distribute the host.

In the changing room under the altar, a map divided the crowd into giant rectangles bounded by rope barriers. Each had its own number. In a system well known and laid out weeks before, my name was penciled in for twenty-eight, a suitably junior posting to the left and almost to the end of the long *piazza* before the palace of the Spanish kings who once ruled Naples.

A fussy little bishop came over and said, "Father, there are more people than we anticipated. Once you have finished twenty-eight, would you please help out at thirty-four?"

"A pleasure." I didn't correct him. Brother, Father, he didn't care. He needed bodies and slick fingers. I've seen experienced priests distribute nearly thirty hosts a minute without mumbling too obviously. You have to say in the language of the mass "the body of Christ" to each communicant as you pass the host. One priest's trick is that the Latin *"Corpus Christi"* is universally acceptable, and a bit faster. I'm not the fastest host-giver in church, but I'm no slouch; a twenty-two-a-minute man at my peak.

We must have been an impressive sight, a long, thin black and white line filing toward the altar to pick up hosts for communion. Most priests have their own ciborium and are honored to use it at a papal mass. I didn't, of course, nor did I have a ciborium for the hosts, but I lucked out when picking randomly among the spares as we waited to go on. It was big and had heft; heavy enough to be solid silver. It was old and beat-up; its original owner had probably gone to his reward long since.

Out in zone twenty-eight, hundreds of people were waiting for me. I walked slowly along the rope, passing the host to communicants in front, and then, leaning forward, to those in a second row behind them. *"Il corpo di Cristo . . . Il corpo di Cristo . . . Il corpo . . ."*

By the time I got to the end of the line and walked back to start again, the people who had received communion had been replaced by two new rows of at least temporarily devout Catholics with open mouths.

Sometimes, funny things happen when you pass out the round, unleavened hosts. People faint. They choke. Young kids pee. People drop the host and curse violently as they scrabble on the floor to recover their very own piece of eternity. But in Naples everything went smoothly. These were Italians, and they knew their communion.

I scurried along with scarcely a hitch, seeing more bridgework than faces, although there were a few worth remembering, and, ultimately, one that I would not forget.

After fifteen minutes, my arm was beginning to ache and the ciborium was heading toward empty. I was eyeing the crowd, trying to guess whether I'd have to do a loaves and fishes: breaking in half the remaining hosts to be sure of having enough for all. That's when it happened.

I leaned forward into the second row, coming face-to-face with a swarthy young man with a thick droopy black mustache. Not Italian. A Latino, my mind registered automatically. Most communicants' eyes are reverently downcast as they receive the host, but his burned with hate.

As I pressed forward, the host in my right hand, so did he. I sensed rather than saw the long blade as it came lancing toward me. I moved reflexively, catching the edge of it with the metal ciborium, jarring it off-course.

Hosts went flying, I heard fabric rip and simultaneously felt a searing along my forearm. I staggered, winced in pain. It must have looked as if I had slipped or was having an attack.

"*Padre, Padre,*" people were shouting. A young man ducked under the rope and steadied me. A security usher came rushing over.

"Blood. You're bleeding, *Padre.*"

"I'm okay, I'm okay," I said. As people gathered the spilled hosts and someone handed me a crisp white handkerchief, my eyes parsed the crowd.

He was gone. He had had only a few seconds to break away and he had used them well, for I could catch no glimpse of the Latino who had come to communion to kill me.

At least the pope was safe. By the time I caught up with Tredi in an indoor arena, he was sitting in a tall-backed throne with two magisterial arms and a tall, carved frame. The pope's meeting with young people was being staged as a dialogue between pope and people. Groups of students would act out a scene while a narrator read a passage of the laboriously assembled morality it was supposed to illustrate. Then the pope would respond, adding a lesson of his own. Vatican planners had borrowed the routine from the travels of the Holy Pole. It was the first time Tredi had tried it, and I could see from his body language that he thought it was boring.

I was late because it had taken a while to work my way to an aid station where a tut-tutting young doctor obligingly sewed up my forearm. I told him I had fallen against a metal stake, and so after the stitches and bandages there was a further wait while they tracked down an obligatory tetanus shot. He gave me a handful of pain pills and sent me on my way, tut-tut, to fall no more. By then, of course, the Vatican motorcades were long gone and I was marooned with half of Naples on the streets around me. Mercifully, the combination of my dog collar and a Vatican credential was enough to convince a cop to give me a ride to the youth meeting.

"Hey, Paul, how are you? Great show, isn't it? I think he's really enjoying himself." Diego Altamirano's eyes were bright with enthusiasm as he joined me at the foot of the stage.

"Yeah, great."

"Man, I don't know about you, but I need a shower, the hotter the better." He stretched. "I feel like I personally gave communion to that whole crowd. Talk about pushing and shoving."

"Shower'd be good."

"It was my first time. What a rush. Didn't I see you out there, too?"

"I was there."

I had thought about reporting the attack to the police and to Vatican security and decided not to. I had been that day's target, and the knifer would have as much trouble as anybody else moving around the pope-choked city. He was not likely to try twice the same day. Still, it would have been unprofessional not to have at least alerted Diego. He was the pope's last line of defense, after all.

"Diego, somebody has told the cops that there's a *loco* on the streets with a knife and a grudge against the pope. Tall, skinny, black eyes, droopy black mustache. Keep your eyes open."

"Brother Paul, you know I will."

The drudgery on the stage limped to a close to lukewarm applause, and for a moment I thought we might be able to escape, but an unctuous young monsignor jumped up with a microphone.

"Holy Father, as you know, students come from all over the world to Naples to study at our fine universities. As a special treat, some of them have prepared a musical salute to celebrate your own Latin American heritage."

Seven or eight musicians filed nervously onto the stage with a bizarre continental melange of instruments: guitar, charango, a bombo, a Mexican horn, even a quena. It had the makings of a disaster. They were scruffy for the most part, and young, except for one striking woman with the beginnings of a rice 'n' beans ass who carried maracas. Tredi smiled wanly.

They had me halfway through the first number; alive, rhythmic, come-and-get-it, bursting with life and color. I don't know if it was folk music, or salsa, more of a Naples-born combination, really, but it pounded deep into my past, and spoke to my soul. I was soaring. By the second number, the arena was rocking, alive, vibrant. Standing next to me, Altamirano was moving in time to the music. I could see the pope's toe tapping.

It was the third number, or maybe the fourth, that did it. Tredi stood up, gave a sinuous wiggle, and clicked his fingers above his head. He sloped over to the band and spoke to the woman with the maracas. I couldn't hear the words, but I could read his lips: two words in Spanish.

"Bailamos, linda," the pope invited. You had to be Latino

to understand the affection and kinship in the invitation. The Vatican Press Office reported with political correctness that the pope had asked, "Would you like to dance, Señora?"

In an instant, a whole palette of emotions raced across the woman's face: surprise, shock, rapture that was born with a huge smile of pure joy.

And so His Holiness Pope Pius XIII bobbed chastely around the stage, holding the woman at arm's length. It was an old-fashioned, brother-sister sort of dance that didn't last long and never quite meshed with the throb of the beat but had a lot of wiggle.

Pandemonium.

The arena was on its feet. Young people's cheers burst in wave after wave over their dancing pope. The pope's dance would make every TV news and every front page. In the jubilant aftermath, I decided to ride home with the reporters: more fun than the Vatican crowd, every time.

"What a showman, Paul. What an advertisement for the faith." Tilly was high on delight. But Tilly the reporter as ever dueled with Tilly the ardent Catholic. She asked more seriously, "Do you think it was planned?"

"Spur of the moment. Didn't you see the music turning him on?"

"And you don't suppose he happened to know about Carmen De Lama, the woman he danced with?"

"I'm sure he never set eyes on her. Who is she, anyway?"

"Oh, Carmen is from Panama; she's in Naples teaching a specialists' seminar in the medical school. Turns out she just happens to be a very Catholic mother of four who may also be the best pediatric surgeon in all of Latin America."

Maybe he did know, at that.

It was a happy ride home, and it never occurred to me that there might be another side to the pope's dance until Rome, when I bumped into Maria as she left the second press bus. Her hair was tangled, her shoulders slumped, the light absent from those wonderful eyes.

I asked, "Has it rained on your parade, *linda?*"

"I'm sick, sick at heart."

"Tell Uncle Paul."

She was on the verge of tears. "Popes don't dance, Paul. Real popes don't dance at all."

I made some reassuring noises. I couldn't share her view, but I could understand it. My own high spirits were pretty good though. My arm hurt like hell, true. But I'd know the knifer if I saw him again. And it had occurred to me on the bus where I might go looking for him before he found me.

20

I HAD NO time to dwell on threats or jitterbugging popes when I got home. There was a crisis at St. Damian's that only doughty Brother Paul could possibly resolve. That's what Father Rector said when I tracked him down, grim-visaged and alone, after finding a message from him at the portico to the house and another on my bed. At least there were no carnations: just a lonely old man's appeal to wrestle with human nature.

"This has happened before, of course, it is only to be expected. But this case is, shall we say, flagrant. There is a confession," the rector said from behind a dark wooden desk from which he had intimidated generations of future priests. Making a teepee of well-manicured fingers, he dryly recounted the details of the crime. There was an elaborate counseling system for seminarians at St. Damian's, and he knew I knew that. We both also knew he was retiring at the end of term. He wanted to go gracefully, and he was determined to go quietly.

"What exactly would you like me to do, Father Rector?"

"Well, I want you to resolve it, Brother Paul. Fix it. You must know how. I . . . these things . . ."

There are some basic facts of life, even at the Vatican, and one of them is that even if you lock up young men who have a strong vocation to be priests in the most antiseptic surroundings, even if you send them to school all day and pray them all night, even if you exhort them spiritually and exhaust them physically, they will still have sex drives. I thought about telling Father Rector that sometimes even the pope woke up with a tumescent penis, but then I thought better of it. If he choked on his false teeth, sure as churches have candles somebody would call Brother Fixit to resuscitate the old goat.

The first thing I did was to wash off the travel dust, and that required finding plastic bags to wrap around my arm so I wouldn't, tut-tut, get the dressing wet. Did you ever try to find plastic bags in a house for seminarians in Rome on a Sunday night? All of which did not improve my appetite for the second thing I had to do, which was to march into the room of a seminarian named Piotr Muesen, a phlegmatic—I thought—Dutchman in his second year of theology.

He was a tall, thin young man with a sharp Adam's apple and one of the best minds in the place. He cringed when I walked in. "Bless me, Father, for I have sinned," he said from the far corner of the small room, his head on his knees atop a neatly made bed.

"I am a brother, not a priest, Piotr. And I'm not here to talk about sin but to ask you a favor."

"I am sorry, Brother. I thought the Father Rector . . ." He was swimming slowly through deep waters. "To ask me a favor? Have you not spoken with the Father Rector?"

"Yes, I have spoken with him, Piotr. He tells me that you have had feelings of carnal desire toward one of our classmates."

"But it is true, Brother Paul. It's Augustus," he said, naming a dark-haired, well-built first-year student from Austria who had more muscles than brains. "Augu is beautiful. I want to touch him."

"Does Augustus know you care for him? Have you actually, uh, touched him?"

"No, of course not. I am so ashamed."

Rector, schmector.

"Let me see if I understand this. This is a desire that came over you in the past few days. And you rushed to tell the rector. And now you think that you are not fit to be a priest."

Quavering lips, the beginning of tears. Hangdog heaven.

"Piotr, the rector has asked me to mention to you, and I am sure he did himself, that at some stage of their training every priest faces such temptations. That is what they are. Temptations. They are sent to try us. It might have been women, or drink, or even theft. Temptations exist to be conquered. And once you have conquered them, you will be a better priest for having endured them. That is what the rector asked me to tell you."

What the dessicated old bastard had said was, "Get him out of this house, Brother. Do it now." What was I supposed to do? Send the poor kid to sleep in the railroad station?

I am only a brother, but I am also an authority figure. Some of my hot air seemed to have hit home. I could see Piotr readjusting his mental position, so I forged ahead.

"What I'd like you to do is help a priest friend of mine who is in the hospital. It is not an easy assignment, so if you think it is too difficult, please say so." He was sitting straight-backed and attentive at the edge of the bed now. "Father Luther is recovering from a grave injury, but he has had some traumatic memory loss. I want you to become his companion, and to help him regain his memory."

"But, how will I know . . ."

"You will go to classes as usual each morning. When you get to the hospital afterward, you must recount to Father Luther in detail what you have learned that day. Bring him your books. If he remembers that he knows about a particular subject, you will stop and tell him something else. If he has not remembered, you will tell him all you know; read him your notes on a particular course from the beginning if necessary. You will eat your meals at the hospital and sleep there until Father Luther believes he can cope without you. Can you do that, Piotr?"

"Yes, Fath . . . Brother. I can! I will!"

Luther was a VIP at the hospital, so nobody even bothered to tell me that visiting hours were over when Piotr and I showed up a little while later. He was talking with a companion monk when I walked in.

"Hey, look who's home from the ball. Who'd *you* dance with, Paul?"

"Under Vatican rules, only bishops and above may dance. The rest of us must trudge."

I explained about Piotr. "Good deal. My guys are stretched thin enough without having to baby-sit me on the night shift," he said. And after the other monk left, Luther gestured toward the bulky dressing that a long-sleeved shirt did not quite hide, and said softly, "Tell me about the arm, Paul. It must have happened in Naples."

I told him about the mustachioed attacker. His eyes narrowed and I saw some of the old fire return.

"Come at you like that, there's no defense. While you're giving communion. Scum. Lucky about the ciborium."

"Yeah, but the good news is that it's me they're after. Maybe it has nothing to do with the pope. That's what I keep hoping. Forlornly, I'm afraid."

We kicked it around a bit, trying to smother fear with familiarity, I suppose, but there was no realistic way that I could slice the apple without seeing the pope as its core. There was a narrowing of focus, payback closing in.

One. Two. Three.

Jimmy Kearns. Luca Caruso. Gustavo Vidal.

Three priests, three papal allies. Murdered.

Four was Brother Paul. Still hanging on. But Luther already a casualty; collateral damage.

If that was the logic, the progression, if that is how the drums of vengeance were beating, then there was no way it could stop there.

Five.

His Holiness Pius XIII.

And then Luther said, "The guy who shot me, Paul, I don't remember much, but I have this image, the shape of the face, really. I wouldn't know him for sure if he came to change my bedpan, but there was no mustache, no mustache at all. I'm sure."

Two hit men? One for me. Another one for the pope?

As I was leaving, Luther said, "One thing about this kid Piotr. He's supposed"—Luther paused to think through what he wanted to say—"this stuff he's supposed to teach me. I probably know some of it from what I've picked up. But I'll bet a lot of it is going to be pretty deep. I'm not sure I can do it."

"Don't sweat that. There's an easy solution."

"What?"

"If you find yourself over your head intellectually, you can still become a simple brother."

He laughed again, the old Luther laugh. Back from the brink. There were tears of thanksgiving in my eyes when my aching arm and I left the hospital.

The next morning I spent in Franco Galli's office, surfing through computer pictures of civilians and clerics with Vatican passes.

A hunch, and it paid off, for I was back at the hospital before noon with some faces for Luther to check out. Among them was the picture of a Mexican named Luis Cubillas. His mustache in the photo was crisp, to the point, when it was taken two years before as he began work for the Keys.

It was shaggier these days—now that he was slashing people who offered him communion. He was there in Caruso's address book, too. Shaggy Cubillas, it turned out, was not a priest. Not a brother. He was a deacon, a sort of halfway rank to accommodate lay people with a yearning to be religious while at the same time pursuing civilian ways of life.

Deacons could be married, or they might be priests-in-the-making. Either way, they had the right to wear ecclesiastical clothing in certain circumstances.

Which meant that Cubillas could have been the figure in priest's clothing that nearsighted Father Pevec had seen with Caruso in the walkway.

Did Cubillas also stuff Vidal into the piano? His name wasn't on the guest list that night, but that didn't mean anything in a freeloaders' heaven like the Vatican. And Cubillas was certainly tough enough to have done the job.

Galli was delighted that I had at long last produced an honest-to-God suspect. But Luther didn't help.

"None of these, Paul, not even close." Luther shook his head emphatically and handed me back the stack of pictures. Cubillas, front and side view, was number three among them.

I tried to cover my disappointment. "As long as you're sure."

"I'm sure. It was, I don't know, younger, a better face, rounder, softer; a face I might have known. Sorry, but it runs away from me."

The next couple of days I spent nosing around for Deacon Cubillas. I watched people going in and out of the smoke-stained Keys headquarters. Nothing.

I even paid a late-night visit to the address that Cubillas had given the Vatican as his residence in Rome. A quiet apartment in a green and expensive quarter of the city. Second floor, two bedrooms, nice place. Juvenile locks. Unlived in. Echoingly empty. Cold as the grave.

• • •

When I got to his apartment one evening later that week, the pope was staring fixedly at a computer screen. He waved me in.

"I thought it might be fun, solving the problems of the church, the world. Well, let me tell you, it's a royal pain," he said. "There are days when I wish that, in the conclave, the Holy Spirit had led me to vote for that squinty-eyed Brazilian."

Tredi's maiden papal visit to New York was approaching, and Diego Altamirano had told me that he was working so hard on his speeches that not even cardinals could get fifteen minutes.

If ever anybody had needed a change of pace . . .

I asked, "Are you suggesting grilled or sautéed?"

"Huh?"

I nodded toward the computer. "The word around is that you're working on a recipe book for tilapia—"

"Blessed tilapia!" It did me good to hear him laugh. "Fact is, the damned things died, my brother says. I got word this morning. A virus or something; killed a whole generation of the fish of the future. Bobby's very upset. I tried to call him, but he's gone off somewhere. Heaven only knows what he'll get up to next."

I didn't have to wait long to find out why Tredi had asked me to come, for he tossed me a thin file of papers in a black folder. "Some light reading for you while I finish my speech," he invited. The cover bore a one-line message: "For the Eyes of the Holy Father Only."

"Sister Gertrude did it for me. Do you know her?"

"By reputation." Everybody knew Sister Gertrude by name. She was a tall Irish nun and the Vatican's premier computer wizard, an almost legendary figure who had almost single-handedly transported Vatican bookkeeping from the fifteenth to the twenty-first century.

"Even more impressive in person," the pope muttered, turning back to his own machine.

"Analysis of certain CD-ROMS left anonymously at the Porta Sant'Anna gate," the nun began. I read with great attention.

"The disks contain current financial and administrative data documenting systematic illegal activity by the Society of the Sacred Keys," the report said. And went on with a luxury of detail to say that the Keys received large regular transfers of money—millions too much for a religious institution—from banks in Colombia, Miami, Switzerland, and the Cayman Islands. The money flowed into the Vatican Bank, and most of it went back out again to accounts in Luxembourg and Guernsey. Elaborate, but not terribly sophisticated.

A big-time money laundry. Drug money. What else? I knew from my own researches that all the money jobs at the Keys were handled by civilians; most holies around the Vatican can't count past the number of beads on their rosaries. I'd bet the Keys spiritual types like Bishop Beccar never had a clue.

Still, the disks should provide the leverage Tredi needed against the Keys. Malfeasance by officials within the church is as old as the church itself. So, too, the church's way of dealing with it. As an institution, the church thrives on indirection.

"Well, this is what the doctor ordered, isn't it?" I said, when the pope finished the assault on his keyboard with a machine-gun burst.

"Yeah, that should do it," he replied. "With the stuff that Gustavo Vidal, God rest him, brought back from South America, this just about closes the circle."

"The Keys and the Caballeros. I still can't believe it. You're going to zap the Keys, aren't you?"

Tredi just grunted. Then he sandbagged me. "What do

you know about those computer disks left like a convenient orphan at my front door, *hermano?"*

"I'm not all that bad with computers, you know. CD ROM disks, for example, are an easy and portable way to store a lot of information; they've replaced the bulkier old reel-to-reel tapes almost everywhere by now. The technology . . ."

He glared at me for what felt like a long time. I guess he knew I wouldn't lie to him directly. There had been no time to copy them. I felt twinges of conscience about the fire, but none about the actual theft. Besides, the worst of what had happened in the old *palazzo* was collateral damage. Like Luther.

In the end, Tredi let it go. I guess we both understood that there are some secrets popes should not know. With a long sigh, the pope stretched his back, rolled his shoulders, and trundled over to a portable bar in the corner. He poured two longshoremen's shots of a single malt whiskey he favors when he's not drinking rum and brought mine over.

"Cheers," the pope said.

Tredi had deep lines of fatigue on his face and pouches under his eyes I had never seen before. He kept squeezing his eyes with a thumb and forefinger, as if to drive away pain. I hadn't had a chance to tell him about Naples, and when I got to the part about the knifer with the shaggy mustache, I could almost see new weight settling on his shoulders.

It occurred to me then how much I loved this man, this holy and solitary figure, thrust by ambition and history into a role canted more to frustration and suffering than to success.

Suffering was the constant, wasn't it? For a moment I saw the tragic and haunting Doctor Longhi who had been Caruso's lover, studying a soulless X ray that spelled death for their child.

Maybe Tredi was reading my mind, for he asked, "Will you find who's behind it, Paul? Behind Caruso and Vidal? The man who shot Luther?"

"I think so. I think the Mexican did Vidal and Luther.

Maybe Caruso, too. There's somebody else, bigger, and I'll get him, too—sooner or later."

"I'm going to honor them, you know, Caruso and Vidal. Not by name, but they'd understand. I know He'll understand." Tredi's forefinger pointed up, straight up.

"Caruso's, uh, friend, the doctor, she'll be pleased," I said. "She made a very strong impression on me." It was an understatement. I thought about her a lot, without knowing what to do about it.

Tredi nodded. He got up and started to pace. "Yes, the beautiful doctor and her even more beautiful dying daughter. Thanks for telling me about them. I invited them in, did I tell you? We had a good, long talk. She hates the church, you know. I tried to explain that I loved Luca Caruso as much as she did, but I don't know if she was able to believe that truth."

The pope walked some more in silence, a bear of a man striding across the brittle skeleton of an antique church. At length, he said, "Paul, you don't suppose Caruso's the only priest who ever fell in love with a beautiful woman? Do you think he's the only one who ever wanted to?"

"We're all of us human, Rico." Did he know about Tilly?

"And the church? Jesus was divine, but also human. That's what we believe, isn't it? So the church must tread a line between the two, must it not—interpreting the divine and the good to the fallible and the human."

No room here for the simple brother shuffle, so I kept my mouth shut and paid attention: Tredi was testing aloud something he'd just hammered into the computer.

"But, there are huge differences between the church's interpretation and the public's acceptance on key issues, aren't there? Contraception, celibacy, women priests, divorce, moral relativism. Can you be a cafeteria Catholic, taking what you like of church teaching and leaving the rest? Are you still a Catholic if you do that? You could say there are huge differences of opinion on all these questions, Paul,

but chasms is more like it. Deep, angry, unbridgeable. There
are great gulfs, and they threaten to pull us apart."

I listened.

"I'm not afraid of these questions. But if I pick one, hack
at it, the danger is that all the others will fester. Still, I can't
ignore them either, can I, dig deep dogmatic shelters and
hunker down? They won't go away." He took a last swallow
of whiskey. "But what if I say that all the problems need to
be addressed and that I'm going to attack them all at the
same time? That ought to rattle a cage or two, no?"

Or set the church on fire, I thought. Schism. The one word
that everybody around the Vatican hates worst.

But then Tredi explained how he was going to do it.

"Maybe I'll be gone by the climax," he said, with a shrug.
"If I am, the next guy can worry about it." Tredi drained his
glass, and I saw that the fire had returned to his eyes. "What
do you think, *hermano?*"

"I think you're a genius." I raised my own glass in salute.
"A lot of people will think you're a saint—"

"But," he finished the sentence for me, "others will curse
me for a heretic." He chuckled. "It's an occupational hazard,
comes with the territory."

Claudio Russo, the wiry Vatican security boss, was hovering as I left.

"Brother Paul, if you please . . . " He led me into a quiet
waiting room. "There's something I think you should see."

When he handed me four stiff white cards, I understood
why.

Russo said, "The Holy Father gets much mail, as you
know, and not all of it is flattering, so there is a procedure for
problem letters. Most are from cranks, but these . . . well,
they have come over the past few weeks and we think they
may signal a serious threat to His Holiness."

Hard to disagree. Each card bore a drawing in a red ink
that I knew so well. All of them showed a cartoonish view of

a stick figure wearing papal robes. The pope was dead in each one, dripping blood.

"Were these delivered together with flowers, by any chance?"

Russo seemed startled. "No, why, what flowers? Just the cards, in the Vatican mail."

We were being taunted by a killer. First me. Now the pope. Target four. Target five. That's what I thought. But I was wrong, for another victim was also on the killer's list.

"I agree that this is serious, Claudio," I told Russo. "I think the Holy Father should know. And pass the word—the Italians, the Americans, Interpol . . ."

My next carnation came without a note. It was delivered to St. Damian's on a sunny morning two days later, but I didn't pay great attention to it because that was the morning on which Tredi destroyed the Sacred Keys.

It began with the Vatican Press Secretary tossing a mortar at his routine noon briefing. Announcement number five of nine, that sort of thing.

As a contribution to the unity and most pressing needs of the church, and the expansion of basic religious instruction, he explained, the Society of the Sacred Keys had agreed to a suggestion from the Holy Father that it transform itself into a missionary order for the education of primary school children in needy countries of West Africa.

From where, it was implied but never actually said, the pope would eternally welcome no news of the society's good works. Consistent with its new mission, publication of current Keys books and journals would cease, with the society's presses diverted to the work of printing urgently needed Vatican-approved catechisms in the various African languages.

"Beccar looked like death. Even if it wasn't an outright suppression, it's just as good, because they can't do anything they set out to do. They might as well fold up and die." Tilly had called to gloat after attending the Keys's farewell press conference. "Beccar said he had met at length with the Holy Father to discuss the changing needs of changing times and that as a servant of the church he would carry out the Supreme Pontiff's wishes. A class act, I'll give the old bastard that much."

There was no further Vatican comment, but there somehow fell into the hands of key Vatican reporters a number of internal documents and articles from Keys publications that were described, never officially, as blatantly schismatic and even heretical. When I eventually poked through them, I realized that the most prominent articles—then smoking gur s—had been written by Luca Caruso and Gustavo Vidal.

The papal crackdown on the Keys had left the Vatican reeling. I wondered how Tredi had woven drugs and money-laundering into what surely had been a polite-as-poison theological exchange between a pope and a brother bishop. By the time it was over, Beccar must have realized, religion aside, that drug sleaze robbed him of any defense, tolling the death knell for his society.

I was delighted at the news, reasoning that the decline of the Keys would give Tredi breathing space; more room to maneuver. But Luther had thought it through.

"Paul, if the Keys are so important to the drug gangs, there's no way it will go quietly, no matter what the old bishop may say. The druggies will fight. Bet on it," he cautioned.

"What can they do, for heaven's sakes? Tredi has leveled the Keys."

"I know that, Paul. Except that the Keys still exists, right?"

"Yes, but only in name. They're finished . . ."

Luther looked at me. "But suppose, Paul, some new pope comes along and says well, oops, Tredi was wrong. Welcome back, Keys. How long do you imagine it would take them to get back to the laundry with their old friends—or some new ones?"

"But Tredi's young, strong. He . . ."

But then I saw it, too. Destroying the Keys had forced the Caballeros' hand. They would have to move quickly now to kill the pope.

21

THE NEXT MORNING I talked turkey with the Vatican cops. I hammered at Galli and the pope's personal security boss, Russo, until I was blue in the face and they were both ashen. A Colombian drug family was gunning for the pope because he had frustrated them long ago when he was still working in the Caribbean. That was my story. I couldn't say where the information came from, I said, but they should accept it as if it had descended from on high. I didn't say what Tredi had done to anger the Caballeros, and they didn't ask. I was careful never to draw any direct parallel between the threat and the Keys. But Vatican cop Franco Galli wasn't stupid.

"Monsignor Caruso and Father Vidal," he asked, "did the drug family kill them, Paolo?"

I nodded. "Not because of drugs but because they were papal allies. They were gathering information for Tredi; they grew to know too much."

Russo asked the question all of us were wrestling with silently.

"These killers, do they have people within the church, Paolo? Are they *within* the church?"

"I am afraid that is a real possibility."

The killers were growing steadily bolder. I argued that the Colombians could strike against the pope at any moment. Galli and Russo agreed. More security outside the Vatican, and in. Tighter screening of people at his public audiences. Above all, no papal wandering. Everybody within the Vatican to watch out for a shaggy mustachioed man who might be wearing priest's garb. Or, for that matter, might have cut off his mustache by now. They had Cubillas's picture, and quietly they distributed it.

If Tredi stayed inside the Vatican and behaved himself, I was confident that he could be protected there. Russo, Galli, and I, some Italian cops they called in for consultation and American Secret Service agents who came running, all understood that the pope would face his greatest risk on the New York visit.

"I don't suppose the Holy Father would consider postponing the trip until we get this guy, or at least scale back his activities?" asked the angular Secret Service commander who was coordinating the New York security.

"No. I didn't think so." She answered her own question with a sigh, after a long silence from the rest of us.

As an assassin, I ranked Cubillas as semi-pro at best. I beat the alarm drums warning against him with great enthusiasm, but privately I had concluded that if Cubillas tried to kill the pope in New York he would fail—or be caught before he could actually launch the attempt.

I was wrong on both counts, as it turned out, but there had been no trace of him on either side of the Atlantic when I wandered over to Tilly's a few afternoons after the Keys suppression. I had been hoping for a dinner invitation and maybe even a lingering dessert, but it was clear—pots boiling, table set for two—that she was expecting another guest.

I was a tad jealous, to tell the truth, but when I tried to go, Tilly stopped me. "Stay, Paul, please. There's plenty of food and I'll put out another plate. Maria's coming. She needs a lot of cheering up."

She did, too. For a beautiful young woman with Olympic gold on her mantelpiece and the world as her oyster, Maria was a mess. She came in bedraggled and glum, hadn't even painted her eyes. Why did I think she was in theological mourning? Black silk blouse, black jeans, black pointy cowboy boots, black scowl, not a shred of jewelry.

"Maria, who died?" I tried, the light touch. Like a sledgehammer. A mistake.

"We know who died, Paul. The Society of the Sacred Keys. And we know who the murderer was—the pope, damn him."

Well, gee.

Tilly fluttered around like a mother hen, clutching Maria to her bosom, pushing back the tangle of uncombed hair, fixing her a transfusion of cold Pinot Grigio.

It was a touching if improbable ballet between opposites and I must have seemed a bit bemused, for Tilly said tartly, "Maria and I disagree about where the future of our church should lie, Paul, but we both have the gift of great faith. We are together. Sisters."

Maria grinched, "Sisters in a church that is going to ruin. I suppose that you haven't heard yet that Bishop Beccar, an honest and holy man, has resigned from the Keys, and with the pope's permission will enter a contemplative monastery of silent monks in Andalucia. What an incredible loss."

"There, there, we agreed not to talk church politics," Tilly comforted. "We'll talk about men, clothes, money, sex. Anything but church politics."

Maria sniffled awhile, but then she brightened. They may have talked about men and hemlines after I left, but while I was there, fueled by the wine, we had a wake for the Keys. Maria, it turned out, was not a full-fledged Keys member, just an enthusiastic volunteer. Her connection with the Keys, she said, had started almost as a hobby and grown to become the centerpiece of her life in Rome, sharpening and narrowing her views of the church along the way.

"They were *mi gente*—'my people'—as we say in Spanish. We spoke the same language, believed the same things. I'm sorry you did not get to know them, Paul, while there was time."

I nodded with feigned sympathy. It occurred to me that it would break Maria's heart, and probably Beccar's and those of thousands of true believers like them, if the Keys's drug connection ever became public. Not from me.

As ever, Tilly was Mother Practical. "The Keys was a fulfilling part of your life, but you'll find other things to replace it. You're a professional journalist, a good one. It's a calling that can lead you in many different directions, offer great satisfactions. Holding on to that idea can work wonders. Believe me, I know."

Maria squeezed Tilly's hand with affection. "I suppose you're right, *querida,* but right now I feel empty. Empty and angry."

Dodging *motorini* is instinctive among Romans as they walk along narrow cobblestoned streets in the old quarter of the city which has never known sidewalks. Pedestrians hearing the waspy buzz of a *motorino* coming from behind understand it is a warning. Make way.

I was walking home after dinner at a stroller's relaxed pace, thinking about Tilly and Maria, about Tredi and Luther, about this and that. It must have been my subconscious that registered the bone-white *motorino* pass me as I skirted the traffic circle in the Piazza Venezia. Maybe it was an old cop gene that alerted me the second time. Its driver sheathed in a big blue helmet with red stars, the motorbike was parked before the tall black fence that protects the Teatro Marcello when I turned right into the Piazza

Campitelli. It's a favorite spot for riders to stop for an out-of-traffic cigarette, but he wasn't smoking. Maybe it was my guardian angel, but when I heard a *motorino* bearing down on me a minute or two later, I knew instantly it was the same man.

Half-turning, I saw him sitting rigidly upright, like a horseman in his stirrups. Raised high in his right hand was what looked like a sword, glinting evilly in the moonlight. I could hear his scream above the roar of the engine.

Cowering with my hands over my head in the shelter of a small brown Fiat, I felt the air from the terrible blow as it missed me by inches and glanced off the trunk of the car, bright sparks illuminating the blackness.

He had spun the bike around and was beginning another run by the time I had lurched to my feet, casting desperately for a place to hide. I ran out of the piazza and into an ancient lane called the Via dei Delfini.

As he made his second charge, I high-stepped across a pile of cobblestones and into a shallow pit of sand in which street workers obviously intended to relay the stones the next morning. I had a clear view of his weapon as he swung past: a machete. It was new, gleaming, maybe even silver plate, the sort of pretentious, engraved self-advertisement that Latin American ranchers and agro-businessmen bestow on one another to celebrate a champion bull or the birth of a grandson. I knew who the helmeted rider was without seeing his mustache.

I diverted the third charge by bowling some of the loose cobblestones into his path. They are called *sanpietrini*, rounded on top but pyramid-shaped underneath in the part you never see, to make them easier to lay. Señor Machete dodged them easily and came around in a skidding turn for another charge. I ran diagonally past him and into an even narrower alley. There were two cars parked there, and beyond them metal scaffolding sheathing the hulk of a derelict old *palazzo*.

Leaping on to the back of the first car, then to the roof, I evaded a scything blow, but he converted it into a swordlike thrust at the last second and I felt fire lance across the back of my leg. When his momentum carried him past, I skittered to the second car and on to its roof. Then it was a race; a very close thing. At the last second I jumped from the car at the scaffold, grabbed a rusty crossbar, and swung my legs up under me.

The scaffold shook as the machete struck it a few inches from where I had been an instant before. And he must have overbalanced, for I saw the machine skid and slide out from under him.

While I clung there struggling for breath and purchase, he sprang off the bike and on to his feet. He discarded the machete like a batter who has struck out, tossed away the helmet, and whipped a knife from a pocket inside his leather jacket.

"You are a dead man," he said in Spanish. Levering himself onto the lowest level of the scaffold, the shaggy-lipped knifer from Naples, the Keys administrator that Vatican records listed as Luis Cubillas, began to climb.

He was angry. Three times he had failed to kill a middle-aged cleric caught unaware: on the staircase that night, at the Naples mass, and here in the alley. And me? My injured arm burned, and I was scared, but I could feel the old fury returning, that black lump that Ivan had worked so hard to neutralize. I had come a long way with a lot of false turnings. I would never be distinguished and not a lot of people would remember me. But I would not die on a rickety scaffold, bushwhacked by some Grade-B Latin knifer sprung from my past. *Ya basta!* Here was a chance that I would not get again. I was going to take the machete man, and I was going to make him tell me who sent him.

Metal scaffolds are an everyday feature of Roman urban architecture, and this one was an archetype of its breed. It was a narrow, Erector-set structure hung from the crumbling facade of a sixteenth-century *palazzo*. Cubillas, if that was his name, was grunting now, not cursing, making heavy weather of the thin metal steps dimly seen. Probably there would be access from the scaffold to the roof, but I couldn't count on it.

The *palazzo* was on an unlit alley, perhaps ten feet wide, that did not seem to go anywhere. Once it had been a graceful Renaissance residence, but now the tired old building was abandoned, a hulk, windows without glass yawning behind splintered, half-closed shutters. As I climbed, I glimpsed floors with planks missing, walls with holes, scorched fireplaces with sagging lintels.

The scaffold was old and fragile. It hung with bolts and anchors from the crumbling façade, its feet nominally leveled by blocks of wood on the street. Narrow ladders led up from one floor to another, where passageways were narrowed by construction materials and the detritus of workers.

Running the whole length of the scaffold, top to bottom, was a rope with a hook on the end that ran to the street from a pulley fastened above the scaffold near the roof. It was a simple and effective way for a worker on the ground to run buckets of cement and stucco, and perhaps an occasional bottle of wine, up to working levels. Unused, the bucket rested out of the way up next to the pulley, the rope dropping vacantly down.

Three-quarters of the way to the top, I was in agony, puffing like a chain smoker. My muscles ached, the leg was bleeding, and the knife wound in my arm had awakened into a throbbing ache. To gain a few seconds, I kicked chunks of rubble from the scaffold platform into the knifer's path. As I rounded the top of the penultimate flight of steps, the scaffold supports above me let go with a weary sigh and a cascade of plaster and dust. We both nearly went off right then.

Then I found what I wanted. When he breasted the next turning, snorting for breath, hair and face white from the dust, I was waiting.

It was a mason's hammer, rusty from age, the handle slick from use, the pointy head resting crookedly in its notch. Someone had forgotten it. I had found it. Finder's keepers. I took him by surprise. He had been the attacker, the lion, and I the frightened zebra. Now it was my turn. With a guttural yell, I charged, hammer swinging. He took two steps back, and as the knife came up, the scaffold gave another convulsive jerk.

I feinted, he parried. I was forcing him back toward the lateral edge of a scaffold that had begun to buck in a battle of its own against gravity. He thrust with the knife, but I grabbed his hand. I was strong, invincible.

Fending off the blade, I swung the hammer, and he put up his left hand to shield his face, but we both knew it was too late.

The hammer came sweeping down toward his skull like an avenging sword. And then the hammer's head flew off, glanced off the building wall, and ricocheted harmlessly into space.

The reprieve gave him new strength. I had trouble with the knife arm then, and for an instant watched in almost third-party fascination as it pointed down toward my chest.

He was heaving, showering me with spittle and grunted half-curses. I kneed him, and when he grunted in pain, the knife wavered. I slapped his arm away and staggered up the last flight of steps.

The scaffold was swaying ominously, too heavy, too old, too tired. Like simple Brother Paul. I was at the end of the road then, nothing left above me but the pulley and its bucket, and above it the roof itself. I was too old, too slow, too tired.

I needed a weapon. There was nothing. Last round then, Brother Paul. Desperation. I would kick and I would claw and I would gouge and at least I would take him with me. *Arrivederci.*

He came reeling around the corner to the top platform, his

knife ready in one hand, the other clutching a handrail for support as the scaffold sagged. Then he smiled in triumph. He knew as well as I did that the end had come.

I saw it by chance: a rounded piece of iron about the length of a crowbar. Not as good as the knife but better than nothing.

He was out of breath, too, and there was an angry red streak along the left side of his face: the hammer handle had done more damage than the feckless head.

I could see him gauging the threat from the iron bar and poising himself for a final attack. But the bar was not for the knifer. I jammed it into the rotting stucco where the top support of the scaffold rested. The anchor surrendered almost instantly, surging from the wall with a tormented screech.

I spun, leapt empty-handed with another scream and wild-eyed fury at the knifer. He took a reflexive step back, falling as the scaffold started to go.

I let momentum carry me to the rope, and I hung on as the knifer and scaffold slid down into the alley with an orchestral bang. My feet fending carefully off the wall, I dropped gingerly into the welter of rusty pipes.

The knifer wasn't going anywhere. He was pinned by the wreckage, at least one leg broken. Maybe his back, too. Tough luck.

"Help me, *Ayúdame*. Father, please . . ." He was babbling in Spanish and bad Italian. Did he think I was a priest? He knew better. Still, I shifted some debris and bent close.

He blessed himself feebly. "Bless me, Father, for I have sinned . . ." he began.

"Make a good confession, my son. Who sent you? Confess. Tell me."

"Uhh," he said, not really there, and lapsed into a keening babble that soon stopped, too.

Nobody lived amid the hulk *palazzi* of scaffold alley, and nobody had yet appeared to find out what had made all the racket. But it was only a matter of time, and I had it all worked out. I would say Cubillas was my friend—walking past, just fell, terrible accident. And I would ride with him to the hospital, where I would identify myself as a Vatican cop and Cubillas as a homicide suspect. Better not to say murderer right off the bat, but I'd roust Galli from bed soon enough. Tossing in pain at my feet lay the break we needed to crush the Colombians who had come to kill the pope.

I crouched there for a moment, catching my breath, nursing my damaged arm and the assorted cuts and bruises of scaffold souvenirs. Cubillas's pulse was shallow but steady, considering that he must be drifting into shock on top of everything else that ailed him. Romans, I understood, are like big city folk around the world in that they hear only what they want to hear. Still, some nosy soul, a grandmother, was bound to poke her nose out of a window before much longer. Someone finally came, just as Cubillas moaned and I had bent forward again to see if he had anything useful to confess.

That is what saved me, for I actually felt the wind from the bullet as it pierced the space that my head had filled an instant before. It ricocheted with a tremendous racket among the scaffold debris. The second shot came close behind it, but by then I had abandoned Cubillas and was scrambling on my hands and knees through twisted strings of old metal and toward the far end of the alley.

The shooter was good, very good. The third shot chipped at medieval brickwork a few inches above my head, but in another few seconds I had skidded around the corner and was on my feet in a lurching run. I could hear the shooter pounding down the alley I had left, but the scaffold got in his way. He made a tremendous racket at first, but then he must have quit, for I limped unmolested into the well-lit Piazza Venezia, and its insurance policy traffic and pedestrians.

At the far end of the piazza, there is a police station, and I hollered at the young guard outside that a passerby had been trapped by a collapsing building. When he dashed inside to raise the alarm, I scuttled into a phone booth up the block, where the Vatican police patched me through to Franco Galli at home.

He picked me up there fifteen minutes later, and when he asked where to go, all I had to do was gesture toward the swarm of flashing blue lights in the distance.

"It's Cubillas, if that's his name. He attacked me and got stuck under a collapsing scaffold." I had trouble keeping the triumph out of my voice. We had them now.

"But you are not hurt badly yourself?" the Vatican cop asked.

"Just rattled. It was a near thing."

"Well done, Paolo."

Galli put on some blue lights of his own and pulled up behind the procession of cars and rescue trucks.

"You seem a little, shall we say, tired, and a bit dusty, Paolo," he said gently. "Let's not alarm our carabinieri friends. Wait here and I will find out to what hospital Cubillas has been taken."

He started to get out, but I laid a hand on his arm.

"Cubillas brought backup, a man with a gun. He's probably long gone, but tell them to be careful. *You* be careful."

So I waited a fretful fifteen minutes. When Galli came back, he slid silently behind the wheel and laid his forehead against its cool surface.

"What's wrong?" I demanded.

"It is true that a scaffold has collapsed, perhaps from a gentle temblor not even the neighbors felt, and it is also true that one victim has been found in the wreckage."

"Cubillas. I told you that."

"Alas, the victim was dead."

Oh, shit. So near, and yet nowhere. "Damn. He was hurt, but I didn't think he was dying."

Galli stared hollowly across the violent night.

"You were right."

"What does that mean?"

"The man is dead because he was shot, Paolo."

A huge shiver engulfed me and I must have drifted away, because the next thing I remember Galli was shaking me gently.

"Paolo, Paolo, are you all right? Shall I take you to a hospital?"

It took me a minute of fierce concentration to corral my mind, stop the shaking.

"Just a delayed reaction to tangling with Cubillas in the alley," I said, and I must have persuaded him, for Galli drove me home in the strained silence of two cops who understood that it was late in the game and it was the bad guys who had the ball.

NEW YORK

22

THE PLANE BOUNCED again high over the Atlantic, but by then I had lowered the glass below spilling level. Organizers would be fretting. Papal flights are as exquisite a feat of aeronautical planning as you'll find, bar the occasional clouds, and they are never accepted gracefully.

The Vatican having no planes of its own, every pope trip begins with Alitalia, the feather-bedded Italian national airline. Like his predecessors, Tredi rode in a special compartment in the front of the plane complete with his pontifical seal on the bulkhead, at least four special first-class seats, and newspapers and magazines in half a dozen languages. On intercontinental flights like the Rome-New York, the pope's place became a two-room suite with a bedroom. He slept when he could. Tredi had once confided that his personal vision of hell was perpetual jetlag.

Everybody gets first-class service on a papal flight, but there's no pretense of equality. Fifty journalists traveling with the pope, including Tilly, Maria, and the other reporters, rode in the back of the plane. They were a pampered bunch: special credentials, advance texts of papal speeches in at least two languages, reserved hotel rooms, buses back and forth from the airport, to papal events, to special press centers, to their hotels. The *Vaticanisti,* as they are called, pay enough for their privileges to virtually underwrite the cost of the charter.

I sat in the middle business-class compartment on the outbound flight with members of the Secretariat of State, the Vatican foreign ministry, clerics of the pope's staff, invited guests, the Vatican press officers, special guests, and a handful of Vatican security cops. I was once again in black suit and dog collar, but among the clerics Diego Altamirano and I were the only ones without the distinguishing splash of purple or red that denotes bishops and cardinals respectively.

Papal security is risible by the standards of American presidential travel, but on the plane were a handful of Vatican security professionals, most of them Italian, as committed—and as good—as the Secret Service. They'd stay close to Tredi and liaise with the battalions of New York cops who'd become responsible for papal safety once we touched down.

The papal security boss on the New York trip was Claudio Russo, a wily former detective inspector from Venice who stayed in shape by climbing mountains in the Abruzzo east of Rome.

"*Ciao,* Paolo." Russo tossed me the yellow-and-white pin that would identify me to the local cops as a go-anywhere member of the papal party for the two-day visit. No one but the security chief knows what color badge will be used until after the plane takes off.

"*Ciao,* Claudio. What are you hearing?"

"The New York police are a little nervous. Opening-night jitters. We don't hear anything special."

The stewardess spoke stiffly with the throaty French-like "r" that is a giveaway for Milan. She cradled a world-class bottle of Brunello, and she, too, was nervous. It happens to everybody on their first pope flight.

Me, I felt as good as could be expected, all things considered. I'm not saying I was normal. I've not been what you'd call normal for many years. But among that segment of the population which sometimes hears inner voices and has occasional strange visitations, I think you could have ranked me serviceable that bright morning as Pope Pius XIII flew to his date with New York.

"Historic Papal Mission," headlined the *Corriere della Sera* that I had bought at Fiumicino that morning.

Let that be all it was, I prayed silently. The killers were ever more aggressive. The pope had had a steady barrage of red-ink threats by mail since the murder of the *motorino* man. I had had my share, too. Personal, intensely nasty, almost obscene.

Tredi knew the risks, and he knew odds. One morning we had breakfast after he said mass in his private chapel, and I told him about the scaffold and everything else he needed to know, except that I had suffered what Ivan delicately called "a minor incident" in the debris.

"I'm okay, but it's all coming down soon. I can feel it. You have to be especially careful."

"Paul, there are legions of committed people putting themselves on the line to protect me. All I can do is what I must."

Time was pressing: he understood that as well as anybody. If the Caballeros had any hope of reversing the damage to the Keys, they would move quickly. Is there any city in the world easier to find an assassin in than Olde New York? A few frontierlands in Colombia, maybe, but in New York the assassin menu is larger and more accessible: down-home skinheads and hopheads, dissident Kurds, Arab extremists, former KGB officers from Russia and nowher-estans galore, renegade Jewish zealots, disaffected Koreans,

Japanese; Latin Americans from a dozen different countries. Take your pick. All the cops—the Americans, the Vatican security team—could do was try to be everywhere. Among them, what I could do was to pick my spots, try to be smart; look for bruises in the Big Apple.

Before lunch, I wandered back to the reporters' section of the plane, where I encountered Maria deeper in piles of turgid Vatican press handouts than any self-respecting reporter ought to be. She was looking continents better than when I had last seen her at Tilly's. We chatted and Maria made no attempt to hide the bitterness over Tredi's kneecapping of her beloved Keys, but I could see that Tilly's ministrations seemed to be paying off. She had come to Rome as a journalist and was flying to New York as a journalist; it was best not to mix professional responsibilities and personal beliefs, Maria assured me solemnly, in a line we both knew had been scripted by Tilly.

"The Keys will be reborn one day in Rome, and its ideals will never die," she said, with great seriousness. "In the meantime, I shall grieve as I would grieve for the loss of a big scoop—or a good man," she added, in a slick change of pace. We both laughed at the Tilly-ism that left one of us wondering how many good men she'd had.

"A healthy attitude."

"Yes, the wound will heal. I just pray that God gives the pope sufficient courage and vision not to tinker further with the principles of our faith. That could be very dangerous." The violet eyes raked me. "Do you know what he will say in New York?"

"Anything's possible," I lied neutrally.

As a matter of fact, I had a pretty good idea. The rumors, sublime to ridiculous, were predicting everything from a Vatican offer to take control of all the world's nuclear weapons to a bombshell announcement that the church would capitalize its treasures and be listed on the New York Stock Exchange. It is, after all, one of the world's largest

corporations, stockholders everywhere, if you want to look
at it that way. Instead, what Tredi intended to do, and never
mind the shadow of threatened assassination, was to pro-
claim a revolution.

Journalist she might be, but Maria was one of those
Catholics who saw change as a personal affront to eternity.
She wasn't going to like what Tredi had to say. No way. And
no sense getting her fired up in advance, when she might
claw out my eyes. Or Tredi's.

So Uncle Paul changed the subject and got Maria talking
about things besides the one true faith for a change. She told
me about growing up on a family winery in Chile's Central
Valley, of her six brothers and sisters, who by now included
two nuns, a priest, a mother of four, and a farmer even more
prosperous than her traditionalist Catholic father. There was
family tragedy, too: one brother, a former air force pilot and
founder of an airfreight company, killed in a crash in the
Andes.

"You're not a priest, Paul, but there's nothing to say you
can't help other people talk through their problems now and
then. It can help you to understand your own better," Ivan
had lectured me a long time ago.

So I particularly welcomed Maria's company that day: it
kept me from dwelling on the mess of my own life and the
murderers I hadn't caught. I got her talking about the great
strain and joy of running competitively, about her days at the
university, torn between track and a half-hearted religious
vocation, even about a boyfriend or two.

"You're nice, Paul. No wonder Tilly likes you so much,"
she said at one point.

Twice in the course of a conversation that cascaded
through lunch, the retrieval of trays, coffee and beyond, I
sensed that Maria's leg lingered against mine for burning
instants longer than was strictly necessary. I was glad that
Tilly was sitting further to the back of the plane, conspiring
about arcania with other *Vaticanisti*.

I was deep into a long and largely true and apparently engrossing account of life as an almost-priest when we were interrupted by a bright *"Buenos días"* from His Holiness, the Supreme Pontiff.

The intercontinental jets are so big that the passengers on papal flights make scarcely a dent in the acres of seats. From the perspective of fifty accompanying journalists spread out in distant economy seats, Tredi in his distant compartment might as well have been on the moon. The plane's great size, with the Vatican retinue as a buffer in the middle business-class cabin, was at once a blessing and a boon to him, the pope had once told me.

"It's great to be alone and able to move around. But boy, on some of the long flights, it can get boring, let me tell you."

Perhaps that is why Tredi had burnished the Holy Pole's early practice of a walk-through among the journalists on the outward leg of a long trip. All off-the-record, of course.

With the pope looming above us, Maria leapt to her feet and I followed with avuncular gravity. It didn't fool Diego Altamirano, who winked, or Tredi, who waited until Maria bent to kiss his ring to give me an instant's eye flash that meant he wanted me to come see him up front.

I thought I knew why. One afternoon when Ivan gave me post-scaffold furlough from circuit realignment, I had tracked down drug cop Andy Ridgeway. Deputy Director, no less.

"A favor, Andy—again." With friends you don't need to beat around the bush.

"Paul," he said, drawing out the name the way a third-grade teacher might regard a student who runs with scissors, "the last time you started a war."

"Who won?"

"The good guys, as a matter of fact. But who could countenance that sort of behavior?" He was teasing. "What now?"

I gave him some names.

"Do you want to fill me in, Paul? Do I want to know what you are up to? Or shall I just wait until the networks break in with bulletins?"

"Andy, you know me. I'm a simple man from the land of the palm trees." That broke him up. It was the first line from the glorious song "Guantanamera," which might as well be the Cuban national anthem.

That afternoon, Ivan and I relieved Piotr at Luther's side for a couple of hours while he walked an extraofficial set of scaffold fingerprints over to a shadowy soul at the American Embassy on the Via Veneto.

When I got to the pope's lonely cabin in the whispering jet, he was staring moodily out a window.

"Paul, how are you?"

"Fine, great," I said. His look reminded me that Tredi and Ivan talked more about Brother Paul than I'd like. "Okay, I'm jumpy about New York, but I'm keeping. Ivan says I'm fine."

"That's what I hear. I'm glad you didn't kill that guy on the scaffold."

"Me, too. But it would have been self-defense."

"I don't doubt it. But no more killing, Paul. There's been too much killing, too much death . . ." He waved his hands in a dismissive, get-thee-behind-me gesture, and I suddenly realized that the pope was hurting.

"Rico. What . . . Who . . . ?"

The polished stage mask dissolved. "My brother, Paul." I could hardly hear him. "My brother Bobby is dead."

"I'm sorry. Wh . . . ?"

"They told me just before the plane left. He was found at a beach house not far from where we lived as kids. We used to play there, pretend it was a fortress we were defending against pirates . . ."

"Was he killed?"

"They seem to think Bobby just died, Paul. Too many cig-

arettes, too much weight, too much alcohol. He'd been sick
on and off for years, a sick man wandering around, full of
grandiose schemes but hiding, really, afraid to go home. But
then he went home. Natural causes, they say."

"Don't you believe it?"

"Would you?" the pope asked softly.

"No."

He knew as well as I did that the DEA had identified the
fingerprints of the dead knifer, Keys worker, and scaffold
victim as belonging to Ernesto Carvajal Lopez. And, lo and
behold, he turned out to be an ambitious Caballero family
cousin. We had made the direct link.

The Caballeros were back. Back in drugs. Back in killing.
I thought that Bobby had been victim number four: Kearns,
Caruso, Vidal, and the pope's brother. We hit a patch of turbulence and the seat belt sign came on. I murmured condolences, Tredi and I exchanged an *abrazo* and I left the pope
to his grief and his revolutionary's plans for a giant church.

I sat alone as the big jet let down off the sea and watched
New York swim out of the afternoon haze. I would have
given centuries of Purgatory time to have known who was
running the reborn Caballeros. Droopy Ernesto was a pawn
for his boss—the man who'd killed him as he lay in the tangled scaffold wreckage. Was the Caballero heir already in
New York? Would he come after me first? He had tried
before. Or go for the pope? The ultimate target.

The trouble at Yankee Stadium started near third base.

From where I was standing halfway up the tall altar in
centerfield, it looked as if a gay rights group, "Priesthood for
Lesbians," charged some young men whose black-and-red
T-shirts proclaimed them "Commandos for Christ." There
were scuffles, fistfights, and a toing and froing as more and
more people became involved.

Security ushers were there quickly. I saw them carry away
one woman with a bloody head, and wrestle a troublemaker

to the ground. Helmeted New York cops came, swinging clubs, and that seemed to cool things for a few minutes, but then fighting started on the first-base side of the stadium: between middle-class blacks and leather-jacketed Latinos, it looked like.

I couldn't tell if violence was being provoked or was simply a microcosm of a fecund and divided church, but the swirling mob, the angry blows and shouts were not the best augur for the celebration of holy mass by the Supreme Pontiff of the world's largest church.

We had come straight from the airport. It was Tredi's salute to a gritty city that he loved. The last time a predecessor pope had visited New York, he had said mass over in New Jersey. A nice orderly, respectful crowd who drove to the stadium, had tailgate parties in the parking lot, bought souvenirs, and filed in happily to cheer the pope and to receive his benediction.

But Tredi had chosen Yankee Stadium, knowing as well as anybody that it is in the Bronx and that the Bronx hadn't been the happiest borough in New York for long decades.

"We're going to do it in the stadium, Paul," he had told me in Rome. "Nobody else likes the idea, but I love it. To me, the stadium *is* New York."

If I had asked him, I know he'd have said that since Yankee Stadium was probably the most famous ballfield in the world, no baseball fan would be caught dead saying mass in a suburban football stadium.

But that's not why we went there. We went to the Bronx because it was once a vibrant middle-class part of the city that had gone spectacularly to pot. The Jews, the Irish, and the Italians had moved out. The blacks and the Latinos had moved in. It had become a Third World ghetto in the richest city on earth, a place of violence, degradation—and genius. Too many of its children paraded through the old Bronx County Courthouse on their way to jail; but another strand of Bronx kids swept through some of the city's top high

schools on their way to amazing achievements in science
and the arts, commerce and the military. The Bronx was
fighting back. It was Tredi's sort of place.

About ten minutes before the scheduled start of the mass,
the violence took a nasty turn. I heard pops, bangs, yells. I
wasn't thinking papal assassination, but chaos and big-time
trampling seemed a real possibility.

Everybody had been frisked within an inch of their life on
the way in, but maybe not well enough. I watched young
men with red crosses on their arms and vests fight their way
clear of the tangle with four stretchers. Pilgrims fainting,
people fighting, pressure groups jostling, they are all part
and parcel of every papal mass. There had been a mass once
in Santiago in Chile's bad old days when riot police had
fired tear gas against protesting Marxists near the altar while
the pope was consecrating the host. The Holy Pole, eyes
streaming, had never dropped a stitch.

This much hassle before the mass, though, was scary. It
looked to me like a storm building. Add to that the chance
that there was a Caballero family assassin biding his time
somewhere in the multitude, and I was not a happy camper.

A few minutes later, Diego Altamirano came by, stared
with stricken eyes for a few seconds at the mob, and touched
my arm. "The Holy Father wants you."

I followed him to a cavernous hall under the temporary
altar. Officially, it was the vesting chamber, though only Vatican bean counters actually called it that. It's the backstage
at every papal mass, where clerics change from their street
clothes into their robes for mass. In some of the best of
them, there's also a place to pee and somewhere to wash
your hands and comb your hair. The hall was jammed with
distinguished prelates vested and half-vested, milling about
like the players they were, waiting for their cue to go on
stage. For many of the priests and obscure bishops who
would march behind the pope and sit at the altar, concelebrating this mass was the chance of a lifetime.

Tredi had his own room, separated from the others by a red curtain. Behind it, the pope lounged in a comfortable armchair while chaos swarmed around him. He was in his robes, vested except for the heavy chasuble and his miter, perched lopsidedly on a dummy head next to the chair. His staff of office leaned against the wall. Tredi was the only man in the room not transfixed by a video monitor high on the wall. Surveillance cameras panned from one to another pockets of unrest, perhaps a half dozen in all. The scuffles defied appeals for order from a young priest at the altar microphone that alternated with equally ineffective go-go religious music. Some hands were clapping; too many others were punching.

Maybe a thousand people in a crowd of nearly a hundred thousand were involved; most of the rest either didn't know or didn't care—for the moment. But you could taste the incendiary pressure, contagious and potentially deadly; it could blow the stadium sky high.

I knew many of the priests in the inner room, by sight or by reputation. Besides Altamirano, they were the usual suspects: Reilly, the genial Irish master of ceremonies who knew more than anybody about the mechanics and protocol of a mass, any mass; Nocilla, the polyphone Italian Secretary of State who had a potbelly and the eyes of a fox; a few factotum monsignors; the ornery, hard-line cardinal archbishop of New York, and a few others keening nervously, who must have been locals in the cardinal's retinue.

Tredi winked at me as I came in. Everybody else was riveted on a red-faced civilian in an expensive suit, dueling with the cardinal.

"Wait a little while. Can't go out there now . . . These things flare up and are gone. Reinforcements are on the way . . . " He must have been the police commissioner, for a New York liaison cop named Dillon, who had come with us from Rome, stood directly behind him with a studiously neutral expression, staring at the floor.

". . . must absolutely guarantee the security of His Holiness before . . ." the cardinal was saying at the same time.

"Perhaps we might reconsider," said the Secretary of State.

"Too much risk," murmured one of the New York bishops in unctuous echo.

I looked over at Tim Holden, an FBI guy who had also flown in with us. He was a terrorist specialist; punch-ups were religion's answer to soccer hooligans. Not his bag. I looked at Russo, the grizzled Vatican security chief. He shrugged. Russo had been in the worst of the tear gas that Friday afternoon in Santiago and never reached for his handkerchief.

"Gentlemen." Tredi stifled the babble with a word. He pointed at me.

Took my breath away.

"For those of you who don't know him, this is Brother Paul. He's our expert in the psychology of crowds; the best in the business, I'd say."

Crowd psychology, *tu madre.* The pope eyed me levelly, his face once again his public mask.

"Go, or no go, Paul? Do I go out there? It's your call."

Hijo de la gran puta!

But that is what friends are for, aren't they? The Caballeros might well try to kill the pope in New York. But not that afternoon in the huge and historic stadium, not with every cop in New York on red alert. The stadium threat was of another sort. It was religious, populist, an affair of the church. It was the kind of threat on which my friend the pope would never turn his back. He would, literally, rather die.

I didn't even give that gawking mob around Tredi the satisfaction of pretending to think it through, weigh the consequences.

"Do it. *You* do it."

This was conversation by subtext, and I think only Tredi and I could begin to count its levels. Nobody else in that room had known him as a crusading cardinal who had put his life on the line time and again. No one else had felt his power on a mountain top.

Better than anybody else in that stadium, I understood: wild horses wouldn't keep His Holiness Pius XIII away from that altar. I told him what he wanted to hear so that he could do what he was going to do anyway. Dead simple, even for a simple brother.

And a graceful thing for Tredi to have dragged me in as the apparent decision-maker. If disaster fell, I'd be the villain; the pope's personal security specialist—Tilly and her friends would invent a title for me—who overrode the experts and needlessly, foolishly, dangerously, unacceptably, choose a damning adverb, put the Holy Father's life at risk.

No hole too deep for him, no hell too hot. And no blame for the boys in New York, or the real Vatican security crowd.

Tredi shushed the dissenting chorus with action. In a few moments, the pope was vested in all his glory. He squared his shoulders, reached over and picked up his shepherd's staff, and summoned the Sicilian cardinal who was his Secretary of State.

"Hold the parade, Calogero," he instructed.

Then, alone, the pope walked to the side entrance of the hall. Altamirano and I and a few of the others made to follow, but he held up his hand: Stop.

"God bless," the pope said, and strode out into the tumult.

I've watched the tape time and again since that night. It's some of the best television ever made.

In the hubbub, Tredi becomes visible first at the left-hand edge of the altar, which had its back to the closed end of the stadium. An excited buzz goes up in what are usually the right-field stands. Then he works his way to the front, staring straight ahead, walking slowly, purposefully. By then, everybody in the stadium sees him. There's more shouting, yelling. He ignores it.

Some wizard at the control board, maybe one of those Bronx kids, dims the stadium lights and hits the pope with a soft spotlight. His shadow's in front of him as he ever so slowly begins to mount the forty-one steps to the altar.

He's come with something to do, you can see that. But it's been a long day. He's an office worker trudging home from the job, a truck driver with aching arms and a throbbing head, a teacher with piles of homework to correct, a weary miner up from the pit. By the time he's three-quarters up the stairs, people are forgetting to fight.

The pope is there, he's alone. A man, a symbol, an idea. At the head of the stairs, he bows deeply to the altar. He turns to face the giant crowd for the first time; close up, you can see the concentration on his face.

This is when the mass should start. There should be fifty-three prelates out there with him in elegant robes, eighteen altar servers: three incense bearers, well-rehearsed readers of the Old Testament, the Epistle and of the Gospel; Reilly, who makes great ceremony of taking the pope's miter and folding it oh so gracefully, who turns the pages of the altar Sacramentary in perfect sequence, who never lets him bow in the wrong direction.

But there is nobody there on the yawning stage.

The pope is alone. He should start mass. Instead he walks over to the microphones.

"My friends," he says, in an English that is not only perfect but also tastes of New York when he wants it to, for that is where he went to university, "I'm delighted to be here with you tonight, and I see that some of you decided to start the excitement without me."

There are some laughs, a rustling. "Free choice for women," comes a cry from near second base, but it dies without echo. People are listening to the solitary figure.

"We are many. We are one," he says. "I have come here tonight to celebrate mass with you. Just you, me, and"—a finger raised—"God. That's all we really need, isn't it? In fact, you don't really even need me. With God, it takes only two to tango." Another laugh, some more cries, but of lessening impact now, an annoyance.

"I know most of you have come to join me in the magic and mystery of the mass. If there are those who have come for other reasons, to express your concerns about issues that affect you, I respect that. But I ask you in turn to show courtesy to those who have come to pray together. Put down your placards, put down your fists. Stay with us to share this ceremony, I invite you. If any do not wish to hear this mass, please leave now. Go in peace."

Reporters would later find a few hundred who said they had marched out in protest, but watching on the monitor I saw little movement in the crowd. The vesting chamber itself was quiet enough to hear a communion wafer drop.

He stands there in electric silence for a couple of minutes, as if waiting for huge numbers of people to go. Then the pope says, "Since tonight is such a special event for all of us, I'd like you to join me in a favorite prayer of mine, a prayer that unites all Christians everywhere. We say it at every mass:

"Our Father . . ."

The crowd prays along. Then Tredi turns to the altar. He sheds his staff and his miter without ceremony, walks around the altar to face the crowd, and begins the mass.

"He has no Sacramentary! The Holy Father has no book!" The cardinal of New York is apoplectic. There's a great scurry. Normally the book for mass is already on the altar on the celebrant's left when he gets there.

But the pope's altar is bare.

In a minute or so, the missal appears, a bulky red-covered thing, and I can see a fight brewing over who will carry it to the pope. The only possible winner is the New York cardinal himself, but I hadn't reckoned on Monsignor Reilly, the Vatican overseer of all altar orthodoxy.

"The Holy Father does not require the Sacramentary, thank you, Your Eminence. He knows the mass for today."

"But the readings, the Gospel . . ."

Reilly and Nocilla stand with Altamirano in a skirmish line near the door. They look as if they'd tackle the nearest book-bearer.

"Please, Your Eminence, the Holy Father will manage," says Nocilla, who, as cardinal secretary of state, outranks the cardinal archbishop of New York by about two stars.

At the altar, Tredi completes the opening prayers and the Gloria and he looks up. "There are three readings for today's mass, but I don't have my Lectionary. Can somebody lend me one?"

Another bustle in the crowd, a collective gasp. Pope's forgot his book! After an awkward minute or two, a helmeted riot cop jogs up the stairs with a borrowed missalette. I could see the red ribbons marking the pages of that day's readings.

The pope says, "I don't have my glasses, either. Would you do the readings, please?"

Altar dumb show. Cop looks around; nobody else there. Points at self. Me? Pope nods.

Me!

"Please," the pope says.

Cop takes off her helmet, shakes her head to release a mass of tight black curls, and reads the two lessons in a clear, clean voice. Maybe her name's not O'Berry, but it could have been.

When she's finished the pope walks over, kisses her on both cheeks, and says a few words. By now, the stadium is mesmerized. Nobody's been to a mass like this.

In the hall under the altar, nothing moves, but when I look over, Reilly's hands are clasped as if in prayer or victory, I think Altamirano looks like a kid whose father just hit a home run, and something is brimming in Nocilla's eyes.

The time comes for the Gospel, and after a shorter pause this time, a black kid with huge sneakers and a funny haircut bounces on to the altar.

He nods at the pope, goes to the microphone, opens his

missal: "The Gospel according to St. Luke," he begins, and
the giant crowd rises to its feet.

Tredi gives a short, upbeat homily. "We are a church that
respects and listens to many voices. We look to the future.
We welcome those who think differently because they, too,
are our brothers and sisters," he says.

Reilly disappears a few minutes before the offertory, and
when it's time for the wine and the bread to come to the
altar, a Latina in tight jeans and a blond kid with yellow and
white "Usher" bands on their left arms bring them to the
pope.

I passed out a lot of communion that day, and never felt
better about doing it. I was in centerfield, thanks, so of
course I thought of DiMaggio and Mantle and imagined
what it must have been like to play with them.

But I thought of Tredi, too, for I had understood from the
start that the real reason he had gone out into the crowd
alone was not just pride. He hadn't wanted anybody else to
get hurt, if that's what it came to.

That night, the FBI got a call that dampened my private
pleasure at Tredi's performance while everybody else was
doing somersaults of praise. Maybe it was the picture that
did it, the backlit pope plodding alone up those stairs. Every
TV news opened with it, every newspaper splashed it. "A
compelling message of unity from the world's loneliest
man," said the city's best paper. One of the tabloids was
more piquant. "Pope to City: Get a Life." Probably polish
my image if the word got out that it was me who sent him
out there alone; maybe they wouldn't make me take the
numerology class again next year. The *Vaticanisti* played the
story as fearless Tredi in the lion's den, no mention of a
gutsy crowd psychologist, but I didn't learn that until later,
because that night I spent in the bowels of Queens.

There, I watched Feds pop a big wholesale Colombian
drug operation with dispatch, enthusiasm, and a dazzling

array of electronic glitz. It was a DEA raid, but the FBI went along because of an outside chance of some terrorist link with the pope. I was an invited guest. Raiders found a couple of million dollars' worth of cocaine in cases marked "Colonial Furniture," and enough firepower in the warehouse to have saved the Alamo. They nabbed a handful of scruffy Latinos, no shooting, thank God, but I didn't see anything that interested me.

"Penny-ante freelancers. Not for us, is it?" said my FBI guide.

"No. I think for Tredi it'll be one guy, working alone. Probably won't even try it here; you guys are too good."

"We're trying, Paul, God knows we're trying. That's one hell of a pope. Don't want him done on our watch."

Or on mine, *amigo.*

23

THE POPE WAS also a hit the next day at St. Patrick's. The soaring cathedral that is one of New York's greatest landmarks glistened in the late afternoon sun as his popemobile carved a triumphant passage up Fifth Avenue. He had been on television all day, at meetings with nuns and priests, with the homeless, with leaders of other religions. And still hundreds of thousands of New Yorkers jammed the broad sidewalks for a glimpse of the tall figure as he floated past in what one reporter called his New Age, electric-powered, environment-friendly answer to the old Doges' gondola.

The stadium mass had wrung me out; too keyed up to sleep much afterward. All morning I had been tense, waiting for some word, some sign, some warning of a Caballero attack.

Nada.

Inside the cocoon of his bulletproof showoff wagon, Tredi seemed as safe as a vault. The security looked impenetrable, cops thick on the ground, motorcycles in a tight V around the popemobile, snipers on the roofs, helicopters overhead.

God knows how many plainclothes cops were in the crowd, but when I asked Chet Dillon, the New York liaison cop, he had grinned. "Lots." It was all very reassuring from where I sat in the Vatican staff bus as we eased through the heart of the nation's greatest city. Except, like every cop in town, I knew that a madman willing to swap his life for the pope's would always have a break-even chance.

I'm not much for cathedrals usually, but I went into St. Pat's. I didn't go to see history in the making. I went because my hands itched, my throat was dry, and a big weight was pressing on my head. I was nervous. I had persuaded myself that the Caballeros would run at Tredi while he was in New York. A church can be a better place than a stadium, if assassination is your bag.

At St. Pat's, anybody who was anybody was jammed into a polished wooden pew. Being Catholic was okay, but hardly essential. The Protestant President and her husband were there, New York's Jewish mayor, leaders from more religions than ever made it into the Bible, and a couple of thousand of the city's best and brightest—or at least most photographed.

I found Dillon prowling around the back of the church during the mass, a bird dog questing for a scent. I took that as a good sign.

"No weak rafters, no tottering columns. No crazed monks. No killer viruses," I ventured.

"Don't even joke about it," Dillon growled. "You happen to be standing in the squeakiest-clean piece of real estate in the whole world at this moment. At the cost, by the way, of pissing off every bishop in the house: we made them all take off their pectoral crosses before going through the metal detector."

"They'll get you in Purgatory for that."

"Be worth it. Everybody likes this pope. And we're squeaky clean here. The closest thing to a threat we've had all day is a flower in one of the confessionals. Nobody knows how it got there."

"A flower, that's ni. . . ." I went cold. "Was it a red carnation?"

"What do I know from flowers? It was red. A flower."

"A carnation. Find out. And was there a message with it?" I must have said it funny, because I saw alarm flash through his eyes as he started muttering into a microphone on his lapel.

We waited for a response and he probed. "Something I should know, Paul?"

"Probably nothing. Just a little jittery, I'm sure . . ."

But Dillon was communing with electronic friends. "Right, ten four," he said to somebody, and then, to me, "They think it may have been a carnation. No card that anybody remembers, but it's history by now. The flower's in some garbage truck we couldn't find if we wanted to."

Before I could absorb that, he said, "Do we have a situation here, Paul? Talk to me."

I told him what he had to know. "There have been some threats—in Rome—involving a red carnation. This is probably a coincidence; carnations are pretty common."

"Coincidence. But you don't like it," he said.

I shrugged. He could see that I didn't like it, so I asked, "You have a fallback way to get the pope out of the cathedral after mass, don't you?"

"We have three fallback routes," the New York cop said, with pride and a touch of asperity.

"Then use the one that looks closest to routine and it'll be cool."

That's what they did, but I had lied. Nothing could ever be cool under the Caballero shadow.

When thunder struck after mass, it had nothing to do with the pope, and everything to do with Tilly. She and I were working our way to the buses when a tall woman on the sidewalk started yelling, "Sister Jean! Sister Jean! Over here!"

The woman waved a truly hideous pink-and-fluorescent-green placard reading "God She Wants Woman Priests" that stood out like a toothache in the forest of hand-sized yellow-and-white Vatican flags waved by adoring spectators.

"Jean! Sister Jean!" It sounded like a foghorn.

Walking alongside me, Tilly glanced over with what I thought was professional appraisal, as if the woman might make a line in her story.

I was wrong. Tilly stumbled. I caught her arm. She was bright red, a sheen of sweat coated her forehead.

"Tilly! What . . ."

She shook me off. "I'm okay. It's . . . I'll see you later." She broke away and headed for the sidewalk, where a cop glanced at her papal press badge and let her slip under the barrier. After a moment of indecision, I went after her.

Of course in my priest suit with its Vatican go-anywhere button, it took much longer to persuade the cop to let me pass. By the time I got there, the ugly placard was leaning against the wall and Tilly and the tall woman were in a tight embrace.

The stranger was a well-shaped lady, I couldn't help noticing, in attractive black slacks and a white blouse. Then I saw the bluff, almost abstract silver cross around her neck and things began to make sense. It was identical to the one that Tilly usually wore.

When Tilly looked up and saw me finally, there were tears in her eyes.

"Oh, Paul, you shouldn't have . . ." but then she segued into a mumbled introduction, "This is . . ."

"I'm Mother Ruth, nice to meet you, Father," the woman said, extending a long, thin hand and an appraising stare. She was a few inches under six feet, I guessed. Her hair was short and jet-black with a sprinkling of gray. Around eyes the color of smoke, she had wrinkles of the sort that come from being too long in the sun. She was one of the most striking women I had met in a long time.

"Clara . . . uh Mother Ruth and I were roommates for years," Tilly began.

"In the novitiate, back in the Age of the Flood." The tall woman smiled.

She turned to Tilly. "I knew you had left the order—ages ago, wasn't it? But nobody could ever tell me where to find you. Gone, no forwarding address. And it's not easy looking from Tenotenango, believe me."

"I never wrote, too embarrassed. I'm a reporter now. You know how it is. I'm truly sorry, Clara, not to keep in touch. It was a stupid and disloyal thing."

The crowd surged around them. Somebody started banging a big drum and people started singing. The two women never heard any of it.

"If not keeping in touch with friends is the worst sin any of us every commits . . . a reporter, huh? And covering the pope. Big time. Glamorous!"

"Not really. And you?"

"Oh, I've become what we all used to hate: a Mother Superior. For nearly ten years, I've run a convent in the highlands of Guatemala. About forty nuns, teaching and nursing sisters, mostly. We keep busy. This is the first vacation I've had in years. Isn't it glorious? Do you know the Holy Father? Can't you talk some sense into him?"

Tilly a fallen-away nun! Why hadn't it occurred to me before?

I left them there and walked to the hotel, figuring Tilly would call to cancel our dinner date so she and her buddy could catch up on old nunnery days.

But she didn't cancel, and we went to a Mandarin place in the East Sixties. We chatted companionably about the trip, the odd chemistry of tight-mouthed clerics forced into close quarters with reporters they had been trained as a breed to hate, about the decline of American foreign correspondence, about New York prices, about the weather.

Finally, I said, "Do you want to talk about it?"

She chased a shrimp across her plate with chopsticks. "No," she said.

"Okay."

We drank more tea.

"Yes," she said a few minutes later, hands knotted tightly around a cup.

"This is the Sister Jean Story, no commercial interruptions. Disjointed, 'cause that's how I feel. If you get lost on the curves, too bad." She sipped and stared deep into the cup. "Okay, I became a nun for all the right reasons, and all the wrong reasons, and I loved the life and the people and the church—and I still do. But the world changed, Paul, faster almost than I could keep up with it, and I changed, too. I wanted to serve the Lord. Nuns get wedding rings when they take their final vows, did you know that? Brides of Christ.

"A beautiful concept, really. But what happened was that as I began to change, I came to realize that we nuns were cheap labor for the church, the ones who did the scut work: teaching, nursing, cleaning, cooking, all the lesser jobs that it didn't take a man to do. And that began to rankle, especially since it wasn't long before I had met a whole slew of holy women—like Clara—and I had also met a fair number of priests who were drunks and some who were randy old coots who just happened to brush up against Sister all the time, sorry, and a few men I thought were truly evil."

She paused and fished a handkerchief from her bag. I poured more tea and kept my mouth shut.

"So after a while it got to be a power thing. Who did *they* think they were, the *'they'* being the men in general and in particular the gerontocracy that runs the church on any given day. *We* women were oppressed, had always been oppressed,

by the church, and probably always would be. An old story,
isn't it? So I demonstrated, and I marched and I conspired
and I wrote angry letters and attended endless meetings and
seminars. Once I even got arrested. All of this took years,
mind you, but one day it occurred to me that there was no
way I could possibly hope to win change by working within
the system. Clara is still fighting from inside. I couldn't
stomach it. I left."

Tilly was quiet for a long minute, staring deep into the
leaves in the small cup. I warned off a patrolling waiter with
a shake of my head. She had more to say.

"But it wasn't that simple, was it? The power fixation was
only part of it. I'd have to say that, if I want to be honest. The
rest of it was sex. S-E-X. I never had any, never knew much
about it. I went into the novitiate when I was seventeen, a
few fumbling moonlight clinches after high-school dances,
that sort of thing. At first I never even thought about it much.
Nuns don't *do* sex. Period. But then I got interested, looked
around at the rest of the world, started fooling around with
myself a bit, and started to wonder if I wasn't missing something good. Gradually it became more and more important
to me. I never actually got laid while I was still a nun, but
there were a few close calls, let me tell you. Ever since, man,
I've been making up for lost time."

She looked at me quizzically. "Have I ever given you to
believe you were the first one?" I shook my head. "Or even
necessarily the only one?" Another shake. "Well, that's
good, because you weren't and you aren't, or may not have
been. In fact, now you are. But that's not what's most important. What matters most is that sex is my all-time favorite
sport, and I'm damn good at it, if you hadn't noticed."

She banged the cup onto the table. A gesture of defiance.
Or perhaps disgust.

"And I've made my way, haven't I? When I left the Order,
I had a pretty good education, but I had never had a job,
never had sex, didn't know much about what we called The

World; not all that many years ago, really. And here I am, a big-time foreign correspondent and the sweetest lay on the pope's plane. Not bad, huh?"

"Great." It didn't matter what I said because I could see what was coming.

"And then how come, Paul"—a little girl's voice—"how come when I saw Clara out there today, I suddenly felt empty, and somehow dirty?"

Some questions need no answers. I paid the bill, and we walked back to the hotel. We rode up in an empty elevator together, and when we got to her floor I gave Tilly a chaste kiss on the cheek and watched the doors close behind her.

Not tonight, Brother. Sister has a heartache.

By next morning the bad news was that all the cops in Gotham hadn't found any sign of a would-be assassin. The good news was that nobody had shown the remotest interest in killing Pope Pius XIII by the time he showed up, bang on time, at the United Nations.

High noon. Once he was inside the riverside skyscraper, the greatest threat to Tredi would be from hot air, so I wandered over to the reporters' gallery for the speech.

"Got a spare text?" I asked a French reporter sitting near the door.

"No text, there is none."

"Strange."

"Never happened before, damn Vatican."

Reporters groused, but I wasn't surprised. That's the sort of thing you'd expect from a media-savvy pope when he doesn't want leaks. Particularly if he has things to say that will rattle the roots of his church.

Ever since, people have wondered if Tredi was right to make that speech in a secular setting. Then again, they'll also be debating the impact of what he had to say for decades to come. Which is exactly what he had in mind.

The President of the General Assembly that year was a

short, rotund individual with a spade beard from someplace indeterminate east of the Urals and short of the Pacific. He made a short, accomplished introduction in Russian, and Tredi stepped to the podium.

Alone again. After that magical mass in the stadium, the United Nations assembled in their giant wood-framed hall gave him a standing ovation before he even opened his mouth.

"Sisters and brothers, thank you for your welcome." He was speaking crisp statesman's English. "I come here today to explain to you some ideas to make my church a more constant and effective companion in the global search for peace, material well-being, and spiritual fulfillment. I want to share with you a blueprint-in-the-making for an old church in a new century."

Tredi said it slowly, with emphasis, portent. He might as well have fired an electric bolt through the press corps. It is not the world's hardest working journalistic outpost, but sluggards need not apply. Reporters sensed what was coming. *"O mio Dio,"* I heard the *La Stampa* man mutter, as he reached for his cell phone. I watched the Associated Press Vatican expert run the back of his hand across dry lips and play his fingers over the open laptop before him. The Catholic News Service bureau chief was unconsciously tweaking his beard, eyes closed in fierce concentration. In the next row, Maria looked as she must have looked waiting for the starter's pistol at the Olympics. Tilly was rigid. The Reuters man next to me was talking hard into a phone, "No text, but it's big. Very big. I'll be dictating. Ride with me on this one. Stay with me, now."

An institution two thousand years old must take a long view of history, the pope was saying. It could not by its nature be hostage to fashionable ideas that were born and died in the blink of a few years or mere decades. But neither, he said, could the church turn its back on changes that had revolutionized the way the world worked and its people lived. He named a few: the rise of democracy, the globalization of the market economy, the information revolution, the planet-threatening menaces of environmental destruction, and apocalyptic over-population.

"In this new century, the Four Horsemen must never ride again on this planet," Pius XIII said. "That must be our solemn undertaking. Without in any way abandoning the moral principles that guide us, we must all of us examine our institutions to see if they are best adapted to these new, accelerating realities. The Catholic church is particularly aware of these challenges because its members live in virtually every nation. And nearly everywhere, women and men of goodwill openly question principles that have governed their church through long centuries.

"We are asked why women cannot be priests, why priests cannot marry, why Catholic couples cannot use artificial birth control, why we deplore the untrammeled materialism that is rampaging through formerly Communist countries, why, in the Third World, the church does not take a more active role in the political arena as a promoter of the social justice it so earnestly seeks. There are good reasons for the church's position on all of these issues, just as there are good arguments against them."

Listening to the pope, I realized that his ideas had evolved over months of hard and patient thought at the Vatican, and that on our night rides and meals together I had heard snatches of the themes he had harnessed into an extraordinary symphony for debut at the UN. There had been a dozen burning issues facing Tredi when he'd assumed the Chair of St. Peter. Confronting any of them individually, controversially, would become a hallmark of his papacy. The issue of married priests, for example, cut to the bone of the church. For the first thousand years, priests, like the apostles themselves, had been married. For the second thousand, they were celibate by church command, but only nominally in many societies. As it entered the third millennium, the church was growing in places like Africa and Asia, where it was a newcomer, and by the millions in Latin America, where there were more Catholics than anywhere else.

Yet there were not enough priests—anywhere—to effectively serve old Catholics, or new. Everybody believed that vocations would pick up dramatically if priests could be married, but no one at the Vatican dared say so. Still, insistence on priestly celibacy was church law, not God's law: a pope could change the rule, although it would be breathtaking if he did. So, too, a pope could alone or in union with his bishops, reverse the church prohibition on artificial birth control; more church law. Change would anger some Catholics but please most, and effectively reshape the face and the image of their church. In sum, there was a daunting list of fundamental and conflictive issues on which a pope could leave his mark—if he had the audacity, the commitment, and the courage to attack one or two of them in the name of unity and modernization.

But that was not Tredi's way. Not for him to tilt at one windmill and leave prickly others for his successors. No. He was going to go after all of the great issues, the whole nine yards. And he was going to do it all at the same time in one giant, calculated blow. There was only one way to accomplish that. I'm not the most religious card in the pack, but what he intended even took *my* breath away, because what he had in mind reached way beyond his own church, to all religions, and by extension, to all countries, all governments, all societies. He was convoking a sweeping global examination of conscience; a morality X ray of the human race.

Across two millennia, the pope explained to the rapt assemblage, church fathers had met, sometimes for years, to consider the state of their institution and its place in the world. The Council of Trent in 1545 had been a response to the Reformation. The First Vatican Council in 1869 and Vatican II in 1965 had restructured and modernized the church in response to contemporary problems.

"The church has a structure handed down divinely and maintained in good times and bad across the ages. Basic principles can never change. The church will never accept, for example, that morality can be relative, a matter of personal convenience. But at the same time, we perhaps should not make principles of matters that prove, on close examination, to be of lesser moment. I think we must look at contentious issues and address them in the context of ancient teaching and modern life. We live, after all, my friends, in a world where change is almost exponential. New generations of knowledge in one field after another are telescoped into a few years; even less.

"I think that it is time for my church to once again systematically examine itself and its role for the benefit of its own future and, I fervently hope, for the well-being of all mankind. This is what I have come to tell you, and to invite you—all of you, whatever your beliefs—to join with us."

Tredi was speaking without a text, without notes, without flaw. Just as well, too, that the UN reporters' gallery is glassed off from the General Assembly Hall, for madness was abroad there, correspondents listening to the pope while simultaneously screaming through telephones and computers in half a dozen different languages.

"And then, the church will examine the results in a way that we have done at twenty-one historic turnings since the death and resurrection of our Lord."

"A Council! Is he going to call a Council?" a Spanish reporter screamed. "I don't believe it."

"Yes! A Council! Yes, a Council!" A German was on his feet cheering.

It was a new pope's invitation to a moral and ethical revolution encased in the public examination by the world's largest religion of its fundaments and the relevance of its teachings. Every reporter and most of the diplomats understood the universal implications of that.

Tredi's flow never broke. "I announce to you here today

that in exactly one decade—ten years from today—the
church will convene Vatican Council Three in Rome. I invite
our brothers and sisters of other faiths to share their own
thoughts with us at the same time. Our Council will examine
all key issues with a fresh eye and in light of the information
that we come to possess about them between now and then.
Some will say that Vatican Two was only yesterday as the
church measures time, and in the historical context I would
agree. But as the world measures change, decades now are
the equivalent of many centuries in earlier eras."

Among delegates, there was a great stirring. Among the
reporters, there was pandemonium. The press room stank
of sweat and tension. Tilly and a lot of the Italians were
jubilant. Maria sat scowling amid a thin-lipped group of
traditionalists.

Tredi paused to drink from a glass of water. Then he
brought it home. "I hope I am pope then to see this new self-
examination take place. If I am, I will study and I will listen
and I will change what should be changed about our great
church, and I will leave untouched, nay, I shall reinforce,
those things which need keeping forever. If I die before the
Council convenes, I charge my successors to enter into its
deliberations willingly and with an open heart and mind. I
beseech them to search for the just and peaceful accommodation of our ancient and true church with its myriad believers—and with its global neighbors—in these early hours of
this twenty-first century."

He stopped then, a theatric pause. He let it linger until it
gathered momentum, building tension around the great hall.

Then Tredi spread his arms high, staring upward, seeking
the light like the lonely priests who come to pray by night in
the Dome of St. Peter's Basilica.

"May God bless us all," Pius XIII begged in valediction.

24

ON THE WAY back to Rome, champagne flowed even before the plane got off the ground. The clerics were exuberant at Tredi's success and the prospect of a historic Council; it would paint every Vatican department with excitement and importance. Among the reporters, the *Vaticanisti* were equally jubilant. Most of them were too experienced and cynical to take a hand in the ideological divisions within the church, but they all recognized a sure thing when they saw one. By summoning a Council, which by its nature would require a cast of thousands and stories by the bushel, Tredi had assured them of steady work and experts' luster for many years to come.

I drank quite a few fizzy glasses. Nothing to do with church business, either. I still hadn't figured out why the Caballeros had let him go unchallenged, but Tredi's performance in New York had buoyed me more than all the blues and yellows in Ivan's magic pill basket.

I shared a glass with Maria, but I could see her heart wasn't in it.

"Cheer up. It could have been worse. It's not as though Tredi's ordered some great shift overnight, or overturned some key point of policy."

"True," she said. "What he has done may even be worse."

"How can that be?"

"Don't you see? He has taken his finger from the dike. We can't know what the Council will do, but in the coming years everything will change, all the people who want to cheapen our faith will try out their ideas. They'll experiment without rhyme or reason and with great fanfare because a Council is coming. People will pay great attention to them. By the time the Council arrives, the church will be a laughingstock, a circus. A joke. And it is all the responsibility of the pope—he is the clown."

I fled Maria's gloom and doom with a sinking suspicion that she might be right, and wandered over to where Tilly and a liquid bunch of progressive co-conspirators were reworking the church in their own well-oiled image. I told them what one of the Curia monsignors had told me in the bus on the way to the airport: a Council itself, while of supreme importance in the decision-making life of the church and a great vehicle for reform, could never offer any panacea for the church's ills; they were too deep, and too regional: what bugged one continent hardly itched another. Besides, a lot could happen in the years before the Council convened, and even when it met, whatever changes it endorsed were almost by definition bound to be incremental. Of course, I said it as if I had thought it all up myself.

"We know all of that," Tilly rejoined. "But the key point is that this pope has summoned a Council. It's what that decision says about him and his views that is ultimately so exciting to us. His mind is open, receptive, looking ahead. He's the pope that this century needs." She stopped dead in her tracks. "My God, what a great headline for an editorial."

I left them to it and repaired to a quiet corner with a pilfered bottle of Brunello to mull matters more pressing. New

York had been peaceful, against all odds. What did that mean? Probably only that the killers felt more comfortable operating in Rome. They were bound to strike again. What gambit might I try back home to short-circuit the next Caballero attempt—against me, against Tredi?

The overnight flight, quiet, safe, was a perfect chance to let the mind wander while the adrenaline dissipated. Thinking about it, cooled by the jet's air conditioning, warmed by the elegant wine, I tried to persuade myself that the worst might in fact be over.

Foreign trips are high risk. The pope is more exposed more often than he ever is at the Vatican. I'd have to assume that there was one scheming assassin to worry about in Rome, the boss and murderer of scaffold-diver Ernesto. But Latinos don't make good suicide killers. And they are not the most patient of God's children, either. If I could keep Tredi elusive enough long enough . . . That might force the assassin to show his hand against me again. I'd be waiting.

When they brought dinner, I ate with the reporters in the big rear economy cabin. Attendants brought too much good food, a bane of papal flights, and of course I ate every scrap, from the lobster to the cream trifle. Feeling like I weighed three hundred pounds, but otherwise about as mellow as crazy Brother Paul ever gets, I slept through two movies and some moderate turbulence. I woke only once to go to the bathroom.

There was only a single pool of light in the giant cabin suspended in space, so far from the forward compartment of the proud and lonely man they earnestly pursued it might as well have been in another dimension. And perhaps it was.

The light was Maria's. She sat upright by the window, still enough to be asleep but she wasn't, just staring at the seat in front of her.

"A peso for your thoughts." I perched on the armrest of the aisle seat.

She smiled wanly and spoke soft Spanish. "Night and

stars. Time moving fast but too slow. Sad, but also happy, decisions taken, bridges to cross."

"Wow. And at this hour. If it isn't Neruda, it should be," I said, though I knew it wasn't.

That won a warmer smile this time and I leaned forward and kissed her lightly on the forehead. She ran her hand across my cheek and I reached up to flick off her light.

"Sleep well, *linda.*"

"You, too, Paul."

Breakfast came with dawn, too early, and I was half hung over, too grumpy to eat much. Afterward, I moved back into the middle cabin with the Vatican crowd so I could gather my gear before landing.

As usual, the handful of reporters selected to meet Tredi for a picture-taking and quick quote began filing past not long before the seat belt sign for landing. I was chatting with Reilly, the master of ceremonies, who was proving much more human than the altar automaton everybody assumed him to be.

"The Holy Father was winging it there at the stadium mass, wasn't he?"

"About as much as you were, Crowd Psychologist." Reilly was smiling.

"Well, I fake nearly everything. But can he do that? I mean, a mass . . ."

He laughed a soft Irish laugh. "Lad, the Holy Father can do anything he wants to do."

A glowing Portuguese radio reporter waved on the way back from her papal minute, and an American TV reporter followed, the redhead with the hard-nosed reputation. She came out smiling, both hands wrapped around a gift pair of papal rosary beads. I was asking Reilly what he'd do if the pope forgot his lines at a complex mass when Maria went by, escorted as far as the curtain to Tredi's cabin by an assistant Vatican press secretary.

She didn't see me, but she was as ever hard to miss. Maria

had painted her face and affixed a polite empty smile, but she looked like hell. Her body language said she was tense, angry.

A bit early in the day for a reporter to chew out a pope, but if one ever did, it would be Maria Lourdes Lopez del Rio.

"I heard once there was a papal mass on one of the Pacific Islands when . . ." and there I stopped.

It took a fatal few seconds, but it came to me. Too slow, Paul.

Tense, angry, resolute . . . "Sad but also happy, decisions taken, bridges to cross" by the beautiful runner, reporter, and Catholic extremist Maria Lourdes Lopez del Rio. Lopez! The scaffold-diver. Ernesto Lopez.

"Maria!"

The name burst from me like a howl of pain.

I was halfway out of my seat, scrambling, driving forward, when I heard a small pop from the pope's cabin. I was the first one there, pushing into the cabin past the startled Vatican photographer who had been waiting to go in. But I arrived an eternity too late.

Diego Altamirano stood there, wide-eyed, mouth open. He was holding a small pistol, the smoking gun. Maria lay in a compact heap on the cabin floor.

Tredi seemed frozen, halfway out of his chair. Then he was bending over the still form. I could see there was no hurry. The entrance wound was marked by a darkening circle under her left breast. Through the heart. She was dead. Instantaneous, the blink of an eye.

Diego looked like a madman, staring at the pope. He took one zombie step forward, another, the gun waving loosely.

"She was so pretty, came in smiling, and I thought she was reaching for her own camera, some of them bring their own camera, you know, but then her hand came out—"

"Diego, pull yourself together," I said sharply, maneuvering to stand between him and the pope.

He looked up at me, as if at a stranger. Then Diego handed me the gun with shaking fingers.

". . . came out with that. I grabbed it to push her away. To push her, that's all. It went off. I'm sorry, God forgive me, I am so terribly sorry."

"Sit down, Diego," I said. He looked as if he'd faint.

Tredi sank to his knees, made the sign of the cross, and began to pray for the soul of the South American who had come to kill her pope.

I pocketed the gun and slumped down beside the pope.

VATICAN CITY

25

ON A SOFT Roman afternoon I was lounging on Tilly's terrace with a vast Sunday edition of her newspaper when she came in from the kitchen bearing two glasses of cold white wine and the bottle wrapped in a towel under her arm. She hadn't bothered to put many clothes back on, so I understood that the wine was a comma, not a period. Squeezed on the chaise lounge beside me, she scissored through the bulky paper until she found her own story, a thousand words about Tredi's new dreams for his old church.

"Good piece," I said.

She raced through it. "Ugh, butchers." Editors, she meant.

It was a companionable and domestic day, the sort I had come to treasure in the aftermath of Maria's death and the great pain I carried inside because of it. It was a wound that had not healed across long weeks and too many what-ifs. Tilly felt it, too, I knew, but she was different. She mourned as much as I. But Tilly was a newspaperwoman; she couldn't live without tension. Apropos of nothing at all, she said, "I still don't buy the Vatican story on Maria. It's been bothering me for months; from the very beginning. Now that I've given you a great lunch, great wine and even better sex, you can 'fess up. The whole story; it's bullshit, isn't it?"

We had buried her from an old church along Via della Conciliazione near the Press Office. Everybody had been there, except Tredi. He had wanted to go, but the Curia went berserk, and for once common sense had prevailed. He sent Nocilla, the Secretary of State. Another cardinal, a Latin American, gave the eulogy. He played the strange-ways-of-God concerto: a young, vibrant, professional woman, a former international athlete, struck dead while being received by the Holy Father for the first time. We were left to imagine the great surge of excitement that had so tragically overloaded her poor soul.

Brain hemorrhage. The Big Lie. What did you expect? The truth. Oh, sure.

Imagine the banner headline:

REPORTER KILLED IN PAPAL ASSASSINATION PLOT
DIES ON PLANE IN STRUGGLE WITH PIUS XIII AIDE

And how long before the tabloids began to wonder:

WAS SLAIN REPORTER POPE'S LOVER?

Not cool. Big-time uncool. The Big Lie was better. Safer. Told with polish, conviction. It was the sort of thing that Vatican functionaries have uttered with great eloquence in mellifluous tones and seemingly total sincerity for centuries.

Maria's body was not disfigured and, only right, the shocked and solicitous Holy See had seen to its preparation, even offering a special resting place in holy precincts for its burial with a special papal dispensation.

Her relatives dutifully flocked in tears from Chile, but why would it ever have occurred to any of them to examine the body, so beautifully arrayed by the time they arrived?

She looked so peaceful. That is what they were supposed to say, and that is what they said. The word "autopsy" was never even mentioned. The whole charade turned my stomach, to tell it straight, but I went along with it.

The issue is not truth, my friend. Or justice. The most important thing was to protect the pope, protect the church. Tredi himself would have played it differently, I am sure. But sometimes the truth is too impossible; lies are easier to believe. And Tredi's ultimate obligation was to the institution. In the end he had surrendered with ill grace, too.

It had been a small gun. The single muffled pop never got further than the first few seats in the business-class sections where the elderly prelates who might have heard it could be forgiven for having thought from personal experience that it must have been another champagne bottle.

In the papal compartment, I had prayed for a few shocked seconds. Then I did something even more useful: I quickly blocked the entrance, standing there alone until ashen, dry-retching, wall-eyed Diego Altamirano recovered wits enough to help.

"Holy Father's fine, no problem," I had lied in three languages to the clutch of flight attendants and clerics gawking at me. "A reporter has been taken ill, that's all. The Holy Father is helping. The doctor is coming."

Russo, the Vatican security boss, had come hurtling forward, followed by Giordano, the papal physician, and Amato, the press secretary. While they had oohed and aahed and worked it out for themselves, I'd crouched down next to Tredi.

His eyes were closed. He was gray. "Did you see anything?" He shook his head.

"Nothing. It was almost as if they were embracing for a few seconds. And then the shot. Why, dear God, why?"

Kneeling beside a fresh corpse with a gunshot wound was no place for the pope. There was a fleck of red on the hem of his cassock, but I never could figure out where it had come from unless it was wine; the bleeding had all gone on inside Maria.

"Holy Father"—I addressed him formally and forcefully—"would you please go back into your bedroom for a few minutes while we sort out this unfortunate incident?"

He did, and we did. The doctor's hands flew across the body, found no life signs, found the deadly round hole, fluttered uselessly. His mouth opened in a shocked "O" and he looked at me, eyes bugging. I raised my hand, an appeal for silence and conspiracy.

Nobody spoke for what seemed like a long time. I had the press secretary, Amato, down as a wimp, but he surprised me. He nibbled for a second at his pencil-thin mustache and set the lie. "I am afraid she has had a bad hemorrhage, hasn't she, Doctor? We'll need a stretcher."

"My men will take care of it. No need to bother the plane crew. We're only a few minutes from landing," said Russo, without missing a beat.

Maria was bundled into an ambulance as soon as the plane landed, and sirened off to emergency surgery in a Catholic hospital, where, sadly, she died a few hours later, even as her colleagues and Vatican worthies prayed together in the hospital chapel for her safe delivery.

That is the Official Story. If you wish to challenge it, you will find detailed confirmation in the death certificate and in the minutes of the death inquiry, both made available to reporters by the Vatican Press Office. The witnesses' testimony, including Brother Paul's, being so straightforward and conclusive, the coroner found no reason to solicit an account from His Holiness, who had not been present in any case when the unfortunate woman was stricken.

"There was nothing wrong with her brain. I mean, Maria was an athlete; strong, healthy, young," Tilly was saying perceptively.

"It happens sometimes to athletes." The Vatican had found battalions of doctors to say as much.

"Nonsense. What really happened was that she was flirting with one of the Vatican security guys, one of those Italian studs everybody wants to snog; both of them standing there in that tiny anteroom in front of the pope's compartment. There's some slap and tickle, one thing leads to another, and bang, somehow his gun goes off. That's the real story. Isn't it?"

Tilly was lying half across me, face close to mine, her arms pressing mine back high above my head. She was a good reporter, all right, for she'd just recited one version of the backup story that Amato, the press secretary, had prepared.

"It's the true story. Tell me it's true. You were there, weren't you?" She bit my cheek. "You're always turning up places."

"You know I was there—after she was stricken." Give her a little bit. "But Maria was already out—unconscious. I helped with the stretcher, that much is true. The rest . . . there's no conspiracy. Sorry."

"Hmm, I don't think I believe you." She rolled off me and stood up, pulling me after her. "And we have a special way of dealing with liars where I come from."

To Luther, I had told the truth. The doctors had released him from the hospital and he was getting stronger every day. He was bound for that special place high in the mountains that Tredi would transform into an elite university for the training of one priest-in-the-making. Luther would study and think and walk for however long it took, and come back robust to be formally ordained. Sounded like heaven to me, except the ordination part.

I told Luther what I said to the pope and to the handful of Vatican insiders who also knew the true story. "We had all heard Maria complain about Tredi messing with her perfect Catholic world, disturbing old traditions and true defenders of the faith like the Keys. She bitched all the time, Luther, but I always took it as the sort of griping you hear from players about their coach. It never occurred to me she was a threat to anybody. Who would have imagined . . ."

Luther mused, "She was strange, though, Paul. All bottled up. Something was there, waiting to burst out. Funny, I could have sworn it was sex; guess it was something else."

"Sex? I didn't think she liked men that much. Still . . ." I remembered her brush touches on the plane.

We were walking in Old Rome, and by unspoken agreement we wandered into a pizza joint where a neighborhood wizard worked magic with crisp dough, spicy tomato sauce, mozzarella, and anchovies. We ate two pieces each, cut from a steaming tray, and while Luther was finishing his beer I asked a question that had been troubling me. "The night you got shot. Could it have been Maria?"

He swallowed deep and let out a long sigh. "Been thinkin' about that. But I'm not sure. I remember a face under a red cap on backward, young, a face I knew, or should have known. A woman hiding her hair? Could have been . . ."

"It's not important."

Certainly not to sore-tried Franco Galli and his suddenly jubilant Vatican cops. My friend Franco was the cat who ate the cream, stamping murder cases "Solved" with gleeful abandon. If he'd been a priest, they'd have made him a bishop. As it was, they'd probably make him a papal knight.

In Galli's world, Vidal was killed by droopy, mustachioed Ernesto because he had learned too much about drugs on his trip to South America. Caruso, by contrast, had pitched to his death in a tussle with the athletic Maria, who resented the danger he represented to the Keys, and who in increasingly psychotic zealotry, went on to become the vehicle and foil of a cocaine clan's plan to assassinate the pope.

Nobody had yet drawn a direct connection between Ernesto-the-slasher-Lopez and Maria-the-would-be-papal-killer-Lopez—the name is as common as Johnson in Latin America—but Galli got lucky there, too. A little quiet investigation by what Galli liked to call "friends of the church"—

and probably meant security police—had turned up an interesting fact. When Maria's pilot brother had died in the Andes, he'd happened to be flying a load of chemicals of the sort used in refining coca into cocaine.

Even if the story ever leaked out—and there was no reason it ever should—the villains were outsiders. Vatican honor was unsullied.

Neat. Your Vatican Police in Action. Trumpets. Curtain.

Too neat for me, but I wasn't on the force. Maria's motive was a problem. I didn't see her as a killer. Murder violated all the big-name holy principles she stood for, didn't it? They couldn't all have been part of her cover. Why bother? Galli finessed that by assuming that the Maria-Caruso Dome scene was part of an internal Keys fight, one act in the passion play that had consumed and twisted Maria.

Was it really Maria who'd finished off Ernesto in Scaffold Alley? Had she sent the poison pen threats to me, and to the pope? There was one more thing I couldn't figure out that I also kept to myself: How, flaunting what were probably the strictest airplane security checks on earth, had Maria sashayed onto the papal plane carrying a pistol?

I was still probing such tender scars weeks later when I had a call from an American who said his name was Wes, a friend of a friend, he said. We had coffee by the Pantheon, where it turned out he had a message from Andy, my old DEA buddy.

"Andy says the analysts have reworked the family tree in Washington. A favor, he said. I don't know what family he's talking about, by the way, and I don't think I want to, but I assume you do," said earnest young Wes. I nodded.

"Andy says they think that when the crazy bastard, he emphasized 'crazy bastard,' chopped down the tree he might have missed one branch," he continued. Yes, Wes, he was crazy. Loco. "It's not entirely certain, according to Andy, because of all the, uh, collateral damage, but it looks like 'the crazy bastard' might have missed the youngest son; kid named Luis," Wes plowed on.

Interesting. But it didn't sound right to Brother *Loco*.

The young agent took a breath, an actor summoning lines for the next scene. "At least, his body was never positively identified, and lately there have been stories he's still alive. Andy thought you should know."

Wes recounted some specifics and then he looked up like a schoolboy relieved his recitation had ended. "That okay?"

"Fine, great. Perfect." But it wasn't. Suppose he was right? The youngest Caballero would be near thirty now. "Where do the stories put this kid? At home? In the States?"

"I think if Andy knew, he'd have said. But he does say that if you need help—anything at all—just holler." He looked at me appraisingly. "Andy's a star. You really must be a good friend."

"We go back, Andy and I. Please tell him I said thanks. Say that 'the crazy bastard' will be grateful when I pass it along."

When the agent left, I had a Campari and soda and mentally recounted the Caballero sons.

There had been four. One had gone sniveling to the gallows with his father. The snakecatcher had counted the others, two, three, four, at the funeral, the youngest standing a bit further back when the rocket exploded between the two coffins, hurling smoke, coffin splinters, and pieces of freshly dead and expensively embalmed Caballeros indiscriminately into the still-blue sky.

Nobody had been left standing when the snakecatcher had scrambled off the hillside that morning. But who could say for sure what had really happened? I certainly hadn't waited to count. Explosions can be capricious. Maybe the youngest boy had been somehow shielded from the blast by his big brothers.

One thing was sure: if Luis Caballero was the dark force behind the plot to kill Tredi and me, he had planned his revenge for a long time. He wouldn't quit easily, or soon. I thought about where he might shelter among Rome's Latin

American community, and so I poked around and kept my eyes open, told the Vatican cops and Diego to pay strict attention, and begged Tredi to keep out of the public eye as much as possible. Maybe the pope modified his schedule, or maybe it was just the pressure of work at the Vatican, but it did seem to me that he flitted about Rome a bit less frequently.

Tilly wandered off to the Middle East for a few weeks, St. Damian's was quiet, Luther went north, and I drifted along, enjoying the city, the sunshine, and the food, but casting an eye over my shoulder about twice every minute. Nothing wrong about thinking you're persecuted when there's a good chance somebody's out there plotting to persecute you, Ivan soothed. At one point, just for a change of pace, I talked my way into a week-long graduate seminar on St. Francis, did all the readings, participated in the conversations, and actually learned some worthwhile things. A great saint, Francis, and a tragedy what Italian earthquakes have done to his cathedral in Assisi.

One slow night the phone rang.

"What do you think about pepper?" We hadn't talked in almost a month.

"As in salt and . . . as in sausage and—"

"As in baseball."

Pepper is a game that is played by one batter and a couple of fielders standing around fifteen feet apart. The fielders toss the ball and the batter slaps it back on a bounce or two. It's useful for sharpening both the batting eye and fielding skills. I told the truth. "I'm not sure my knees are up to pepper."

"Nonsense. I'm older than you, and I'm good at it."

"Why pepper?"

"Because I'm feeling old urges, and because I'm pope I can't have what I really want most, so I make do with pepper."

I think he had had some rum.

"What is it that you want most, Holiness?"

"A batting cage. Twenty minutes a day, that's all. Is that unreasonable?"

"Of course you can't have a batting cage. The world would think you'd sold out to the Americans. Besides, who ever heard of a pope distributing communion with calluses on his hands?"

"And I'd tell the world that four of the best hitters this season happen to come from my part of the Americas." Tredi paused, and I thought I heard him swallow. "But you're right, of course. So we'll do pepper. It will be an unadvertised special on my private retreat this weekend." The thought seemed to please him.

"Umbria," he said, naming a green, hilly region north of Rome that is famous for its fragrant white wine and its ruins and tombs of the mysterious pre-Roman Etruscan civilization.

"Saturday morning," the pope commanded. "Take the early train to Orvieto. Somebody will meet you. Bring your mitt, shorts, and gym shoes. But, oh, you'd better wear your dog collar. I'm sending Diego off to get a master's degree in the States. There'll be a reception for him before lunch; a few Vatican types and a quick *spumante*. Then pepper and a picnic. Just the three of us."

"What if it rains?"

"It had better not rain."

26

FOR THE NEXT four days and four nights, heavy, insolent rain drenched Rome and all central Italy. By Friday, the news was full of rising rivers, buckling bridges, and moping farmers, but the sky was only cloud-streaked when I lumbered up the hill Saturday morning to catch the train. It didn't look like baseball weather to me. Still, obedient servant of the church, I hopefully carried my mitt in a tattered old gym bag.

For centuries popes anxious to get away from Rome for a weekend, or a pestilential summer, have traveled southeast to Castel Gandolfo in the Alban Hills, where there is a papal summer palace and a village of rich peasants who thrive off the tourists it draws. The Holy Pole had expanded papal vacation boundaries, though. A vigorous outdoorsman until age and infirmity had imprisoned him, John Paul II had loved to walk in the mountains and delighted in the consternation he caused with spur-of-the-moment skiing expedi-

tions outside Rome. Tredi had extended the skein, weekend-
ing in different parts of Italy as whim and season commanded. Officially, the escapes were described as private
papal retreats; a chance for His Holiness to reflect and
recharge his spiritual batteries. Sometimes Tredi took his
personal confessor among a relative handful of aides and
watchers. And sometimes, I knew, he took his glove and a
handful of precious wooden baseball bats.

Normally, Orvieto is only about ninety minutes from
Rome, but that Sunday it took nearly an extra hour, what
with storm-weakened trestles and soggy switches. Still,
there was a big smile on a familiar Irish face when we finally
chugged in.

"Top of the mornin' to you, Brother Paul," said Daniel
Reilly, with an exaggerated brogue.

"And to you, Monsignor. What's the occasion?" I hardly
merited the papal master of ceremonies as my trainspotter.

"The man's saying mass by himself this morning, and I'm
wanting some fresh air."

Reilly drove with exaggerated care, ignoring horn-heavy
Italian drivers trapped behind us on a lovely two-lane road
that lazed across a series of picturebook ridges. The pope
was in high spirits, Reilly confided, resting at a hilltop eminence owned by a noble and felicitously absent Roman family in a wooded area known for its views, its wild
mushrooms, and its ruins. From what I could see as we
passed a gate watched by two bored young cops and turned
into a long driveway flanked by cypresses, the ochre-painted
villa was isolated but not what you'd call inaccessible.

Neither the cops nor the tall stone boundary fence enclos-
ing stands of vines and olive trees would stop a pro with a
grudge against the pope. I wasn't happy about it. What
occurred to me, though, as Reilly crested the drive, was that
the pope might have heard something to make him believe
that danger had passed.

For one thing, Tredi was sending his live-in bodyguard

back to school. For another, his first real sally from the Vatican since the New York visit was a relaxed weekend with low-level security. What had changed? I decided to ask the pope, but I never got the chance.

A seductive aura of peace and languor lay over the lovely old villa. It was echoed at the all-in-the-family reception for Diego.

"I wish you well, Father, and hope to have you back with us soon," said the papal chamberlain, a monsignor unctuous by breeding and training.

"To have served with all of you, Excellency, has been the greatest experience of my priesthood," murmured Diego Altamirano in polished reply.

"When will you be leaving?"

"This very afternoon, I'm afraid. Right after lunch."

There were about a dozen of us in a baroque salon with splendid views of woodlands clinging to steep hillsides under a glowering sky. Everybody but me was a member of the papal household: secretaries, aides, and less specific hangers-on who have been integral cogs in papal retinues for centuries. Tredi hadn't yet made his appearance, but from the way all of them kept looking over at a tall wooden door at the end of the chamber, I knew he wouldn't be long.

Until then, Diego was the center of attention. Most of the people seemed genuinely sorry that he was leaving. My own emotions were mixed. Luther was gone, and I wasn't happy about seeing the pope abandon his last line of protection. On the other hand, I was not one of Diego Altamirano's greatest fans. I thought he was too slick by half, cocky, arrogant. You'll say my judgment was clouded by jealousy, because having the young priest around as a companion-confidant meant that Tredi had less time, less need, for Brother Paul.

Okay. *Touché.*

But our own special kinship was still there, for a few minutes later, when I bowed to kiss his ring, His Holiness Pope

Pius XIII inquired out of the side of his mouth, "Did you bring your glove?"

"Yes, coach."

Tredi grinned. "Good. This'll be over soon. Stay with Diego."

It was and I did, and soon Diego and I had both changed out of our black-and-whites and into T-shirts and sweatpants. I sported a Marlins cap; his was Cardinals. Diego vanished into the kitchen and emerged with a big basket, the picnic lunch. He was like a little old lady, I thought, nervous and fussing. "I know that no matter how hard I try, I'll forget something." He grinned.

Couldn't blame him, having the pope for lunch. Following Diego into the garage, I carried two scuffed old bats and a canvas bag with six new American League balls. He lugged everything else. We stowed it all in the back of a 4x4 with Vatican plates and swung around to the front. In a couple of minutes, Tredi appeared in black sweatpants, a plain white knit pullover shirt, and a kelly green cap adorned with the intertwined letters HS.

"Does that stand for High School?"

"Holy Spirit High," he said. "Illinois, I think. Haven't won a game in four seasons. They sent it to me with an appeal for help. I'd pray, but I suspect that sending them a pitcher or two from back home would be quicker."

Diego drove expertly down a muddy track to a tall green gate, which he opened with a remote control.

I asked, "Where are we going?" Tredi shrugged, kneading his glove. But it was not an idle question. In security terms, the pope was now naked— literally out in the woods and completely out of touch with his Vatican minders.

"Not far," Diego replied. "There's a good place to play near an archaeological dig that I thought you might find interesting, Holy Father."

Driving with great care, Diego negotiated a slick and bumpy decline, stopping where the track turned back into

the trees. We were on the lip of a long, very steep hillside
scored by a dark and turbulent stream lancing through the
debris of an old landslide.

Diego cut the engine at the edge of a forest glade so beautiful it looked as if it had been sculpted. It was nearly flat
and roughly triangular, framed by trees on all sides with a
tempting view of a lake at the southern end. The grass was
short and almost Irish green.

Tredi was grinning in anticipation. "Ah, new hardships for
the Holy Father."

He and I played catch to loosen up, ignoring a few drops
of rain. I felt strong, together. Carrying the lunch basket,
Diego had vanished off to where the glade met the hill. I fan-
cied I heard the old-friend sigh of a cork coming out of a
bottle as the ball disappeared into Tredi's glove with a
friendly snap. I was beginning to sweat lightly.

In a few minutes, Diego jogged over with a bashful grin,
pounding his glove. "Lunch is ready when you are, Holiness," he said.

"Pepper first," the pope commanded. "I hit."

He grabbed the bat and we played pepper. After about fifteen minutes, I was wringing wet, and long-becalmed muscles were beginning to ache, but I could feel old skills
slowly reawakening.

I was batting and we were all fairly muddy, when Tredi
called a halt. By then the rain was falling in earnest: the
prospect of a picnic didn't seem a great idea. Diego must
have seen my face, for he said gaily, "We'll eat snug and dry,
Brother Paul, I promise." We followed him into an
amphitheater of stone alongside the stream, which was
sluicing the hillside with great energy.

"This way, please," Diego called. "Watch your head. The
entrance is a little low."

He ducked down and walked into the hill. It was a cave, I
realized as I followed Tredi inside, and maybe nature had
started it, but man had certainly finished it.

Diego was smiling in the half-light of an enclosure around eight feet high and ten feet across. He handed each of us a towel and by the time I had dried my face and hair, he had conjured up three glasses with cold white wine. Nectar.

"What is this place?" Tredi asked. The air was cool, flushed by currents that seemed to swell up from below.

"It is a partially excavated Etruscan ruin, Holy Father, a bit unstable perhaps, but perfectly safe," Diego replied. "This is an antechamber leading to a series of tombs first built nearly three thousand years ago. What is interesting is that one of them later became an ancient Christian chapel. We, uh, the scholars, think that early Christians met secretly to pray here in the first centuries of the church, when the faith was still forbidden by the Romans. There are some rough stone carvings further back."

"Fascinating," Tredi said.

"If you are ready, Holy Father." Diego gestured at the picnic spread out on a flat-topped rock, *prosciutto,* baby artichokes in oil, cheese, chicken, fresh roasted peppers, black olives.

"Let's see the chapel first, Diego. I'd like to say a prayer there."

"It will be wet and slippery because of all the rain, Holiness. I cannot recommend it."

Diego should have realized that was like waving a red flag at a bull. Or maybe he did, for Tredi announced, "Nothing ventured, nothing learned, Diego. Light your lantern and lead the way."

The pope looked over at me inquiringly. "Paul?" He knew I didn't like enclosed spaces.

"Right behind you," I promised, trying to hide my unease.

The trip to the chapel was not great as distance is measured, but it spooked me. First we edged through an opening at the end of the antechamber and then slithered on hands and knees along a slippery stone tunnel with water running briskly on the floor. We passed a series of empty niches that must have been ancient tombs, and then, turning right, descended another level.

The whole way I kept my eyes fixed on the bulk of the pope before me and the glimmer of light that marked Diego and his lantern. Once I dislodged a large rock with my knee and it gouged nastily along my calf. By the time we got to the chapel I was sweating, and getting angry. This was no place for a pope.

Tredi disagreed. We stood in a rock chamber about twenty feet across that was lit in some eerie way from above the high ceiling. There must have been a seam in the rocks up there, because the air was fresh and water sprayed into the room. It gathered on the rough stone floor and was already lapping at my sneaker tops, but there were more important things to notice first.

On the longest wall of the chamber an elongated cross had been carved into the white *tufa* stone, longer than it should have been, and not quite straight. But as moving in its way as his faith must have been to the artist who carved it nearly twenty centuries ago. Tredi surveyed the chamber with a smile on his face and his arms spread, palms open, before him.

"Thank you, Lord, for this sight, and for the vision of all those who have gone before us in Your name," the pope said.

Diego sloshed over to where a narrow makeshift altar had been carved under the cross. He laid the lantern on the altar and strode into the shadows.

"Here are some farewell gifts, Holiness, from me to you."

The pope walked forward. "Diego, how nice, you shouldn't have . . ." but then Tredi stopped, because he had read the address label on the half-open lid of the center box. "But these are addressed to my family, back home."

Tredi opened the lid, then turned sharply.

"What is this, Diego?" the pope demanded, his face suddenly flushed with anger.

27

DIEGO ALTAMIRANO LET the question hang for a pregnant moment. When the pope repeated it, he at last replied in a parched monotone.

"It's heroin, Holy Father; the best money can buy—or prayers. All ready to go. Vatican diplomatic mail. Overnight delivery. Usually we send it to your brother, Bobby, but he's permanently indisposed, isn't he?"

It's hard for me to describe what I felt then. But all the pieces came rushing together the instant I saw the heroin. I understood.

Murder, the Keys, a scaffold killer and the heroin; ever so much more fashionable in a new century than pedestrian cocaine. As all the realization came flooding in, I guess I mostly felt ashamed, for once again I had arrived too late.

"The package on the left, which is soon to be the property of your family, is a ninth-century chalice. On the right, is a jeweled song bird that was a gift to the pope from an

Ottoman emperor in the seventeenth century," the young priest continued, with rising cadence. "Both have been quietly 'borrowed,' in the pope's name, from the storerooms of the Vatican Museum."

"Diego!" the pope thundered. He was gaping in astonishment, blinking hard, trying to work it through. It was time to end the charade.

"His name is not Diego," I said softly. The pope spun to glare at me. "He's Luis Caballero."

I saw Tredi's eyes widen in understanding.

"Well, well, Brother *Loco,* good for you," Caballero taunted. "You've figured it out."

"Enough."

"I doubt it." He edged a careful two paces further away from me. "I know it may be difficult, *Loco,* but try not to do anything stupid. And you, *Your Emptiness,* stay right where you are."

"It was you who killed Cardinal Soliz, wasn't it?" the pope said suddenly. "Murdered him in his cathedral."

"Yes, I had that honor. I snapped the cardinal's neck. Pop! Poor Cardinal Soliz. Your beloved brother was even easier; a phone call."

The scene belonged to the drugs scion who had called himself Diego and pretended to be a man of God. He played it with manic *brio* as chill water swirled through the eerie chamber.

"How easy it was to deceive the church and all of its cretins," he boasted. "To pretend, to toady, to burrow eventually right to the heart of the throne. Just being in Rome was enough. But no—I couldn't believe it—I was summoned to become bodyguard for the man I had come to kill. You cannot imagine the vistas that opened. What wonderful irony."

Luis Caballero enjoyed explaining how clever he was. With a mixture of cold rationality and hubris, he bragged

about deception and murder as the light gradually dimmed
and water inched coldly up my leg.

"Cardinal Soliz told me about you," the pope interrupted
almost conversationally. "He took you in, treated you like a
son, sent you to Rome. But he never told me you were a
Caballero."

"Ah, but he never knew, and he never asked. But he was
quick enough to accept the big contribution my family's
friends made to his church, wasn't he?" For the first time I
saw the gun in his hand. "The precious cardinal dreamed
that I would become a long-robed fraud like him. Like you.
I stayed for long and empty years because I needed a place
to hide. To plan. You dishonored my family, pope. And you,
Loco, destroyed it."

Enough is enough. By then I sensed what elaborate
scheme had led us to the underground chamber. I doubted
that I could divert Caballero from it, but I had to try.

"Destroyed it. Sure, I killed them, killed them all," I said.
"Big deal. That's old news, but I'm the one, me, *cabrón.* He
doesn't know anything about it. Let the pope go."

I saw the naked hatred rake across his eyes, but Luis
Caballero controlled it. "Oh, no, *Loco.* I want him just as
much, more even." He pawed at it silently for a moment.
"Can it be that you really don't know why? Didn't your precious idol ever tell you how his family and my family were
partners in the drug business?"

That stopped me, all right. I looked over at the pope. His
eyes were expressionless, opaque.

"*Loco,* are you really the last to know? Did he never mention, in the spirit of confession, perhaps, how much cargo we
moved together, a relay, my family in South America, his
through the Caribbean? All those tons, all that time, until the
day came when money was no longer enough, until uncon-
trolled ambition overwhelmed the man who desperately
hungered to be pope? That is when he betrayed us! The

Cocaine Cardinal! In more ways than one! I spit on you!
Thief! Priest!"

"You're wrong. Let the pope go."

I don't know where Tredi's mind was, but I was looking
for an opening. I had failed once to kill Luis Caballero, and
I'd never get a third chance.

"But being a pretend priest—all those meaningless
vows—was not so wasteful in the long run, was it? No. I
made it work." Caballero was bragging. "How absurdly
easy it was to dupe those morons at the Keys; to hijack
their organization. We made millions moving heroin in
shipments of Keys books and magazines, my friends and
I. And millions more using Keys accounts to launder our
money. I am richer than my father ever was! What do you
think about that, pope? My father would have been
proud."

Quietly, I said, "The last time I saw your father, his face
was purple, veins bursting in his head. He died like the pig
he was."

Luis Caballero was marching to internal drummers, but
he heard that, all right. A bullet howled off the rock face a
few inches from my head and ricocheted dangerously
through the chamber.

"I remember, *Loco*. I will die remembering. My father
and my brother hanging from that tree; at their funeral the
coffins suddenly vanishing before my eyes in the brightest
flash of light I have ever seen. But I survived. I survived to
avenge him, my brothers; all Caballeros, every one. When I
leave here today, another name, another passport, my real
life begins. I drove the Holy Father and his friend to a place
they knew, I returned, and I caught the afternoon train as
everyone knew I must. 'Go with God, Father Altamirano.' It
will be days before you are found. By the time they even
think to look for me, Father Altamirano is gone, vanished.
The priest who never was."

He needed us to see how smart he was. And you had to hand it to him—it was pretty slick, waiting until the last instant before making a play.

"Spare us the melodrama, Luisito," I interrupted. "Think about poor Brother *Loco*. I ought to get my money back."

"What!"

His eyes were black diamonds. Even in the gloom the bore of the pistol looked like a tunnel.

"When you buy expensive weapons to eradicate scum, you'd think they'd kill all the scum. But you escaped with just that lovely scar on your cheek, Luisito. Not fair. Was it from your father's casket? I am very disappointed. Still, it was fun. Shall I tell you how your brother squealed as he twisted from the rope?"

"Paul!"

It was the pope, but I ignored him. I watched Caballero's face go red, the scar incandescent. I saw his finger tighten on the trigger, and then relax suddenly. He had other plans for me, I had worked that out. Maybe he'd pull them off, but the rage was on me and that wouldn't make it any easier for him.

"Go ahead and shoot, Luisito. You're good at killing. Let's see. A cardinal, Father Vidal, your asshole cousin Ernesto in the alley. And Maria. You probably did Caruso, too, didn't you?"

"How smart you are today, *Loco*! Applause for Brother Crazy." The sarcasm dripped. "Yes, I killed Caruso; he was getting too close to the Keys. An anonymous appeal for mutual comfort and prayer, that's all it took to get him into the Dome. The rest was easy. Vidal was hardest, you know. All those people around and I was supposed to be protecting the pope. But Vidal knew too much. He had tales to tell."

The light was worse, the water higher. I was edging away from Tredi; away from the lantern rays, one careful inch or two at a time.

"Maria, though, she was another easy one," Caballero continued. "Poor Maria, another kitten, a walk-on. Do you know how simple it is to buy a gun in New York? Do you know how easy it is to get the gun onto a plane if you're walking next to the pope? No metal detectors for *His Holiness.*"

He paused for a second to let us appreciate how clever he had been. "Still, I felt bad about Maria. She had cotton for brains, but she was beautiful and I wanted to fuck her. But Maria had to go because you—both of you—had to think that the threat was over. So that nobody would be suspicious and I could set up a final act in our little play, like, well, like this one.".

He gestured in the air, an architect pleased with his creation.

"You should have shot straight in the Ghetto that night. It's me you want, Luisito. I love killing Caballeros."

Caballero fired another shot above my head and Tredi and I crouched with drawn breath while it pinged around the chamber. Caballero seemed not to have noticed the dangerous ricochet. He stamped his foot in the water and unconsciously clapped one hand to the scar-side of his face.

"Oh, dear, we really shouldn't have let Brother *Loco* out of his madman's cage after all. He's not as smart as we thought. I shot who I aimed at in the Ghetto, *idiota*! Luther was the threat to me, not a crazy, bumbling fool like you. He was at the Vatican, watching the pope, watching everything. He was too close, too smart. Luther cramped my style."

When Tredi spoke, he sounded a trifle disingenuous, one step off the pace. "You've had dozens of chances before. Why this charade, this elaborate production now?"

"You really don't understand? Of course I could have killed you at almost any time. But death is not enough. No one will mourn Brother *Loco,* and to kill you without leaving a clear message would be only to create a martyr. No good. Death is coming, but it will be almost incidental. The real pain for you—the Caballero revenge—is that you will die in humiliation and in scandal that the whole world will see, pope. Like my family. Brother *Loco* can tell you."

"He doesn't crave just your death, but your disgrace, Rico, and the disgrace of the church. He wants to make it look as if I killed you. He intends to leave us here. That stuff on the altar will make it seem there was a falling-out among thieves who were defrauding the church. He wants your death to be as empty and your memory as scarring as his father's."

The pope looked at me with supreme disdain. "Nonsense," he said.

"No, no, *Loco* is right for once," Caballero said excitedly. "It's all for the cameras, for history. Give that *Loco* a prize."

He pointed to a small stool next to the altar. "There is a tape recorder, *Hollowness*. And with it a sheet of paper. You will record what it says. Try to disguise your voice if you like. That will make things even more exciting later."

The pope waded across and silently read the paper. "Preposterous. Who is this Ramón supposed to be? Do you imagine anybody will believe it? I won't read it."

"Ramón is just a name. People will believe it; governments, newspapers, the church will spend millions, years looking for him. And, yes, you will read the message, because if you don't start within five seconds I will kneecap Brother *Loco*."

"Don't do it, Rico."

"One . . . two . . . three . . ."

"*Ciao*, Ramón," the pope began, reading in Spanish. "Here's another little something, top grade from out East. I recommend you take it to our old friends in Los Angeles, give the Miami boys some time to get hungry again . . ."

Caballero was watching raptly, his face frozen in a rictus grin, his eyes fever-bright.

" . . . you should filter the chalice and the figurine through more or less reputable dealers in New York and London," the pope continued. "I doubt anybody will spot them as Vatican stuff; they haven't been on display before. Next month . . ."

I didn't hear the rest, for I went for Caballero, one giant step through the water and a low dive. There had been no chance to signal my play to the pope, but he must have been anticipating one, for I caught a glimpse of the tape recorder tumbling through the air just before it smashed against the lantern.

The light went out as Caballero fired.

I felt the bullet howl past my head and heard it whine off the stone wall. Then I was on Caballero, half-kneeling in the water with both arms wrapped around his right leg. He was hopping wildly, seeking an instant's stability in which to make a killing shot.

I was pushing, thrusting up with all my strength, trying to bring him down. I heard the pope thrashing around in the darkness somewhere behind me. I hoped he would have sense enough to run while he could.

Caballero fired again.

This time a chip of stone rocketed off the wall and ran hotly across my forehead. For a minute I could taste the blood, but then I had him. With a mighty heave, I twisted the leg savagely and he tumbled backward.

The gun flew into the darkness, but Caballero was on me like a wildcat, punching, clawing, grasping for my eyes and my throat.

I butted him with my head and punched him once hard under the breastbone. But he was an expert and it was an uneven struggle with only one possible outcome. Both of us knew that.

A jab with the side of his hand left my head ringing. He struck a nerve with a straight-fingered punch that sent a terrific jolt of pain lancing through my body and left my left arm twitching and momentarily insensible.

He had me down in the water by then and I felt the blackness gathering when a shadow rose up behind Caballero. I watched with a spectator's detachment as a rectangular wooden box came crashing down on his head.

I glanced back as the pope jerked me behind him through the narrow passage toward the cave mouth.

Luis Caballero was lying on his side while heroin spilled from the wooden box and mixed like sugar in a cup of tea with the cold water flooding the ancient sanctuary.

28

WE NEARLY MADE it. Tredi was back in the antechamber and I was behind him, still scrambling clear of the narrow passageway, when Luis Caballero shot me.

I never knew whether the bullet hit me on a straight run or, more likely, as a ricochet, but my left side exploded and I screamed in pain as I toppled backward, knocking the pope down.

"Paul! Paul!" Tredi was there, pulling me out of the line of fire as more shots rang out. As I lay there panting, I could feel the bones grating. I opened my mouth to welcome the pelting rain.

Tredi asked, "How bad is it?"

Another shot sounded from below.

The pope was watching the cave opening behind us. We had to move. I understood that.

"Ribs, it feels like." I was trying not to moan, but I knew that I could not move. The pope gently probed my side.

"The blood is more or less in a straight line. It's not dark, and it's seeping, not pumping. That's good, isn't it?"

"Good, yeah."

The rain tasted wonderful. I felt as if I could lie there at peace and drink it forever.

Tredi regarded me. Softly, he said, "I hope we're not going to have one of those 'leave me and save yourself' huckleberries, *hermano*."

I don't think I have ever felt such a loving look. I surrendered. "He'll be coming. Let's go."

With my arm around the pope's shoulders, I found that I could maneuver, but walking was easier said than done for either of us.

We had emerged into a maelstrom. Rain pelted the hillside in vertical sheets. Rivulets large and small sliced down the slick surface. Meeting, joining, racing like frenzied drops on a window, they plunged toward the valley below. No more forest friend, the stream had become big and menacing, tripling its width in the short time we had been inside the cave. It dangerously flushed bushes and branches, big chunks of soil and large rocks before it.

We gaped as a tree trunk jammed crossways between two boulders, forming a natural dam. Almost instantly, tons of water backed up behind it, pouring into the cave mouth. The cave must have endured many tricks of nature across the long centuries, but never one with a ransom of heroin and a gunman inside.

"This way," Tredi hollered, pulling me painfully with him uphill across a treacherous skein of rocks. He was leading us back toward the 4x4, but the long way around, avoiding the worst of the stream. I'm not sure that I could have crossed it safely even unwounded.

The wind clawed at our clothes as we lurched upward, fighting gravity and the storm. Leaves and twigs were flying like darts, tree branches pinwheeling before the wind's fury.

A bolt of lightning stunned us, thunder rolling down like some Old Testament admonition. I could smell the sulfur and I saw a large oak shudder and crack in despair higher up the hill.

"Not much further," Tredi gasped.

But it was. The mud was more than slippery. It seemed to have an evil mind of its own, icelike; oozing, traitorously sliding away at the slightest touch. Somehow we breasted the last barrier of rocks and began to turn downhill toward the muddy track where we had left the 4x4 so many deceptions ago.

My side ached and I felt light-headed, but I was strangely reassured. If it had been a killing wound, I'd never have gotten this far.

"Can you make it?" The pope leaned close, shouting against the wind. "I could carry you from here."

Tredi said it with a challenging half-smile that should have warmed me. It didn't. I kept hearing Luis Caballero's ranting. Over and over it rattled through my head. Two families, he had said, Caballero's and the pope's, combining to relay cocaine in its heyday out of South America, snaking it up through the Caribbean and into the United States. It rang true for reasons more than geography.

Caballero had all the reason in the world to hate me, kill me if he could. But why his consuming determination to dishonor the pope? Why did he hate the pope so? And why risk showing it?

Kill me, and no one would mind. Leave even the barest suggestion that he had assassinated a popular young pope and there was nowhere, no time, Luis Caballero could ever rest, under whatever name. He knew that as well as I did.

I wished, there in the rain and the wind, that I could remember the origins of Tredi's great crusade against drugs, but I couldn't, and by the time we could make out the shape of the 4x4 through the driving rain, my mind was aching as badly as my side.

Then the bullets came again. One, two, three, they chipped off the rocks around us and went spinning into the trees. Clumsily, Tredi spun us around.

There at the mouth of the cave, his pistol raised as if in salute, stood Luis Caballero. He looked half-drowned. There was a big gash in his scalp, and when Caballero took a few steps toward us, he limped badly.

But there was no mistaking his determination. A feral scream rose up to challenge the storm. For a tingling second, it smothered the wind and seemed to still the raging water. And again.

I know it was human, because I saw it come from Caballero, but it seemed to me then that I had heard the voice of the devil. Tredi crossed himself. Then he tugged me forward as Caballero issued a third challenge of fury and impotence.

"Wait."

"Why, Paul?"

"Because he can't chase us and shoot at the same time. If he comes up the way we did, he'll never catch us. If he tries to cross the main stream to get closer, he'll get swept away. Let him decide. We'll move as soon as he does."

Out of the wind, I laid my cheek against the cold, protective side of a boulder. The instant that I had time to think about it, the pain whipped mercilessly across me. I watched Caballero and I waited. Tredi squatted pensively beside me, one hand unconsciously exploring the rough fabric of the stone. He was scraped and muddy and wringing wet, but there was an aura about him still. It was a marvelous gift.

"There's something you should know, Paul," the pope said, looking straight at me.

Caballero had advanced a few painful steps up the incline and was brandishing his gun at us. He fired a shot into the air. I should have been counting the bullets, maybe, but you can never be sure these days what load a particular gun carries.

The pope said, "What he said back there about two families cooperating to smuggle drugs. It's true, Paul, I wanted you to know that."

So there it was. I wouldn't have known how to ask him.

Climbing on his bad leg into the teeth of the storm, Caballero had slipped and lay supine, pounding the mud in fury with both fists. There was a lot of blood low on his right leg, and I wondered if he had broken his ankle. He would climb no higher.

"He's going to try the stream. We should get moving." But it was so nice there out of the wind, far from the pain.

Tredi pulled me around to face him. "Did you understand what I just told you?"

"Yes. I think the stream will be too much for him, but we could be cutting it close."

"Paul, this is more important." He said it with great authority.

I looked at my friend.

"It was Bobby, wasn't it?" I had only just seen it. "He must have told the Caballeros that you were helping behind the scenes, smoothing the way, making everything work."

"Bobby, Bobby. Bad Bobby. God rest his soul." The pope said it with infinite sadness. "I never knew who seduced who, Paul, but the Caballeros were hungry and Bobby was wonderfully accommodating. He could be so charming, you know. And, of course, he had a brother who was a big shot in the church. That could make things happen, couldn't it? Wink, wink. I guess everybody had a good laugh about that, didn't they?"

Caballero had the gun jammed into the waist of his pants now. Dragging his leg, he was cautiously exploring the edges of the stream, looking for the safest place to cross. From above him, I had a better overall view of the torrent. Hurt as he was, swollen as it was, Caballero would never make it.

Tredi had never told me the full story of black sheep Bobby, but I bet that he had told me more than anybody else had learned in his years around the Vatican. There are many cardinals who are conservative and some who are liberal, but none who are stupid. There are no princes of the Roman

Catholic Church who would vote for a doper's kin as their pope.

"Of course I never knew until too late, Paul. Why would I even think about such a thing? I was barely keeping my head above water as a bishop, trying to keep churches open, schools running, poor people fed, young people from becoming crooks or revolutionaries. And then, wham, I'm a cardinal overnight. I can't begin to tell you how much I didn't know. How in my wildest dreams could I have imagined that my beloved brother was dealing drugs? Good family, education, money, social prestige. Why would he do that?"

Caballero was still stopped, gauging. Maybe he was praying as well, for there was nothing for him in that torrent but death.

"I never would have known, either, if a gutsy young priest hadn't come to ask could I please move the cases of books and religious materials I was storing in his parish hall because they wanted to hold a dance. What cases? I went to look and there were statues of St. Francis in some, and in the others cans that said 'Sliced Pineapple.' Both crammed with cocaine."

Caballero waded into the stream. On the fringes, water barely reached his calves and he made good limping progress, but I could see that even in shallow water he was having to lean against the swift current.

"Lend me your shoulder. We need to go." Tredi obliged and we stumbled along, me watching Caballero inching closer and closer to his doom. We were sheltered from the worst of the wind and the pope kept talking, as if to himself, purging the unmentionable.

"I knew right away there was only one person who would dare call up a priest using a cardinal's authority to order him to store something. But Bobby wasn't around. Bobby was never around when there were problems, Paul. So the priest and I took the crates and went out to the beach and we broke every statue and opened every can, cut our hands on the tin, made a joke of it at the end, spilled everything into the sea. But it was no joke. Two weeks later, the priest was dead. Automobile accident, the police said."

Luis Caballero was barely halfway across the stream and he was already in trouble. The water was up to his shoulders and its force was irresistibly forcing him downstream. Soon he would lose his footing because the water was too deep or because a piece of debris would sweep him away, and when that happened it would end.

"So that's when I guess I went a bit *loco,* Paul, obsessed—like all crusaders. I went drug-hunting. Pretty soon I was the Cocaine Cardinal. And along the way I found there were a lot of good decent people willing to help me, all over the Caribbean. I never saw Bobby; he was hiding, I guess. It's only been the last few years that I even heard from him again. He always needed money—and I always sent it. He was my brother, after all."

He was smarter than I thought, Caballero. He had found a diagonal series of rocks about ten feet apart. With great effort, he was lunging from one to the other, half swimming. He had started well upstream and by now was nearly level with us. But he posed no threat. Even if he survived the torrent, we would be at the 4x4 by the time he emerged. If there was no key, all we had to do was to walk the path downhill, away from the stream. There'd be a phone and many cops long before Caballero could limp his way out of the woods.

"There's one thing, Paul. One day in the middle of the Cocaine Cardinal thing, never a sign of Bobby, of course, something occurred to me. Knowing Bobby, he never would have risked storing all his stash in a strange place. Just what didn't fit someplace safer. So I went looking, on and off, whenever I got the chance. I finally found it in the rafters of an old fishing shack where my dad used to take us when we were kids: more statues, lots of them."

"The shack where he died? You told me about it on the plane to New York."

"That shack."

"You think he went back? Imagining the cocaine might still be there after all these years?"

"No. Nostalgia, probably. But the real point is I found only a little cocaine in the shack, Paul. Mostly, there was money."

Tredi looked at me, and I felt something walk across my grave.

"A suitcase full of money," he said, almost a whisper.

"That suitcase."

The pope nodded.

"That one."

We were home free. The muddy torrent had finally caught up with Luis Caballero. He had managed better and gotten further than I thought, but in the end rampant nature won.

Caballero was a critical few yards short of the side of the stream where Tredi and I stood, and he was trapped. He could not advance, and he could not retreat. He was clinging to a slick black rock in desperation and obviously waning strength. Nowhere to go. Too bad.

But then His Holiness Pope Pius XIII heard Luis Caballero's shrill cry for help above the thrum of the storm.

"Paul! Caballero will drown."

"There's nothing we can do for him."

"We have to try."

"No, we don't."

"We are Christians, Paul."

Before I could stop him, Tredi slipped out from under my arm. Shorn suddenly of support, I staggered a couple of paces and sat down hard.

"Help me! *Ayudame!*" Caballero screamed.

The pope, damn fool, crabbed about on the stream's edge until he found a storm-victim branch about as wide as a closed fist. He scuttled across three rocks and then lowered himself prone on a fourth that was more or less flat but not nearly big enough to contain his bulk.

As Tredi tendered the branch toward Caballero, I could see his feet desperately churning against the current to keep him level.

I slid into the water, reluctantly, painfully, slowly— against my better judgment. It was cold, dark. It took my breath away, and it gouged my wound so savagely that I cried out. Something covered with fur brushed past my legs.

"Grab the stick! Take it and I will pull you in." I could hear the pope yelling to Caballero. "Quickly. Take it," he commanded.

I waded out to where the water was almost up to my thighs, anchored myself against the upstream edge of a sturdy-feeling rock. Leaning forward was a bad idea, because my side suddenly felt as if it had caught fire, but on my second try I caught one of Tredi's legs, then the other, and grabbed them as tight as I could.

It made all the difference. Tredi straightened out and suddenly the stick was within Caballero's grasp. His left arm was wrapped clawlike around a rock protruding a few inches above the water. He had stopped screaming and was watching the pope with eyes that yawed between fear and determination.

A small tree trunk brushed past me, the bark like sandpaper across the wound. I screamed again, I'm afraid, and I nearly lost it. Tredi, too, must have realized that one improvident chunk of flotsam could take us all in one split second.

"Take it, damn it," the pope thundered.

I watched Caballero's eyes reach a decision. Slowly, his right hand emerged from the water and reached toward the branch.

But the fingers were not open. They were closed. I yanked at the pope with all my might.

The gun was aimed straight and steady, not more than five feet from the pope's forehead, when Luis Caballero pulled the trigger with another one of his howls. I screamed then, too, a cry of fury, a heart-rent cry of anguish. A dirge. But nothing happened. There was no shot.

Nothing happened. Gun too wet, Luisito? No bullets left, Caballerito? Tough shit. Tredi lost his grip on the rock and I jerked the pope savagely back toward shore.

Caballero had been methodically pulling the trigger in disbelieving fury. But then he dropped the gun and lunged with both hands at the receding life-saving branch that Tredi, his head barely above water, still stubbornly extended before him.

Luis Caballero missed by a fatal few inches.

Pope Pius XIII was spared the sight of Caballero tumbling downstream, vanishing under the torrent with a silent scream.

But I enjoyed it.

29

IVAN AND LUTHER were playing *bocce* in the grove with a view of snow-capped peaks and I was pretending to study Scripture, but my mind trekked in other mountains. I was thinking of Tilly.

It was several weeks after that day in the meadow before I next saw her. Tilly had been delayed by riots, coups, who knew what trauma, but when she called one afternoon to say she was back, I toddled over.

"Paul! What happened to you?"

The cast itched like hell.

"Fell off a *motorino*. Like a fool."

"*Pobrecito,* you're too old to be messing around with those things," she said, and rushed off to make me a drink, returning with the inevitable question. "How're things around the Vatican?"

"Fairly quiet. Luther's out of the hospital. Tredi hasn't done much."

"Shame about Archbishop Beccar. I saw a squib in the papers out there."

"Uh, I guess." The former Keys leader. Dead from a stroke in a Spanish monastery.

"And I see that Diego Altamirano has left. His replacement is a Dane, of all things." Tilly gestured to a pile of Vatican news bulletins on her desk.

I nodded. "An expert in Norse legends."

"Where'd Diego go, do you know?"

"South, he went south."

Tilly sat down next to me and gave me a sisterly kiss. Then she leaned back and looked out across the city.

"Sounds good, south." It sounded liked a rehearsed line, and it was, for suddenly Tilly was all business.

"Doesn't it sound good, Paul? South."

"South as in where?"

"How about Guatemala?"

"Guatemala." I understood. "As in a convent in the mountains run by Clara, that old friend of Sister Jean's?"

Tilly nodded.

I said, "Guatemala is supposed to be beautiful. Great place for a vacation."

"More than that," Tilly said so quietly I nearly missed it. "I thought I'd just sort of go, you know, hang out. An open-ended kind of thing. Maybe not for good; certainly not as a nun again. But . . . well, I've got some money saved up, Paul, and the paper says I can have time off . . . kind of a sabbatical. There's lots I can do there, Clara says."

"Sounds like fun."

"I don't suppose you'd like to tag along?" She asked it with hesitation, and, I thought, hope.

Tempting. A fresh start. A new place. Tilly. There was nothing about my life at the fringes of a giant church that would be improved by the absence of Tilly Wright. But no thanks, Tilly.

"For a visit, you mean?" That's not what she meant. "Absolutely. Try and stop me."

My wound was nearly healed and I was bound for the mountains to have my head regeared. Papal orders. When that was over, I'd be back. Rome would be my home and the Vatican my haunt as long as Tredi was pope. It was a promise I had made to myself and, unspoken, to him.

Tilly was crying. "Clara says she's working harder than ever. A lot of vocations, new kids to teach. She says they're so full of joy, of hope. Do you suppose it might rub off, Paul?"

I kissed her.

"Vaya con Dios, mi amor."

That's as close as a simple brother can get: it takes a priest to give a real blessing.

I had thought a lot about Tilly as Ivan ironed mightily at the corrugations of my psyche. And she was lazing cozily through my mind when the housekeeper walked up from the house that day and handed me a letter. Not from Guatemala, for the stamp was Italian, the postmark Siena, the return address a doctor's office. It was from Teresa Longhi, who had loved a man killed in a fall from the Dome of St. Peter's.

Dear Brother Paul:

I know it must have been you who made it possible for my daughter Antonia and me to meet Pope Pius XIII. I write to say thank you, although it has taken me some months to marshal my thoughts.

When the invitation came, I was surprised. Knowing my feelings about the church, you must understand that I almost didn't go. But Antonia, who was rapidly weakening, was very excited and I did not wish to disappoint her. We shopped everywhere to find just the right dress.

It was a rainy Thursday when we got to the Vatican, where I expected that we would be greeted by the pope, exchange a few words, and continue on our way like so many before us. Imagine my surprise when I learned that we were to have lunch, just the three of us.

Antonia and I were too nervous to eat much, but the pope seemed to know all about us and he did everything to make us more comfortable. He talked about life at the Vatican. Antonia hadn't laughed like that in years.

Before we left, the pope turned to Antonia and said, "I want you to know, and never to forget, that your father was my friend. He was a good man, and a good priest."

He cradled Antonia's face in his hands and kissed the top of her head. I think we were all crying by then.

What I must write next is difficult for me, for I am not only a mother but also a doctor.

As I may have told you, even by the most optimistic projection my daughter should be dead by now.

But Antonia's tumor is gone, Paul. That killer black spot in her skull has vanished.

I'll spare you the boring medical details, but the fact is that my specialist colleagues and I can't understand where it went—or why. There is no trace of it. Antonia is gaining weight and plans to return to school soon.

What happened? I wish I could tell you.

Researching the literature, I have found only two similar cases of spontaneous remission, although not at such an advanced stage.

You may draw your own conclusion, Paul, but I'm sure that you'll understand when I say that as a non-believer and as a doctor I was strangely reassured to have found those cases.

I understand that you yourself have been ill. I wish you a speedy convalescence. You will be forever welcome at my home. And Antonia's. Please come and see us soon.

Your friend,

Teresa Longhi

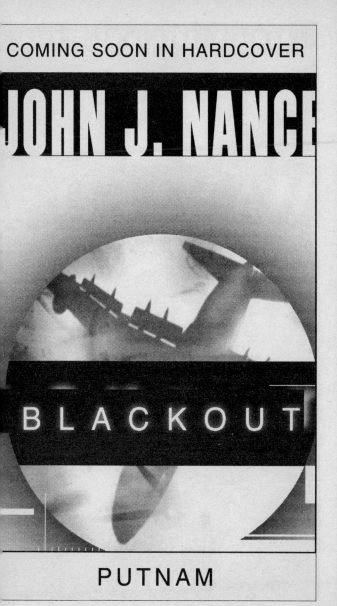